A VIEW ACROSS

A VIEW ACROSS THE VALLEY

Short stories by women from Wales c. 1850-1950

edited by

JANE AARON

HONNO CLASSICS

Published by Honno
'Alisa Craig', Heol y Cawl, Dinas Powys
South Glamorgan, Wales, CF6 4AH

First Impression 1999

British Library Cataloguing in Publication Data

A catalogue record for this book is available from the British Library

ISBN 1 870206 35 5

Published with the financial support of the Arts Council of Wales

Acknowledgements:
Every endeavour has been made to trace all holders of copyright material contained in this anthology. If, however, there are some we have failed to find, the editor would be very grateful to hear from them. 'The Old Song and the New' is published by courtesy of Archifdy Gwynedd. The following have given their kind permission for the reproduction of texts to which they hold the copyright: Mari Elis for 'Nancy on the Warpath'; Katrina Burnett for 'The Poacher'; Mrs N. E. Nightingale for 'Davis'; the Estate of Brenda Chamberlain for 'The Return'; Cassandra Davies for 'The Old Woman and the Wind' and 'A Modest Adornment'; Dilys Rowe for 'A View Across the Valley'.

Cover: Gwen John, *Girl in profile* (detail), late 1910s,

Cover design by Chris Lee Design

Typeset and printed in Wales by
Gwasg Dinefwr, Llandybïe

ER COF AM BARRY PALMER

Contents

Introduction

JANE AARON

In 1954, from a hospital bed, Margiad Evans wrote a poem to her sister Siân on their childhood relationship with one another and with nature:

> Nature and Time are against us now:
> no more we leap up the river like salmon,
> nor dive through its fishy holes
> sliding along its summer corridor
> with all the water from Wales . . .

In their 'unfathomable friendship' with nature, the children experienced themselves as blissfully 'lost' to the adult human world of social concerns. But, startlingly, at the close of the poem, that alternative lost world of the children is presented as constituting in itself the essence of their country:

> All the places were us, and we were all the places,
> and the inscrutable innocent altars of nature. . . .
> For our ways, our fields, our lostness
> were children. So we were our country.
>
> (Margiad Evans, 'To my sister Siân',
> *A Candle Ahead*, 1956)

This formative experience took place, in the case of the Evans' sisters, on the Welsh border, in the neighbourhood of Ross-on-Wye in Herefordshire, rather than in Wales itself. Nevertheless, the sense of union with a natural locality remembered in 'To my sister Siân' is one which frequently recurs in the English-language writings of women from Wales. The central characters of the stories that are to follow in this anthology frequently identify, and feel most at home, with natural rather than human phenomena. One way or another, most of them are alienated from the human communities in which they dwell, but many forge 'unfathomable friendships' with the natural landscape and elements which press closely about their rural or industrial dwellings. They hail as their intimates the wild winds which sweep across the highlands; the sea and its creatures, the seals and the sea-birds; the rivers darting down through the lowlands; the shadows which daily cross and re-cross the narrow valleys; or the sun in its meridian on exposed hilltop places. To such an extent is this the case that if one were compelled to choose one image which might most characteristically represent the many ways in which Wales has been imagined, or has known itself, in pre-1960s women's writing in English, it would be this image of Wales as the wild zone which would be likely to predominate.

It is an image which is at variance with the traditional view of what Welsh fiction in English has to offer. During the 1920s and 1930s, the English-speaking voice of Wales became identified with that of the worker in the coal mines and iron and steel industries of south Wales. Welsh novelists and short story writers characteristically wrote of and for the human communities from which they sprung, expressing and identifying with the struggles of the working class during years of economic depression and industrial strife. That women writers had little part to play in the development of this tradition is historically understandable. Women's exclusion from the paid workforce of the heavy industries, and their marginality within the labour movement which fuelled much of the creative cultural activity of the period, made it difficult for them to imagine themselves as suitable spokespersons for their communities. More significantly, perhaps, the human cost of maintaining the late nineteenth and early twentieth century industrial communities of Wales fell particularly heavily upon the shoulders of the womenfolk. The 'Welsh Mam' was an essential and overworked servant of the industrial machine, as she struggled to rear and maintain healthy manpower in the overcrowded and insanitary terraces. Life expectancy was lower for women than men in the Valleys, for all the health hazards of the men's employment; women died earlier, worn to the bone by childbirth and the incessant effort to maintain standards of hygiene before the establishment of pit baths or domestic water supply. It's not surprising that few women had the leisure or the self-confidence necessary to become authors, and it's not surprising that the few who did tend to regard human communities as inimical to their creative life rather than supportive of it.

It's not surprising either that those women writers who did emerge were less representative of the mass of the Welsh population in terms of their class and ethnic orientation than the typical male writer. Because Welsh industrial development was largely under the control and ownership of English entrepreneurs and capitalists, an indigenous Welsh middle class was slow to develop. But peasant or working-class boys of particular ability could still hope to rise to become leaders of Welsh cultural and political life, as Nonconformist preachers, Liberal MPs, or labour activists, through the direct support of their local communities, which sometimes even clubbed together to fund their further education. Whatever early promise they might show, girls were not afforded the same opportunities. As a result those women who did manage to amass the necessary levels of education, leisure, and confidence to become writers tended to come from the middle rather than the working class, and consequently – in the nineteenth and early twentieth century – to be more Anglicised than the majority. Some of the women whose work is included in the following pages were born in Wales of non-Welsh parentage; others were literally Anglo-Welsh – that is, the off-spring of mixed Welsh and English marriages; others again had but the slenderest of indigenous Welsh connections, but deliberately chose for themselves a Welsh identity. Yet their atypicality with regard to the mass of the Welsh population during the years 1850 to 1950 does not of course in itself render their view of Wales inauthentic.

The wild Wales with which they identify is not tourist brochure Wales: nature is harsh here, life is a struggle not a holiday, and there are few hospitable faces to welcome the wanderer in from the cold and rain. The central characters in the stories that follow tend to be social outsiders, encountering their destinies in isolated valleys, on barren hilltops or rough seas. In those stories which are concerned primarily with the individual's relation to human communities, the protagonists are generally represented as baffled and alienated by the confusing, unsympathetic patterns of social behaviour. From society's point of view theirs is the life of the eccentric and the dispossessed, but their alternative 'lost' world offers to them a way of finding themselves in communion with nature. Their 'view across the valley' gazes *across*, from hilltop to hilltop, rather than dwelling for long upon the doings of the valleys' human inhabitants below. And 'so they were their country': for Wales too, in so far as it can be said to find representation in these tales, is itself imaged as a social outsider. It is figured as a dispossessed, anarchic country, closer to nature than to culture, wild because it has not yet arrived at adult accountability and self-responsibility but is still, in childlike fashion, living its own intense and secret life under the governance of a distant parent.

As far as its Welshness is concerned, it is to be hoped that, with the onset of devolution, this has become, or is about to become, a dated image, as dated as the chapel or the coal mine, in so far as they cannot be said today to be representative of the realities of contemporary Welsh life as a whole. A democratically self-governing Wales cannot again so readily be imaged as a wild, childlike and dispossessed country. And as far as women are concerned, it is also to be hoped that the image of the feminine as particularly associated with the wild zone of nature, and as outside masculine culture and full adult accountability, has likewise become a dated, historically specific, concept. Women's lives have changed, and are changing, in Wales as elsewhere, and it seems by now unlikely that we will ever revert to a situation in which the woman's sphere can only be located outside the world of public responsibilities, in the home or in the wilds. But this anthology is a historical collection, of stories written by women from Wales before the 1960s brought a new wave of protest and change to the lives of both women and the Welsh. It does reflect aspects of the realities of Welsh and female experience during the years 1850 to 1950.

In doing so it also expresses an aspect of the human condition which is an abiding reality for both women and men, and for women and men of all nations. The desire to feel at home in nature and its elements, and to feel in that bond a conscious renewal in adulthood of the all-encompassing sensory experiences of childhood, is not one that is likely ever quite to disappear, while the human animal remains an animal. 'Speaks/Cadair Idris still/with a healthy hiss?' asks Margiad Evans in one of her last poems, 'Old Snowdon/does he still knock/on the small windows?' The mountains, rivers and winds of Wales speak with a very distinct hiss on some of the following pages, and knock most persistently on the windows of human perception. They may not hail us here in that tongue which has been attributed to them by centuries of Welsh-language writers, but at least they do still speak, in the only language available to many of Wales's contemporary inhabitants.

Present-day readers have not been afforded much opportunity to hear the voice of nature, or indeed any other voice, as it has found expression in pre-1960s Welsh women's fiction in English. It cannot be entirely a coincidence that the only writer amongst those anthologized in this volume whose work has remained more or less readily available in print since its first publication is one of the most English writers in the list. Though I like Mary Webb's novels, and I'm glad they have remained in print, I would not say that she is manifestly a better or more interesting writer than Margiad Evans, Hilda Vaughan, Brenda Chamberlain or Dorothy Edwards. Yet not a single novel or short story by these four last-named authors is currently available through book shops. Indeed, most of the stories included in this present collection have not been republished since their first appearance in print. In general, this neglect of Welsh writing in English, which is all too apparent in the case of Welsh men's texts as well, can largely be attributed to the fact that so few English literature students are introduced to Welsh authors in the schools and higher educational institutions of Wales. But when it comes to women short story writers in particular, the lack of recognition from which they suffer is also in part the consequence of the inconsistent manner in which they have been treated by former editors of Welsh short story anthologies.

Since the 1930s nine general anthologies of Welsh short stories have emerged from various presses. The representation of male writers in these collections is remarkably consistent; the same names appear in each anthology, with the effect of establishing those authors as major contributors to the genre. But when it comes to the women, it's a matter of 'now you see them, now you don't': their names bob up and down like corks on the anthologies' contents sheets. In a pioneering 1937 anthology, Dorothy Edwards, Margiad Evans, Siân Evans, Eiluned Lewis, Allen Raine and Hilda Vaughan were all included. That women were never to have it so good in subsequent collections may not be unrelated to the fact that a woman, Elizabeth Inglis Jones, assisted with the compilation of this volume, whereas in all other cases the books' editors were male. The next major anthology, which appeared in 1940, dropped all the English-language women writers apart from Siân Evans from its list, and Eiluned Lewis, Allen Raine and Hilda Vaughan were never in fact to feature in the anthologies again. In 1956, Margiad Evans reappeared, but no other English-language woman writer was included. Dorothy Edwards made a come-back in a 1959 collection, in which Dilys Rowe was also included, but Margiad Evans was now absent, along with all other English-language women writers. A 1970 anthology ignored the women altogether, while a 1971 volume included only the two Evans sisters as representatives of English-language women writers. Both were absent from a 1976 collection, however, along with all the previously anthologized women writers, though Brenda Chamberlain was now included for the first time. She was still in the team in a 1988 volume, which also found space for both the Evanses and Dorothy Edwards. The latest anthology to appear, however, in 1993, includes none of the pre-1960s English-language women writers, although it does feature the same array of male writers from the earlier period as all the other anthologies. As a consequence of all this, no woman writer has been presented by these anthologies as an indispensable contributor to the genre, and no acknowledged foundations have been laid for the development of a specifically female tradition in Welsh story-writing in English.

But that tradition does exist as this anthology hopes to show. It may surprise some readers that this book begins with a mid nineteenth-century author, for current critical wisdom has it that the volume which marked the birth of Welsh writing in English, as a distinctive literary tradition, was Caradoc Evans's *My People*, published in 1915. Yet *My People* was written in part as a riposte to Allen Raine's view of Wales, as popularized in her many end of the nineteenth century novels. And once Allen Raine is included as a full member of the body of Welsh writers in English, then her predecessor, Anne Beale, also becomes a candidate for recognition. Anne Beale's work bears close similarities, in terms of style and subject matter, to that of Raine, and as she was still producing her own very popular novels and serial stories at the time at which Raine commenced publishing, she is very likely to have influenced her successor's work. Beginning in the last century also allows the anthology to include representative pieces from that group of writers who were primarily motivated by the Welsh Home Rule movement of the 1880s and 1890s. Mallt Williams, Sara Maria Saunders and Gwyneth Vaughan were all contributors to the journal *Young Wales*, the English-language mouthpiece of the movement.

Although the particular preoccupation with nature, evident in the later stories included in this anthology, is not so apparent in these earlier pieces, a tendency to identify with the figure of the dispossessed, the social reject or the embattled outsider is a central feature of these texts too. In Gwyneth Vaughan's fable, that figure is directly related not only to the Welsh but to the Celts in general. For Jeannette Marks, as an American observer, the sense of Wales as an outsider translates into a representation of its people as endearingly childlike, in their continuing involvement with folkloric superstition. A *dyn hysbys* or witch-doctor type of figure also makes an appearance in Bertha Thomas's story, but here the context of his actions is a Welsh version of the Romeo and Juliet theme, and involves a young woman's struggle with the prejudices of her society. In Ellen Lloyd-Williams' 'The call of the river', nature represents such a healing antidote to the pressures of life within human communities that the protagonist chooses mergence with it rather than a continued harassed existence. 'The coward' of Kathleen Freeman's story, on the other hand, experiences himself as a coward because his ties to his mother and his familial role mean that he cannot ultimately accept the anarchic, anti-social, type of loving offered to him by a girl whose image is strongly associated with that of the wild countryside surrounding his industrial village. To resist, or to attempt to control and conquer, nature results in sterility, though an entire abandonment of the self to it brings destruction in human terms. In Dorothy Edwards' complex story 'The conquered', while the spirited Gwyneth chooses to identify with the past imperial conquerors of her land and its people, her subdued admirer Ruthie insists on planting an almond tree as a gift for her. Ruthie's tree serves perhaps to symbolize not only the collusive tendency of the subordinated and dispossessed to revere dominance, but also, and more positively, the survival of the meek and the conquered as a living force with different and ultimately more enduring values than those of their conquerors.

'The conquered' is set on the Welsh/English border, and many of the stories collected in this anthology could be categorized as 'border' tales in more ways than one: they are preoccupied with the relation between margin and centre, and with shifts of perspective in terms of what is to be seen as central. 'The Heads of Coed Uchaf' takes a lighter look at Welsh/English tensions on the geographical border, while in Mary Webb's love story the outsider from the margins is for once welcomed to the established hearth. But the subordinated wife in Hilda Vaughan's 'A thing of nought' succeeds in bringing about, in her preacher husband, a reversal of his original centre of values. In this tale Megan Lloyd's self-identification with natural processes – with the 'shadows, as do pass to and fro across the Cwm, and are leavin' no trace of theirselves behind', as she puts it – works as an essential aid to spiritual survival under duress. Indeed, her whole life seems a reflection of the day's cycle of light and darkness as it is experienced in her narrow valley, around which the surrounding hills climb so steeply that only for a brief moment, when the sun is at its meridian, is her home not in shadow. Similarly Megan's shadowed existence is lightened but fleetingly by the golden-haired lover whose features reappear again, miraculously, in the 'child of my dreams' she conceives by her dark husband.

The stories from the 1930s and 1940s which bring this collection to a close continually return to the theme of the outsider, and his or her identification with nature in opposition to social expectations. A trickster figure, allied to an anarchical life force, exposes and shatters social conformities and snobberies in 'The poacher'. In 'Davis' another nonconformist – but one of a very different breed from Mallt Williams's David – also resists integration into the necessary human struggle to control nature and time. The need to resist human patterns of behaviour that lead to unconscious hypocrisy and prejudice is stressed, by implication, in Rhian Roberts' story: in 'The pattern' a bewildered child's eye view is used to expose a south Wales industrial village in war time as itself but a replica in microcosm of the fascist totalitarianism it is intent upon fighting. In both 'The return' and 'The old woman and the wind', natural phenomena, for all their violence, are presented as ultimately less of a threat to the individual's mental balance than immersion in a petty-minded or malign human society. 'A modest adornment', on the other hand, explores the way in which a community's inability to imagine its members as motivated by any except the expected patterns of loving serves to erode a long-term lesbian relationship, and illustrates the loneliness of the homosexual in close-knit but narrow-minded communities. Finally, in Dilys Rowe's 'A view across the valley' a girl escapes on a blazingly hot Sunday afternoon from the confines of her industrial town to the surrounding hills, in search of an alternative perspective of her own on the steel works, the dirty canal, the slag heaps, the chapels and the terraced streets which make up her world. She finds it, but at the cost of her life, as the sun ignites a circle of fire about her on the scrubby hill side.

This last story in particular may suggest that the peculiarly sharp juxtaposition of natural and industrial landscape characteristic of much of Wales's scenery, in the north as well as the south, constitutes one of the underlying reasons for these writers' preoccupation with the embattled relation between man and nature. The surrounding hills do knock most persistently on the small windows of line after line of terraced dwellings in some parts of Wales. To women locked in sweated labour inside those homes by virtue of their social role, they must have called with a particular intensity, and those women's experiences find expression in these stories. The gendered polarization of themes within the canon of Welsh stories in English, with the men focusing on the community and the women on the hilltops, also increases the sense of a destructive split between two incompatible, but mutually vulnerable, worlds. But the stories and divisions discussed here belong to a previous historical era.

As gender segregation grows less prevalent within new patterns of work and relation for men and women in Wales, and as the hills grow greener once more, it is to be hoped that a more integrated balance between the feminine and the masculine, and between the natural and the man-made, may yet prevail. If that balance is to be established on a cultural level, however, the historical contribution of hitherto neglected women writers needs to be made available, so that they can add their weight to the scales.

I

Mad Moll's Story

ANNE BEALE

Mad Moll, or rather, Mary, was not born in Llangathen, but was brought thither when about six years old. She was the offspring of sin and sorrow; and could her unhappy mother now see her child, bitterly indeed would she suffer. Little is known of Mary's early history. She was born probably on the borders of Wales. Her father was a man of station; her mother, his victim, died when she was quite young, leaving her, in the true sense of the word, an orphan. It was supposed, however, that the little Mary was kindly treated and well brought up until her sixth year, living either in or near her father's house. Her recollections of her early days were always lively, and even now visions of her infancy seem to float occasionally through her disordered brain. She has been even heard to say, 'I should not be like this if my father knew it.' That father married, and determined, or perhaps it was determined for him, to break every link that bound him to his child by sending her to a distance. He accordingly gave her into care of a man named John Harries, of whom he knew nothing but that he was a drover who lived at Llangathen, a place far from his own residence. Little is known of what passed between Mary's father and John Harries, – nothing, indeed, but what the latter chose to communicate to his neighbours when he returned home. He was to keep the child, bring her up decently, and do for her as he thought best, for which he was to receive, and did receive, one hundred and twenty pounds – a little fortune to a man in his condition of life. He doubtless promised fairly to the father, or to whomsoever finally settled the matter, and probably, at the time, intended to perform his duty by the child.

It is between twenty and thirty years ago since John Harries and his charge arrived, late in the evening, at Llangathen. He had been absent from home longer than usual, and his wife and children were expecting his return. They were clamorous at the sight of him; and the first question asked by his wife – it was ever her first question – was, 'What money have you brought home?' He chuckled as he introduced the little stranger, who, terrified at the appearance of so many unknown faces, had shrunk behind him. His wife was delighted at the gold he displayed, and was, in imagination, soon established in a comfortable farm-house. She did not so much rejoice in the care which the gold brought with it, but she comforted herself by saying that, as the child was already six years old, she would soon be useful.

John and Kitty Harries had five children; the youngest, a boy of about twelve years, was the only one of them who looked good-temperedly upon Mary when she came to Llangathen. The present Mrs Shenkin, a relative of Kitty's, and at that time a spinster, made one of the family.

Mary was a bright-eyed creature, full of life and natural gaiety; her face plump and rosy, and her little limbs strong and active. John Harries was proud of the admiration she excited among his neighbours, whilst his wife was proud of a new gown and bonnet, the first purchases made from their newly-acquired wealth. Little Mary was neatly, though plainly dressed, and brought with her a good store of clothes for a child of her condition. It was impossible to look at her rosy cheeks, arch black eye, and dimpled mouth, and not be convinced that she was a creature of joy and innocence – one who seemed never to have known check or privation. From her introduction to Kitty Harries she took a dislike to her. She shrunk away from her the first night and clung closely to John, asking him when she might go home again. Her fear daily increased; and although Kitty was, for some little time, kind to her, she never overcame her aversion. She was miserable, and would retire to a corner and cry, unobserved, whenever she could escape from Kitty. If any one asked her what was the matter, she would say she wanted to go home; and when questioned concerning her home, would speak of the friends she had left behind – of her father's visits to her, and of many other little events which had impressed themselves upon her mind, and which have not been effaced from it, not even when her intellects had become disordered, and her powers of recalling the past destroyed. She made one friend in the Harries' family, and only one. This was the youngest boy Willy, who was very fond of her, and whom she loved as a brother. Little Mary's only happy hours were when he returned from school in the evening; for truly she was, like Wordsworth's sequestered 'Violet':

> *A maid whom there were none to praise,*
> *And very few to love.*

John Harries appropriated the money given with Mary to his own use, and improved his circumstances thereby; but it did not seem to occur to him that any portion of it ought to be devoted to the service of his young charge. When Mary was about eight, John Harries happened to visit the place from whence he had received her, and found, upon inquiry, that her father and his family had left it, and gone, no one knew whither. This intelligence released Kitty from the obligation she had imposed upon herself of keeping up a show of kindness towards the child, upon the chance of inquiry being made. At seven years old Mary had much hard work to do; at eight she was a little slave. It was soon remarked that the blooming child became pale and thin – that her eyes were often swollen and red – that she looked terrified when spoken to, and that she was always afraid of encountering Kitty, whose ill temper daily increased. John Harries was a close man, and would never communicate his projects or proceedings to his wife, who saw the money gradually dwindling away, and bringing her no positive good. It is true they apprenticed one of their sons, and were, on the whole, better off than formerly; still Kitty felt little Mary to be a burden upon them, and hated her accordingly. All day long the child was subject to her ill-humour, and by degrees to that of her sons and daughters also, who, Willy excepted, took a delight in annoying and abusing her. The mother was very fond of Willy; and when he was at home Mary had a respite from her troubles, for he always took her part. Sometimes in the cold days of winter, when he returned from school, and found her shivering in a distant corner of the room, and striving to suppress her struggling tears, he would take her hand, and lead her, in spite of her resistance, towards the chimney corner, and make her sit down by his side whilst he played or talked with her. It was fortunate for Mary that Willy had been a spoiled child all his life, and that his mother rarely thwarted him.

But oh! those winter days! No one can tell what Mary suffered. There was a near neighbour who pitied her sincerely. How good-natured Ann Jones's heart ached when she saw Mary with her little hands and feet naked, and covered with chilblains, returning from the brook with a pitcher of water too heavy for her strength, and the tears streaming down her cheeks at the pain she endured; or going to the wood for sticks, and not daring to return without a load sufficient for a strong boy! How her heart ached when she heard Kitty's imperious voice, or, what was worse, her blows, and Mary's heavy sobs! She knew that her remonstrances would be vain, still she could not forbear inquiring what was the matter. The only reply she ever obtained was, 'that it was no business of hers,' and that Kitty was only punishing 'the worst and most troublesome brat that any one was ever plagued with'. The people of the village by this time began to say that the Harries's did not treat Mary well; but an event in their family put a stop to all gossip on the subject.

Willy was taken ill, and all the care and attention of his mother was directed towards him. He had a violent fever, and in the height of his malady Mary was no longer persecuted, but was allowed to sit, unnoticed, by his bedside, holding his burning hand, and crying as if her heart would break. As long as Willy remained sensible he would not allow her to quit him, but if she left the room, always asked whither she was gone. The mother was distracted with grief, for there was, from the first, little hope of his recovery. Mary was now old enough to understand the misery of her condition. When she reflected upon the probability of her losing the only being in the wide world who loved her, her brain became bewildered, and she could neither think nor move. Willy dead! What would become of her? She must die too, for how could she live without him? When he begged her not to cry, and told her that he should soon be well again, she ran into the open air to sob alone and unheard; but when he said that he thought he should die, and hoped God Almighty would forgive him and take him to heaven, she fell upon the bed, threw her arms about him, and wept so violently that she was obliged to be removed from the room. Then she would go to Ann Jones, and ask her if Willy must die.

'God only knows that, my poor child,' was the good

woman's reply. 'If it be His blessed will that he should recover, he will get well yet; and if not, I hope he will go to a better place, for he is a good little boy, Mary.'

'Oh! if I could only go with him,' sobbed Mary. 'If God would take me too, then I wouldn't mind. Oh! if I could die and go to heaven with him, we should be so happy!'

It was in vain for Ann Jones to try to comfort her, for she would not be comforted. She watched the face of her only friend change and become convulsed. She knew that he was dying, and she felt an agony of grief that few, perhaps, have ever known, since few are circumstanced as she was. When Willy turned his dying eyes upon her, and she saw their glazed, fixed look – when Kitty uttered a piercing cry and sunk upon the bed – she knew that all was over, and that her only friend was gone from her. She felt, as she afterwards described it, 'all over giddy'; and when Ann Jones led her from the room, and took her to her own house, she was almost insensible. She remained with her friend Ann until the funeral was over; but whilst the corpse continued in the house she stole over constantly to look at Willy, and nothing that Ann could do or say gave her any comfort. Her only consolation appeared to be in talking of her departed friend and companion.

She returned home and found that Willy's death had not softened Kitty's heart towards her. I should only disgust my readers were I to enter fully upon the long series of persecutions that she had to endure, not only from Kitty, but from Mrs Shenkin and the rest of the family. It is supposed that her present hatred of Mrs Shenkin had its foundation in her recollection of past ill-treatment. Suffice to say, that under the united influence of her tormentors her health and spirits entirely gave way. Ann Jones began to think there was something strange about the child. She seemed to forget events in an extraordinary manner, and talking of Willy was still her only pleasure. She would recall, with painful minuteness, every word he had said to her on any occasion, together with the particulars of his death and funeral, always ending by wishing she had died with, or instead of, him. Sometimes she would start suddenly, as from a train of thought, and ask an incoherent question; but at home she seldom spoke at all, bearing blows and angry words with apparent indifference. This manner made Kitty, and her gossip, the present Mrs Shenkin, more bitter against her than ever.

Ann Jones was one day summoned across the road to the Harries's house by fearful screams. She had before interfered between Kitty and Mary, and she now found the door locked against her. She had witnessed Mary's transgression on the present occasion, and felt assured that she was undergoing a severe punishment. The child had been to the brook for a pitcher of water, and had placed it upon the door-step while she unfastened the door. It was winter, and the stones were covered with ice. Her foot slipped, and she fell against the pitcher, which rolled off the step and broke to atoms. She screamed out. Kitty appeared, gave her a blow on the head, and dragged her into the house. The door was closed after them, and Ann Jones saw and heard no more, until the violent screams I have already mentioned, met her ear. She listened for a few moments to what was passing within. The screams gradually subsided into a low, muffled sound, and then all was quiet. She knocked, and no one came. She knocked louder and louder, and at last the door opened, and Mrs Shenkin appeared.

'Oh! Ann, is that you?' she said, looking as red as suppressed passion could look. 'There's nobody at home but me; and I was just gone into the garden for some cabbages, and I locked the door because there is so many idle good-for-nothings about.'

'Where is Mary then?' inquired Ann, looking her fixedly in the face.

'Oh! she's just gone out for a pitcher of water,' was the reply.

'Who was that I heard screaming just now? You must have been making a terrible noise in the garden by yourself,' pursued Ann.

'Dear, yes, I think I heard it too; 'twas somebody up the lane, I suppose. Shall we go and look?'

'You can't deceive me,' said Ann, with a firm voice. 'I know those screams were Mary's; and if you don't bring her here to me, I'll go and fetch a constable.'

'Go, and look yourself,' said Mrs Shenkin; 'I tell you she isn't in the house.'

Ann went accordingly; she searched the back kitchen, but Mary was not there – she went up stairs, but she was not to be found – she ran into the garden and called, but no one answered; again she returned to the back kitchen, where Mrs Shenkin was standing looking triumphant. A short sob met her ear. She suddenly recollected that there was an old cellar little used, and consequently forgotten by the neighbours. She went to a door covered with dirt and cobwebs, before which was placed a long stool. Mrs Shenkin declared that it was impossible to open that door, and that nobody ever went through it, because the cellar was haunted.

'Well, I'll brave the ghosts,' said Ann, and pushing open the door, descended a few steps into a dark room. The objects it contained were scarcely visible, but Ann determined to prosecute the search. She walked round, and in one corner discovered Mary, stretched upon the floor, apparently lifeless, whilst near her, with a large rope in her hand, stood Kitty. Ann Jones endeavoured to raise the child, but she shrunk back, and screamed as if from pain. Ann spoke to her, but she was not, for a few minutes, aware who she was, mistaking her for Kitty. She was evidently much injured, for she could scarcely move. Ann declared her intention of going at once for a magistrate, when Kitty, in terror, burst out into promises of amendment, accompanied by every possible asseveration, declaring that she would be kind to Mary for the future, and would never lift her arm aganist her again. Ann made no promises, but insisted upon Mary's being removed from the dark cellar to bed, reproaching Kitty, meanwhile, for her disgraceful conduct to the poor orphan child. Kitty was terrified into decency, and poor Mary was conveyed up stairs.

Ann went to the parish officers, but could not obtain no satisfaction, as they said Mary did not belong to Llangathen, and the Harrieses must do the best they could with her. She had no higher authority to appeal to, and was therefore obliged to content herself by bringing the whole village about Kitty's ears. But this was of no service to Mary, and did not ameliorate her condition. She was now seldom visible, but as no great noise was heard in the house, the subject was gradually forgotten by all excepting Ann, who was constantly on the watch, but who seldom caught sight of Mary.

One morning a great bustle was seen and heard at John Harries's. All the household were in consternation, and the neighbours had collected about the house to learn what was the matter. Mary was missing – no one knew where she was, or what had become of her. Kitty said that she went to bed as usual the preceding night, at eight o'clock, and that in the morning she had disappeared. There was such evident truth in Kitty's statement, and such alarm in her manner, that Ann Jones believed the child had made her escape; but others whispered that there was something dark in the affair. The matter was, however, cleared up in a few days, by the appearance of Kitty Harries in the village street, triumphantly dragging Mary by the arm. She had discovered her in a wood at some distance, where it is supposed she had subsisted upon acorns and wild fruits. She looked attenuated, and laughed strangely when the neighbours questioned her upon what had happened to her, making incoherent answers to them. Ann Jones and her children crowded round her when she came near their house; and Kitty told Ann to talk to her, since she could obtain no information from her. Ann asked her many questions, but received no fit answers to any. She fancied that the weakness proceeding from long abstinence had affected her mentally as well as bodily, and begged Kitty to give her food and repose. But Mary clung closely to Ann, and with a piteous cry entreated to be allowed to remain with her. It was vain; Kitty seized her roughly by the arm, and dragged her across to her old prison. She was kept close to the house; and Ann Jones never saw her but through the windows, for Kitty chose to consider herself aggrieved, and now never spoke to her good-natured neighbour.

One Sunday Kitty took Mary to church. Ann Jones boldly approached her, and spoke to her, but she only laughed strangely at her, whilst Kitty was dragging her along. She was no longer the handsome blooming girl that she was when first she entered Llangathen, but was pale, and thin, and haggard, exciting compassion in every one who looked at her. As she walked through the churchyard, on her way back, she made her escape from Kitty, and ran towards Willy's grave. She knew it well, for when she had been allowed some portion of liberty, she delighted in stealing thither, and planting primroses, or whatever flowers she could obtain, around and about it. She seated herself upon the earth, and began to sob bitterly. The people gathered round her, and asked her what was the matter, but she made no reply to their inquiries. Kitty told them, with genuine tears in her eyes, that the child had been very fond of her little boy, and was now lamenting for him. Poor Mary talked very incoherently, and said she saw her dear Willy down below calling her to come to him, and that she would not leave him any more, but must go to him and live with him. Kitty at last forced her from the grave; but Ann Jones, and every one else, now saw that the child's reason was fast departing.

Still she had cunning enough again to elude the vigilance of her tormentors. This she effected one night when Kitty was on a visit to a friend, and John Harries absent on business. No one knows how she escaped from the house, or whither she went, but all search for her this time was vain. Years passed, and she was not heard of, and the inhabitants of Llangathen soon forgot that she ever existed. Even Ann Jones and her family began to speak of her less often; and when she became the subject of their conversation, they alluded to her as one dead. It was never ascertained what became of her during this period; but it was supposed that she wandered far away, a destitute and lone creature.

Homeless beside a thousand homes she stood,
Beside a thousand tables pin'd and wanted food.

Three or four years had elapsed, when one evening, towards dusk, there appeared opposite Ann Jones's house a beggar-girl of a strangely wild appearance. She looked about fifteen or sixteen years old, much weather-beaten, and very poorly clad. Ann spoke to her, and asked her who she was, and what she wanted. 'I won't go there,' was the only answer she received, as the girl pointed to the Harries's house. Ann looked at her; and she said, 'Mayn't I go in with you. Just you hide me away – you won't beat me – you won't kill me, no, I'm sure you won't.' Ann looked again earnestly into her face, and in the now wild black eyes, matted raven hair, and bronzed features, recognised the once lovely little Mary. She caught the poor girl in her arms, and almost carried her into the house. How shocked was she to find that reason, sense, recollection, were now entirely departed! An occasional glimmering of memory in the darkened chambers of her mind was all that appeared to show they had once been there. Ann talked to her on every subject that had once interested her, and endeavoured to recall the past; but she might as well have uttered her words to the northern blast. She seemed to have a partial recollection of Ann personally, that is to say, she unconsciously looked to her for kindness. The only subject that awakened any thing like memory were the Harrieses, at the mention of whose names she would look wildly about her, and seek to hide in some corner of the room. When Ann spoke of Willy, she became silent and subdued, and appeared to endeavour to recollect the past. A casual mention of her father produced the words, 'If my father knew of it, I shouldn't be like this;' but no sooner had she uttered them than total forgetfulness succeeded. Ann Jones could not refrain from tears; and when Mary saw them flow, she knelt down by her side, took her hand, and looking wistfully into her face, said, 'Ah, yes! poor Mary – you're kind and sorry, and don't laugh and make sport!' She was then silent for a few minutes, putting her hand upon her forehead, as if to summon thought to her aid, and then added, 'You used, didn't you, . . . yes, you used to . . .' but before she could finish the sentence the light was gone, and her mind was dark again. Ann could make nothing from her wandering discourse of the life she had led for the past four years. She saw that she was mad, and rejoiced that it seemed a quiet madness – a mere loss of reason, without any fierce and terrible impulses. Her mind had gradually sunk under a repetition of cruelties, and was now a void. Ann prepared a bed for her, but it was with difficulty she could induce her to lie upon it. 'Won't they come?' she asked, 'won't they beat me?' Ann at length quieted her fears, and watched until she saw her sound asleep before she went to bed herself; but the next morning she was gone.

Ann Jones awoke with the sun, but no Mary. She spoke of her appearance and disappearance to her neighbours; for though she had been seen in the village, she had not been recognised. A slight search was made, but not diligently prosecuted, for the parish officers thought it better to let her roam about at will. The Harrieses pretended to be sorry that they had not seen her; and there the matter ended. As time passed on, however, Mad Moll – for so the poor creature was called – was occasionally seen in the neighbourhood. The Harrieses left Llangathen, for nothing prospered with them; and it was said that John Harries was afflicted with much inward sorrow and remorse for their treatment of Mary.

Nearly twenty years have elapsed since Mary left Llangathen, and she is a lone wanderer still, and will not voluntarily remain under any roof even for a day. When they once confined her she became frantic. Her mind has, in a slight degree, recovered its powers, particularly that of memory, for she seems sometimes to have snatches of the past. She wanders the country over, appearing for a few hours, or a day, in some particular haunt, but never remaining long. She visits fairs and public gatherings, where she is the sport of many an unfeeling or unreflecting spectator; but she seldom appears in a place more than once in a twelvemonth. She is in general treated with kindness in her periodical rounds, and never forgets such treatment. There is one poor consolation in reflecting on her present condition: she is not unhappy, – she goes where she likes, and amuses herself as she likes, singing and dancing the livelong day. She procures food here, and a garment there, and, mindless as she is, is contended; whilst He who feeds the ravens is not unmindful of her!

II

David

MALLT WILLIAMS

It was the close of a September day, fifty years ago. The shadows were lengthening fast, and David Lloyd quickened his steps, as he went gaily down through the little blue-roofed Aber village. He was a tall, well set up young fellow, swarthy and sun-burnt, like a typical Cymro, and in his Sunday suit of black he looked what he was, a prosperous, superior young farmer. As he crossed the ford of the rocky rushing river, on which Aber stood, a little old man, very poorly dressed, came down the opposite bank.

'Good even to thee, Uncle Bili,' sang out David in his sonorous Cymraeg. 'I'm uncommon glad to be back home agen. Indeed, an' the town canna' hold a candle to Aber, I'm thinking.'

Uncle Bili stood and regarded him earnestly.

'David,' he said, in his quavering voice, 'tell me is it true what the brethren sent word from Abertowy, that thee ha' been converted? Oh, *bachgen*, don't break my heart by saying no,' he cried earnestly.

David was by nature grave and sedate. Uncle Bili could not understand his present gay mood. How should he? The old man had left his youth so far, far behind him, that even the knowledge that David was going to his love-tryst would not have accounted for his gaiety in his eyes. Instantly a subtle change swept over the young man's face; it was not less happy, but it was a graver happiness. He answered in a lower, but eager tone, –

'Indeed, and it's truth they speak. I ha' given my word to tell the brethren of Aber the story of it at the next meeting.'

'An' that's the morrow's even, on Pen yr Allt. Wilt be there, *bachgen*?' asked Uncle Bili, quickly.

'I'll not fail,' answered David, with his candid eyes fixed upon him.

'Praise the Lord,' said Uncle Bili, fervently, and they parted. David turned off from the road into the fields, presently paused by an old ash tree, that commanded a view of a substantial yellow farmhouse, and putting his hand to his lips, gave a clear musical call. In a few minutes, a young girl came running up the field, a little blue 'turn-over' shawl thrown over her head; her pretty face was flushed, her lips parted with her rapid breathing.

'Oh, David,' she cried, as he seized her hands, 'I was afraid I couldna' come when I heard thee call, for the squire is sitting with father in the parlour, and I had to wait upon them.' She paused a moment to gain breath, and then went on. ''Twas of thee they were talking, and sore grew my heart, indeed, to hear them. 'Deed, David,' she broke out passionately, 'what's come over thee after thee went to Abertowy? *Thee* gone over to those low Methodist people. Thee attending their meetings, and whimpering and praying. David, David, I'd never ha' thought it o' thee; but now thee'll forget these new notions, thee'll come back to the old ways, and be my own dear David again.'

She clasped her two hands round his arm, and her pretty face looked coaxingly up at him. He had listened quietly to her, only his face had grown very sober. Now he spoke.

'Gwen *anwylaf*,' he said gravely, 'I canna' be the same David, I'm thinking, in this world ever agen, thank the Almighty who led me to the house of Jonas Dafydd at

Abertowy. I went there bent on earthly gain, and behold I find the pearl o' great price; there I received conviction of sin, and there, God be praised, I was converted.'

Gwen Jones looked at him with a great scorn in her bright blue eyes, –

'One would think thee had never entered the church's door in thy life, David Lloyd. Must thee go the long weary way to Abertowy to hear what the parson tells us every Sabbath? Thee ha' gotten a bit silly, David, I am thinking.'

'Parson never brought it home to me,' answered David, earnestly, 'and *anwyl, anwyl*, it's never at peace will I be until I see thee, too, converted, saved for time and eternity.'

'If thee likes to think thyself a great sinner, David, I'll thank thee to leave my name alone,' cried Gwen indignantly. 'Me, indeed, going to church regular, happen there's service, and drinking tea twice a year at the Rectory.' Then, her mood changing, – 'David, thee'll never let these wild new notions come between us, for I never would stand my man being pointed out as a Ranter.'

He held her hands in a strong grip.

'Gwen, it's more than life to me. I canna' go back from my word.'

'David, thee knows the squire is at the house with father, and he said afore me, that given what he ha' heard of your new Methodist leanings be true, thee shall be no tenant of his, and your cousin, Morgan Lloyd, shall rent Pannau.'

All the light died out of David's expressive face. Pannau was the little farm where he and Gwen had hoped to begin their happy married life. It had been the goal of his ambition for years.

'The squire ha' promised it me. He canna' be so unjust to go back from his given word,' he burst out vehemently.

'He never promised a Methodist,' rejoined Gwen, 'and I for one canna' blame him.'

'What would thee ha' me do?' asked David, in a strangely dejected tone. The possible loss of Pannau was a terrible blow.

'Break with the whole lot of Ranters. Why, in the Aber they'll be calling thee Uncle Bili Bali's shadow. Thee should ha' more respect for thyself, David. It would ha' broken thy poor mother's heart. Think how thee ha' vexed the squire and the parson, and thy Uncle Ifan.' Then using a more personal plea, and more likely to be effective with her lover, – 'Give it all up for my sake,' she whispered, and laid her fair cheek against his swarthy one. The strong arms holding her pressed her more closely; he bowed his head on her bright hair; she could hear the heavy throbbing of his heart. Something of awe prevented even Gwen from breaking the great silence. At last he spoke, –

'And if I say no, what then?'

'Why I'll never be wife of thine, and that's plain speaking.'

'But if thee love me. Love is for ever,' cried David. 'Oh *anwylaf,* I never thought thee'd throw me over. If it was wrong I'd done, it's not asking thee to marry me, I'd be; but it's trying to walk upright in a wicked world I am, and thee should be the verra' one to give me a helping hand, for it's weary walking among the briars and thorns and stones.'

'I love thee, David; it's not ashamed I'd be to say it to the whole world, but if it broke the verra' heart in my breast I'd never take a Ranter for my man.'

She withdrew herself from his arms, and, in David's eyes, she had never looked lovelier, as she faced him in her wilful, defiant mood. The sight unmanned him. 'God forgive me, for I canna' make up my mind to say the word that will part us for ever,' he said, brokenly. 'Give me time to think and pray over it, Gwen.'

'Thee knows o' the meeting on Pen yr Allt, the morrow's night, I doubt na'. Well, go there, and stand up preaching and praying, and never will Gwen Jones give thee word good or bad again. That's my word, and I'll no go back from it, David Lloyd.'

She drew the little shawl over her head, turned, and went quickly down the field, without word of farewell to her lover. He stood looking after her in a dazed sort of way. It seemed to him as if his merry, kind-hearted Gwen were possessed by another spirit than the one he had heretofore known. He watched her till she was lost to sight, and then, feeling as if the light of his eyes had indeed gone from him, he too left the old ash tree, and went striding up the dingle, not caring whither he went. A fierce battle was raging in his heart, – the old conflict between good and evil, – self crying out against the sacrifice demanded of it. 'Anything but this, and I will do it,' was his utterance. All that night he passed on the hills; walking was a relief to the throbbing heart and brain. At last, worn out as much by mental anguish as physical fatigue, he stumbled over a loose stone, fell forward, and lay face downwards on a bed of dry heather. So he lay mute and motionless for hours.

He had left the mountain-top, he was walking on a broad white glistening highway, going gaily to his tryst with Gwen. Then before him on the road he saw a stranger-form, drawing with difficulty some heavy burden. As he came nearer, he saw it was a great cross, blood-stained, and blood was falling from the bearer's face and hands upon the smooth white road. David's heart was full of generous impulses. He ran forward, and laying hold of the cross, exerted all his strength to drag it along himself. He could not see the cross bearer's face, but a great happiness filled his heart. He broke out into a hymn of joy, and then two hands pressed his arm. Gwen was beside him, putting forth her strength to draw him away. She looked so beautiful,

David could not deny her. He released his hold on the cross and taking Gwen's hand, turned away. Yet, as he did so, he looked back, and the cross-bearer lifting his head, looked upon David, a look so reproachful, so sweet, so soul-piercing, that David's heart was like to break within him with contrition.

The night passed, dawn came, and David, awakening, lifted up his head in a dull wonder as to where he was. Then a sudden cry broke from him, for, casting his eyes downwards, he saw a long narrow valley stretching before him, and nestling at the mountain's base was a smiling well-cultivated little farm. He looked, and drew a long breath of pain. He knew every one of those fields by heart, and the comfortable yellow farmhouse and pile of outbuildings. He loved Pannau Farm, – it was the summit of his ambition to reign master there. Every thought of his heart had centred in Gwen and Pannau. And now? Must they be given up? Could not he effect some sort of a compromise between them and his conscience? Could he not retain the outward signs of a good churchman, and follow his new convictions in secret? But it was not in vain David had dreamed his dream of the cross-bearer. Imagination recalled the sad reproachful gaze of the divine eyes, and David writhed upon his bed of heather; it seemed to him now that, in accepting Gwen's decision, he would be guilty of the fearful sin of denying his Redeemer. He lifted himself to his knees, and poured out his heart in fervent prayer. The hour of weakness passed, – he was strong as he had never been before. Earth, for the moment, had passed out of his heart, and earthly things. He could look calmly on Pannau itself when he rose from his knees.

A mass of rock stood out boldly on the wild hill-side, and

in the serene autumnal night, dark-robed figures crept towards it, as to an appointed goal. From the four points of the compass, singly, or in twos and threes, they came, silently, softly, without speed or sound, until some fifty or sixty souls were gathered in the hollow below the rock. A preacher mounted the natural platform and gave out a well-known Welsh hymn. They sang it softly, in a sweet, sad, minor key, – the plaintive sad refrain was in harmony with their lives. They were very poor, they were persecuted, many of them had come long distances over the hills, and were foot-sore and faint for food; but to feed the spiritual hunger the needs of the weak flesh were unheeded. The slowly rising harvest moon sent long shafts of silver light before, to herald its coming, and the figure of the young man, who now advanced onto the rocky platform, was visible to all in the crowd, as he stood in the growing radiance. He did not see the up-turned expectant faces, or the little thrill of interest that stirred the congregation at his first appearance there, for his eagle glance had leapt beyond, and fixed itself on one form standing on the outskirts of the crowd. Shawled and muffled as she was, he read her through her disguise; she had come to prove him, and for a moment his resolution faltered. She threw back her hood with a little defiant movement, and their eyes met, – anger and pain and a challenge in the one, a sorrowful leave-taking in the other. No one knew what it cost David Lloyd to kneel down and say the brief introductory prayer, no one guessed what he was giving up. At first, in the tumult of his spirit, he could only close his eyes, while his lips moved voicelessly. Then it seemed to the enthusiast that the Master Himself unsealed his lips, and he preached as he never would again. God and the devil, heaven and hell, death and judgment, were living realities to him, and the passion, and the zeal, and the fire of the enthusiast were upon him; his heart was bursting to save his fellow-sinners from the wrath of an offended Creator, to lead their wandering steps into the way of peace.

When the meeting broke up, he went home with Uncle Bili Bali. It was day-dawn when they reached Deri Farm, David's home. His Uncle Ifan, with whom he lived, was coming out of the gate, with his men and young Morgan Lloyd, his nephew, all armed with reaping hooks, and bound for the corn fields. He stopped when he saw David and his companion, and his brow grew black as night as he addressed his nephew.

'An' it's now thee art returning from meeting, David? Thee'd better go back to thy praying preaching friends. I ha' told thee once for all I'd ha' no Methodees round Deri, and sorrow I ha' to think it is my own brother's son I am speaking to. All you men here bear witness and remember what I swear now, – that the portion intended for my nephew David Lloyd shall go to his cousin Morgan. Get thee gone, David,' he re-iterated, in a voice choked with passion. There was a taunting laugh from young Morgan Lloyd. Without a word David turned and went. Uncle Bili Bali overtook the young man, and laid a detaining hand upon his shoulder.

'What wilt thee do, Dei *bach*?' he faltered.

'I shall na' starve; I ha' health and two hands to work,' said David, answering the old man's anxious look with a re-assuring smile. 'One thing thee need na' fear. This will na' make me give up being a Methodee.'

'God be thanked,' said Uncle Bili, solemnly.

'I must seek a lodging in the Aber,' went on David, in a lighter tone. 'Happen I'll find a room there.'

'Come home with me, *bachgen;* thee art welcome to bit and sup as long as I ha' a roof to cover me. I'm fain to ha' thee, David, for it's a bit lonesome whiles.'

'Thee shall never ha' to say that agen, Uncle Bili,' said David, kindly.

It was a changed life for David Lloyd from that day. The

rising young farmer, the betrothed of handsome Gwen Jones, the favourite nephew of a well-to-do man, he sunk at once to the level of the labourer, toiling monotonously for daily bread.

In the summer, he hired himself out to the farmers, in winter he worked with Uncle Bili at his trade of shoe-making; summer and winter he sat far into the night over his books. Study had become a passion with him; his one ambition was to enter the ministry. Such a powerful preacher had a call, his new friends said, to God's special service. He lived as straitly as any ascetic, – no meat ever passed his lips, his drink was water, his clothes of the coarsest. He made no friends; he was a grave, silent recluse outside his work. The wounds of disappointed hopes and misplaced affection were slow in healing; because he made no moan, he suffered the more. He went down into the cleansing fires of life's discipline, and came out purified.

The winter had been a mild and humid one, the drip, drop, drip, drop of rain sounded steadily day after day, the mists lingered in the valleys, and never quite left the mountain-tops, and spring brought no health-giving purifying winds sweeping over the land. There was wailing and moaning round Aber, for the terrible scourge of small-pox had broken out in the country side, and death was reaping a rich harvest. Round Aber, house after house was stricken, and so terror-struck were the inhabitants that those who escaped the disease refused to come forward and nurse the sick. In one of the upper windows at Pannau Farm a dim light was burning at midnight, – sure token of the dread visitant. In that upper room Gwen Jones, – Gwen Lloyd now, wife of Morgan Lloyd, – sat nursing her delirious boy in the adjoining room; her husband lay dead of the same disease. She was alone in the house, all her servants had fled, no neighbour dare venture to share her most lonely vigil. She was dead-tired; no food had passed her lips all day, she had wept all her tears away, nothing could relieve the dry aching of her heart. She had to put forth all her strength to keep her boy in bed. The door opened noiselessly, and a man in the garb of a minister came in and stood by the bed-side. She lifted her weary eyes and recognised him. She had never given him sign or greeting in thirteen years. She knew he had long ago left the village to take charge of a church at Abertowy, but she was too dazed and heavy-hearted to feel surprise at his presence at Pannau.

'Go and lie down awhile, cousin Gwen, I'll mind the little lad,' he said gently.

'I canna' leave him; he shall die in his mother's arms,' she cried, passionately. 'Oh, my *anwyl*, my *anwyl*,' and she tried to restrain the child's efforts to leap out of bed, but she had little strength left, and it was the man's strong hands that laid him back on his pillows.

'Indeed, and we hope he'll not die whiles yet,' said David Lloyd, cheerfully. 'Trust thy lad to me. I ha' learnt how to nurse the sick, and thee needs rest sadly, Gwen.'

'Ha' thee no fear, David?' she asked, as he bent over the poor little body, one mass of disease.

He gave her a sweet strong look. 'I've given my life and all I ha' into my Maker's hands, whiles back; happen he ha' taken the power o' fearing out o' my heart. I came over from Abertowy to see Uncle Bili Bali die, and down at Aber I heard of thy trouble, and I knew then my work was here. Get thee to rest, Gwen, in peace.' The weaker will yielded to the stronger. She rose and left her boy in his hands.

The lad did not die. David's devoted nursing saved his life, the doctor said; but the day the little invalid was pronounced out of danger David left Pannau, and dragged himself wearily to his lodging in the village, feeling in throbbing head and aching limbs that the disease had fastened on himself. For weeks he lay on a sick bed, and when his strength came back again to him, and he was once more able to go out and mix in the world of men, he knew he would carry the brand of disease upon his face all his life long.

Gwen Lloyd and her little son were returning home, after a sojourn at the seaside, and as they drove up the steep hill road to the farm in the evening quiet, they saw the figure of David Lloyd coming down the Coed-cae side. She stopped the gig and dismounted, telling the man to drive on to Pannau. Then she stood in the roadway waiting David's approach. He walked slowly, leaning heavily on his staff, and when he reached her side, he sank down wearily on the sloping bank, and signed to her to do the same, but she chose to stand and front him. As she saw the fearful ravages disease had made in his once handsome face, she cried out sharply, –

'Thee ha' been at death's door, David, and through me and mine. Woe's me, for I ha' done thee injury all my life.'

'*Taw sôn, y fach,*' said David, soothingly. 'Indeed, an' I am uncommon glad to ha' seen thee agen, cousin Gwen. I bide na long at Aber, and I ha' wished to say farewell to thee.'

She pressed nearer him.

'You are not going to die,' she said breathlessly.

He looked up at her with his old bright smile.

'Na, na, I'm thinking I'll be whiles longer on this airth. It's going to foreign parts I am, Gwen.'

She stared at him in amazement that made her silent. He went on dreamily, –

'"The earth is the Lord's, and the fulness thereof, the world, and they that dwell therein." I aye thought to live and die among my own valleys and hills in my dear Cymru;

but it's been borne in upon me lately that happen the world is the Lord's, there's many a thousand soul living therein, who ha' never so much as heard o' the Lord's name, and I'm thinking happen thee ha' the light thyself, thee should e'en take it to them who lie in darkness. One of the great missionary societies is sending me to the South Seas with others, and I set out for London the morrow's morn.'

He paused a moment, then repeated, –

'Indeed, an' I am pleased to see thee looking thyself agen, and well and happy, cousin Gwen.'

She could not say so much for him.

They made a contrast, those two on the wild hill road. She looked a comely matron in her handsome black garments, her face round and ruddy, not a line on the smooth brow, – her blue eyes bright and undimmed as of yore. You could see hers had been a pleasant, prosperous, unruffled life. He was thin and finely drawn as an ascetic, the clean-shaven face full of lines innumerable, his iron-grey hair was turning to white on the temples, – he was branded with the mark of a loathsome disease, he stooped, he was poorly, coarsely clad. With it all, he looked possessed of a latent strength and mental vigour, and his eyes had the old ardent fire.

'Wish me God-speed, Gwen,' he said, holding out his hand.

She did not take it.

'Thee need not go to outlandish wilds, but bide at home in comfort. Things are not what they were, and I remember thee had the making of a good farmer in the old days.' The colour left her ruddy cheek, her voice faltered. 'Bide here and manage the farms for me. It is more than one woman can do and make it pay.'

The enthusiast, buried in his own dreams, did not read her meaning. He looked at her with his clear candid eyes, but his thoughts were far away. Vaguely she felt that she was making him some sort of offer, that she meant to be kind.

'Thank thee kindly, Gwen, there's many an honest man will be ready to serve thee and take pride in the doing of it, while I ha' my own bit work to mind. Fare-thee-well, cousin. The Lord bless thee, and bring thee into His kingdom of peace.'

Then he clasped his hands over his staff and bowed his head upon them. He had forgotten the woman at his side. Once they had been all in all to each other; she, now in her ease and prosperity, was less than the least of God's creatures to him. They had not a thought together in common. All these years he had cherished his higher nature; she, her lower. She had no delicate perception, or she would have left him then. Instead, she took a step nearer.

'I am so lonely,' she muttered, drooping her head.

David heard without comprehending her. He was wrapped in contemplation of the Eternal, to whom, in the after years, he would be drawn by the fiery path of martyrdom.

Gwen Lloyd went home, and put her bonnet carefully away in her best band-box. She smoothed out the rumpled satin strings with a meditative face. 'I must ha' been a bit silly to bid David stay. It's laughing they would be at him in market, – it's too innocent he is to make a good bargain, and there isn't a man in the country-side but would jump to be master at Pannau. I'll bide quiet a wee, and look round.'

III

Nancy on the Warpath

SARA MARIA SAUNDERS

The relations between Mr Morris and his son were very strained. They met in the chapel; but they never spoke to one another, and neither had ever crossed the other's threshold since the day of Edward's marriage. It was said that old Mrs Morris was feeling the estrangement badly; and when Edward's boy was born, she declared to her husband that she was going to see her first grandchild, whether he liked it or not! Mr Morris looked at her; and she quailed before him: when you have been under subjection for thirty years, you lose the capacity for self-assertion; and poor, weak Mrs Morris went back to the parlour, and said nothing! People wondered how Mr Morris would act on the occasion of the baby's christening, and many were the theories advanced. But on the eventful night he announced that a baptism was to take place, then sat down in his seat, and read his hymn book until that part of the service was over. Neither by word or gesture, did he own to any feeling of interest in the ceremony. Both Edward and Nancy were much hurt at this display of indifference, and the former would have joined another denomination, if only his wife had been agreeable. But loyalty was one of Nancy's strong features, and she would not consent to leave the old chapel, which was associated with the happiest events of her childhood. Five years thus passed away, and then Edward Morris had a severe illness. The doctor gave but little hope of his recovery, and Nancy, with tearless eyes, bade me go over to Cwmdwr to tell the father and mother of their son's condition. I gave my message with a brusqueness that was almost brutal; it seemed to me that the cruel old man deserved to suffer, and I did not try to pick my words. If I imagined that I would make any impression upon him, I was mistaken. He listened to my story with a stolid indifference that I found very hard to bear. I was just leaving the room when I thought that I heard a moan, and I looked around; it came from a distant sofa by the wall, which in the uncertain light I had not noticed. Scarcely knowing what was right to do, I went across the room, and saw Mrs Morris huddled up in a corner of the couch. 'My boy is dying, dying, dying!' she wailed.

'Come with me to see him,' I said suddenly, forgetting for an instant the old autocrat and his power.

'I daren't come, oh, I daren't,' she moaned, 'if I only dared!'

'Young man, it is time for you to see to your own business, instead of troubling with what doesn't concern you: there's the way out.' He pointed with his finger to the door, and I felt compelled to go.

When I got to Bryn Croynan, the doctor had just left the house. 'If there's no change before morning he will die,' Nancy said very quietly, 'and I haven't much hope; well, what did his father say?' I told her everything; she said nothing, but I saw her go into the parlour where little Edward was playing with his bricks. She stooped down and kissed him, then ran up stairs. A few minutes later she came down dressed as for a walk.

'Are you going out?' I asked in surprise.

'Yes,' she said, 'I'm going to do what I hope my boy's wife would do for me if I were in such sore straits as *she*, poor thing. I'm going over to Cwmdwr to fetch Edward's mother to her son.'

'He won't let her come,' I said stupidly.

'I'll make him let her come,' she answered.

'Well, its sheer waste of time,' I retorted, 'Why do you leave your husband's side when you know how . . .'

'How short a time I may have him,' she finished quickly, 'I don't pretend that it is easy to go, but my heart aches for that poor woman yonder, and I *must* go to her.' It seemed to me that any king might have been proud to call Nancy his queen that moment. She looked regal as she stood ready to start on her errand of mercy. I followed her, Mrs Rogers was keeping guard in the sick room, and I believed that it was Nancy who needed me most at that hour.

She walked very quickly, and it seemed but a few seconds before we stood outside the door of Cwmdwr. Then, for a moment, she hesitated. 'I thought once of going through the back door into the kitchen,' she said quietly, 'but I've changed my mind, Edward's wife ought to enter her father-in-law's house through the front door.'

She knocked, and presently one of the maid servants opened the door. She held up her hands in dismay, 'You here, ma'am!' she cried.

'Yes,' said Nancy very quietly, 'don't make any fuss. I want to see your master and your *mistress*.' She laid particular stress on the last word.

'They're at supper,' the girl said slowly, 'you'd best not disturb them, master's not himself to-night.'

Nancy waved her aside imperiously, and unceremoniously walked into the parlour where Mr and Mrs Morris were sitting by the table. Mrs Morris staggered to her feet, 'He's gone, oh! he's gone!' she said dismally.

Nancy was beside her in a moment, 'No, he's not gone yet,' she said tenderly.

'I should like to know why you are here,' said Mr Morris very calmly.

Nancy met his gaze unflinchingly. 'I've come here to fetch Edward's mother to her son,' she replied steadily. 'Ann,' to the servant, who was staring stupidly at the door, 'fetch your mistress' bonnet and shawl; Mr Harris, will you get the mare put into the car, we'll be out in a few seconds. Mr Morris, your son is dying, so the doctor says, and I, his wife, who love him more than life, have left his side to give you another chance. You are an old man, and you can't live many years longer in the nature of things, and I'd like you to be able to feel, when you lie on your dying bed, that you hadn't this cruelty on your conscience, the cruelty of having kept a mother from her only child when he was on his death bed.' She placed her arm around the frail old woman and led her out without another word. The trap was ready, and I almost lifted Mrs Morris into it. Then we drove away in the darkness! Once, and once only, did Mrs Morris speak. 'Oh my dear,' she said plaintively, clutching hold of Nancy's hand, 'if Mr Morris 'll be in Heaven, I think I'd rather not go there!'

When we got to the house, Nancy led her mother-in-law upstairs to Edward's bedroom, he was lying, as we had left him, moaning and groaning, tossing about from one side of the bed to the other in the utter abandon of fever. His mother sat beside him, and once when he was semi-conscious for a moment, he seemed to recognize her; and placed his hot hand in hers. Towards morning he sank into a restful sleep, and the watchers realized that the worst was over. Nancy stole down stairs very early, 'He's sleeping like a child,' she said huskily, 'now that I have hope, I feel that I can cry, but, Mr Harris, tell me, ought I to ask old Mr Morris to come here?'

'I think you've done enough,' I said gruffly, 'he's got no more heart than a stone, and it's a case of casting pearls before swine to go and plead with him; no, I wouldn't go.'

She left the room, and ran lightly upstairs, but she only

remained away a couple of minutes. 'Just think, mother,' she said to Mrs Rogers, who was sipping her tea by the fire, '*he* has actually come, he must have slipped in when I was down here before, he's upstairs standing looking at Edward sleeping. Isn't it fine?' I stole upstairs, scarcely daring to believe Nancy's story, but she was quite right, he was certainly there, gazing intently at his son's face. I went downstairs at once, I believed it would be better to leave the three together. We were all tired, and I suppose that we fell asleep, I was wakened by the sound of wheels outside. I sprang to my feet and looking out, saw Mr and Mrs Morris in their trap disappearing round the corner! So this was the meaning of Mr Morris's visit; he had come to fetch away his wife! Nancy burst out crying, she had been so pleased with her success the previous evening, and this disappointment was hard to bear! Edward recovered his health very quickly, and in a few weeks he was sufficiently well to go about his usual duties, but the breach between him and his father had grown wider, and it seemed to me, that nothing short of a miracle could ever bring them together again.

I think that it must have been about six months after this that I heard incidentally that old Mrs Morris was ill. I carried the news to Bryn Croynan, and Edward seemed deeply affected; but steadfastly refused to go to Cwmdwr to see his mother. Nancy and I argued with him for an hour, but all in vain. 'I'd do anything for my mother,' he said, 'if I could only get her away from that house, but go there *I cannot*.'

'Well,' Nancy said resolutely, 'if you won't go, I will. Your mother is not going to be ill with no one to tend her but servants; perhaps when I've smoothed the way a bit for you you will not be afraid of venturing,' she added a little sarcastically.

'What's the good of going there to be insulted to your face?' Edward asked warmly, 'I don't go to Waterton market past

Cwmdwr, because seeing it irritates me, and I'm in a bad temper all day in consequence.'

'I don't think you are right,' Nancy said calmly, 'you ought to go past Cwmdwr to market, just because there is a chance of your mother getting a look at you. Oh,' she added, the tears springing to her eyes, 'don't I know very well, that I'd be at the window, watching if my little Edward was likely to be passing near by, that's the way mothers are; you men don't understand.'

'I'm sure there's no one who thinks more of his mother than I do,' Edward said stoutly, 'only, poor little thing she's been downtrodden all her life, and every bit of spirit has been crushed out of her. I have been tempted again and again to go to see her, when I know that my father was away; but I felt that it would only mean more pain to her afterwards, – my father would say a few words that would bruise her more than a thousand kind words from me would soothe her.'

Nancy shook her head. 'You're are all wrong, Edward,' she said quickly, 'to hear you saying that you loved her, and thought about her, and spoke about her to your little boy would be something that she could treasure up in her heart, and if your father did throw a little cold water on things, he couldn't throw enough to cool her happiness. You've tried your way for nearly six years, try my way for once.'

That night there was a service at the chapel, and knowing that his father would be there, Edward walked over to Cwmdwr to see his mother.

'You were quite right old girl,' he said to Nancy, 'I wish I hadn't been so stubborn now, but bless me! it's dismal there; it's enough to give one the blues to spend half-an-hour there. There she was sitting upstairs in the bedroom with a little bit of fire not large enough to burn your hand; I asked her if my father begrudged her coal; and she began to cry and to say that I was always down on him, that it was her own fault about the fire, that she didn't like to trouble the girls to carry coals upstairs: there's a life she has led! and yet, I suppose they would call my father a good man, ugh!'

Nancy did not say much, but she rose early the following day, finished her work betimes, then taking little Edward with her, she went out after dinner. Her destination was Cwmdwr. She saw her father-in-law outside, and she walked up to him as naturally as if she were going to meet a friend. 'Good day,' she began, 'I have called to see my mother-in-law, perhaps I'd better leave little Edward with you while I go upstairs; there sonny, stay with grandfather while mother goes away for a bit.' It took the old man a few seconds to recover himself; then he said aloud, 'The impudent hussy!' But Nancy was upstairs by this time; she did not talk much, but she busied herself in putting the room neat, she built up the fire and ordered a bucketful of coals to be brought up, then she went downstairs, and to the amazement of the servants prepared a dainty little tea for the invalid, who looked quite bright and happy after Nancy's capable fingers had properly adjusted things. She said nothing about her boy, judging that the old lady was too weak to see him that day.

'Now, goodbye,' she said brightly, 'I hope you'll sleep nicely to-night, I have made your bed comfortably, and very soon I'll be round again, and will see to things.'

'My dear, you'd better not,' Mrs Morris said feebly.

'Oh, you leave things to me, I'm a good one for getting my way,' Nancy said gaily. She went downstairs and sought for Mr Morris, he was in the parlour writing; and when she opened the door, he said gruffly without looking round, 'Your child's in the kitchen, and I'll thank you to go home, and to remember that no one comes to this house excepting at my invitation.'

'I'm not going to leave this room till you and I have settled matters,' Nancy said firmly, closing the door as she spoke, and standing close to it. 'Now Mr Morris, I am ready as soon as you can leave your writing to attend to me, I'll tell you all I have to say, but of course, if you are busy, I'll stay till you have a little time to spare.'

The old man got up and faced her. 'Do you know to whom you are speaking?' he asked angrily.

'Oh yes, I am speaking to my husband's father,' Nancy said calmly, 'and you have got to listen to me either here or in chapel next Sunday, whichever suits you best. You know my mother, I think; well, I'm her daughter, and my mother's daughter has never yet been afraid of anyone, *and she's not afraid of you.*' There was so much determination in Nancy's face that the old man visibly recoiled.

'Well, say what you've got to say and begone,' he said roughly, 'I've no time to waste with your sort.'

'Very well,' Nancy said quietly. 'First of all, I want to tell you that you are a cruel husband, your wife is upstairs ill, and she has fewer comforts and poorer attendance than the wife of any one of your workmen.'

'That's a lie, a down right lie,' Mr Morris said fiercely.

'Oh no it isn't,' Nancy retorted, 'I'm not saying anything that I can't prove. A workman's wife, even if she were ill, would have some kind neighbour to tidy up her room and to talk with her sometimes: my poor mother-in-law was sitting in a dirty room, crouching over a handful of fire, she was languid for want of food, just because she was afraid to trouble the servants to bring her up coals and food.'

'And whose fault is that?' the old man asked angrily.

'Yours, of course,' Nancy replied, 'you knew that an invalid required attention, and you knew that you had to ask me, your son's wife, to come over, and I'd have come gladly, and now I'm going to give you your choice of two things; either you let me take Edward's mother to Bryn Croynan, so that I may nurse her there, or you must drive down to-night to fetch me from home, and put me in authority here – no one has as much claim upon me as Edward's father and mother; so whichever suits you best will suit me.'

'Do you think that I am a fool? Do you think I'll take to be dictated to by you?' Mr Morris asked, his face white with suppressed passion.

'Well,' Nancy replied, 'it's one or the other, and if you refuse both, then I'll call the attention of the church to your conduct, and I'll ask them if they consider that a man who has rejected every advance on the part of his son, who allowed his only son to be on the brink of death without stretching out a finger to help him, who leaves his sick wife to the tender mercies of a lot of stupid, ignorant servants. I'll ask them if they think that such a man as that is fit to be a deacon? I'll tell you, Mr Morris, you'll have no chance; let a person but put a match to the gunpowder that's in that chapel and you'll not forget the blaze in a hurry. Now, which is it to be? It wants just ten minutes to five o'clock; at five I'm going, and it'll be too late for you to stop me from striking that match.'

She looked him straight in the face, and in a few minutes the old man said quietly, 'Perhaps you'll kindly move from the door, I want to get out.'

'Certainly,' Nancy said at once.

He walked across the passage, opened the kitchen door, and said quietly to the astonished servant, 'Bring in my tea, and bring an extra cup for my son's wife, the boy can stay in the kitchen, and tell Joshua to put the harness on the gray mare, and to have the trap ready in half an hour.'

When he returned to the parlour, he offered Nancy a chair, and seating himself in his easy chair, read the newspaper. Tea was ready presently, and Mr Morris said authoritatively. 'You had better pour out the tea, it's woman's work.'

She obeyed him, and they ate and drank in silence.

Immediately they had finished, Nancy and her boy climbed up into the dogcart, and Mr Morris drove them home. He waited by the gate, while his daughter-in-law made a few preparations for leaving her home, 'You must get mother to manage here,' she said to her husband, 'I'll run over as often as I can, and mind that you come to see us.'

Edward went out half sheepishly to speak to his father, but the latter was not in a talkative mood. 'You've married a woman of spirit, Edward,' was his parting salutation, as he and Nancy drove away.

IV

The Old Song and the New

GWYNETH VAUGHAN

It hath been told that on a bright spring morning, in one of the years that are lost in the past when the world was young, the strong sons and fair daughters of the people that dwelt in the Isle of the Mighty came together to feast and make merry under the shadow of the sacred oak tree, nigh a broad river of clear water, which drew its strength from the running mountain streams, and for all the ages never paused on its journey to the sea.

And so happy and glad of heart were those strong sons and fair daughters that they fell a singing joyously; meanwhile there were amongst them some that played sweet melodies on many various kinds of harps and pipes, and others that could not but dance gaily in their mirth. For the seeds of corn had all been laid in the meadows, and the grass of the fields was becoming once more green. The leaves of the trees were springing forth anew, and flowers were appearing upon the earth. In truth it was a time of joy for youth and maidens, this spring time of the year. And the songs which they chanted so blithely in chorus were all in praise of their own land. They sang of their snow-capped mountains, those peaks whereon the eagles made their dwelling places, and the purple-hued hills of heather, the home of the lark. Nor was it in them to forget the woods and dales where the thrush and the blackbird led the choir in a great outburst of melody to welcome the King of day. Then they sang the praises of the sea, the never-ending blue waters of which won the love of their hearts one day, and the next became their terror in the mighty greatness of its storms. Yet was it their delight, that wilderness of waters so strong, and so silent, the ever-restless sea, illimitable in its vastness to those children of the mountains and the forests that daily looked upon the deep from the heights. They saw and loved the beauty of their God's great temple – those isle men and isle women of long ago.

While they were thus singing and making merry in the spring sunshine, they beheld drawing near unto them a goodly company of men, clad in long white robes reaching their feet; and he that was chief among them had a circlet of gold round his brows, and a wreath of the sacred oak leaves was set upon the gold, which, when the sun cast its beams thereon, became so brilliant that the light therefrom gladdened the hearts of men. Around the waist of the chief was a girdle of finely wrought silken cord of deepest blood-red hue; and upon his breast was the bow-shaped broad gold band hanging from the neck which was the band of Justice and gave to the owner thereof power over his fellowmen. In his hand he held a drawn sword, which glittered in the sunshine, but upon approaching the young men and maidens, he sheathed his sword within its scabbard and cried in a loud voice:

'Peace be to you, and game in plenty. Ye shall find not amongst the sheaves ears empty of corn, for the sun by day and the moon by night keep guard over the land. When the foeman cometh to savage and defile ye may become conquerors in more ways than one. Be ye therefore of good cheer, and make merry this day, ye children of the Isle of the Mighty.'

When the youths and the maidens beheld the company of

white robed men drawing nigh, he that was their chieftain took up his horn, and blew a loud blast; and all of his folk of one accord – women as well as men – gave an answering shout, until the hills resounded with their voices. For right happy were they in their glee that it had pleased the servants of their Great God to come forth and bestow upon them their blessings on that their feast day.

After the shout there was silence, for the fair daughters bethought themselves it was meet they should place before their guests food and drink, and some of them filled the horns with the mead, while others busied them with the meat. When they had broken their fast, and drunk their fill of the mead, and were refreshed thereby, they departed thence, leaving the youths and the maidens to their merrymaking.

Then the harpers smote their harps and the pipers blew their pipes until the heavens sang with the great noise, yet was every note in tune, and the melody as sweet as that of the spring chorus in the woods. Thus they continued to hold high revelry until the day was far spent. Then did he who was their chieftain cry out, saying, 'What is it that I see drawing nigh to us on the bosom of yonder broad river? Methinks it is a ship that hath no sails yet is it exceeding trim. What hindereth you men to run to the bank for I would fain know whether the craft carries friend or foe.'

And they sped thither, but though they bestirred themselves, yet the ship that came up the broad river so swiftly with neither flapping of sails nor the sound of oars had cast anchor before they had reached the place of landing, and a fair damsel had leapt ashore, and was coming forward to greet the youths of the Isle of the Mighty.

Then the young chieftain spoke to her, saying, 'Whither goest thou? What seekest thou?' And he saw that the damsel was very fair, and was richly clad in a robe of diverse colours that glittered in the sunset, as a rainbow shineth upon the clouds after rain.

Quoth the damsel, drawing near to him, and smiling, 'Chieftain, my name is Sunder, and I have come forth to tell thee and thine of other lands, and fair isles where ye may fear no foeman from the land of the cold north, neither him that cometh from the hot south, to enslave strong men, and capture fair women.'

And lo! as the damsel thus spake the hearts of the strong men became overburdened with sorrow, and the faces of the fair maidens of the Isle of the Mighty were sad to look upon; and the land was covered with a gloom, for a thick mist rose from the river, and the night dew fell upon them.

Then spake the damsel whose name was Sunder once more, and said, 'Strong sons and fair daughters of the Isle of the Mighty, not for long will this isle be for you all. Alas! a great army cometh, and they will count your white-robed Druids for naught. They are those that understand not Justice, and they will fight you with weapons that ye wot not of. They will speak you fair, and play you foul, those robbers of the sea, and ravishers of those that dwell in fair isles.'

And while the damsel thus spake, the mountains became dark like unto thunderclouds, and there was a wailing of the wind among the oak trees, and the sun departed unto the unknown region where the sea and sky met. Then he who was their chieftain hid his face with his hands as a man sore burdened with grief, but he spake nought, for his sorrow was too great for words.

Then came forward a fair daughter of the Isle of the Mighty, and said she, 'Damsel, I will follow thee to the isle of beauty which thou wilt lead me to. My harp I will take in my hand, and those of my kindred that desire a safe keeping may bear me company. The isle I will call by my own name, for methinks I shall but seldom again see the Isle of the Mighty.'

And one of the sons lifted up his voice and quoth he, 'Shall it be said that a fair daughter of the Isle of the Mighty dared that which a strong son may not venture? I will also be led by thee, damsel, into a new island where the sea robbers may not come, where those that are of my house and kin may learn to sail ships, and we will take of our merchandise to other lands.'

Then another son spake, saying, 'If I enter thy ship, thou damsel whose name is Sunder, thou wilt take me not to another isle, but to a corner of a far-off country, among mountains such as thine eye beholds, where the sea waters wash their feet; and where there may be green meadows to grow food thereon, and vineyards for the wine, for alas! we may not drink elsewhere of the mead of the Isle of the Mighty.'

And once again a maiden spake and said she, 'I will enter not thy ship, thou damsel in the many coloured raiment, but I will seek refuge in the uttermost part of this Isle of the Mighty, and the rocky cliffs of its sea shall be my safe haven; and my castle shall be the birthplace of the greatest of kings, of him who shall be the chief of warriors and the flower of knighthood.'

'Nor will I leave my mountains to the ravisher,' spake another fair daughter, 'nor the inheritance of the princes of the Isle of the Mighty to be the dwelling place of a sea robber. And when in other days ye will come back to greet me, ye shall hear my voice and that of my kindred answering to the call of you all in the language that is spoken this day here and now. The foeman may kill and plunder, but he may not steal my tongue.'

Then he who was their chieftain spake, his face shone, and was exceeding beauteous, and they all harkened to his voice, for he was well-loved by his kindred, this tall son of the Isle of the Mighty: 'Here will also be my abiding place. My home will be amidst the snow-clad mountains of the north, and the fair islets of the sea, nor shall the lochs of my land belong to another. My great rivers will carry greatness to me and mine, and no stranger shall cross them to possess my country. The foeman may array himself for battle against me, but he will not conquer my people, and in the days to come I will reign over him.'

When they had all spoken the damsel whose name was Sunder murmured within herself, saying: 'Their parting is not for all time, they will come back, and I may sunder them no more, for they shall be as one kindred again as heretofore, these strong sons and fair daughters of the Isle of the Mighty.'

While she thus mused, the darkness of the night gave place to the grey dawn, and the chieftain spake: 'I would fain hear once more before we part the old song.'

And the strong sons and fair daughters of the Isle of the Mighty took up their harps and their pipes, and fell to singing an old song of their people to the morning light, the song that was so like the glad carolling of the lark. But, alas! the old melody was no longer jubilant, for the eyes of the singers were wet with unshed tears, and the cadence of sorrow entered into their song; and there was a note the less at the end of their music which finished in a sob.

And thus they parted leaving with each other but the memory of a lost note, and the echo of a song into which sorrow had entered.

The ages came, and the ages went; great battles were fought, and great kings reigned; yet in the days that are gone and in other days that have come in their stead did the strong sons and fair daughters of the Isle of the Mighty make good their words. The foeman came but they infused into him of their own blood, and their sons reigned over him. Withal their song never lost its cadence of sorrow, and the notes of their music held the memory of a parting pain – the lament for the days of old.

Thus it fell upon a day that a strong son of the north became of one heart with a fair daughter of the west whose name was Hope, she who dwelt in the beauteous Isle of Avallon, beside the cave where slept in a long sleep he who was chief among warriors, the flower of knighthood – Arthur the greatest of all Kings.

And the son of the north sought the daughter of the west to wife. But the maiden answered, 'Nay.' 'For,' quoth she, 'I may wed no man until the days of my waiting are over, and the King awakens from his sleep, and I shall speed me with his royal commands to all those of his kindred nigh and afar.'

Then spake the youth: 'So will I be with thee, wheresoever thou goest. I am thy Knight of Union, and without me, fair maiden Hope, thou canst achieve nought.'

While he was yet speaking a light as of the noon day sun shone upon them, and there was a sound of the clinking of armour, and the maiden's beauty became wonderful to behold. Then was brought to them on the wings of the wind words of great moment: 'Go thou my Knight of Union, with my faithful maiden Hope, and call my kindred from all lands, for it is my pleasure to see them united once more – the strong sons and fair daughters of the Isle of the Mighty.' And the voice was like unto the sound of silver bells at a distance.

Then the maiden spake: 'It is the King. Arthur is awake, let us carry the glad tidings to our kinsmen and kinswomen.' And they sped them into the Emerald Isle, where dwelt the fair daughter Erin, and from thence to the Isle that was Man's, and to the land which had become his 'Mam Vro' to the Breton. Then they hied them to the West – the birthplace of their King; and to the Highlands of the north, the home of the chieftains; and last of all they betook themselves to the Cymric mountains, where dwelt a people that for all the ages had spoken to their God and to each other in the language of the strong sons and fair daughters of the Isle of the Mighty. Then the kindred of Arthur the King gathered together from all lands, and stood once more under the shadows of the oak trees. And they smote their harps, and blew their pipes, and their song knew not the cadence of sorrow, for their eyes held no unshed tears, and instead there came a triumphal paean from thousands of voices; nor had their music a note the less because it had become a sob, but clarion notes of joy filled the Isle of the Mighty from one end to the other, like unto the carolling of an innumerable company of larks to the morning light. And the new song was jubilant as was the old song in the days that were gone, for the earth no longer held a foeman to them who had made all countries their own, and darkness could not cast over them a gloom, for the sun never sets in the lands of the Celts.

V

Home, Sweet Home

ALLEN RAINE

It was September, and at Bronwylan Farm the drowsy stillness and the clean-swept hearth showed it was afternoon, when the menservants no longer clattered about in their wooden shoes, for they were away in the cornfields, and little Anne, the milkmaid, who generally sang at her work, was busy in the hayloft looking for eggs. The sun shone straight through the open door. Sometimes a wasp would buzz noisily in, and quickly fly out to the sunshine again. Everything showed it was afternoon, when old Nancy Vaughan, becloaked and hatted, came into her kitchen. She was old, the story of her life was over, or ought to have been, and she would have been much surprised to find any one gave her a thought, for she had long been accustomed to neglect and loneliness. Nevertheless, she had not lost her interest in her surroundings, for she still loved the old farm which had been the scene of her happy married life, when the unrest and indecision of the days of courtship had ended in her marriage to the man of her choice, and she had settled down to the peaceful monotony of Bronwylan.

It was in the kitchen of the same old farm that she was now standing, ready dressed as if for a journey, her iron-grey hair cut straight across her forehead, as had been the fashion in the days of her youth; above it, the full frill of her lace cap, kept in place by a kerchief of black silk tied under her chin;

over this her broad-brimmed high-crowned hat. A long cloak of mulberry cloth hung from her shoulders; in her soft-veined hand she held a crutch-stick, upon which she leant a little, as if weary. She looked round at the old familiar room with all its signs of rustic plenty, its platters and bowls, its hams and flitches, at the old fireside at which she had crooned to her babies in the content of a perfectly happy marriage, and where her husband had shared her joys with her.

One thorn only had there been in their nest, and that was the obstinate and selfish character of their only son; this had often ruffled the smooth flow of the river of their lives. From what old ancestor he had inherited his churlish disposition it would be difficult to say – certainly not from his parents, who were both of remarkably amiable and placid temperament.

In the course of time their daughters had married, and had gone to their own homes, and John the disturber had succeeded to the ownership of the farm, where, after his father's death, his mother had continued to live with him, supported by his charity, and that but grudgingly. Lately he had married, and the buxom, rather hard-featured girl, who passed in and out of the kitchen with bustling, hurrying manner, was his newly made wife.

'Must I go, then?' said the old woman, looking round the room with sad eyes. 'Couldn't you find a little corner for me here, in the hayloft or in the barn?'

'Don't talk nonsense!' said her son roughly. 'I wonder you talk about sleeping, after all the trouble your bed has given us.'

'It was unfortunate,' she answered meekly; 'but what harm was it if my bed did happen to lie across the line between two parishes? 'Tisn't as if I wanted relief from them,' and the delicate cheek flushed with a glow of pride. 'They might know that none of the Bronwylan family would trouble them!'

'Well, well!' said John. 'There's no need to talk any more about that; you are going to live with your daughter Jenny for the rest of your life. You'll be all right with her.'

'Yes, Jenny was a nice lass,' said the old woman pensively, as if trying to reassure herself; 'but I don't know will her husband take to me. 'Tis hard to make a new home when you're old.'

'Well, don't talk any more about that now. We've gone over it so often. You'll be all right when you get there. Better come outside. I hear the cart coming round.' And reluctantly she turned to the open doorway.

'Well, good-bye, Jane!' she said to the busy housewife, who scarcely looked up from the curds to answer her. 'I would have tried not to be in your way, for well I know it is not right for the old mistress to interfere with the new. Good-bye, then, merch-i, you'll let me come and see you sometimes when Jenny's husband goes to the fair. I am sure he will bring me in the cart with him; my heart will be here with you and John.'

'Oh, of course!' said Jane, drying her hands. 'Good-bye, then; come when you please to see us.'

One look round as she passed through the doorway, and the old woman was out in the farmyard, where the rough red cart awaited her.

Seated on the front board, her little box of clothes under her feet, she shook hands with the man whose bad temper had often disturbed her night's rest – the son, who, in spite of his hardness, with a mother's blind infatuation, she still believed incapable of acting cruelly towards her.

'I would like to have patted "Corwen" once more,' she said wistfully, as she caught sight of the cows filing into the farmyard.

'Pwr "Lucy" and "Pinken"! I would like to milk them again.' And seeing that the tears were brimming over in her eyes, John hurried the departure.

With a 'Commop, Rattler!' the carter cracked his whip, and with a pink-and-white spotted handkerchief to her eyes, Nancy Vaughan was driven away from her old home.

It was some time before she recovered herself sufficiently to notice her surroundings. 'Why are you driving me?' she said at last, seeing a stranger at her side. 'Where is Will?'

'Oh! they were all busy on the farm, so they asked me to drive you,' he answered reticently, for he had been well tutored by John before starting.

''Tis eight miles to Llain, my daughter's house, isn't it?'

'About that,' said the man.

'I am sorry to leave my old home,' she said again, in excuse for the tears which would fall on the old hands resting on the crutch-stick.

'No doubt – no doubt,' said Owen Jones, with another crack of his whip, for he found the sudden lurch that followed this action a good means of interrupting Nancy Vaughan's questions. For several miles they rumbled on without further conversation, but as the evening drew on, and the sunset light began to gild the scenery, she asked again, 'Is it much farther to Llain, I have not been there often, and I suppose I forget the way. I thought it was all uphill.'

'Oh no – good road – and all down hill,' said the man. 'We won't be long now.'

'Well, indeed, I am glad,' said Nancy, 'for I am tired. Dear anwl! I must brighten up a bit before Jenny and the little children see me.'

'Bt shwr!' said Owen Jones. And they relapsed into silence, until at a turn in the road they came in sight of a low-lying valley, through which a broad river meandered. In the soft twilight the little town of Tregarreg lay peacefully resting in the arms of the hills, the smoke of its chimneys rising straight into the pale evening sky, where a faint moon hung over the valley. 'Dear anwl! What is this place?' she asked. 'I didn't know we would pass a town on the way to Llain.'

''Tis Tregarreg, 'tis all right,' said the driver. And the woman's gentle face grew full of interest, for well she remembered how she had ridden there one day to the midsummer fair, how she had met her lover there, as well as his rival, how her staid and cold manner to the latter had delighted the heart of Ben Vaughan, how he had summoned courage to ask her to marry him, and how, when she had consented, they had ridden home together in the first flush of young love, when the present seemed all that was beautiful, and the future stretched before them like a happy dream. To-night, as the rough red cart drew near the town, the light from the setting sun that illumined the scene around her reminded her of that long-past sunset ride, and there was a radiant look in the grey eyes and a tender smile on the sunken mouth that made the old face look beautiful.

The sun had reached the horizon; he was sinking fast behind the line of hills. Suddenly he was gone. The golden light vanished, and the red cart stopped in front of a square white building. Owen Jones jumped down, and opened the gates, which led into a large kitchen garden.

'Stop! Stop!' said Nancy. 'Surely we have no right to go through there.'

'All right,' said the man, leading the horse down between the grass-edged beds of cabbages.

'What place is this?' said the old woman, in a voice that trembled, 'this great white place – these big doors? Surely I have heard of Tregarreg Workhouse! Owen Jones! you haven't brought me there, have you?' And it would be impossible to describe the bitterness, the horror, in the woman's voice.

'I have brought you safe whatever,' said the driver, knocking at the workhouse door with his whip handle. In a few moments it was opened by a red-faced, burly man; behind him, the kindly though brusque matron, who, coming forward, stretched up her hands to help the newcomer to alight.

'Oh, no, no!' cried the latter. 'I am not coming here! I am going to Jenny, my daughter! Yes, indeed, that's what John told me. Has he deceived his mother, and has he sent me to the workhouse? For this is the workhouse, isn't it?'

'Yes, yes, all right. Come you down,' said the matron; 'supper is ready.' But Nancy Vaughan, trembling and sobbing, clung to the red cart as long as she could.

They were used to such unwilling arrivals in that cheerless home, and it was not long before Owen Jones and the matron together had lifted the frail woman out of the cart and over the threshold. The door was closed, and Nancy was patted on the back, coaxed, and at last threatened, until she had allowed herself to be led into the long, bare, common room, where about twenty women were seated at their supper, consisting of bowls of 'cawl', with hunches of barley bread.

At home, at Bronwylan, with the cat purring on the hearth, and the firelight dancing on the tins and coppers, Nancy Vaughan would not have turned from the simple fare; but here, alone and frightened by the rows of stolid faces, each framed in the calico frill of the workhouse cap, her very soul shrank in terror, and she drew back from the seat on the bench which an imbecile woman invited her to share with her.

'Come, sit down,' said the matron, 'take your supper, and then off to bed! You'll be all right to-morrow, and Mali here shall sing you some of her songs about the crow and the cuckoo, to make you laugh.'

'Oh, no, no!' said the old woman. 'I will not stay here. I

cannot sleep in the workhouse. I am Nancy Vaughan, of Bronwylan. There are nine cows in the "boidy", and seven stacks in the haggard. Open those big doors for me, put me outside, and I will find my way home again.'

'Twt, twt!' said the matron. 'Come upstairs to bed, and you, Mali and Ruth, you've finished your suppers, come along with her for company.'

'Come along!' said Mali, the imbecile woman. 'I'll sing you to sleep, merch-i, like I do Ruth here every night.'

Ruth looked back with a scowl. 'Sing me to sleep! Fool!' she said, as she led the way through the long, bare passage, up the stairs to a large whitewashed room, in which were a row of iron bedsteads.

'Now,' said the matron, 'there's your bed. Undress and go to sleep. No more nonsense!' And she turned on her heel, intending to leave the women to themselves; but old Nancy Vaughan ran after her, clung to her arm, her gown, beseeching, weeping, imploring, 'Oh! put me outside the door!'

At last the matron's patience was at an end.

'Look here!' she said, in a stern tone; and leading the old woman back to the grim iron bedsteads, she pointed to one, and said, 'Now, listen. There's your bed. Get in, and lie still, or if you don't,' and, lowering her voice, she added, 'Mali, there, will give you a box on the ears.' And Nancy Vaughan, the gentle and timid woman, who should have been sitting by some warm hearth, with kindly faces around her, and the words of love to brighten her last days, sat down on the hard bed, listening in terror to Ruth's snoring and to the maunderings of the imbecile Mali, who might at any moment start up and box her ears.

The darkness crept on, the moon looked into the gaunt, bare rooms, where on one bed a dark form sat motionless through the night – motionless except for the heaving shoulders, which were the only signs of the sobs stifled in

Nancy's sodden pink-spotted handkerchief. As the dawn approached, she took off her broad-brimmed hat, and, in sheer exhaustion, fell sideways on the hard bolster, still refusing to lift her feet from the ground.

'What, go to sleep in a workhouse? No, no, no! God have mercy upon me, and let me die sooner!' was her last thought as she sank into a heavy, dreamless sleep.

No one around her knew what bitter thoughts had bowed that grey head, what sorrowful feelings and wounded pride had torn the loving heart, while the big workhouse clock told the hours as they dragged on heavily. How her memory, which she thought had been dulled by age, awoke in all its pristine vigour, bringing before her the scenes of youth and happiness, which had long faded into forgetfulness! And always it was John the callous and ungrateful who figured in her brightest visions, and the cry of her heart was, 'Oh, my little lad that I loved so much! That he should have turned me out of my home in my old age, and sent me to the workhouse!' No wonder that the tears fell like rain, and that the bent shoulders heaved with sobs, while Ruth snored heavily, and Mali babbled of the fields and the cuckoo and the crows.

For Nancy recalled how in the summer evening she had sat on her stool to milk the sleek cows in Bronwylan farmyard; how her husband had come whistling by, with the little lad astride on his shoulders. She shed no tears for her husband, for she had long learnt to think of him as safe at the end of the journey which she should soon accomplish herself. But her boy! – her boy! And with cruel distinctness memory recalled every harsh word, every grudging gift, every cold look with which he had repaid her tender love. Would that she had died with her husband, for the wound in her heart threatened to rob her of her reason; and the deadly weariness under which at last she had sunk on the hard workhouse pillow was a merciful relief to her sorrow-laden spirit.

In the course of a few days she had become so far accustomed to her unhappy surroundings that she no longer wore herself out with weeping, but seemed to have fallen into a stolid and silent indifference, which was in reality only the result of complete prostration. She had no more tears to shed, she was too weak to sob. At night she no longer refused to stretch herself on the hard bed. At meal-time she partook of the coarse fare as far as hunger compelled her to do, retiring afterwards to a straight bench by the white-washed wall, sitting there silent and in dumb grief, which was too deep for words.

'Come, cheer up!' said the matron, who, in spite of her hard face, was not an unkindly soul. 'Cheer up! On Friday is the meeting of the Board, and they'll settle something about you then. Perhaps they'll send you home, after all!'

Nancy looked up with so much misery in her eyes that even the matron turned away with a muttered, 'Poor thing!' She never spoke except in answer to a question; nevertheless, the hope that she might be discharged at the next meeting somewhat revived her drooping spirit.

She had been allowed, in consideration of her position as a farmer's widow, to retain her own clothing, instead of donning the hateful workhouse garb, and her quaintly picturesque peasant dress looked strangely out of place amongst the blue-gowned, cap-frilled, workhouse women.

On the day of the meeting, when called into the Board room, she followed the matron, dazed and bewildered, but upheld by the fervid hope that the consultation would end in her deliverance from what was to her the bitterest captivity. It was a terrible ordeal to the timid woman, who had been thus thrust for the first time in her life from the shelter of her home, and had she been arraigned at the bar of justice for a deadly crime, she would scarcely have endured more shame and horror than she felt when standing at the green baize table, confronted by that stolid group of Bumbledom known as 'The Board'.

With pathetic simplicity she looked from one to the other of the irate faces of the two guardians, who disputed the obligation to support her owing to the fact that her bed had lain exactly across the boundary between two parishes.

A letter from John Vaughan was read, in which he stated that the farm of Bronwylan was heavily mortgaged to his father-in-law, and that he, John Vaughan, was allowed to occupy it only in the capacity of farm bailiff to his wife, and that it was impossible for him to keep his mother on the farm, as his father-in-law objected to his doing so, and she thus became chargeable to the Tregarreg Union.

Nancy Vaughan wept no longer. Her tears were dried up. Once only she wrung her hands with a pitiful cry of, 'Oh, John, my little lad!'

'Hush! Silence!' said the chairman. 'Don't interrupt the business of the Board.' And she shrank back into herself as if she had been struck and stood in silent endurance while her fate was being decided. It was not very clear to her, until the matron came up, and laid her hand on her arm; then she understood it all, and allowed herself to be led away.

'Hello! come back like a bad penny?' said Mali, as Nancy entered the large, bare room where some of the women were sewing, but most of them sitting with empty hands, and faces that grew daily more dull and hopeless. 'Come on then, merch-i, and I'll sing you a song.' And, following Nancy to her usual seat, Mali stood before her and sang, in a cracked voice, imitating the notes of the two birds:

While on the wing I love to sing,
Cuckoo, cuckoo, cuckoo!
Oh! silly song, 'tis all day long
Ringing the valley through.

From rock and scar 'tis better far
To sing craa craa, craa craa!

The women laughed as if they had never heard the song before, but Nancy Vaughan seemed not to hear.

'Come, come,' said the matron, 'we are very kind to you! You've your own clothes to wear, plenty of food, and a clean bed. What do you want more?'

But Nancy was silent, her thoughts wandered far beyond the precincts of the workhouse walls. Old Bronwylan rose before her in all its pleasant homeliness: the cows were in the yard, she could see them, knee-deep in the straw; the tabby cat was purring on the hearth; the kettle boiling on its chain.

Ah, how she loved it all! And while the slow hours dragged monotonously on, she lived her life alone in dreams of the past, and in visions of the home which would only fade from her memory with her last breath.

When bedtime came, while Ruth grumbled and Mali sang her foolish songs, she knelt to say her simple prayer. 'God bless my dear daughters both! bless my dear John, and soften his heart to me! and in mercy, Lord, let me not die in the workhouse!' Nightly, hourly, she breathed this prayer: 'Let me not die in the workhouse!'

December came with its bitter cold, its sleet and rain. The plum pudding and roast beef of Christmas Day, looked forward to for weeks by the other inmates, were nothing to her; the meal almost choked her as she tried to eat to please the matron. She had grown thin and pale, but a pink flush dyed her cheek, and her eyes burned with a feverish glow which the matron took for a sign of increasing health.

'There's well Nancy Vaughan is looking; in my deed she must have been a beauty once,' she said to her husband one day.

'Of course she was,' said the master; 'I have heard my

father say she could have her pick of the best men in the parish.'

'Poor thing! she's more contented than she was whatever.'

They little guessed that in Nancy Vaughan's heart the longing for the old home was growing in intensity. It shaped her dreams at night, it filled her with a fictitious strength by day, it burned in her eyes, it glowed in her cheeks, it nerved her to do and dare to regain the freedom for which she pined.

She was old! She knew it by the increase of weakness in her limbs; she knew it by the panting breath, the failing eyesight. Oh yes! she knew the signs of age, for she was no fool. But she knew, too, that she had within her sufficient strength and energy to help her to escape from these unfriendly walls. She had watched, she had seen, that, across the bare yard beneath the barred window, one of the big doors which had struck terror into her on her first arrival was frequently left ajar. Could she but reach that door in safety! Even now, while they were all at supper, she alone left in the dormitory with a headache! Even now she must summon all her strength to her aid, and cross that yard in the falling twilight.

Old? Surely no! They were the winged feet of youth that bore her so swiftly from the open door to the workhouse gate. No one had seen her. Fate was kind. Old? No! This was the fire of youth that coursed in her veins. Weak? No, indeed! she could run with the fleetest.

The night was darkening, but she could still see her way on the broad white road – yes, whiter and whiter, for the snow was falling lightly, and as it fell, it froze. Bitter, cold! But, thank God! she had escaped. She would yet see Bronwylan. She would yet sit on the warm hearth, hear the old clock ticking in the corner, and see the grey cat sitting by the fire!

In the workhouse nobody had missed her, nobody had

asked, How is Nancy Vaughan's headache? 'Let her be,' said the matron. 'Let her be without supper; she'll go to bed, and be all right in the morning.' And the stolid women had filed into the room, each in her blue linsey dress and coarse apron, and her frill-cap of calico. They had undressed and gone to sleep without noticing that Nancy's bed was unoccupied, for the light was dim, and the imbecile Mali, who slept next to her, was generally given as wide a berth as possible by her companions.

While they huddled in under their blankets, and tried to get warm in the black, biting night, up the bare mountain road a bent figure was toiling through the fast-falling snow. The spurt of energy was gone, the flame of unnatural strength was dying out, her knees were trembling, her breath came with difficulty in the frosty air, and Nancy Vaughan knew now that she was old and weak and worn out.

The darkness increased, the road grew heavy with a dead impalpable softness, the snow fell thicker and faster; but she pressed on, slowly and painfully, yet with a paean of joy in her heart, for she was free! She was going home! No grim workhouse walls closed her in!

What mattered it that the icy cold was gripping her! What mattered it that she was weary, for here by the roadside she would rest awhile. This big grey boulder would shelter her from the blast. Ah, how cold it was! How tired she felt! How sweet to rest, to stretch the tired limbs, to close the drowsy eyes! But not for long – oh no! She would soon press on again, for she was going home, thank God! Home! home! home! And she sank into a calm sleep, with a smile upon her lips, and a vision of Bronwylan in her heart.

Next morning, when the shivering workhouse women turned out of their beds to dress, Nancy Vaughan was missed. The matron was called, the master consulted, the long, bare rooms were searched, but all in vain; there was no sign of her anywhere.

Outside the ground was wrapt in a thick mantle of white. No footsteps marked the smooth, untrodden snow. What could have become of her? Old and frail as she was, she could not have gone far, and the search was renewed through ward-room and passages and yards, but in vain; there was no sign of Nancy Vaughan, and it was Mali at last who threw a gleam of light on the subject.

'Well, she's gone home, of course,' she said, 'to that place she was always bothering about. But I don't believe there was such a place; but 'tis there she's gone, be bound! Oh! course, she's gone home. Why wouldn't she go when the door was open last night? I saw it.'

The master looked at the matron. 'No doubt Mali was right!' And in less than half an hour two men were sent up the mountain road, with strict injunctions that they were to search until they found Nancy Vaughan, even if they had to trudge the whole way through the snow to Bronwylan.

The men were delighted, for it meant a change in the monotony of their lives, and they toiled on bravely until about four miles from Tregarreg, and half-way to Bronwylan they came upon a long, low mound that lay in the shelter of a big grey boulder.

'Is that her, I wonder?' said old Billo Pensarn, and clearing the snow away, they found Nancy Vaughan sleeping calmly the sleep of Death, with the pure white snow for her winding sheet, and the big grey boulder for a headstone, and on her face a smile of peace and content, for she had reached Home.

VI

An All-Hallows' Honeymoon

JEANNETTE MARKS

Intermittently the wind whined and raced, howling like a wolf, through the Gwynen Valley; and intermittently, too, the rain doused the bridge on whose slate coping Vavasour Jones leaned. It was a night when spirits of air and earth, the racing wind, the thundering water, the slashing rain, were the very soul of this chaos of noise. Still, cosy lights shone on either side of the bridge, the lights of Ty Ucha and Ty Usaf, where a good mug of beer could be had for a mere song to a man of Vavasour's means. And the lights from all the cottages, too, for it was All-Hallows' Eve, twinkled with festive brilliance upon the drenched flags of the street. Indeed, there was not one of these houses in all Gwynen whose walls and flaggings were not familiar to him, where Vavasour Jones and his wife Catherine had not been on an occasion, a knitting-night, a Christmas, a bidding, a funeral, an All-Hallows' Eve. But to-night his eyes gazed blankly upon these preliminary signs of a merry evening within doors, and he seemed unconscious of the rain pouring upon him and the wind slapping the bridge. He moved when he saw a figure approaching.

'Hist! Eilir!'

'Aye, man, who is it?'

'It's me, it's Vavasour Jones.'

'Dear me, lad, what do ye here in the dark and rain?'

Vavasour said nothing; Eilir peered more closely at him. 'Are ye sick, lad?'

'Och, I'm not sick!' Vavasour's voice rang drearily, as if that were the least of ills that could befall him.

'Well, what ails ye?'

'It's All-Hallows' Eve an' . . .'

'Aren't ye goin' to Pally Hughes's?'

'Ow!' he moaned, 'the devil! goin' to Pally Hughes's while it's drawin' nearer an' nearer an' – Ow!'

'Tut, man,' said Eilir sharply, 'ye're ill; speak up, tell me what ails ye.'

'Ow-w!' groaned Vavasour.

Eilir drew away; here was a case where All-Hallows' had played havoc early in the evening. What should he do? Get him home? Notify Catherine? Have the minister? He was inclining to the last resource when Vavasour groaned again and spoke:-

'Eilir, I wished I were dead, man.'

'Dear me, lad, what is it?'

'It's the night when Catherine must go.'

'When Catherine must go? What do ye mean?'

'She'll be dead the night at twelve.'

'Dead at twelve?' asked Eilir, bewildered. 'Does she know it?'

'No, but I do, an' to think I've been unkind to her! I've tried this year to make up for it, but it's no use, man; one year'll never make up for ten of harsh words an' unkind deeds. Ow!' groaned Vavasour, collapsing on to the slate coping once more.

'Well, ye've not been good to her,' replied Eilir, mystified, 'that's certain, man, but I've heard ye've been totally different the past year. Griffiths was sayin' he never heard any more sharp words comin' from your windows, an' they used to rain like hail on the streets some days.'

'Aye, but a year'll not do any good, an' she'll be dyin' at twelve to-night, Ow!'

'Well,' said Eilir, catching at the only thing he could think of to say, 'there's plenty in the Scriptures about a man an' his wife.'

'Aye, but it'll not do, not do, not do,' sobbed Vavasour Jones.

'Have ye been drinkin', lad?'

'Drinkin'!' exclaimed Jones.

'Well, no harm, but lad, about the Scriptures; there's plenty in the Scriptures concernin' a man an' his wife, an' ye've broken much of it about lovin' a wife, an' yet I cannot understand why Catherine's goin' an' where.'

'She's not goin' anywhere, Eilir; she'll be dyin' at twelve.'

Whereupon Vavasour Jones rose up suddenly from the coping, took a step forward, seized Eilir by the coat-lapel, and, with eyes flickering like coals in the dark, told his story. All the little Gwynen world knew that he and his wife had not lived happily or well together; there had been no children coming and no love lost, and, as the days went on, bickering, scolding, harsh words, and even ugly actions. Aye, and it had come to such a pass that a year ago this night, on All-Hallows' Eve, he had gone down to the church-porch shortly before midnight to see whether the spirit of Catherine would be called, and whether she would live the twelve months out. And as he was leaning against the church-wall hoping, aye, man, and praying that he might see her there, he saw something coming around the corner with white over its head; it drew nearer and nearer, and when it came in full view of the church-porch it paused, it whirled around, and sped away with the wind flapping about its feet and the rain beating down on its head. But Vavasour had time to see that it was the spirit of Catherine, and he was glad because his prayer had been answered, and because, with Catherine dying the next All-Hallows', they would have to live together only the year out. So he went homeward joyfully, thinking it was the last year, and considering as it was the last year he might just as well be as kind and pleasant as possible. When he reached home he found Catherine up waiting for him. And she spoke so pleasantly to him and he to her, and the days went on as happily as the courting days before they were married. Each day was sweeter than the one before, and they knew for the first time what it meant to be man and wife in love and kindness. But all the while he saw that white figure by the churchyard, and Catherine's face in its white hood, and he knew the days were lessening and that she must go. Here it was All-Hallows' Eve again, and but four hours to midnight, and the best year of his life was almost past. Aye, and it was all the result of his evil heart and evil wish and evil prayer.

'Think, man,' groaned Vavasour, 'prayin' for her callin', aye, goin' there hopin' ye'd see her spirit, an' countin' on her death!'

'Oh, man, it's bad,' replied Eilir mournfully, 'aye, an' I've no word to say to ye for comfort. I recollect well the story my granny used to tell about Christmas Powell; it was somethin' the same. An' there was Betty Williams was called ten years ago, an' didn't live the year out; an' there was Silvan Evans, the sexton, an' Geffrey his friend, was called two years ago, and Silvan had just time to dig Geffrey's grave an' then his own, too, by its side, an' they was buried the same day an' hour.'

'Ow!' wailed Vavasour.

'Aye, man, it's bad; it'll have to be endured, an' to think ye brought it on yourself. Where's Catherine?'

'She's to Pally Hughes's for the All-Hallows' party.'

'Och, she'll be taken there!'

'Aye, an' oh! Eilir, she was loth to go to Pally's, but I could not tell her the truth.'

'That's so, lad; are ye not goin'?'

'I cannot go; I'm fair crazy an' I'll just be creepin' home, waitin' for them to bring her back. Ow!'

'I'm sorry, man,' called Eilir, looking after him with an expression of sympathy: 'I can be of no use to ye now.'

Across the bridge the windows of Pally Hughes's grey-stone cottage shone with candles, and as the doors swung to and fro admitting guests, the lights from within flickered on the brass doorsill and the hum of merry words reached the street. Mrs Morgan the baker, dressed in her new scarlet whittle and a freshly starched cap, was there; Mr Howell the milliner, in his highlows and wonderful plum-coloured coat; Mrs Jenkins the tinman, with bright new ribbons to her cap and a new beaver hat which she removed carefully upon entering; and Mr Wynn "the shop", whose clothes were always the envy of Gwynen village; and many others, big-eyed girls and straight young men, who crossed the bright doorsill.

Finally, Catherine Jones tapped on the door. Within, she looked vacantly at the candles on the mantelpiece and on the table, all set in festoons of evergreens and flanked by a display of painted china eggs and animals; and at the lights shining steadily, while on the hearth a fire crackled. Catherine, so heavy was her heart, could scarcely manage a decent friendly greeting to old Pally Hughes, her hostess. She looked uncheered at the big centre table, whereon stood a huge blue wassail-bowl, about it little piles of raisins, buns, spices, biscuits, sugar, a large jug of ale and a small bottle tightly corked. She watched the merriment with indifference; bobbing for apples and sixpences seemed such stupid games. There was no one in whom she could confide now, and anyway it was too late; there was nothing to be done, and while they were talking lightly and singing, too, for the harp was being played, the hours were slipping away, and her one thought, her only thought, was to get home to Vavasour. 'Oh,' reflected Catherine, 'I'm a wicked, wicked woman to be bringin' him to his death!'

The candles were blown out and the company gathered in a circle about the fire to tell stories, while a kettle of ale simmered on the crane and the apples hung roasting. Pally began the list of tales. There was the story of the corpse-candle Lewis's wife saw, and how Lewis himself died the next week; there were the goblins that of All-Hallows' Eve led Davies such a dance, and the folks had to go out after him with a lantern to fetch him in, and found him lying in fear by the sheep-wall; and there were the plates and mugs Annie turned upside down and an unseen visitor turned them right side up before her very eyes.

Then they began to throw nuts in the fire, each with a wish: if the nut burned brightly the wish would come true. Old Pally threw on a nut, it flickered and then blazed up; Maggie tossed one into the fire, it smouldered and gave no light. Gradually the turn came nearer Catherine; there was but one wish in her heart and she trembled to take the chance.

'Now, Catherine!'

'Aye, Catherine, what'll she be wishin' for, a new lover?' they laughed.

With shaking hand she tossed hers into the fire; the nut sputtered and blackened, and with a shriek Catherine bounded from the circle, threw open the door and sped into the dark. In consternation the company scrambled to their feet, gazing at the open door through which volleyed the wind and rain.

Old Pally was the first to speak: ''Tis a bad sign.'

'Aye, poor Catherine's been called, it may be.'

'It's the last time, I'm thinkin', we'll ever see her.'

'Do ye think she saw somethin', Pally, do ye?'

'There's no tellin'; but it's bad, very bad, though her nut is burnin' brightly enough now.'

'She seemed downcast the night, not like herself.'

'It can be nothin' at home, for Vavasour, they say, is treatin' her better nor ever, an' she's been that sweet-tempered the year long, which is uncommon for her.'

As she fled homeward through the dark, little did Catherine think of what they might be saying at Pally's. When Vavasour heard feet running swiftly along the street, he straightened up, his eyes in terror upon the door.

'Catherine!' he cried, bewildered at her substantial appearance, 'is it ye who are really come?'

There was a momentary suggestion of a rush into each other's arms checked, as it were, in mid-air by Vavasour's reseating himself precipitately and Catherine drawing herself up.

'Yes,' said Catherine, seeing him there and still in the flesh, 'it was – dull, very dull at Pally's; an' my feet was wet an' I feared takin' a cold.'

'Aye,' replied Vavasour, looking with greed upon her rosy face and snapping eyes, 'aye, it's better for ye here, dearie.'

There was an awkward silence. Catherine still breathed heavily from the running, and Vavasour shuffled his feet. He opened his mouth, shut it, and opened it again.

'Did ye have a fine time at Pally's?' he asked.

'Aye, it was gay and fine an' . . . na . . .' Catherine halted, remembering the reason she had given for coming home, and tried to explain. 'Yes, so it was, an' so it wasn't,' she ended.

Vavasour regarded her with attention, and there was another pause, in which his eyes sought the clock. The sight of that fat-faced timepiece gave him a shock.

'A quarter past eleven,' he murmured; then aloud: 'Catherine, do ye recall Pastor Evans's sermon, the one he preached last New Year?'

Catherine also had taken a furtive glance at the clock, a glance which Vavasour caught and wondered at.

'Well, Catherine, do . . .'

'Aye, I remember, about inheritin' the grace of life together.'

'My dear, wasn't he sayin' that love is eternal an' that . . . a man . . . an' . . . an' his wife was lovin' for . . . for . . .'

'Aye, lad, for everlastin' life,' Catherine concluded.

There was another pause, a quick glancing at the clock, and a quick swinging of two pairs of eyes towards each other, astonishment in each pair.

'Half-after eleven,' whispered Vavasour, seeming to crumple in the middle. 'An', dear,' he continued aloud, 'didn't he, didn't he say that the Lord was mindful of our . . . of our . . . difficulties, and our temptations, an' our . . . our . . .'

'Aye, an' our mistakes,' ended Catherine.

'Do ye think, dearie,' he went on, 'that if a man were to . . . to . . . na . . . to be unkind a . . . a very little to his wife . . . an' was sorry an' his wife . . . his wife . . . died, that he'd be . . . be . . . ?'

'Forgiven?' finished Catherine. 'Aye, I'm thinkin' so. An', lad dear, do ye think if anythin' was to happen to ye the night, – aye, *this* night, – that ye'd take any grudge away with ye against me?'

Vavasour stiffened.

'Happen to *me*, Catherine?'

Then he collapsed, groaning.

'Oh, dearie, what is it, what is it what ails ye?' cried Catherine, coming to his side on the sofa.

'Nothin', nothin' at all,' he gasped, slanting an eye at the clock. 'Ow, the devil, it's twenty minutes before twelve!'

'Oh, lad, what is it?'

'It's nothin', nothin' at all, it's . . . it's . . . ow! . . . it's just a little pain across me.'

Catherine stole a look at the timepiece, – a quarter before twelve, aye, it was coming to him now, and her face whitened to the colour of the ashes in the fireplace.

To Vavasour the whimpering of the wind in the chimney was like the bare nerve of his pain. Even the flickering of the flame marked the flight of time, which he could not stay by any wish or power in him. Only ten minutes more, aye, everything marked it: the brawl of the stream outside, the rushing of the wind, the scattering of the rain like a legion of fleeing feet, then a sudden pause in the downpour when his heart beat as if waiting on an unseen footstep; the very singing of the lazy kettle was a drone in this wild race of stream and wind and rain, emphasising the speed of all else. Vavasour cast a despairing glance at the mantel, oh! the endless *tick-tick, tick-tick,* of that round clock flanked by rows of idiotic, fat-faced, whiskered china cats, each with an immovably sardonic grin, not a whisker stirring to this merciless *tick-tick.* Aye, it was going to strike in a minute, and the clanging of it would be like the clanging of the gates of hell behind him. He did not notice Catherine, that she, too, unmindful of everything, was gazing in horror at the mantel. Vavasour groaned; oh! if the clock were only a toad or a serpent, he would put his feet on it, crush it, and – oh! – Vavasour swore madly to himself, covering his eyes. Catherine cried out, her face in her hands – the clock was striking.

Twelve!

The last clang of the bell vibrated a second and subsided; the wind whimpered softly in the chimney, the tea-kettle sang on. Through a chink in her fingers Catherine peered at Vavasour; through a similar chink there was a bright agonised eye staring at her.

'Oh!' gulped Catherine.

'The devil!' exclaimed Vavasour.

'Lad!' called his wife, putting out a hand to touch him.

Then followed a scene of joy; they embraced, they kissed, they danced about madly, and having done it once, they did it all over again and still again.

'But, Katy, are ye here, really *here*?'

'Am I here? Tut, lad, are *ye* here?'

'Aye, that is, are we *both* here?'

'Did ye think I wasn't goin' to be?' asked the wife, pausing.

'No-o, not that, only I thought, I thought ye was goin' . . . to . . . to faint. I thought ye looked like it,' replied Vavasour, with a curious expression of suppressed, intelligent joy in his eyes.

'Oh!' exclaimed Catherine. Then, suddenly, the happiness in her face was quenched. 'But, lad, I'm a wicked woman, aye, Vavasour Jones, a bad woman!'

As Vavasour had poured himself out man unto man to Eilir, so woman unto man Catherine poured herself out to her husband.

'An', lad, I went to the church-porch hopin', almost prayin' ye'd be called, that I'd see your spirit walkin'.'

'Catherine, ye did that!'

'Aye, but oh! lad, I'd been so unhappy with quarrelling and hard words, I could think of nothin' else but gettin' rid of them.'

'Och, 't was bad, very bad!' replied Vavasour.

'An' then, lad, when I reached the church-corner an' saw your spirit was really there, really called, an' I knew ye'd not live the year out, I was frightened, but oh! lad, I was glad, too.'

Vavasour looked grave.

'Katy, it was a terrible thing to do!'

'I know it now, but I didn't at that time, dearie,' answered Catherine; 'I was hard-hearted, an' I was weak with longin' to escape from it all. An' then I ran home,' she continued; 'I was frightened, but oh! lad dear, I was glad, too, an' now it hurts me so to think it. An' when ye came in from the Lodge, ye spoke so pleasantly to me that I was troubled. An' now the year through it's grown better an' better, an' I could think of nothin' but lovin' ye an' wishin' ye to live an' knowin' I was the cause of your bein' called. Och, lad, *can* ye forgive me?' asked Catherine.

'Aye,' replied Vavasour slowly, 'I can – none of us is without sin – but, Katy, it was wrong, aye, a terrible thing for a woman to do.'

'An' then to-night, lad, I was expectin' ye to go, knowin' ye couldn't live after twelve, an' ye sittin' there so innocent an' mournful; an' when the time came I wanted to die myself. Oh!' moaned Catherine afresh.

'No matter, dearie, now,' comforted Vavasour, putting his arm about her, 'it *was* wrong in ye, but we're still here an' it's been a sweet year, aye, it's been better nor a honeymoon, an' all the years after we'll make better nor this. There, Katy, let's have a bit of a wassail to celebrate our All-Hallows' honeymoon, shall we?'

'Aye, lad, it would be fine,' said Catherine, starting for the bowl, 'but Vavasour, can ye forgive me, think, lad, for hopin', aye, an' almost praying' to see your spirit, just wishin' that ye'd not live the year out?'

'Katy, I can, an' I'm not layin' it up against ye, though it was a wicked thing for ye to do – for any one to do. Now, dearie, fetch the wassail.'

Catherine started for the bowl once more, then turned, her black eyes snapping upon him.

'Vavasour, how does it happen that the callin' is set aside an' that ye're *really* here? Such a thing's not been in Gwynen in the memory of man'; and Catherine proceeded to give a list of the All-Hallows'-Eve callings that had come inexorably true within the last hundred years.

'I'm not sayin' how it's happened, Catherine, but I'm thinkin' it's modern times an' things these days are happenin' different, – aye, modern times.'

'Good!' sighed Catherine contentedly, 'it's lucky 'tis modern times.'

VII

The Madness of Winifred Owen

BERTHA THOMAS

'Not from an old face will you ever get the same fine effect as from an old house.'

The old saying was brought to my mind by the sudden sight of an exception to the truth of it in the person of Mrs Trinaman, landlady of the 'Ivybush', at Pontycler, in the heart of South Wales.

It was in the summer of 1899, when the cycling fever was at its height in all spinsters of spirit. I and my 'Featherweight' had come three hundred miles from our London home, nominally to look up the tombs of forgotten Welsh ancestors in undiscoverable churchyards; more truly for the treat of free roving among strangers in a strange land. So much I knew of the country I was in – that Wales, the stranger within England's gates, remains a stranger still.

At Pontycler, a score or so of cottages dumped down round a cross-roads tavern in a broad green upland valley, I thought to halt for the night, but was met by objections. The accommodation at the 'Ivybush' was not for such as myself. So the striking-looking woman above named plainly intimated.

A woman well on in the fifties, stout and grey, form and features thickened by years and the wear of life; a woman substantially and spotlessly clad in black stuff skirt, white apron and cross-over, and crowned by a frilled cap as awe-instilling as a justice's wig. Yet, to look at her was to feel that there, once, stood a beautiful girl. There was power in the face, there was mind; but it held you fast in girl's fashion by some indefinably agreeable attraction.

'Board and lodging that are good enough for you are good enough for me,' I thought, and said so.

At that she fairly laughed, and agreed to house me, for one night only.

While the room was preparing I strolled out on foot. Led by a habit of avoiding the beaten track, I presently left the road for a lesser lane; the lane for an approach to a farm; the farmyard for a rough upward track between pastures screened from view by hedgerows so tall as nearly to meet overhead.

On a sudden break in the left bank I saw, close by, on higher ground, an old house looking down on me as it were in surprise at the intrusion. A small, grey-stone, slate-roofed house, in a curious stage of dilapidation. The sash windows, carved wooden porch, broad grass-plat in front shaded by a lofty ilex and dense foliaged yew, also some handsome wrought-iron gates beyond, marked it as a dwelling-place of another class to the snug thatched farm just passed, or the jerry-built Pontycler cottages. Some steep stone steps in the hedge-gap led me up to the little green; and through the broken front windows I saw inside – saw solid mahogany doors and marble mantels, but ceilings coming down, floors falling in, and no sign whatever of present or recent occupation.

An elderly shepherd, escorting a few sheep up the track I had left, told me that Cilcorwen – so the house was named – belonged to distant folk who, unable to agree as to its use and upkeep, let it go thus to decay.

I remarked that it bore traces of better keeping at some time or other.

'Ah,' he said meditatively, leaning on his pitchfork, 'that was when Dr Dathan had it, twenty, thirty years back, when I was a lad. Twelve years or more he was living there.'

'Rather an awkward, out-of-the-way residence for a medical man,' I let fall.

'Ah, well, but he – Dr Dathan – was not one who went doctoring the sick, unless in some sudden great need,' said my informant. 'He was always at his books – and other things – studying – studying – all the time. A man who knew a lot more than others. Too much, they used to say.'

'Oh, a witch-doctor, was he?' said I jokingly, but catching at the notion like a trout at the fly. It suited the weird little place so well.

'I do not know. Some would call him a conjuror, and feared him like a ghost,' the Welshman admitted, adding, with a sour smile, 'As a boy I wasn't afraid of no ghosts, nor anything, unless it was a mad dog or a bull, and that one man, Dr Dathan. And I thought he was a ghost! He looked like one.'

'What became of him?' I asked.

But my frank curiosity made my friend cautious and suspicious. He shook his head repeating: 'It is all long ago. I was a lad. There are those here who could tell you more than I.'

'Mrs Trinaman, at the "Ivybush", perhaps?' I hazarded, explaining that I was stopping there this night.

'Winifred Owen? She at the "Ivybush"?' His eye – his tone – woke up. 'Yes, indeed,' he said, nodding gravely and mysteriously. 'She should know. She should remember. I believe he did cure her once, when she went clean off her head – crazed, as you say; and was given up by the regular doctors.'

'What?' I exclaimed, startled. Here was a fact stated, more unexpected, more inconceivable than any tale of demonology or witchcraft. For if ever woman stood up looking like Sanity in thick shoes, it was surely my landlady at the 'Ivybush'.

'Aye. It was the talk of the parish! She was keeping house then for her father, Evan John David Owen, at his farm, away down yonder by Pontycler bridge. She went from here after that, rather sudden; and we never saw her no more till two-three years ago she came back to her people, and set up at the Pontycler Inn, to be near her old home.'

His sheep were bleating to him to come on; we exchanged courtesies after the custom of the courteous country, and went our opposite ways.

The vision of the old house, posed there as if for a picture, stayed in my mind's eye as I retraced my steps to the 'Ivybush', there to find, to my dismay, that my hostess had vacated her own bedroom to give it up to me. It was too late to remonstrate. Nay, later on I encroached still further, forsaking the cold comfort of the 'parlour' for a snug corner of the oak settle by the kitchen hearth, watching Mrs Trinaman step to and from the bar serving many comers – greybeard village chatterboxes, tired quarrymen, beery carters, pert cyclists, and tramps; customers very various, but all impatient and out of temper, for a wild wet evening had set in, threatening worse. Half the conversation being carried on in the local dialect – elusive as a secret code – was to me unintelligible; but only to listen and watch her was to perceive she found the right word, way, and tone for each. No need to teach man or boy how to behave in her presence. By-and-by they ceased to come; the storm had burst forth on a heroic scale.

She closed the door, observing, 'Wherever a man is now to-night, there, if he can, he'll stay.'

Ten minutes later she was sitting opposite me with her knitting, and we were having a friendly chat. Her remarks, her questions, showed a knowledge and understanding of men and things acquired in a wider world than Pontycler;

and she readily resumed touch with it, opportunity offering. She obviously believed in class distinctions, accepting these as a social fact, without attributing to the fact such sinister importance as to resent its existence. She neither proffered her company and conversation, nor refused them when invited and welcome. But never have I been more conscious of personal and mental inferiority than in the presence of Mrs Trinaman. She simply towered – not by dint of any self-assertion – but by the sheer sense she conveyed of force of character.

Demented? She? Never! Her part in the shepherd's tale I dismissed as a fable. But I spoke of Cilcorwen and the gossip I had picked up by the wayside concerning its sometime occupier.

'Dr Dathan,' she said, quite freely. 'Yes, I knew him.'

'Was he a pretender to magic, pray; or only a quack?'

'Certainly not a quack,' she replied. 'He – he – never put his hand to cure any one if he could help it. For the rest – well, they said he practised black magic. But I, for one, should be sorry to believe any harm of him since to him and his "sorcery" I owe my life.'

'How could that be,' I asked, 'if, as you say, he left the healing of the sick to others?'

'Not "my life" in that sense.' She smiled enigmatically. 'Yet in more senses than one.' Her grave eyes seemed taking a long view – a backward sweep; her strong, expressive, face told of deep and lasting emotional experience undergone – yet not of the sort that corrupts or warps the soul. 'It's an odd story,' she resumed. 'One that wouldn't be believed here even now – *as it happened* – which is why I never tell it.'

But as we sat there over the smokeless, glowing hearth, with the storm-wind howling round, she told it me, as follows.

'I was a little girl of ten when I first remember him. I think he had not long come to Cilcorwen, but wonderful tales went abroad about him from the first. A doctor who took no patients, yet who was not taking his ease and his leisure but toiled hard all day; some said, all night! Ned the poacher, whose habits took him out and about mostly at bedtime or in dark hours, vowed the light was always burning at Cilcorwen. Two of the lower rooms were kept locked, and not even the old woman, lodging in the lean-to hovel attached, who cooked and so on for him, was permitted to meddle with them. We children used to take to our heels if we saw his figure coming down the road. I don't know why. It was odd-looking, and seemed not to belong to these parts. He wasn't of a tall make, but spare and flexible; and he wore his black hair longer than is customary. He dressed carelessly, but always like a gentleman, a London gentleman – in black, not squire or sportsman fashion as they all do here. He was sharp-featured, with eyes like two burning fire-devils; his skin wrinkled and white – yellowish white, like a buried thing dug up again, as they say.'

'And they took him for a ghost,' I said.

She laughed.

'More than likely it was the natural effect of a life spent poring over books; and breathing the unwholesome fumes and vapours of the chemicals in his laboratory. Only the pure, keen air of our Welsh hills kept him alive. Perhaps that was why he had settled down here. But the boys said it was because Pontycler being so out of the way and behindhand he could practise his forbidden unholy arts there without risk of being found out.'

'What sort of arts?'

'Nobody knew; but they whispered he spent his time making experiments on living animals – besides dissecting dead ones; studied poisons; could cast spells; knew incantations that would poison your food. Another story said he was an anarchist and made bombs, but I think that was only because he always wore a crimson tie! Oh, there was no end to their tales. Pat Coghlan, an imp of an Irish farm-hand, boasted that, spying round Cilcorwen one winter evening and seeing the blind awry and the light burning, he climbed up on the window-sill, peeped in, and saw . . .'

'Saw what?'

'Dr Dathan in his shirt-sleeves raising the devil. So he assured us; but it's my belief he was too scared to see anything. For the doctor turned his head, and Pat dropped away and ran for his life. "Corpse-candles was a-burning in the garden," he told us. "If he had set eyes on me it's a dead boy would be telling you this now!" We believed every word.'

'Did he make no friends, no acquaintance, here?'

'He avoided company, never cared to see the neighbours, rich or poor, unless on business. But he was in correspondence with great doctors and learned professors all the world over; the letters he posted and the stamps on those he received showed that. Sometimes a visitor from town would come down for a few nights – some one in his own style; and now and then he went there himself for a week, always leaving Cilcorwen securely locked up. Yes, though he harmed no one, he was a mystery, and something of a terror; but no one molested him and he stayed on so long that we got used to him and forgot to wonder or to pry. He never took the faintest interest in anything or anybody here, but was always civil-spoken and always paid his way.'

'One evening father sent me on a message to the "Ivybush". A handy-man had been repairing the roof there, and I was to urge him to come to-morrow to make good some damage done at our farm by a heavy gale the night before.

'Finding no one at the bar, I walked straight into the

kitchen, and was taken aback at the sight there of two men – foreigners – Englishmen, that is. One was a little redcoat, and was babbling in the foolish, rambling way of a man who is the worse for drink. The other wore a plain dark-blue uniform, and I took him for his mate, but he had such a pleasant, open face and quiet, determined look that I was not afraid to stay waiting. I noticed the tact and judgment with which he treated his companion, keeping him from making a worse fool of himself than could now he helped. In a few minutes the innkeeper came back and told me that the handy-man had gone off to another job, a day's journey from Pontycler. I was very much put out, for skilled labour here is scarce. So I stood bemoaning our predicament, and the landlord shaking his head and chiming in "What a pity!" when the man in blue, who had been lending an ear, spoke – I seem to hear his voice – saying:

'"Now, if you'll listen to me, I'll tell you how you can do what you want done yourselves."

'And he described very precisely and clearly how the thing could be managed. But I could not follow him, I had learnt English and thought I knew it, little knowing then how much there was to know. He soon saw I was puzzled outright.

'"Well," said he, with a funny side-glance at the little redcoat slouching sleepily on the bench where you are sitting now, "I'm stranded here for to-night. You live near, you say. If you like I'll step over first thing to-morrow and do it myself."

'I was shy and suspicious of strangers – as we all are here – but somehow I never once thought of refusing his offer, or even asked myself whether I could trust this man, so knowing he seemed, and yet so simple-spoken! My head was full of what seemed to be quite a little adventure as I ran home. But I remember my father scolded me sharply for giving the job without bargaining for a price, and I was vexed to death that he, when the man called next day, began haggling with him about the charge. He laughed outright; said he was no journeyman tinker, and wanted no pay for lending a helping hand to a fellow-Christian. That so hurt father's pride that he walked off in a huff. The other turned to me with a sort of merry appeal in his eye. "Come, there's no pleasing you Welsh!" he complained.

'"Don't say that!" The words slipped from me without thinking; then I felt overcome with confusion – hot and red. Our eyes had met for a moment, and I turned away, my heart beating fast.

'Well, he made short work of half a dozen jobs – leaks, broken panes, and what not; refused payment, but stayed to take a cup of tea at our table.

'He told us he was a seaman in the Royal Navy, and that he and the soldier-man had first met in the train yesterday afternoon. He had managed to keep his half-tipsy fellow-passenger quiet, till, on nearing Pontycler, the booby tried to pull the communication cord, then wanted to fight the stationmaster, who turned him out of the train as unfit to travel. Just to save him from further scrapes, the sailor threw in his lot with the culprit, piloted him to the safe shelter, for the night, of the "Ivybush", and had packed him sad and sober, off to Cardiff that morning.

'All the time I was thinking, "Presently it will be thank you and good bye – and all over!" sadly. For I liked him. Then, just as he was taking leave, he told us how, last night, Dr Dathan had come to the inn on exactly the same errand as myself, and persuaded him to stay and help patch up the roof at Cilcorwen. And (father had been called off for a moment) though he didn't say so, he let me know he was glad to be detained, because of the chance offered of seeing me again; and my heart gave a thump of rising joy.

'So we did meet, once or twice; but along with the gladness of it I was sorely, sorely troubled. He seemed very far off;

and if he and his speech and ways gave me a chink view into a new life and world, it was one with which I had and could have nothing to do. For one thing, he was a servant of War. War was wicked, and all fighting men servants of sin; so said every teaching and preaching man I had ever heard. A stranger too, one of an alien race; while I, born and reared at Pontycler, belonged body and soul to the little Welsh world of my fathers. Add to that I was as good as promised to another man – Vaughan Hughes of Bryngolau, who had been courting me for some time – and father had made up his mind he was to have me. He was a farmer in a larger way than ourselves; and all the girls I knew envied me the flattering offer, and said spiteful things about the power of a pretty face. And though I hung back, feeling shy of the man, no one believed my bashfulness would last long. We were not brought up to consider our fancies, for father was a very masterful man. I knew that with his old and confirmed prejudice against the English and his heart set on the marriage with Vaughan Hughes, he would be frantic if he knew how I was feeling now.

'Well, a sailor's wooing is short. The fourth time we met – very gravely, very quietly, very tenderly, Walter – that was his name – asked me to be his wife.

'Then the whole trouble of it plumped like a shower of stones upon me. Walter would not and could never understand why, since he had won my heart, he should not have my hand for the asking. There was no stopping him. He went straight to my father for his consent, startling him out of his wits, poor father! He went into a violent rage; then, as Walter persisted, unmoved, he broke into taunts and abuse, shouting out that all sailormen drank, had a wife in every port; loudly treating the offer as an affront to an honest Welsh girl. Walter, stupefied, turned silently to me. I stood up to father, for the first and last time, said that I loved and wished to marry the man who had spoken; and that, come what might, I would never marry Vaughan Hughes.

'Then father broke out in the old Welsh tongue of his forefathers. Oh, he could use it and make it work, in ways Walter could never conceive of. He reproached me as treacherous and unfeeling – a girl who, for a light passing fancy for a foreign vagabond, could be false to ties of home country, kindred, religion – every holy thing.'

'What? Can you mean that he considered that for you to marry an Englishman would be a disgrace?' I asked in wonder.

'Well, no,' she half smiled. 'I won't say. Perhaps had there been money or advantage in the match he might, though not liking, have thought it his duty not to forbid it. He knew as little about the English as you – pardon my saying it – do of Welsh people; and he judged them from the worst sort that come here because they have gone wrong in their own country. Walter's quiet assertion that he was in a position to support a wife, he scouted. Here, he had made up his mind, was a tippler, an unbeliever, a spendthrift, whose dupe I should never be if he could help it. Oh, you might just as well have tried to move the Black Mountain yonder as to reason with father on the point. The difference of language rose up suddenly like a wall between them, and father seemed to lose his power of understanding or expressing himself in any but his mother tongue. Even Walter was discouraged; felt it was hopeless to argue or to pray.

'He had to join his ship; but bade me take heart, hold firm, and in a few weeks he would come back for my final answer. It was with a sinking heart I saw him go. But he wrote, he wrote!

'The next fortnight felt like a year of torment. Father was confident I had given in, and tried his best to hurry on the affair with Vaughan Hughes, who had heard about Walter and his suit, but was not jealous – not he! – refusing to take it seriously. "What, an impudent English sailor rascal from who knows where try to steal his little girl?" Father, now that Walter was out of the way, had calmed down; but his pleading was hard, too terribly hard for me to resist. When he stood up and spoke you were moved and awed as by one of the prophets or patriarchs in the Old Testament. How could I want to break his heart and bring shame on the family by giving him this godless English vagabond for a son-in-law – I, the only daughter left? My head had been turned for an instant – he could forgive that. But so heartless, so undutiful, as to mean it – he couldn't believe it of me.

'I felt somehow he saw things in a wrong light and would never see them in any other. He was old, too. There was no help anywhere. I was bound to go under. My appointed place in life was here with my people, while Walter, far off in the busy world, would presently forget me. It was bitter, and yet I might have yielded but for the dread of being drawn into the other marriage. After that, no hope in this world for Walter and me – none! My brothers, the neighbours, every one were against me, and full of hard words for him who in passing by had broken, if not destroyed, the peace of our hearth.

'There came the yearly grand fair day at Llanffelix, three miles off. Every one was starting for the town, all the girls in holiday clothes. I was in no humour for sports, and stayed to mind the house. Then, left alone with my trouble, it so possessed me and became so unbearable I half wished I had gone with the rest.

'There were butter and eggs to be taken up to Cilcorwen, and later in the day I went over with them myself. And as I went, thinking of father, of Vaughan Hughes, but mostly of

Walter, whom I must give up – desperate, and at my wits' end what to do, it crossed my head, not for the first time, to consult Dr Dathan!'

'Did you really look on him as a magician?' I asked.

'Well, I won't say that I did not. And only some superhuman power, I thought, could come to my relief. It seemed a wild notion, yet as I walked on in the loneliness – every human creature was at the fair – the determination grew. I knocked at the house door, and receiving no answer, wondered if he too had gone to Llanffelix. The blinds were drawn, but the door opened to my hand, and the passage door into the sitting-room stood ajar. I peeped in. Dr Dathan sat facing me at a table that seemed lit by magic stars. He was so absorbed in watching something in a glass that he never heard me on the threshold. The room, all misty and queer-smelling, was full of strange things whose nature and use were to me beyond conception – mysteriously-shaped bottles, tubes, glasses, and scientific instruments; but the strangest object of all was Dr Dathan, with his peaked, pallid face and lanky hair, under a red smoking-cap. Coming into that sickly-smelling little den straight from the open, the simple fields and feeding cattle, it knocked me stupid. At the moment I believed all the fairy tales I had ever heard of him.'

'Were you frightened?'

'I felt cold; but something seemed pushing me on. Then he looked up at me standing there, and I spoke. "Dr Dathan, I am in a dreadful difficulty. I want to consult you –"

'"I never give medical advice," he said, sharply.

'"Nor do I need that," I answered.

'I had broken up some precious bit of study, and he was impatient and annoyed. But – I was not bad to look at in those days – he hesitated a moment to order me off, and out I came with my story. I made it short. Something warned me not to talk to his pity, but to his power, his wisdom and experience. He knew something of my father and Vaughan Hughes, and had seen Walter and me. Still, having said what I had to say, I felt – oh, so miserably foolish! Unless he were a real wizard, what could he do for me in such a pass?

'"You mean that you cannot hold your own," he said. "Well, in this world the weakest must go to the wall."

'"If I am parted from Walter, what my father wills I shall do in the end. He upbraids, he talks of my dead mother, he beseeches, then he cries and sobs. If I defy him, and go off with Walter, it might be his death. With fury and excitement he will work himself into a fit." My own feelings were getting out of hand, and I broke out helplessly, "Oh, tell me some way to safeguard myself from being over-persuaded into this other marriage at least. I read once of a girl who disfigured herself – spoilt her good looks – to get rid of a suitor. I thought it something too terrible to be true, but feel now that I could do it myself!"

'"That would be a pity," he said, and I heard him mutter as if thinking aloud, "Girl of an uncommon stamp – in more ways than one!" Then he levelled his fire-devils of eyes at me searchingly – suddenly – with an expression so outspoken, I seemed to read it off like writing. It said: "Shall I or shall I not?"

'"You can do something for me," I said hastily. "I see it in your face!"

'He was put out and silent for a moment, glanced down at some papers lying before him, then shot another look at me, as keen as one of his own blades.

'"So you think you would face anything that offered you a chance?"

'"I would face death," I said.

'"Death ends all chances," he said grimly. "Besides, there are worse things than loss of life or lover."

'"What things?" I asked shakily. His manner had changed

from one of indifference and become earnest, and he was watching me now as carefully as the chemicals in the glass when I came in.

'"I dare say you have heard horrible things told of me," he began – "that I make a study of the hidden things of darkness – poisons, and so on."

'I assented in silence.

'"It is a necessary part of the physician's art. Disease is a poison they have to deal with, and that we men of science are occupied in tracing to its origin. You or anybody can understand the principle of what we call the 'anti-toxin treatment', namely, that by introducing a small dose of some particular poison into the system we bring about a mild attack of the particular complaint, which secures immunity from all danger from it in the future. The extension of this principle is bringing us to the verge of discoveries of tremendous importance. Now I have in this glass a certain liquid," he laid his hand on a small tube. "Were I to use it on you it would hurt neither you nor your beauty, yet it might bring about, in the natural course of events, all that you desire. Say that I were to inject a drop of it into your veins . . ."

'"What will happen?" I asked, all of a tremble.

'"Ah!" The smile on his face made me shiver. "Since the experiment is one I cannot make usefully on myself, and no other human subject is forthcoming, I can only tell you what I believe will happen. It will affect one organ only – your brain. After a few days you will probably suffer from definite mental derangement. You will think, act, and talk absurdly, just as in a dream."

'"Do you mean that I shall go mad?" I asked, scarcely believing my ears.

'"Well, your memory, your reason, will be temporarily disordered. The disorder will pass away. But you will find Farmer Hughes will have cooled in his suit. A man like him thinks twice before wedding a girl who has been out of her mind. Ask yourself! What passes here would of course remain our secret."

'I shrank, scared at what I thought a demoniacal offer. "Oh, Dr Dathan, I cannot!"

'"Well, well, in that case there is no more to be said," he replied, his tone changing quickly. "Go home! I was only joking, you little fool!"

'Never joker looked and spoke as he had done! I knew better. "Why, they would put me away, shut me up in an asylum," I stammered out.

'"Even if they did, you would be released soon. But I think I can prevent that. I shall interest myself in the case, and will talk to any other doctor they may summon, and provide an attendant for you at home if necessary. No special treatment will be needed, and in three weeks I say you will be well – and rid of Vaughan Hughes's attentions."

'His urgency and confidence were gaining ground on me. "But say I consented," I faltered, "there is Walter. What of him?"

'"Oh – he – the Navy man – leave him to me. In any case you will be relieved of what you tell me you dread most. To your lover I will – well, I'll tell him something; not all – but enough. Think, now. Will you or will you not?"

'I was agitated, as never in my life before. But the excitement, the eagerness that seemed to devour him, and heaved under his ordinary manner, was a thing I couldn't describe or ever forget.

'"Mind," he said, pulling himself up, as it were, "the only certain risk is mine. I have gone farther into these studies than most; and it may be long before certain processes of protective treatment I would advocate are recognised as safe and proper. I am defying law, public opinion – endangering private and professional standing by proposing this to you.

And if you consent, you must speak of this to none – not even to Walter – until after my death. Observe, I am trusting you, as you will trust me."

'His audacity and zest caught and clutched me like a hawk, and carried me away. "Yes," I said, "I am willing. Will it – will it – hurt much?"

'His whole person lit up with elation and excitement. "Oh, a pin-prick," he said, with the laugh of those who win.

'A pin-prick, and it was done.

'Then, from an evil spirit tempting me, he seemed to become a human being; and talked to me kindly and cheeringly, as to one who has rendered you a service. I went home palsied inwardly with fear, but repeating over to myself his last words: "Don't think. Don't worry. Wait. Let what will happen; hold on and trust to me. All will be well at the last."

'The blessed, blind trust we put in doctors helped me to do as he said, at the first. Soon, awful fears came like big waves to swallow me up. He seemed to know – for sure. But suppose he was mistaken – had miscalculated; and the effect were to destroy my mind – make of me a madwoman for life! Had I perhaps committed a sin, though unknowingly, in consenting to let him try the experiment? I perhaps deserved this most terrible punishment. I had seen in his face that it would be nothing to him what became of me. All he cared for was to study the effect on me of the treatment.

'In the long after-years I have been in lands where they still offer up human sacrifices to their gods. I thought once or twice then of Dr Dathan.'

'Well, what did happen?' I asked, deeply curious.

'For a few days – I don't know how many – I went about my work as usual. Then one morning I was smitten by an awful headache; could scarcely see or speak. As by chance,

Dr Dathan looked in at the farm that very day, spoke cheerfully to me, and advised me to keep very quiet.

'It's little or nothing I can tell you from my own knowledge of anything after that. They say I went completely off my head; talked and behaved just as he had foretold, as senselessly as in a dream; persuaded that impossible things were happening; persons there who were not; one thing changing, melting into another. I was incapable of understanding what was said to me, or of making myself understood. My father and brothers were as scared as if I had turned into a goblin or a ghost. They fetched Dr Dathan in a hurry – he being so near. He managed to quiet them a little, till the Llanffelix doctor came, who was perplexed, and not particularly hopeful. Dr Dathan professed to leave me in his hands but let him know that he held a different opinion. He offered to watch the case for the other, and was as kind as could be, coming every day; and, while confessing he had never seen an attack like it before, predicted that in due time I should recover.

'And so it happened; gradually – as I was told – but to myself it seemed as if in one happy hour, I shook off a nightmare – a heavy cloud; and my wits became clear again, though I was as weak as a little child. "Patience," Dr Dathan whispered to me. "You will soon be as well and strong as before." And so it came to pass!

'But the whole parish knew I had been off my head, and some whispered, since Dr Dathan gave no pills or draughts, that he had cured me by a charm. Vaughan Hughes behaved just as the doctor had foretold. There must be madness in the family, he supposed. Certainly I seemed to be Winifred Owen herself again; but the attack might recur. He had inquired, and heard how rare it was that patients, though discharged from asylums as cured, remained permanently sane. I don't see that he was to be blamed for his caution, but he offended father by his plain-speaking, and they had some words. Just then Walter came back; and Dr Dathan took a lot of trouble – got hold of him and talked to him in private, in the first place.'

'What did he tell him?'

'That he felt certain mine had been a case – a rare case – of blood poisoning, and that there was not the slightest danger of a relapse. To father he hinted that a thorough change of scene and circumstances would be a desirable thing for me on all accounts. Other admirers might behave like Vaughan Hughes; while here was Walter, with a bundle of badges and testimonials from his superior officers, ready and eager to wed me. Father gave in; Walter Trinaman was married to me three weeks later, and away with me to England – to Plymouth – and the Fleet.'

Five-and-thirty years ago she went out with him into a new and complicated world, the world of infinite good and evil, from which Pontycler prudently still keeps its face averted. Yet had she been blessed in her deed. Walter Trinaman proved of the good leaven, one of the best in a line of life where all must be of the better sort. His officers, his mates, knew it; and his Winifred came to know.

'And when I said I owe my life to Dr Dathan, I mean Walt's life and mine that we led together!'

Much had she seen, 'places and men'. Sorrow she had known, 'Our little son – we lost!' And that sorrow, I felt, was unhealed. 'But we had two dear daughters.'

Both married young, she told me; and two years ago Walter Trinaman, then in the coastguard service, was one of the six lives lost in rescuing others from a memorable wreck on the coast of South Devon.

'My own life seemed ended and lived out. Of my girls, one was settled in Canada; the other in Glasgow. My heart turned suddenly – so strangely and unexpectedly – to Pontycler and the old country, and I came over, to find father still living, though going on for ninety years old. My brothers carry on the farm. The people at the "Ivybush" were leaving, and so it came to pass that I took it.'

'And Dr Dathan,' I asked, 'what became of him?'

'It was about three years after I went away that I read a notice of him in the paper. He was found dead in his bed at Cilcorwen by the caretaker who brought up his breakfast one morning. At the inquest the doctor said his whole frame was wasted and perished, and that it was a miracle he had lived so long, not ailing, apparently; as he might have dropped off at any moment the last twelvemonth. There are those here like Caleb Evans, whom you met to-day, who still half believe that the devil came for his own and fetched him away. That is not fair. What became of his researches I never heard; nor do I think he cared to be famous – only to find out, and to know.'

On leaving the 'Ivybush' regretfully the next morning, I suggested enlarging and improving the inn, since so pleasant a halting-place as Pontycler could not fail to attract numerous summer visitors of a better class. Surely it would be worth while.

'If you mean that it would be more remunerative,' said Mrs Trinaman plainly, 'I, or any one who knows anything about it, can tell you this kind of thing pays much better!' And that, I felt, was the proper answer to my commonplace, middle-class suggestion. But her last words were in another key, as, standing before her door, a serving hostess to every passing wayfarer, to the fit and unfit alike, she wished me good speed. 'So long as I stay,' she said wistfully, 'it shall stay as it was when I first met Trinaman – I've told you where and how!'

VIII

The Call of the River

ELLEN LLOYD-WILLIAMS

You would not remember John Evans, Tŷ Bach; he was almost before your time – a little dark, spare man with high cheekbones, and eyes not black, but a clear deep brown, like turf-pools in sunshine. He was a man of no fixed trade – a peat-cutter in the season, at other times hedger, bee-keeper, gardener, and an excellent farrier on occasion, the beasts trusted him as they trust few men. It was with children as with the dumb creatures, for they would flock around him wherever he went, to hear his tales of the days when the Fair Folk came to buy in Carmarthen market, or when the miner in his narrow alley underground would pause a moment, to hear the tap-tap-tap of goblin hammers beyond the narrow wall that hemmed him in. Or he would point to the Pwca's lantern hovering at night above the deep waters of the bog, or hold up a silencing hand as he listened for elfin music on the edge of rings trodden green upon the hill-side.

'Stuff and nonsense,' would say the old grandmother with whom he lived. 'It is not from my folk that you got such foolishness!' But John would only laugh at all her anger.

'Is it my fault then, *mam-gu*,' he would say, 'if I was born of a Midsummer Night with the moon at the full?'

Indeed he was a queer soul, with eyes that saw more than those of other folk. Many a time, as we came home across the fields, he would stand stock-still in the path, and 'Stop,' he would say, and ''Sht now,' he would say, and turn his head about to listen; though I would hear nothing but the sleepy call of birds that comes with the setting sun. 'What do you hear, John?' I would ask him, and he would answer, 'I almost heard Them then – I heard Their voices . . .' 'They! Who?' I asked him once, for it was foolish talk. He only looked at me with puckered brows. 'I don't know . . . I'm not sure . . .' he said, his eyes puzzled and doubting as a child's, his voice trailing off into vague murmurs. I let him be after that. He was a lovable, kindly fellow; and if he was a little odd over his 'voices', surely it was a small matter, and did no one any harm.

Tŷ Bach – it is long pulled down – stood close beside the bank of Ayron river. The ripple of water echoed all day long in every wall of that little, thatch-roofed house. It whispered the folk to sleep at nightfall, and woke them again next day with the glancing sunlight that danced from the little waves to the leaded panes and back again. John had been born to that faint, murmuring sound; one might have fancied that his ears were dulled to it. Yet, when he was needed, it was always by the river I would find him – and sometimes, coming on him unawares, I would hear him talking in a low, gentle tone, as though he spoke to someone very close. It was his earnestness, maybe, and the strange folly of the man infecting me, but it seemed to me as though the river answered him with a hushed, laughing cadence like a woman's voice. He was crazed, of course, and I a fool whose ears deceived me.

Crazed or not, there was one woman at least who set her fancy on him; and she was the daughter of Blaenpant, and a very fair match indeed for John Tŷ Bach, with his uncertain livelihood and restless ways. Her father was reckoned to have put by in his time; and the girl was pretty and plump and rosy-cheeked. The rosy cheeks turned pale as she waited for John; at first her father would not have it, and would have married her elsewhere, but John Tŷ Bach she would have, and her folk gave in.

But John himself hung back and said never a word, though his grandmother said words enough for twenty. 'Are you a man or are you not, John Evans? Will you waste all your time roaming the fields? You will make no fortunes yourself, and here comes a fortune tossed into your lap! I have no patience with you.'

'But I do not love her,' John would say, with his troubled child's eyes upon the old woman.

'Love!' she would answer, choking with disgust. 'As if that mattered! She can keep your house! But if you want love, any fool could see she has enough for two – and you are breaking her heart for her, John Evans.'

It was that, I think, which won him in the end – him who had never hurt a soul in all his days. One evening, late, I found him after many hours of absence. He was kneeling upon the river-bank, and there was a pain in his voice that cried out, though the words were low. I could not find it in my heart to call him, and I stood still and waited in the shade of a crooked willow.

'It is good-bye, then,' he said. 'O, my dear, my dear. Goodbye, since you will not come to the warm fireside and the living hearts of men. And I must go away – away from the sound of your silver voice and the rippling fall of your laughter, and the sight of your deep dark eyes and your smile alight in the sunshine . . . Oh, I cannot leave you behind me – come out of your world to mine!' But the river rippled on with a sound like a woman's tears.

After awhile he went back into the house, walking heavily; and I never stirred till he had gone. Folly, all folly, of course, but that hour was his own. The next day he was promised to the daughter of Blaenpant.

Oh, but the grandmother was pleased! They were to have a cottage on the hill, close by the turbary where John worked in the season; and she was glad to leave the low ground of the valley. The marriage would be early, for what need had they of waiting? The Blaenpant girl's cheeks bloomed again; her father beamed his content. Only John himself went his way, kindly as ever, gentle and tender with his promised bride – more silent, it may be, than was his wont.

'He is a fine bridegroom,' said the old woman, as we sat in the house a night or two before the wedding. 'Even his sweetheart can get scarcely a word from him. In my young days I would have thrown a lad over for less than that; but everyone has his own taste, and perhaps it's just as well.'

It was a black night, stormy, with little gusts of wind and rain. I was for going home early, but the old woman would not have it, and made tea, and boiled fresh eggs, and made lightcakes dripping with butter, saying she could not let me go without supper on so comfortless a night. Every now and then she would cast some little mocking remark at John, who sat in the chimney corner very quietly, with a curious strained look upon his face as though he were listening for something. The sounds of the night came very clearly in to us – the wailing wind about the house, the angry tossing of the storm-swept, straining trees, and, above all, the rushing sound of the river, swelled by recent rain. It silenced us all at last, and we sat closer round about the fire.

There was a sudden blast of wind that seemed to shake the house. The door swung wide open; the house was filled with the echo of swirling water, and above and through it something that seemed a call, high, penetrating, sweet, imperious. And, as if in answer to a summons that he understood, John rose abruptly and stepped out into the night. The door crashed to behind him.

We never saw him again. The morning dawned and showed no trace of him – not though we dragged the river's shallow reaches from end to end, to the mocking laughter of the little eddies. We never found him, though even that swollen tide had hardly strength to sweep a man downstream and out to sea. But that day, and the next day, and the next, the ripples rang like a peal of silver bells.

IX

The Coward

KATHLEEN FREEMAN

The landlady's daughter opened the door of my sitting-room, and carried out the supper-tray.

'Good night, sir,' she said gently, and flushed all over her fair, pretty face.

'Good night,' I said, and my heart beat violently. I sat again to my books; but my body was on wires. At last I took a pipe from the mantelpiece, and climbed the stairs to the room above my own.

My friend the foreman roadmender sat at his table, sorting and arranging his specimens. Hundreds of cubes of rock lay before him, all ticketed. He fondled them one after another in his horny palms. In this way he spent all his evenings, never going out after his day's work was done, and reading nothing but books on geology and quarrying. He was good to hear, with his tales of quarries and caves and roads, and good to see with his massive head and golden beard. I sat down opposite him at the table.

'Young man,' he said, fixing his bright blue eyes on my face, 'your blood's restless. Why don't you find a wife?'

'Rot,' I said, startled.

'Find a wife,' said he, 'and quickly; one of the sort that trips in at supper-time with a savoury dish, and all you have to say is, "What have you got there, Mary, my girl? Something tasty, I'll be bound." And Mary sits down to serve it out, glowing and smiling as if you'd told her that her eyes were like the stars in the heavens. Ah, you town cubs; you're not strong enough to live alone.'

'Rot,' I said again. 'A man can live alone and be happy, unless he's a fool or a coward.'

'Or has sins to think on,' said he.

'It's the same thing,' said I. 'Conscience makes cowards, you know.'

He stared away from me at the wall. 'The man that said that was a wise man,' said he. 'I know the man. 'Twas he who said there were sermons in stones. Shrewd sayings, both. I could vouch . . .'

He stopped. Then, taking up one of the cubes of stone, he passed it to me.

'Can you read that?' he said.

It was a piece of iron stone, and the ticket attached to it bore a name and a date.

PENALLT. OLD SHAFT. 18 –

'That came from the hill on which I was born,' he said. 'I used to live in a cottage about half-way up the hill, in a belt of wood. There was iron in the hill; my father had lived most of his life there, working in the mine. By the time that I was old enough to work, the iron mine had been shut down – it wasn't yielding enough ore to give a profit – and a quarry had been started on the south side, where there was red sandstone. When I was sixteen, my father was killed – he fell down one of the shafts of the mine in which he had worked nearly all his days – and I and my mother lived on at the cottage, as well as we could on what I earned.

'We were happy, too, I tell you. We never went off the hill except to buy food. I crossed the top every day from our cottage on the west slope to the quarry on the south-east; and when I came back in the evening, she'd be looking out for me at the gate. Sometimes, she'd come along the track to meet me. I can see her now coming through the bluebells, a sea of them all moist among the trees, and you couldn't tell where they ended. I was always angry when the foxgloves came pushing up and over-topping them, as though to say, "Give over admiring those frail creatures; see how sturdy and fine we are!" As for me, I always hated their gaudy flaunting looks. I suppose I took that from my mother. She was strange about that. She never would come to meet me in foxglove time; and it's always through the bluebells that I see her coming.

'For three years we lived like that. Then my mother began to grow frail and white. For a long time, she made no plaint; but one day I found her on the bed crying. I went to her, and touched her on the shoulder. She turned and clutched me tight and close round the neck.

'"Joe, my boy," she said, "there's something very wrong with me. My limbs – they're somehow not mine, I feel. Joe, I'm afraid – afraid. What will you do if I'm gone? Oh, my dear, we've come to a rough patch of ground at last."

'We clung together affrighted. I believed what she had said. From that day onward, I knew in my heart that our happiness was over. Somehow, I seemed to have known always that it couldn't last.

'I brought a doctor from the village. He told her that all she had to do was to keep very quiet and not worry; to go to bed, and not move at all; and while I was out, a little girl must be there to look after her; and if she did as he told her, she'd probably get well. She didn't believe him. She knew better. After he'd gone, she called him fool and liar. When he got me alone downstairs, he put his hand on my shoulder, and said:

'"My poor lad, I'm very sorry for you both."

'"How long?" I said.

'"Eight months," he said. "Probably less. Her blood is turning to water."

'So I did the work of the house, and went to the quarry as before; and no one met me on my homeward road. It wasn't so bad in the winter – it was January when she fell ill, and she always waited for me by the fire in winter, when the light had gone before I got home, – but when bluebell time came, I cursed the ground beneath my feet for sending up that blue mist like nothing else in the world. I used to go in amongst it, and lie on the ground till the scent of them made me wild. Then I would crush them under my boots, and curse them. I was thankful that year when the foxgloves came.

'One evening, in foxglove time, I was walking home from the quarry, not looking at the foxgloves, nor caring enough about them to be angry at their stupid pushing ways. On my way, I passed a small quarry, long left idle, a shallow square cutting, with an opening at one end on to the track. I looked down the entry, from old habit; and there, with her back to me, was a girl, standing very still, watching something on the ground. I wondered if she was scared – sometimes one finds snakes in an old quarry – and I walked down the entry, treading heavily so as to let her know I was there.

'She didn't turn, but waved a hand behind her impatiently. "Sh-h," she hissed.

'And there, five feet away from her, was a weasel, stepping out of the bush with his bright eyes dancing. He gave us one clever little glance, and back he slipped into his bramble-bush.

'"There," she said, "you frightened him away, you great oaf. Now he won't come out again. What was he, do you know?"

'"Just a common weasel," I said. "Have you never seen one before?"

'"No. I've lived all my days in a town. I've never, never seen a weasel before. Think of that now! Ah, Mr High and

Mighty, but maybe I could teach you a few things. How to treat a weasel when I find one, say. You're so used to them, you don't think. You country people are all, alike – don't value what you've got. Look at the foxgloves, now. I daresay you never take any notice of them. You don't see anything wonderful about foxgloves, I suppose?"

'"I don't like foxgloves," I said, "but . . ."

'"There you are. Oh no, you don't see anything in foxgloves. They always grow here, and why make a song about it? I have lived in a town, and worked in an eating-house, I've been better brought up than that. I know what to look for in the country, yes, and how to treat what I find. I'll bring a basket to-morrow, I will, and take a load of them back down there. Good-bye." And away she went, swinging down along the path up which I had come. I stood looking after her. She stopped, picked a foxglove, waved it to me, and was gone.

'When I went up the stairs to my mother, she said:

'"You're late, aren't you?"

'"Not more than a minute or two," I said.

'"Time seems long to me, lying here," she said, and turned away from my kiss.

'A fortnight later, I met the girl again. I sat beside her in the old quarry, on a ledge of rock. She told me that her name was Nancy, and that she worked in the public-house below in the valley. It was better, she said, than the eating-house in the town. They gave her more free time. And she felt at home, somehow, in this hill country, perhaps because her grandmother had been a gypsy. People always said that she had her grandmother's eyes and hair. Then she said:

'"Do you know, I never thought I could like a man until I met you?"

'I said, "Do I come first?"

'She said, "Yes."

'"Do you love me?" I said.

'"Yes," she said again. "Now keep quite still. I'm going to kiss you."

'I shut my eyes and she kissed me, very lightly and slowly, on the lips. The blood rushed to my head.

'"Shall I kiss you now?" I said, "in my way?" And I moved to take her in my arms. But she snatched herself away, and ran from me. I sat there, hoping she'd come back, fearing to go home.

'For twenty days I saw nothing of her; and I forgot her, because those days were a St Martin's Summer for my mother and me. Our hopes rose. She grew stronger. She was able to leave her bed, and lie, wrapped in shawls, by the open window. She ate the food that I brought her, and we talked, yes, and laughed, sitting through the evening hours together. She would put her white little hand on mine, and laugh at the difference, she would laugh at the yellow down growing on my face, and call me her only chicken. The hopes grew on, and even she, who never lied to herself for comfort's sake, was drawn on to make plans for future days.

'"When winter comes," she said, "you'll be home earlier. The days won't seem so drawn out then. I'll sleep all the day, and when you come in, you shall lift me out, and set me by the fire, and I'll knit while you read. I'll be strong enough to knit, maybe, when the winter comes."

'And I, so cautious, so sure, deep inside me, that our happiness was over, for a little space forgot that winter lay beyond the allotted time.

'One evening, we sat by the window, as the sun was sinking, and up the hill road came a girl walking. We watched her, and neither spoke a word. My heart stood still when I knew it was Nancy. She looked up then, and waved to me. I raised my hand, and she passed on. My mother said:

'"Who is that?"

'"A girl who works in the village," I said.

'"How did she come to knowing you?" said my mother.

'"I met her once on the quarry road," I said, "and she asked me a question, about an animal she'd seen, what it was. It was a weasel, and so I told her."

'My mother questioned me no more. After a while, she said:

'"Carry me back, Joe. Put me into bed again. I feel cold."

'"The sun's gone down," I said. "You mustn't stay up after sun-down."

'But I knew that my voice had betrayed me.

'After that, my mother weakened; and our misery was the blacker because of the hope that we'd opened our eyes to see. All through the June evenings, when I came home from my work, I stayed beside her bed. Yes, and sometimes the night through. But now I did not forget Nancy. I would sit watching my mother asleep, and on a sudden, I'd feel Nancy's lips touching my neck; and I'd let my thoughts loose; I'd chase her down the forest track, till I caught and held her. I'd feel her body warm against mine and her hands clutching my shirt collar, cold against my throat and breast. The little bedroom – I'd want to heave the roof off it with my shoulders. I'd pant for the open air, the hot sunshine stinging my back, escape from that stifling agony of imprisonment and vigil. And the shame that followed after was cruellest of all to bear.

'The summer days went by, and still my mother grew weaker. Now she would turn away from the food that I brought her. Now her eyes would turn on me with fear in their depths, the look that I've seen in the eyes of an animal in the slaughter-house, in the midst of the shambles and the smell of blood. That look made me lie to her, bid her hope; but we'd told each other the truth too long. It was too late now for one of us to cheat the other with lies that we'd always scorned. And I prayed to God to take away the torture from her poor body, and set it upon mine, who dared to stand before her in my strength, and lust after a woman while I stroked the hand that death would soon stiffen, and the earth rot away. So there were two tortured bodies in that small room.

'One evening in July, there came a tap at the front door. My mother was asleep. I crept away softly. Big and clumsy though I was, I'd learnt to move without raising a creak from one board of that rickety floor. On the doorstep was Nancy. She came straight in, shut the door behind her, and clung to me. At last she looked up.

'"Is she dying?" she said.

'"Yes," I said

'"Poor love," she said, "poor love." She drew my head down to her, and wound my arms about her. She kissed my breast and stroked my throat with twining fingers. She pressed against me, till I went mad, and picking her up, carried her to the room where I slept, under my mother's, for there I could best hear her knock the floor in the night-time. And there like a wild beast I made her mine.

'There came two knocks on the floor. We started. Then again two knocks; my mother's summons. I staggered out of the room and up the stairway, clinging to the rails. The bedroom was in darkness.

'"Joe, Joe," came my mother's voice, "where are you?"

'"Here," I said, "don't be afraid, little one. I'm here."

'"There's some one with you," said my mother. "Who was it that came?"

'"Only a girl from the Inn, mother," I said. "They sent you some flowers." I ran from the room, and down the stairway. On the passage floor were the roses that I'd seen in Nancy's hands; and the front door was open. I carried the roses up the stairs, and laid them on the bed.

'"Light the lamp," said my mother.

'I lit the lamp; she took up the roses.

'"Beautiful they are," she said, holding them in her arms, and smelling them one by one. Then she thrust them away.

'"Take them," she said, "the scent's too strong – for the dying. Take them away."

'And I turned sick with fear, as though I'd stopped her breath with my hand over her mouth.

'After that night, she hardly spoke, but lay still. I never left the house. The sunlight blazed outside, and the nights brought scents to our window. A week later, when I sat at dawn with one arm beneath her head, she opened her eyes, and said with a look of terror that will be stamped and burnt for ever on my brain:

'"I'm going. Oh, save me. Quick, quick."

'When the doctor had come from the village, she was dead, and now, in death, she was smiling. All that came said, "How peaceful she looks!" That night, I crept up the stairs to look at her. But she was not peaceful. No, her lips were drawn back and the teeth gleamed. That was not peace. It was fear. Or was it wrath? Next morning I went again with a neighbour into the room; and then her face was calm, in bitter coldness.

'A week later, I was lying in the old quarry, with the sun blazing down on me; and Nancy came.

'"Joe," she said, "Joe, why are you grovelling here? Why don't you stand up and go to your work, like a man?"

'"Work?" I said. "'Tisn't that, Nancy. I'll go to work this day. But it's the house. I don't know why; but I can't get fresh air into it. I can't drive out the smell of the coffin wood, and the flowers they brought."

'She took me by the shoulders.

'"Are you a coward?" she said.

'"No," I said.

'"Look at me, then."

'I looked, and bent towards her. She held me away.

'"If I thought you were a coward," she said slowly, "I'd spit in your face. You think I'm yours now, maybe. But the truth is, you're mine; and if I found you out to be a coward, I'd flick you off me, big as you are, like a burr from my sleeve."

'"And what if I'm not a coward?" I said.

'"If you're not a coward," she said, "you'll know what next to do."

'I lifted her in my arms, and carried her down the track to my house in the wood.

'And now it was she who came along the track to meet me in the autumn evenings, she who waited for me at the fireside when the days grew shorter. Never a soul came near us; the men, my work-mates, and the folk of the village, grew small and far away to me as though I saw them from the hill-top; unreal, as though I saw them in a dream. Nancy, her nearness, her warmth, the dread that she'd leave me, these were my world and the living images that peopled it.

'My mother's room I had locked up; and now I never climbed the stairs to it by night or by day. But often at night I would wake and start from my bed, thinking that I heard the double knock of my mother's stick on the floor. Often in the day I would get up from my chair, and go into the passage to listen, thinking that I heard her voice, calling "Joe, Joe!" sharply, as she had used. Nancy would watch me, and when I came back to her, her lips would smile wryly.

'One day she said to me:

'"Joe, fetch me the thimble that your mother used."

'"Where shall I find it?" I said.

'"Where did she keep her sewing?" said she.

'I went up the stairs, and found it where she had left it, in the work-basket by her bed-side.

'The next day, Nancy said:

'"Joe, I want new stockings. Give me money to buy them."

'"You mustn't go back to the village, Nancy," I said. "You mustn't leave here. Tell me what you want, and I'll bring it to you."

'"No, no," she said. "You can't buy what I want. Go, then, and look if there are any here."

'I gave in, for fear that she would leave me. I went to that room, and brought from my mother's chest the stockings that she had knitted and laid by.

'Each day she would lack some new thing, and each day I would go to that room and bring it away, treading softly, like a thief. At last she said:

'"Joe, I'm tired of this room. To-night I shall sleep in the room above. Come or not, as you please."

'I followed her; and all night I lay awake beside her. In the morning she said to me:

'"Did you sleep well, my friend?"

'I made no answer.

'"Come," she said. "Tell me. Haven't I the right to know? Your face is as white as my apron. Is it the cold you're feeling? Tell me. What's a woman like me for, if it's not to keep her lover's blood warm?"

'"Nancy," I said, "for God's sake don't torture me more. I love you. I can't live without you. Come with me, away from this house. In the name of my dead mother, marry me and let's make an end of this."

'And I went and knelt to her where she sat. But she stood up and laughed aloud.

'"Marry you!" she said. "Not I! No, I'll not have you for husband. Marry you, to save you from your mother's curse! Marry you, so that when you kiss me, you needn't look back over your shoulders, lest you see her standing there, pointing at you! Did I show fear, when I came to you and comforted you when she lay dying? Your mother hates the woman who comforted her son? Then good-bye to you both. I'll not have a coward for husband or lover. Stay here, and drown your fears in drink, or throw yourself down the shaft for want of me. Once a coward, always a coward. Afraid of the dead, afraid of love, afraid to live alone."'

He ceased suddenly, his face twisted and his forehead damp with sweat. At last he turned his blue eyes slowly on me, and said:

'So now, my friend, you know how a coward was left alone with his bad conscience. Many a mile I've tramped with none but him for company . . . But what does all this matter to you? All you town cubs have to do is keep your job, find a good wife, and read the daily paper night and morning, and you'll never see more of the devil than a tip of his tail. But start young. I saw to-night by your face that he'd flicked you.'

And my friend the foreman roadmender turned again to his cubes of stone.

X

The Conquered

DOROTHY EDWARDS

Last summer, just before my proper holiday, I went to stay with an aunt who lives on the borders of Wales, where there are so many orchards. I must say I went there simply as a duty, because I used to stay a lot with her when I was a boy, and she was, in those days, very good to me. However, I took plenty of books down so that it should not be waste of time.

Of course, when I got there it was really not so bad. They made a great fuss of me. My aunt was as tolerant as she used to be in the old days, leaving me to do exactly as I liked. My cousin Jessica, who is just my age, had hardly changed at all, though they both looked different with their hair up; but my younger cousin Ruth, who used to be very lively and something of a tomboy, had altered quite a lot. She had become very quiet; at least, on the day I arrived she was lively enough, and talked about the fun we used to have there, but afterwards she became more quiet every day, or perhaps it was that I noticed it more. She remembered far more about what we used to do than I did; but I suppose that is only natural since she had been there all the time in between, and I do not suppose anything very exciting had happened to her, whereas I have been nearly everywhere.

But what I wanted to say is, that not far from my aunt's house, on the top of a little slope, on which there was an apple orchard, was a house with French windows and a large green lawn in front, and in this lived a very charming Welsh lady whom my cousins knew. Her grandfather had the house built, and it was his own design. It is said that he had been quite a friend of the Prince Consort, who once, I believe, actually stayed there for a night.

I knew the house very well, but I had never met any of the family, because they had not always occupied it, and, in any case, they would have been away at the times that I went to my aunt for holidays. Now only this one grand-daughter was left of the family; her father and mother were dead, and she had just come back to live there. I found out all this at breakfast the morning after I came, when Jessica said, 'Ruthie, we must take Frederick to see Gwyneth.'

'Oh yes,' said Ruthie. 'Let's go to-day.'

'And who is Gwyneth?'

Jessica laughed. 'You will be most impressed. Won't he, mother?'

'Yes,' said my aunt, categorically.

However, we did not call on her that afternoon, because it poured with rain all day, and it did not seem worth while, though Ruthie appeared in her macintosh and goloshes ready to go, and Jessica and I had some difficulty in dissuading her.

I did not think it was necessary to do any reading the first day, so I just sat and talked to the girls, and after tea Jessica and I even played duets on the piano, which had not been tuned lately, while Ruthie turned over the pages.

The next morning, though the grass was wet and every movement of the trees sent down a shower of rain, the sun began to shine brightly through the clouds. I should certainly have been taken to see their wonderful friend in the afternoon, only she herself called in the morning. I was sitting at one end of the dining-room, reading Tourguéniev with a dictionary and about three grammars, and I dare say I looked very busy. I do not know where my aunt was when she came, and the girls were upstairs. I heard a most beautiful voice, that was very high-pitched though, not low, say:

'All right, I will wait for them in here,' and she came into the room. Of course I had expected her to be nice, because my cousins liked her so much, but still they do not meet many people down there, and I thought they would be impressed with the sort of person I would be quite used to. But she really was charming.

She was not very young – older, I should say, than Jessica. She was very tall, and she had very fair hair. But the chief thing about her was her finely carved features, which gave to her face the coolness of stone and a certain appearance of immobility, though she laughed very often and talked a lot. When she laughed she raised her chin a little, and looked down her nose in a bantering way. And she had a really perfect nose. If I had been a sculptor I should have put it on every one of my statues. When she saw me she laughed and said, 'Ah! I am disturbing you,' and she sat down, smiling to herself.

I did not have time to say anything to her before my cousins came in. She kissed Jessica and Ruthie, and kept Ruthie by her side.

'This is our cousin Frederick,' said Jessica.

'We have told you about him,' said Ruthie gravely.

Gwyneth laughed. 'Oh, I recognized him, but how could I interrupt so busy a person! Let me tell you what I have come for. Will you come to tea to-morrow and bring Mr Trenier?' She laughed at me again.

We thanked her, and then my aunt came in.

'How do you do, Gwyneth?' she said. 'Will you stay to lunch?'

'No, thank you so much, Mrs Haslett,' she answered. 'I only came to ask Jessica and Ruthie to tea to-morrow, and, of course, to see your wonderful nephew. You will come too, won't you?'

'Yes, thank you,' said my aunt. 'You and Frederick ought to find many things to talk about together.'

Gwyneth looked at me and laughed.

Ruthie went out to make some coffee, and afterwards Gwyneth sat in the window-seat drinking it and talking.

'What were you working at so busily when I came in?' she asked me.

'I was only trying to read Tourguéniev in the original,' I said.

'Do you like Tourguéniev very much?' she asked, laughing.

'Yes,' I said. 'Do you?'

'Oh, I have only read one, *Fumée*.'

She stayed for about an hour, laughing and talking all the time. I really found her very charming. She was like a personification, in a restrained manner, of Gaiety. Yes, really, very much like Milton's *L'Allegro*.

The moment she was gone Jessica said excitedly, 'Now, Frederick, weren't you impressed?'

And Ruthie looked at me anxiously until I answered, 'Yes, I really think I was.'

The next day we went there to tea. It was a beautiful warm day, and we took the short cut across the fields and down a road now overgrown with grass to the bottom of the little slope on which her house was built. There is an old Roman road not far from here, and I am not quite sure whether that road is not part of it. We did not go into the house, but were taken at once to the orchard at the back, where she was sitting near a table, and we all sat down with her. The orchard was not very big, and, of course, the trees were no longer in flower, but the fruit on them was just beginning to grow and look like tiny apples and pears. At the other end some white chickens strutted about in the sunlight. We had tea outside.

She talked a lot, but I cannot remember now what she said; when she spoke to me it was nearly always to tell me about her grandfather, and the interesting people who used to come to visit him.

When it began to get cool we went into the house across the flat green lawn and through the French window. We went to a charming room; on the wall above the piano were some Japanese prints on silk, which were really beautiful. Outside it was just beginning to get dark.

She sang to us in a very nice high soprano voice, and she chose always gay, light songs which suited her excellently. She sang that song of Schumann, *Der Nussbaum*; but then it is possible to sing that lightly and happily, though it is more often sung with a trace of sadness in it. Jessica played for her. She is a rather good accompanist. I never could accompany singers. But I played afterwards; I played some Schumann too.

'Has Ruthie told you I am teaching her to sing?' said Gwyneth. 'I don't know much about it, and her voice is not like mine, but I remember more or less what my master taught me.'

'No,' I said, looking at Ruthie. 'Sing for us now and let me hear.'

'No,' said Ruthie, and blushed a little. She never used to be shy.

Gwyneth pulled Ruthie towards her. 'Now do sing. The fact is you are ashamed of your teacher.'

'No,' said Ruthie; 'only you know I can't sing your songs.'

Gwyneth laughed. 'You would hardly believe what a melancholy little creature she is. She won't sing anything that is not tearful.'

'But surely,' I said, 'in the whole of Schubert and Schumann you can find something sad enough for you?'

'No,' said Ruthie, looking at the carpet, 'I don't know any

Schumann, and Schubert is never sad even in the sad songs. Really I can't sing what Gwyneth sings.'

'Then you won't?' I said, feeling rather annoyed with her.

'No,' she said, flushing, and she looked out of the window.

Ruthie and Jessica are quite different. Jessica is, of course, like her mother, but Ruthie is like her father, whom I never knew very well.

Next morning, immediately after breakfast, I went for a walk by myself, and though I went by a very roundabout way, I soon found myself near Gwyneth's house, and perhaps that was not very surprising. I came out by a large bush of traveller's-nightshade. I believe that is its name. At least it is called old man's beard too, but that does not describe it when it is in flower at all. You know that it has tiny white waxen flowers, of which the buds look quite different from the open flower, so that it looks as though there are two different kinds of flowers on one stem. But what I wanted to say was, I came out by this bush, and there, below me, was the grass-covered road, with new cart-wheel ruts in it, which made two brown lines along the green where the earth showed. Naturally I walked down it, and stood by the fence of the orchard below her house. I looked up between the trees, and there she was coming down towards me.

'Good-morning, Mr Trenier,' she said, laughing. 'Why are you deserting Tourguéniev?'

'It is such a lovely morning,' I said, opening the gate for her; 'and if I had known I should meet you, I should have felt even less hesitation.'

She laughed, and we walked slowly across the grass, which was still wet with dew. It was a perfectly lovely day, with a soft pale blue sky and little white clouds in it, and the grass was wet enough to be bright green.

'Oh, look!' she said suddenly, and pointed to two enormous mushrooms, like dinner-plates, growing at our feet.

'Do you want them?' I asked, stooping to pick them.

'Oh yes,' she said; 'when they are as big as that they make excellent sauces. Fancy such monsters growing in a night! They were not here yesterday.'

'And last week I had not met you,' I said, smiling.

She laughed, and took the mushrooms from me.

'Now we must take them to the cook,' she said, 'and then you shall come for a little walk with me.'

As we crossed the lawn to the house she was carrying the pink-lined mushrooms by their little stalks.

'They look like the sunshades of Victorian ladies,' I said.

She laughed, and said, 'Did you know that Jenny Lind came here once?'

Afterwards we walked along the real Roman road, now only a pathway with grass growing up between the stones, and tall trees overshadowing it. On the right is a hill where the ancient Britons made a great stand against the Romans, and were defeated.

'Did you know this was a Roman road?' she asked. 'Just think of the charming Romans who must have walked here! And I expect they developed a taste for apples. Does it shock you to know that I like the Romans better than the Greeks?'

I said 'No,' but now, when I think of it, I believe I *was* a little shocked, although, when I think of the Romans as the Silver Age, I see that silver was more appropriate to her than gold.

She was really very beautiful and it was a great pleasure to be with her, because she walked in such a lovely way. She moved quickly, but she somehow preserved that same immobility which, though she laughed and smiled so often, made her face cool like stone, and calm.

After this we went for many walks and picnics. Sometimes the girls came too, but sometimes we went together. We climbed the old battle hill, and she stood at the top looking all around at the orchards on the plain below.

I had meant to stay only a week, but I decided to stay a little longer, or, rather, I stayed on without thinking about it at all. I had not told my aunt and the girls that I was going at the end of the week, so it did not make any difference, and I knew they would expect me to stay longer. The only difference it made was to my holiday, and, after all, I was going for the holiday to enjoy myself, and I could not have been happier than I was there.

I remember how one night I went out by myself down in the direction of her house, where my steps always seemed to take me. When I reached the traveller's-nightshade it was growing dark. For a moment I looked towards her house and a flood of joy came into my soul, and I began to think how strange it was that, although I have met so many interesting people, I should come there simply by chance and meet her. I walked towards the entrance of a little wood, and, full of a profound joy and happiness, I walked in between the trees. I stayed there for a long time imagining her coming gaily into the wood where the moonlight shone through the branches. And I remember thinking suddenly how we have grown used to believing night to be a sad and melancholy time, not romantic and exciting as it used to be. I kept longing for some miracle to bring her there to me, but she did not come, and I had to go home.

Then, one evening, we all went to her house for music and conversation. On the way there Ruthie came round to my side and said, 'Frederick, I have brought with me a song that I can sing, and I will sing this time if you want me to.'

'Yes, I certainly want you to,' I said, walking on with her. 'I want to see how she teaches.'

'Yes,' said Ruthie. 'You do see that I could not sing her songs, don't you?'

In the old days Ruthie and I used to get on very well, better than I got on with Jessica, who was inclined to keep us in order then, and I must say it was very difficult for her to do so.

When we got there, right at the beginning of the evening Gwyneth sang a little Welsh song. And I felt suddenly disappointed. I always thought that the Welsh were melancholy in their music, but if she sang it sadly at all, it was with the gossipy sadness of the tea after a funeral. However, afterwards we talked, and I forgot the momentary impression.

During the evening Ruthie sang. She sang Brahms' *An die Nachtigall,* which was really very foolish of her, because I am sure it is not an easy thing to sing, with its melting softness and its sudden cries of ecstasy and despair. Her voice was very unsteady, of a deeper tone than Gwyneth's, and sometimes it became quite hoarse from nervousness.

Gwyneth drew her down to the sofa beside her. She laughed, 'I told you nothing was sad enough for her.'

Ruthie was quite pale from the ordeal of singing before us.

'It is rather difficult, isn't it?' I said.

'Yes,' said Ruthie, flushing.

'Have you ever heard a nightingale?' asked Gwyneth of me.

'No,' I said.

'Why, there is one in the wood across here; I have heard it myself,' said Jessica. 'On just such a night as this,' she added, laughing, and looking out of the window at the darkness coming to lie on the tops of the apple trees beyond the green lawn.

'Ah! you must hear a nightingale as well as read Tourguéniev, you know,' said Gwyneth.

I laughed.

But later on in the evening I was sitting near the piano looking over a pile of music by my side. Suddenly I came across Chopin's *Polnische Lieder.* It is not often that one finds them. I looked up in excitement and said, 'Oh, do you know the *Polens Grabgesang*? I implore you to sing it.'

She laughed a little at my excitement and said, 'Yes, I know it. But I can't sing it. It does not suit me at all. Mrs Haslett, your nephew actually wants me to sing a funeral march!'

'Oh, please do sing it!' I said. 'I have only heard it once before in my life. Nobody ever sings it. I have been longing to hear it again.'

'It does not belong to me, you know,' she said. 'I found it here; it must have belonged to my father.' She smiled at me over the edge of some music she was putting on the piano. 'No, I can't sing it. That is really decisive.'

I was so much excited about the song, because I shall never forget the occasion on which I first heard it. I have a great friend, a very wonderful man, a perfect genius, in fact, and a very strong personality, and we have evenings at his house, and we talk about nearly everything, and have music too, some times. Often, when I used to go, there was a woman there, who never spoke much but always sat near my friend. She was not particularly beautiful and had a rather unhappy face, but one evening my friend turned to her suddenly and put his hand on her shoulder and said, 'Sing for us.'

She obeyed without a word. Everybody obeys him at once. And she sang this song. I shall never forget all the sorrow and pity for the sorrows of Poland that she put into it. And the song, too, is wonderful. I do not think I have ever heard in my life anything so terribly moving as the part, 'O Polen, mein Polen,' which is repeated several times. Everyone in the room was stirred, and, after she had sung it, we talked about nothing but politics and the Revolution for the whole of the evening. I do not think she was Polish either. After a few more times she did not come to the evenings any more, and I have never had the opportunity of asking him about her. And although, as I said, she was not beautiful, when I looked at Gwyneth again it seemed to me that some of her beauty had gone, and I thought to myself quite angrily, 'No, of course she could not sing that song. She would have been on the side of the conquerors!'

And I felt like this all the evening until we began to walk home. Before we had gone far Jessica said, 'Wouldn't you like to stay and listen for the nightingale, Frederick? We can find our way home without you.'

'Yes,' I said. 'Where can I hear her?'

'The best place,' said Jessica, 'is to sit on the fallen tree – that is where I heard it. Go into the wood by the wild-rose bush with pink roses on it. Do you know it?'

'Yes.'

'Don't be very late,' said my aunt.

'No,' I answered, and left them.

I went into the little wood and sat down on the fallen tree looking up and waiting, but there was no sound. I felt that there was nothing I wanted so much as to hear her sad notes. I remember thinking how Nietzsche said that Brahms' melancholy was the melancholy of impotence, not of power, and I remember feeling that there was much truth in it when I thought of his *Nachtigall* and then of Keats. And I sat and waited for the song that came to

> ". . . the sad heart of Ruth, when, sick for home,
> She stood in tears amid the alien corn."

Suddenly I heard a sound, and, looking round, I saw Gwyneth coming through the trees. She caught sight of me and laughed.

'You are here too,' she said. 'I came to hear Jessica's nightingale.'

'So did I,' I said; 'but I do not think she will sing to-night.'

'It is a beautiful night,' she said. 'Anybody should want to sing on such a lovely night.'

I took her back to her gate, and I said good-night and

closed the gate behind her. But, all the same, I shall remember always how beautiful she looked standing under the apple trees by the gate in the moonlight, her smile resting like the reflection of light on her carved face. Then, however, I walked home, feeling angry and annoyed with her; but of course that was foolish. Because it seems to me now that the world is made up of gay people and sad people, and however charming and beautiful the gay people are, their souls can never really meet the souls of those who are born for suffering and melancholy, simply because they are made in a different mould. Of course I see that this is a sort of dualism, but still it seems to me to be the truth, and I believe my friend, of whom I spoke, is a dualist, too, in some things.

I did not stay more than a day or two after this, though my aunt and the girls begged me to do so. I did not see Gwyneth again, only something took place which was a little ridiculous in the circumstances.

The evening before I went Ruthie came and said, half in an anxious whisper, 'Frederick, will you do something very important for me?'

'Yes, if I can,' I said. 'What is it?'

'Well, it is Gwyneth's birthday to-morrow, and she is so rich it is hard to think of something to give her.'

'Yes,' I said, without much interest.

'But do you know what I thought of? I have bought an almond tree – the man has just left it out in the shed – and I am going to plant it at the edge of the lawn so that she will see it to-morrow morning. So it will have to be planted in the middle of the night, and I wondered if you would come and help me.'

'But is it the right time of the year to plant an almond tree – in August?'

'I don't know,' said Ruthie; 'but surely the man in the nursery would have said if it were not. You can sleep in the train, you know. You used always to do things with me.'

'All right, I will,' I said, 'only we need not go in the middle of the night – early in the morning will do, before it is quite light.'

'Oh, thank you so much,' said Ruthie, trembling with gratitude and excitement. 'But don't tell anyone, will you – not even Jessica.'

'No,' I said.

Exceedingly early in the morning, long before it was light, Ruthie came into my room in her dressing-gown to wake me, looking exactly as she used to do. We went quietly downstairs and through the wet grass to Gwyneth's house, Ruthie carrying the spade and I the tree. It was still rather dark when we reached there, but Ruthie had planned the exact place before.

We hurried with the work. I did the digging, and Ruthie stood with the tree in her hand looking up at the house. We hardly spoke.

Ruthie whispered, 'We must be quiet. That is her window. She will be able to see it as soon as she looks out. She is asleep now.'

'Look here,' I said, 'don't tell her that I planted it, because it may not grow. I can't see very well.'

'Oh, but she must never know that either of us did it.'

'But are you going to give her a present and never let her know who it is from?'

'Yes,' said Ruthie.

'I think that is rather silly,' I said.

Ruthie turned away.

We put the tree in. I have never heard whether it grew or not. Just as the sun was rising we walked back, and that morning I went away.

XI

The Heads of Coed Uchaf

NANSI POWELL PRICE

Lisa sat in her grandmother's garden overlooking the river, watching the men at work in the cornfields. Since dawn they had been crossing from Coed Uchaf, the Welsh village on the opposite bank, to help in the Commortha, an age old custom that was still kept up in that remote part of the Border. Not even the constant feuds that arose between the two villages, facing each other, had interfered with its performance. Feuds in a mild way there would always be: the river divided not merely two counties, but two countries and two races which had bickered and fought for generations.

Lisa's big grey eyes widened at the possibilities of this reunion of Welsh and English. A wicked flirt she was, never happy unless two men were making themselves silly over her impish face. Excitement and fun were the very breath of life to her, and to secure them she would strain every nerve, use every wile.

So she planned a wonderful joke. And into it she put an Englishman and a Welshman, Dai Lloyd and Will Merton, but not rich George Smith whom she had promised to marry. No one knew about that, yet. She had made George promise to keep it quiet for a bit – long enough for her to have her fling, her very last bit of fun.

The striking of the clock from the church across the river cut into her thoughts. For a moment she considered the heavy masonry of the old building. The church was the one thing for which she had any respect. It roused feelings in her which she half resented, half feared: its mysterious silence terrified her. On its edge, peering down on the green country below, little stoned demons and winged animals were perched, just as if they had been pushed there by the cold marble saints inside. Then there were the bells: the great tenor bell that rang at funerals, tolling the ages, telling the sex of the departed – once for a child, twice for a woman, three times for a man . . . Some day it would ring for her! She caught herself up quickly and thought of other things, less personal, that the tower kept.

Right up in the belfry was a heap of skulls, the relic of a long forgotten battle. People said they shouldn't be there, should be given decent burial. As she thought of them a great idea came into her head. Supposing –

'Lisa!'

Dai Lloyd's gay voice behind her made her start, guiltily.

'Oh,' said the little schemer, looking up at him with an expression of fear that was very pretty and speaking in her up and down Border way, 'You munna frighten me so, Dai!' She liked his long limbs and the merry, deep set eyes, that so cleverly hid the thoughts that went on behind them. 'I was thinking o' them heads,' she nodded her own at the tower, and the black plaits she wore coiled gipsy fashion round her ears, shone with a hundred different lights, 'Yo'll never believe the awful thing Will Merton's vowin' to do. He's set on goin' up church tower, to-morrow midnight, an' to bring one o' them down in his hand!'

She spoke with a rush, just as if the devil was putting it into her mind.

'Merton?' said Dai, sharply, with a quick glance at his rival's burly form in the cornfield, 'What's he doing it for?'

'Maybe someone's dared him,' suggested Lisa, spurring

herself on to fresh efforts. 'But that's how he is, full o' pluck.' She looked at Dai sideways to see how he was taking it. 'Taffy heads he called them,' she added.

'Oh, did he?' said Dai, suddenly flushing. 'He'd better say that to me; I'll "taffy" him!' Suspicion added to his wrath. 'It's only show off to make you care, Lisa,' he said.

Lisa sighed, not sure how to take him.

'I do love bravery,' she told him, softly, 'an' a man who'd dare all that is worth sumat. Onst or twice I've bin thinkin' of settling down, Dai . . .'

'You mean you'd marry him for that!' almost shouted Dai, 'for a hair brain thing like that?'

'Shure-ley it's natural!' wailed Lisa, wiping her eyes with a wisp of a handkerchief. 'My father was English, Dai . . . An' Will's brave – '

'He'll want his bravery to-morrow night,' mentioned Dai under his breath, but not so low that Lisa's little bubble of a heart did not jump with pride. 'He'll not get that head so easily! Supposing there was to be a fight up there,' he went on, looking hard at her, 'you'd take the one who wins. You can't marry both of us, Lisa.'

'No,' agreed Lisa, lifting pansy eyes to his, and thinking how hard it was that she could not. 'I 'ool marry the one I like best,' she promised. And to do her justice she had quite forgotten about George Smith. 'I'm afeard of Will Merton, that I am,' she whispered, her cheek against Dai's.

It was only when Dai was well out of sight and once more at work in the corn that she allowed herself to laugh over the success of her plotting. Then, looking round to see that she was not watched, she went noiselessly over the stepping stones in the river to the other bank.

Inside the church tower the sun shone cheerfully through the loop hole slits in the walls where men had once looked and defended themselves against an approaching foe. As she swung herself up the ladder that led from the belfry to the outside of the tower, she saw the skulls lying in their corner, and flung them an unconcerned glance. In the daylight they seemed no more terrifying than the shrunken poppy heads in her grandmother's garden.

Once outside, a wild, irrepressible feeling took hold of her. She felt so free. By leaning over the edge, she could make out the figures at work in the field, Dai, and further on, Will Merton, whose red head shone fiercely in the sun. It would be easy to manage Will, she thought. All she had to do was to make him jealous of Dai. By his side was George Smith – solid, square shouldered George, who thought there was nobody like her!

She turned round to find herself a hiding place to watch the meeting of the two rivals, and found that by lying down flat on the stone flags she could see right down into the belfry.

Later in the day, Will came round to see her. He was a serious faced young man with prickly views which he called independence, and a temper to match his hair.

'I dunno know what's come over Dai,' said Lisa, when she had him to herself in the garden, 'he'm goin' about sayin' he 'ool make me marry him and he'm set on doin' an awful thing.' Her voice dropped to an awed whisper: 'Vowin' to go up church tower, midnight, to-morrow, an' to bring down one o' them heads – jest to show how much he cares!'

The wicked hussy laid her head on his shoulder and shivered at her trickery, as well she might.

'Yo'll never bring yoursel' to take one o' them heads,' remarked Will, sourly, his heavy jaw well thrust out.

The small Herodias waved helpless hands. She was almost ready to cry at his stony reception of her efforts. 'He'm set on it, Will,' she told him; 'that's how the Welsh are . . . If there's danger – '

'They run away,' clipped in Will.

'They'm brave,' insisted Lisa, her voice thrilling. 'Sometimes I feel like settlin' down, Will, an' incourse it 'ool be natural for me to find a husband from over the river – my mother bein' Welsh.'

'Dai wunna be brave when I've done with un,' boasted Will suddenly. 'An' then yo'll marry me, Lisa.'

'Oh, shure-ley it's a terrible lot for a girl to promise,' protested Lisa, now enjoying herself thoroughly in the shelter of his arms. 'But I'm afeart of Dai, that I am.'

She was in her most contrary mood when George Smith called. But that only made her more attractive in his adoring eyes.

'Why won't you marry me now?' he asked. 'You've only to buy a dress. You'll wear white for me, Lisa? I've always pictured you coming to me in white.'

'Shure-ley I 'ool,' promised the little wretch, putting both her arms round his neck. 'But I do want it kep' a secret for a bit, George. Real love shouldna be talked about, I do think. An' yo' know they'd talk a dell. Couldna we be married quiet like?'

And she looked so pretty with her pink cheeks and shining hair that it would have taken a cleverer man than George Smith to see through her argument.

A thick mist had risen from the river and clung round the meadows like a thick blanket when Lisa climbed the tower the next night. She shivered as she went, for the moon peeped palely through the window slits and lit up the blackened skulls, making them look like anything but poppy heads. When a bird flew, frightened, out of the ivy, she nearly lost her hold of the ladder. Her scared cry hung in the stillness. At her feet the Welsh village lay quiet, each window with its light. A queer shine they gave through the mist. She turned from them uncomfortably. They made her feel an outcast. For the first time doubts began to rise in her mind. Supposing, after all her planning, the two men did not turn up. Supposing Will had thought better of it? Then there was Dai. One never knew what to expect of a man with laughing eyes!

A step on the stairs made her revive. Craning her head forward, she saw Will, standing fearfully over the skulls. Will, alone! Lisa could have cried. Without Dai there could be no fight. And she had counted so much on that. There would be no fun, no thrill, no triumph. Then suddenly a great idea came to her. She would not be done. As Will's hand closed over a skull, her voice came ghostlike through the night air: 'That's my head,' it moaned.

She had some sort of a laugh then, for Will could hardly wait to throw his trophy on the heap before his hurrying feet took him hurtling down the stairs, as if the devil was at his heels.

Before she had stopped her laughing, someone else entered the belfry. It was easy to make out Dai's tall figure.

'That's *my* head,' groaned Lisa, as he picked up a skull.

For a moment it looked as if Dai was going to follow his rival's example. He half turned to go. Then something made him change his mind. Very carefully he began selecting another.

'That's my poor head!' piped the little witch in the ivy, on an agonized note.

'Oh, is it?' enquired the figure below, pleasantly. 'Well, do you mind my borrowing it for a moment to show to a friend?'

Almost before the words were out of his mouth he was scaling the ladder.

'So it's you!' he said, when he reached her. And no name he might have called her could have been worse than that short word. It bit into her harder than the grip of his hand on her wrist. 'You've been a bit too clever this time, Lisa! When Will Merton ran past me just now, shouting "Spirits", I guessed it was one of your wild cat tricks. It came to me that there was only one spirit wicked enough to make fun of the dead. And that's yours!'

He spoke with a rush, just as if he could keep it in no longer. And Lisa sat quite still. She, whom no sermon had ever touched, felt each word as if it branded her.

'You, that talked so nicely of settling down,' continued Dai, mercilessly. 'There's only one place for the likes of you to settle, up here with the goblins and the weathercock!'

And with that he took her, limp and lifeless as she was with his scorn, to the flagstaff. One hand he put round the pole for support, and in the other he placed the skull she had dared him to fetch.

And there he left her.

She heard his step on the ladder and saw the light of his torch on the wall. Then the key turned in the lock, and she knew she was there for the night.

Perhaps she might have been, for she deserved it and more; only the two men she had fooled had no wish that she should die of fright, so after an hour they let her out.

She ran past them with never a word, her hair floating like a black cloud behind her.

And the next thing they heard was that she had married George Smith. It may be that he tamed her in America, where she made him take her, for he was a decent man and worthy of a better fate. Or it may be that out there on the tower, with the wild things of the night to teach her kindness, and the spirit of the Commortha to speak to her of friendship, she had learnt her lesson.

XII

Over the Hills and Far Away

MARY WEBB

Margaret Mahuntleth, in the corner of the big settle, basked in the hearth-glow like one newly come to heaven. Warm light reddened her knitted shawl, her white apron, and her face, worn and frail. It was as if the mortal part of it had been beaten thin by the rains and snows of long roads, baked, like fine enamel, by many suns, so that it had a concave look – as though hollowed out of mother o' pearl. Some faces gather wrinkles with the years, like seamed rocks on mountains, others only become, like stones in a brook, smoother, though frailer, in the conflicting currents. Margaret's was one of these. And though she was a bit of a has-been, yet her face, as it shone from the dark settle-back, seemed young and almost angelic in its irrefragable happiness. For Marg'ret had never dreamed (no, not for an instant!) as she fought her way to Thresholds Farm through weather that made her whole being seem a hollow shell, that she would be invited into the kitchen. Usually she did her work in the barn. For Marg'ret was a chair-mender.

She travelled on her small birdlike feet, all over the county, carrying her long bundle of rushes. With these she mended chairs at farms and cottages and even in the kitchens of rectories and in parish rooms and at the backs of churches where the people from the almshouses sat. She mended chairs mostly for other people to draw up to glowing fires and well-spread tables. She made them very flawless for weddings. For funerals she made them strong, because the people who attend funerals are generally older than those who attend weddings, and the weight of years is on them, and they have gathered to themselves, like the caddis worm, a mass of extraneous substance.

For dances Margaret also made them strong, knowing that in the intervals young women of some twelve stone would subside upon the knees of stalwarts rising fifteen stone.

Marg'ret knew all about it. She had been to some of the dances years ago, but people forgot to ask her to dance. Her faint tints, her soft, sad, downcast eye, her sober dress, all combined with her personality to make her fade into any background. She was always conscious, too, of the disgrace of being only a chair-mender; of not being the gardener's daughter at the Hall, or Rectory-Lucy. So people forgot she was there and she even forgot she was there herself.

She worked hard. She could make butter-baskets and poultry-baskets through which not the most centrifugal half-dozen fowls could do more than insinuate anxious heads. She could make children's ornamental basket-chairs, and she could do the close wicker-work of rocking-chairs for nursing-mothers. Winter and summer she tramped from place to place, over frozen roads and dusty roads and all the other kinds of roads, calling at farms with her timid knock and her faint cry, plaintive and musical, soon lost on the wind – 'Chairs to mend!'.

Then she would take the chair or basket or mat into the orchard or the barn, and sit at her work through the green day or the short grey day, plaiting with her pale, hollow hands. Within doors she never thought of going. She would have been the first to deprecate sheeding rushes all o'er. The warm kitchen was a Paradise to which she, a Peri, did not pretend. Its furnishings she knew intimately, but she knew them as a church-cleaner might know the altar and its chalices, being, if such a thing were possible, excommunicated. Under the bowl of the sky, across the valleys she came, did her work featly as an elf, and was gone, as if the swift airs had blown her away with the curled may-petals of spring, the curved leaves of autumn.

If night drew on before she had done her work, she would sleep in the hayloft. Nobody inquired where she usually slept, any more than they concerned themselves about the squirrel that ran along the fence and was away, or the thistledown that floated along the blue sky.

So Marg'ret had never dreamed of being invited to the hearth-place. It was the most wonderful thing. Outside, the wan snowflakes battered themselves upon the panes like birds, dying. The night had come, black, inevitable, long. And to those who have no house the night is a wild beast. In every chimney a hollow wind spoke its uncontent. There were many chimneys at Thresholds Farm. It was a great place, and the master was a man well-thought-of, rich.

Marg'ret trembled to think she was here in the same room with him. He might even speak to her. He sat on the other side of the hearth while the servant-girl laid tea – the knife-and-fork tea of farms, with beef and bacon and potatoes. A tea to remember.

He sat leaning forward, his broad, knotted hands on his knees, staring into the fire. The girl slammed the teapot down in the table and said:

'Yer tea, master.'

Marg'ret got up. She supposed it was time now for her to creep to bed in the hospitable loft, after a kindly cup of tea in the back kitchen. It had been wonderful sitting here – just sitting quietly enjoying the rest and the dignity of the solid furniture and the bright fingers of the firelight touching here a willow-pattern plate and there a piece of copper. It was one of those marvellous half-hours of a life-time, which blossom on even to the grave, and maybe afterwards. She had never dreamed . . .

She softly crept toward the door, but as she went the master lifted his gloomy, chestnut-coloured eyes under their thatch of grizzled hair, and so transfixed her. She could not move with that brown fire upon her, engulfing her. So he always looked when he was deeply stirred. So he had looked down at his father's coffin long ago, at his mother's last year. So he had looked into the eyes of his favourite dog, dying in his arms. The look was the realization of the infinite within the finite, altering all values. Never once in all fifteen years during which she had been calling here had he seemed to look at Marg'ret at all.

In the almost ferocious intensity of the look she felt faint. Her face seemed like a fragile cup made to hold an unexpressed passion which was within his soul, which must find room for itself somewhere, as the great bore of water that rushes up a river must find room, some valley, some dimple where it may rest, where it may spread its strangled magnificence. She stood. Firelight filled her hollow palms; her apron, gathered in nervous fingers, so that it looked like a gleaner's ready to carry grain; the pale shell of her face.

The servant-girl, perturbed by some gathering emotion that had come upon the kitchen, remained with a hand on the tea-pot-handle, transfixed. Marg'ret trembled, saying no word. How shall a conch-shell make music unless one lends it a voice? She was of the many human beings that wait on the shores of life for the voice which so often never comes.

Suddenly the master of the house said loudly, with his eyes still hard upon her:

'Bide!'

It was as if the word burst a dam within him.

Her being received it.

'Bide the night over,' he added, in the same strange thunderous voice.

She took that also into her soul.

'And all the nights,' he finished, and a great calm fell upon him. It had taken all the years of his life till now for the flood to find its valley.

Then seeing that she stood as mute and still as ever, he said – 'Coom then, take bite and sup.'

And when she was seated, like a half-thawed winter dormouse at its first feast, he said to the servant-girl, who still remained holding the Britannia-metal teapot (which seemed to mock Marg'ret with its inordinate convexity) –

'Make a bed for the Missus!'

He was determined that no misunderstanding should vex his new-found peace, and when the girl had gone, breathing hard like an exhausted swimmer, he remained staring at Marg'ret in a kind of hunger for giving. And she, perfectly receptive, empty-handed as a Peri, let his flaming eyes dwell on her face, let his fire and his food hearten her, and so gave him her charity. And this was how Marg'ret Mahuntleth, the poor chair-mender, without will of her own or desert of her own, as far as she could see, came to be the mistress of the house and lawful wife of the master of Thresholds.

XIII

A Thing of Nought

HILDA VAUGHAN

To her neighbours she was known as Megan Lloyd. In my memory she lives as Saint Anne.

Years after I had lost her, I was wandering through the Louvre, and came upon the picture attributed to Leonardo. I stood before it, happy; and my eyes filled with tears. Megan Lloyd, when I knew her, was older than this wise and gracious mother of the Virgin. Her hair was white as lamb's wool; her face, like a stored apple, seamed with fine wrinkles. Yet there was her familiar smile, full of tenderness and understanding.

She is in my mind now, seated, like Leonardo's homely saint, in the open. Often I saw her moving about the farm-house kitchen, or sitting beside the whitewashed hearth, her fingers, as she stooped to warm them, cornelian red in the glow of a peat fire. Sometimes she had a grandchild in her lap, and another in the cradle that her foot was rocking with slow rhythm. But I remember her best as I saw her often during my last summer in Wales, out of doors, her faded lips parted a little to the hill wind.

She sat on an oaken chair upon the stretch of sward surrounding Cwmbach homestead, where hissing geese paddled to and fro, bobbing their heads on long necks. From the neighbouring buildings, white as mushrooms in the green landscape, came the cheerful noises of a farmyard and a house full of lusty children. Her eldest son, dark and dour, clothed in earth-brown corduroys, her busy shrill daughter-in-law, her tribe of swarthy grandchildren, to me were present only as a background to Saint Anne. They and their home were like the walled towns, the cavalcades of horse-men, the plumed trees, behind the central figure of the Madonna in some fifteenth-century altar piece. They had no connection with my tranquil saint. Their toil and clatter, their laughter, quarrelling and crying did not disturb us, who were the only two human beings of leisure in the countryside.

I was idle and self-tortured throughout that long hot summer. The harsh gales of spring were raging through my mind, unemployed and as yet empty of experience. She was profoundly calm; serene as an autumn evening after a tem-pestuous day, when the wind has fallen and the dead leaves lie still. It was with difficulty that she dragged herself abroad. Her fingers were twisted with rheumatism; she could no longer work. She could not even see to read her Bible. So, during these last months of her life, she sat, content to wait for death, with hands folded, while she watched the shadows of the hills on either side of Cwmbach as they stole across the narrow valley. The shade of the eastern hill dwindled behind the house as the sun reached its zenith; that of the western hill advanced when the sun began to sink. Little Cwmbach was so strait that only for an hour at noon was its whole width lit by sunshine. The mountains rose like walls on either side, shutting out the world. Down in the dingle lay the solitary farm and a stern chapel, square and grey, with the caretaker's cottage clinging to its side, as a white shell to a strong rock. An angry stream, hurling itself against boulders, foamed between these two dwelling places, and a thin ribbon of road wound its empty length up over the pass, where the hills converged.

Day after day I climbed across a waste of heather, moss

and bog, and, scrambling down the channel of a waterfall, flung myself at Saint Anne's feet. I was eighteen. The universe to me was the stage upon which my own tragedy was being acted. I talked by the hour about myself and my important emotions. She listened with inexhaustible patience. When I told her that no one had ever loved or suffered as I did, she smiled, not with derision, but sadly, as one who knew better.

If I looked up at her and found her smiling in that fashion, I fell silent. Then, after a while, she would begin to talk. It was thus I came to know her lover, her husband and her child. Her words were few, but they had magic to conjure up the dead. I knew so well their looks, their manner of speech, their gestures; it is hard to believe that never in my life did I see them, save through her eyes, or hear their voices except as an echo in her memory.

She was eighteen when she went to Pontnoyadd fair and fell in love with Penry Price, son of Rhosferig. He was tall, broad-shouldered, wind-tanned, blue-eyed. His laughter had reached her, gay and good-natured, so that she loved him before ever she set eyes upon his beauty. She edged her way forward through the press of admiring yokels by whom he was surrounded. He was in his shirt sleeves, hurling a wooden ball at an Aunt Sally. With a superb swing he brought his right arm back and flung the ball with such force that the coconut he aimed at flew out of its stand and broke to pieces. A chuckle of applause arose from the spectators. He turned round to smile at them, displaying teeth white and strong as those of a young savage. Picking up another ball, he threw it with all his might, smashing the target as before. One after another, he brought the coconuts down, until a heap of broken winnings lay scattered at his feet. The owner of the booth watched him with apprehensive admiration, and the murmuring of the onlookers rose at last to a shout. Megan could not take her eyes off him. His cap and coat lay on the ground. The sun on the bright hair gave him the splendour of a warrior in a helmet of gold. His shirt sleeves were rolled up, and the hairs on the back of his freckled arms glinted like a smear of honey. The sweat of exertion made his shirt cling close. She could see his muscles swell. To her, who seldom looked on any young man but her own weakling brother, this hero of the fair appeared a god. She held her breath with joy when he turned round and began to distribute his earnings to the children in the crowd. '*There now*!' she thought, proud as a mother. He was as good and generous as he was strong and handsome! 'Any gal 'ould have been bound to love him,' she was wont to tell me, 'he was such a *man*. There was summat about him of a child, too.'

Soon he caught sight of her brother, who had brought her to the fair, and greeted him with a slap on the shoulder.

'This is my sister as you are not knowing,' announced the boy, pushing Megan forward.

Looking down at her eager face, Penry flushed self-consciously. 'And shy, also, like myself,' she thought. 'Who ever 'ould have guessed it!' Should he treat her to a ride on the roundabout, he asked, stammering. She was too excited to answer, but nodded her head, whilst her colour came and went and her green eyes sparkled, like dew on spring's first grass.

She went with him, elated by the scene – the white tents pitched upon the wet and shining field; the dizzy kaleidoscope of colours formed by roundabouts flashing with brass and gipsies' choice of paint; the throng of country folk, forgetful to-day of their Puritanism; the discordant clash of three or four organs playing different tunes, of bells ringing and people laughing, talking, shouting; the holiday jostling and fun of it all.

'There's pretty you are,' said a young man, ogling her. She was glad that Penry heard, and marched her off quickly. She glanced at him from under her straw bonnet. Perhaps she really was good to look upon? Devoutly she hoped so. Her hair was parted demurely in the centre, brushed down each side of her oval face, and twisted in a neat coil at the nape of her neck. She wore her Sabbath gown of black alpaca, and the shawl of white cashmere with a red fringe in which her mother had been married. In a new pair of slippers 'her feet beneath her petticoat like little mice stole in and out'. To the front of her tight-fitting bodice was pinned a posy of cottage garden flowers. Her breasts were small and firm as apples; her waist was slim. She looked winsome, and Penry thought so, evidently, for he stayed close to her the rest of the day, and showed her the many delights of the fair: the gipsy fortune-teller, who promised each of them a faithful and pretty sweetheart; the monstrous fat woman in tights and spangles, the shooting gallery where goldfish could be won; the acrobats and jugglers, the wrestlers and daubed clowns. By all these pagan wonders Megan was enchanted. She drove home that evening beside her sleepy brother in the jolting farm cart with her heart beating and her temples throbbing. For nights after, she dreamed of Penry. The sound of footsteps, a knock at the door brought hot colour to her cheeks.

He came on the fifth day. It was the Sabbath. She was trying to read the Psalms, but closed her Bible quickly as she saw him vault down from his pony. He asked leave to stable it at Cwmbach farm. 'I have come to hear the preacher at your chapel,' he explained to her brother, who grinned.

Penry flushed, and her father replied: 'He's a tidy minister, but I never heard tell as he was noted for his eloquence . . . Still, you're welcome, young man.'

So Penry stayed to tea, and at dusk walked over to chapel side by side with Megan. There, in a dream of Paradise, she listened to him singing in his hearty bass voice.

'What a voice he was havin',' she would say. 'Goin' through me it was, deep down into my heart. Onst I had heard him sing, it was as if I was belongin' to him ever after. He was *here* – always.' And she would lay her gnarled hand, with wrinkled skin loose on the knuckles, upon her shrunken breast.

I did not dare look up at her when she spoke of her lover's singing. At such times I knew that tears were trickling down her checks. Of all the suffering through which she had passed, she could speak in her old age dry-eyed; but not of that happy voice, to remember which was ecstasy.

'They was all listenin' to him in chapel; and praisin' his singin' after. But *I* wasn't able to say nothin'. Feelin' too much, I was.'

After that first Sunday, he came again often from his father's farm which lay twelve miles away over the wind-scoured hills. He was a general favourite, whom Megan's parents welcomed to a meal and heard with indulgent disapproval when he told of fights, fairings and poaching. They were strict Calvinistic Methodists. A pious gloom hushed their home when Penry was not in it. To Megan he seemed a dazzling shaft of sunshine which had pierced its way into the darkness of a tomb.

'I was livin' in a family vault afore he came,' she said to me once. 'Indeed, he was my Saviour, bringin' me hope o' a glorious Resurrection. God forgive me if I do take His name in vain. 'Tis not in blaspheming. For Penry was my life, as Christ is the life o' good religious Christians.'

She spoke to him seldom, being content to listen to his voice, and to his laughter that made her happy, hot and afraid. It was to her he spoke when he addressed her parents or her brother. His tales of daring escapades were told to them in order to amuse her. When she joined, wholehearted, in their reluctant mirth, he grew still gayer. Sometimes he and she exchanged a glance full of understanding.

So she existed from week to week, going about her drudgery in a trance, waiting for Sunday till she should live again. Monday and Tuesday were hateful days, empty and cold. On Wednesday anticipation began to revive. Was it not already the middle of the week? Throughout Thursday and Friday her impatience mounted. On Saturday she was secretly distraught. Tired though she was by long hours of labour, she could scarcely sleep that night, but lay tossing in the darkness, asking herself again and again: 'Will he come to-morrow? Will he come?' If he came, she was supremely blissful, until the hour of his dreaded departure. If he did not come, the day was leaden with disappointment, and another week of interminable length dragged itself out like a life sentence.

One Sunday Penry knocked at the door of Cwmbach farmhouse.

'There he is,' cried Megan, springing up. She had been trying for hours to hide the fact that she was on the alert for his approach. When her mother looked at her with a smile and a sigh, she hung her head, abashed.

'Come you on in, boy,' her father called, and Penry strode into the kitchen. His manner was preoccupied. He neither laughed nor boasted during dinner. The old people noticed nothing amiss, since he spoke with his usual candour when they asked him any question. Only Megan, who knew every fleet change of expression in his eyes, grew troubled. Watching him anxiously, she pushed away her food untouched. His glance avoided hers, until, as they rose from table, she laid her hand timidly on his wrist. She had never touched him before, and she withdrew her fingers as though the contact had burnt them. He stood rooted, gazing down at her. She could have fainted, fearing that he was about to take her in his arms before them all. For an instant he seemed to struggle with himself whilst she held her timid breath. Then, turning away with a frown, he addressed the others.

'I have been thinkin'. 'Tis like this. A boy as is the youngest o' five and livin' at home like I am, he isn't gettin' no manner o' chance to earn money – not even gettin' the wages of a workin' man, he isn't.' He stared at the stone-flagged floor between his feet. 'Workin' like that for twenty or thirty years maybe, and left with nothin' after.'

Megan's father nodded. 'Yes, yes. When there is more nor one or two sons, 'tis better for the younger ones to get out o' the nest.'

'Well, now, I am havin' an uncle in Australia,' Penry resumed gloomily, and Megan's eyes grew wide with fear. 'Writin' to Mother he was some years ago, and sayin' "send you out one o' the lumpers, and I'll see as he shall do well".' Megan's lips parted, but no sound came from them. 'I've a mind to go out to my uncle,' Penry announced, his tone challenging anyone to stop him. Megan leant for support against the dresser and became aware that the kitchen had grown dark. The speech of her parents and brother had a muffled sound as though it came from a long way off. They were agreeing with Penry, but she could scarcely make out what they said. Her life seemed to be coming to an end. She had turned so white that at last her mother noticed it.

'Whatever's on you, bach?' she cried, and all eyes were turned on the girl where she stood, still as a figure of stone.

'I am all right,' Megan murmured, 'only – 'tis terrible cold in here.' She moved unsteadily towards the door and went out into the pale sunshine of early spring that turned to a sad yellow the stretch of sward before the house. The smell of moist earth and the sound of many streams were in the air. The hills, that had been brown and sombre all the winter through, were beginning to grow green, except where a patch of snow still lingered in a hollow. Everything was awakening to new life. Yet Megan felt as though her blood were ebbing away.

After a while she heard her mother's voice calling from the small window overhead. "Tis time to get ready for chapel.'

'I am not going,' she answered, and remained motionless, staring at the wide sweep of open hillside across the valley. From the time she was a little child, the vastness of the hills had brought her comfort in distress. At this moment she could not endure to have them shut out from her sight. So she stayed while the little group of black-clad figures came out of the house, and made their way soberly across the valley.

When the landscape was once more empty, and the silence of the hills unbroken but for the voices of wind and waterfall, Penry also came out of the house, and laid his hand on Megan's shoulder. She started and, turning round, looked up at him with eyes full of suffering. He was gazing at her as he had done when she touched his arm in the kitchen, and her heart began to beat again violently.

'Why are you goin' away?' she made bold to whisper, with a catch in her throat.

'Because it was comin' to me, sudden like, when last I seed you, that I couldn't live no more without you.'

She gave a sob of joy and wonder. 'But you are goin' away from me where I 'ont never see you.'

'Only to make a home for you there, Megan bach,' he answered, and his eyes travelled caressingly over her face, the silky, lustrous brown hair around it, the curves of her slender neck. Then, because he could find no words to say, he picked her up in his arms, and carried her into the house. There he set her on his knee. She sat very still for a long while, with her head drooped on his shoulder. Fear and suffering no longer existed for her; nor did time. In a moment she had been raised from the depths of despair to giddy heights of happiness beyond belief. The upward flight had left her weak, and with a queer sensation of dizziness. She clung silently to Penry, and listened to the throbbing of his heart close to her own. The strength of his muscle-hard arms around her was consoling. They gave her a sense of safety. Nothing, she fancied in this hour of ecstasy, could ever take her from him. She was profoundly content.

After a while, his hand stole up to her small chin and raised her face gently to his. Their lips had never met before. They did not soon part.

Penry came again to Cwmbach oftener than hitherto; and, since the young people were from henceforth admitted to be 'courting', they were allowed to sit up together, according to custom, long after the rest of the household had gone to bed. They sat hand in hand in the glow of a peat fire, and talked in whispers. What they said would have conveyed nothing to anyone else, for they had much to tell which neither could put into words. They looked, sighed, smiled and kissed. Sometimes they laughed low, and sometimes they clung together throughout a long silence. They understood each other perfectly. Their love filled the world for them. There was no serpent in their Eden. Even the thought of the impending parting did not greatly dismay them – they passed it over, and looked forward already to the time when they should meet again and be always together. They believed that such love as theirs must needs triumph over poverty, and that neither time nor distance could make it grow dim. Talking thus, they would throw more peat on the embers. The fire would leap up and the light of it flicker on the low ceiling. Wicked little shadows would run hither and thither, as if mocking the lovers and their happy fancies. But they did not heed – being too glad for fear, until their eyelids grew swollen for lack of sleep and dawn looked in upon them, ghostly grey.

'Cold,' Penry would say with a sudden shiver. 'Is it?' Megan would ask. 'I wasn't noticin'.'

It was not until the autumn, when Penry had gone away, that Megan began to realize the meaning of that dread word 'parted'. Then her longing to see him and to hear his voice became a physical torment, and she would be awake at night struggling with her sobs, telling herself in vain that this separation was but for a little time.

The winter set in pitiless. For months the pass at the top of the valley was snowbound, and even the pious few who attended Alpha chapel in lonely Cwmbach were kept from their devotions. Megan went about her household duties day by day, silent and subdued, finding the weeks and months of waiting, which were to have sped by so swiftly, intolerably long. She wrote to Penry every Saturday night; but letter-writing was to her a labour, exceedingly slow and toilsome; and when the ill-spelt letters, that had cost such pains, were returned to her long after, with 'Not known at this address' scrawled on them, she abandoned herself to despair. It seemed as though she would never hear from Penry, never be able to reach him, now that the unknown had closed upon him. She tormented herself with the thought that he had died on the voyage out; until at last, almost a year after he had gone away, she received his first letter. It was despondent in tone, but still she hugged it to her as evidence that he was still alive, and not irrevocably lost to her.

He had arrived in Australia, so he wrote, to find that his uncle was dead, and that no work was to be obtained in that locality. There had been a succession of droughts, and prospects were very bad; still, he had managed, after great difficulty, to find temporary employment on a sheep ranch. He feared that making a home for his Megan would prove a longer business than they had thought, but, if she would wait for him, he would never give up the struggle.

Wait for him? What else could he fancy there was for her to do? What was she living for but the time when they should meet again? She laughed at him for imagining that she could ever give any other man a thought. She carried his letter about inside her bodice, and slept with it under her pillow, until it was tattered and crumpled. Then, lest she should wear it out altogether, she put it away in the oak chest where she kept the coloured daguerreotype he had sent her of himself before he sailed from Liverpool. It was her most cherished possession, too well beloved to be exposed; to be taken out and looked at only by lamplight and in secret.

Another year went by, and another; and after that, in her loneliness and disappointment, Megan lost count of the seasons that divided her from her lover, and, at length, even from hope. She heard from him at rare intervals. Now he was doing well, and would soon have earned enough to come and fetch her. Now another drought had ruined his employer, and he was again cast on the world, searching for work, whilst his precious store of savings, that meant happiness for them both, dwindled.

He had been gone seven years when she received a short, barely legible letter, written in pencil, much blurred, and in a laboured, childish hand. Luck was against him. She must wait for him no longer. He had been almost starving for the last month, rather than break into the store of money he had laid by. He had enough to come and fetch her now, but where was the good in bringing her out to a country in which he had no home to offer her? Every enterprise he touched failed. He had begun to think that he brought ill fortune with him wherever he went. 'Like Jonah in the Bible,' he wrote. 'I won't never bring you, my love, to ruin, you may be sure. So better think of me as dead.' There followed a cross and his signature.

This was the last letter she ever received from him. With tears dropping on to the paper, she wrote to tell him that she would never give him up. The pathetic, smudged little missive was returned unopened. He had apparently gone away, leaving no address, no indication of his whereabouts. She heard from him no more. She could not hope to obtain news of him, for she knew no one in that far-distant country. He was now utterly lost to her, as though he had passed over to another world. 'Indeed most likely the boy is dead,' her parents told her, and at last she came to believe that it was so.

It was then that the new minister came to Alpha Chapel. He was unmarried, and lived alone with the deaf caretaker in the barnacle cottage clinging to the bleak wall of his house of prayer. The fame of his preaching spread abroad, and people came from far over the hills to be denounced and edified by him.

He was not old; nor did he look young. His aspect was austerely virginal, for he was tall and very thin, with a pale face, and black eyes, in which burned fanatical fire. A spiritual descendant of Savonarola, he loathed the sins of humanity, and saw terrible visions of an avenging God. He would have made a 'bonfire of vanities' and condemned to the flames whatever ministered to the gaiety of life. Religion and self-denial were to him inseparable. He was ready, in the name of his faith, to endure torture or to inflict it. Yet even he was moved to pity by the sight of Megan's pale face. He learned her story from the lips of her parents, at whose house he became a frequent visitor. She herself never spoke to him of her sorrow until one day he met her coming home from market alone, and laid his lean hand on her shoulder.

'My sister,' he said abruptly, 'I know why you are sad.' 'Oh,' she cried, flushing, 'I do hope as I don't let everyone see how 'tis with me. I am tryin' not to hurt others by the sight o' my sorrow. Indeed and I am.' 'Yes, yes,' he answered, looking into her eyes. 'I know. You endeavour to be brave; but you cannot always succeed, is that not so?' She nodded 'Do you know why?' he resumed. 'Because you are proud.'

She stared at him, astonished. 'Proud,' he repeated. 'And spiritual pride is sinful. In your secret arrogance, you strive to bear the burden of your grief alone.' He had intended to preach her a sermon on the duty of casting her care upon the Redeemer, but the grandiloquent words, long premeditated, died on his lips. He found himself saying instead, quite simply: 'Won't you make a friend of me, and tell me all about it?'

She was too overwhelmed to reply; so he took the market basket out of her hands, saying as he did so: 'I can carry this home for you, at any rate.'

Lonely and unused to kindness as she was, she felt her eyes smart with tears of gratitude. 'You are wonderful good to me,' she murmured, 'and you such a great preacher too.'

'We are all alike sinners in the sight of God,' he answered, resuming once more the lofty tone that became his calling.

The following Sunday, Rees Lloyd preached upon the Christian virtue of resignation. His thin fingers strayed along the edge of the pulpit, as though they groped for something to hold fast. His gaze seemed to pierce through the whitewashed wall on which it rested, as if beyond it he beheld a sublime vision. He was in a gentler mood than usual. No longer concerned with death and judgment and the vengeance of an Old Testament Deity, but full of pity for the afflicted. "Blessed are they that mourn for they shall be comforted," he quoted, and again: "It is good for me that I have been in trouble; that I may learn Thy statutes." 'Without suffering,' he cried, 'there is no understanding; be not rebellious then, but resign yourselves to the hand of the Lord, knowing that whom He loveth he chasteneth, that His loved ones may be refined as is gold by the fiery furnace.'

The black-clad congregation sat spellbound, listening to the vibrations of the preacher's voice as it rose to a shout or sank to a penetrating whisper. Down the weather-beaten face of an old man, who had lost his wife and child, tears fell. A girl, who had crept into the back of the building, huddled up in a shawl, shrinking from the contemptuous glances of her respectable neighbours, sobbed unrestrainedly. All who had suffered loss and grief were moved by the sermon. But Megan was afraid, knowing that this eloquence was directed towards herself.

'Did you like what I said to-day?' the preacher asked her that evening when he came to Cwmbach farm. 'Yes, indeed,' she answered, 'it was beautiful.' 'Oh,' he said impatiently, 'but was it *helpful*?'

They were standing beside the hearth in the kitchen, apart from the others, who were busy at the supper table. Megan gave him a look at once timid and thankful.

'Yes,' she breathed, scarcely above a whisper, 'it do help me somethin' wonderful to know as you are feelin' for me.'

'I would give my life to help you,' he whispered back, with such fierce intensity that she shivered and hung her head. 'Look at me,' he commanded in a low tone, but she dared not raise her eyes to his.

'Supper is ready,' her mother announced, and Megan turned away quickly with a breath of relief.

She could not define her attitude towards Rees Lloyd, his absorption in the things of the spirit, his devotion to his faith, the stirring tones of his voice, the penetrating gaze of his eyes, fascinated her; yet she feared him personally, and was never at ease in his presence. When he was near her she would have been glad to escape; but because he, of all souls in this indifferent world, had offered her his sympathy, she felt the need of him when he was gone. Her hopeless love for Penry was in no way abated; but daily the minister took a larger share in her thoughts.

Soon after this, the caretaker of Alpha Chapel died. The elders who gathered together at the funeral were concerned as to what should be done. It was not easy to find anyone who, for the pittance so poor a community could offer, would live alone in the valley where was only one other dwelling. 'If only the preacher were married,' one of them said, 'he and his wife could have the house by the chapel for theirselves.'

'Yes, yes,' they all agreed. ''Tis pity as he isn't married to a tidy 'oman as 'ould look after the place for us.'

When Rees Lloyd came to Cwmbach farm that night, Megan's father repeated to him what the elders had said. They were sitting round the kitchen table in a circle of light thrown down by a heavily shaded lamp. The rest of the room, with its low raftered ceiling and stone-flagged floor, was in semi-darkness; only a red glow shone from the hearth and was reflected in the gleaming eyes of cats that slunk about in the shadows. All the brightness in the room was concentrated on the open pages of the Bible, which lay on the table beneath the lamp. Rees Lloyd, with his hand resting upon the book, arose. His head and shoulders disappeared in the twilight above the lamp. His pale face was still visible, ghostly, with eyes shining in the gloom. He remained thus whilst the grandfather clock ticked through a whole minute, and all the while he looked fixedly at Megan. The old people sat in hushed expectancy, with faces upturned; but their daughter kept her gaze on the Bible and the taut hand clenched in the harsh light upon its sacred pages. She dared not look Rees Lloyd in the face. At length he turned his burning glance on her parents.

'Behold your daughter,' he said, in slow deliberate tones. 'This is the Lord's call to her.' 'No, no,' she cried, starting to her feet, 'not that.' 'Yes,' he persisted, 'the Lord has need of you for His service. You cannot deny His call.'

She looked about her distractedly, seeking a way of escape. The others remained awestruck, listening to this voice that compelled them in the darkness.

'Here is your appointed task in life,' it continued. 'I am a minister of the Most High; I need your help, and in helping me you will serve Him also. He is calling to you, Megan, to forget yourself and your personal sorrow; to live only for others, and for His greater honour and glory.' She made no reply. 'God is calling to you,' cried the voice, louder and more insistent than before: 'He is calling to you through me, because it shall be given to me to lead your wandering soul into the safety of His fold. Will you not come?'

She turned away into the darkness, and hid her face in her hands. 'Answer,' he commanded. 'I do want to serve God,' she whispered at last, 'but indeed, indeed, I can never be your wife.' 'Are you mad, gal?' cried the old people both together. For answer she wrung her hands. Then the voice from the darkness spoke to her more gently.

'I know what you are thinking of, Megan. You have not forgotten your first love.' She inclined her head. 'But I have need of you,' cried the voice, vibrating with passionate appeal. 'I love you.' And after a tense silence, imploringly – 'Will you not come?'

Slowly, reluctantly, as if drawn towards him against her will, she stole into the circle of lamplight, and placed her cold hand in his upon the Bible.

When they were married she crossed the narrow valley from her old home to her new. There she took up the work of the chapel caretaker, and cooked the minister's meals, and kept his cottage in order, waiting on him day by day. He believed that in doing this she was serving God; and he made her also believe it. Therefore she was content with her lot, and her husband in his possession of her. He had not known carnal love before, and he abandoned himself to it, indifferent to the feelings of the woman who submitted herself to his caresses.

So the weeks wore by, each like the last, marked by

Sundays when up the valley and down over the pass the faithful came to worship, black as rooks. When they were gathered together in chapel, they sang their melancholy hymns, set to music in the minor key, older than Christianity, old almost as the race; and Rees Lloyd thundered at them from his high pulpit.

After the people had gone away, the shadow of the western hill stole across the emptied valley, and every trace of the congregation was gone. It seemed to Megan that with the next Sunday might come a fresh generation, for a week and an age were as one to the mountains that had looked down unmoved on the passing of one race after another.

To her husband she did not tell these fancies. It would have been difficult for her to put them into words, though as a girl she had managed to convey all she felt to Penry. But he and she had been as children together, holding hands on the threshold of a darkened room, peering awestruck into the unknown. Rees Lloyd, on the contrary, appeared to her to possess vast learning, gained from his score of theological books, which she dusted reverently every day. His positive assertion and ease of self-expression made it almost impossible for her to converse with him at all. She spoke to him always with hesitation, struggling to translate her thought into the intricacies of language – a language seldom used by the people around her except to communicate the needs of daily life. To have contradicted any of her husband's dogmatic pronouncements would have been open heresy, and she dared be a heretic only in secret. She admired him. She sat demurely listening to his eloquence Sunday after Sunday, aware that his knowledge of many matters was as great as was her ignorance. Yet in the wisdom of her humility, she guessed that he was well instructed rather than wise. His wrath against sinners made her sigh. For his famished lusting after her body she felt a shrinking pity.

He had gone one day to preach at a distant chapel. She stood with arms folded on the stone wall before their home, and mused upon the strangeness of their marriage. Her gaze was on a point where, at a bend in the valley, the road was lost to sight. Something about that lonely road, leading away into a world she had never seen, fascinated her. She often stood thus, staring. To-day she felt unable to take her eyes off it, though it was time she locked up the house and crossed over the stream to her former home. Whenever her husband was away, she returned to Cwmbach farm "for company"; but this evening the profound stillness held her entranced. As she lingered in the mellow golden sunlight, a speck appeared upon the road and grew presently into the figure of a man. When he had come closer, she saw that he was unusually tall, and was swinging along at a great pace. He carried a stick in one hand, and a bundle slung over his shoulder. He drew near rapidly, and she noticed that he wore no hat and that his fair hair and beard glistened like honey in the sun. Her curiosity was awake now, for a stranger was seldom seen in the Cwm. She leant over the wall, intently watching his approach. As he came closer still, she could see that his face was sunburnt, making his blue eyes appear startlingly light; they were fixed upon her. Something stirred within her breast, as though her heart, long dormant, had awakened, and begun once more hotly to beat. The rugged strength of this strange man's features was familiar. The upward tilt of the chin, though hidden by a luxuriant beard, recalled a favourite pose of *someone* whose face she had once known – someone – who was it? The next instant the ground beneath her feet seemed to have given way.

'Did you ever dream as you were fallin' off of a tremendous high place?' she asked me when she was describing the sensations of that moment. 'That's how I was feelin', and I wasn't wakin' up neither, as you are doin' after a bad dream.

I seemed to go on fallin' and fallin' for a long while, and then to hang in the air, as if there wasn't nothin' below me nor above, nor on either side. It was the sound of his voice as brought me back to myself, at last – the same voice, strong and deep as ever, not changed even so much as his face was. Only I was havin' a terrible feelin' as if I was listenin' to the dead; and I was tryin' to pray – "God help me, God help me". But there didn't seem to be a God no longer, seein' as *this* had happened.'

She sat twisting her fingers together when she told me this. 'What did *he* say to you?' I asked at last, caressing her knee. '"Megan," he was sayin', coming close up against the other side o' the wall, "are you rememberin' me?" I was leanin' against the wall, my strength havin' gone clean from me, and lookin' up into his face. I knowed it well, every line of it. It seemed 'twas only yesterday as he'd gone away – only there was more power in his face like, and lines round his eyes, as wasn't there before. Very thin and strong it looked, not so round and boyish; but handsomer nor ever. I wasn't answerin' him for a while, but was lettin' my eyes have their fill of what they'd been weepin' for many a long year. When I could find my voice, I was answerin': "I am rememberin' you right enough – *Diar Anwl*, could I ever forget you?" "You *did* forget me, whatever," says he, "when you married another man. They told me down in Pontnoyadd how 'twas; but I 'ouldn't believe them, no, not one of 'em, till I saw it with my own eyes." He was lookin' at the ring on my hand, as I held by the wall for the weakness in my knees. I looked down at it too, and I turned as cold as if I'd been standin' on top o' the hills in a bitter winter. I couldn't speak for a long while after, to tell him how I comed to get married; but we was lookin' at each other all the time, quite still, and frightened like, same as people that had seen a corpse candle.'

She could not tell me, but I knew what turmoil of emotions

assailed her during this silence that seemed to her tormented soul to last through an eternity. For she knew, as she looked upon Penry, that here was the man who had possessed her heart entirely from the day on which she had first set eyes on him; and that she had no love for her husband, with whom she must live out her days to the end. She looked back on her own passive calm of a few moments ago, as though she were looking across a gulf of time, knowing that the relative contentment of her first months of married life could never again be hers. *He* had returned. He would go away, no doubt, suddenly as he had come, and she would most likely never see him in this world again. But in these threatened moments, as she stood scrutinizing his face, the ecstasy and passion of first love, the yearning of years of hope deferred, reawakened within her; and she knew that never for an instant could she forget him again. The memory of her promise to 'love, honour and obey' another man tormented her. Honour and obey – yes, she could continue to do that, but *love* – was it possible to keep such a promise? Was it right to force anyone to make it? Could she ever again suffer the caresses of Rees Lloyd? At the thought of them she sickened. The future appeared to her so unbearable that she prayed God to take pity on her and let her die, now, whilst she stood looking up at the man whom she adored. But God was without mercy, since He had suffered her to betray Penry's trust. Why had she received no warning that he was yet alive? Why had she not waited for him just a few months more? Wherein had they both deserved this cruel suffering? Was there no compassion, no justice even, in the universe?

I do not know to what depths her soul went down during that long silence. She spoke to me of it once only, and then in broken sentences. She was never quite at home in English, and there are feelings too deep for any language to convey. It was forty years afterwards that she related to me this episode in her life, but as I looked up into those quiet deep-set eyes of hers, I saw such a haunting of anguish that I turned away.

At last they began to talk. Simply, in a few words, they told each other what had happened. Soon after Penry had written her the last letter she received, he had succeeded in finding work with a man who paid him good wages and treated him as a friend. He still had those cherished savings of his. Grown reckless with ill fortune, he sank them all in a speculation into which he and his employer entered together. To his delight and astonishment, the concern prospered. Soon he had doubled his small hoard and wrote to tell Megan that a turn had come in the tide of his affairs, that he would be home within the year to fetch her. That letter, which should have reached her just before her marriage, miscarried.

'Duw, Duw,' she cried, wringing her hands, 'why was I never gettin' it? I didn't hear from you, *diar anwl*, and the years was passin' by, and they was all tellin' me as you were dead.'

'I do wish as I had died out there,' he answered, 'I can't go back to the place where I've made a home for you; nor I can't bear to stay here where you are livin' as another man's wife.'

'What will you be doin', then?' she asked him.

''Deed and I don't know,' he answered wearily. 'Maybe as I 'on't be livin' long.'

It was then that she clasped his hand in hers. At the contact, fire seemed to run through her veins. Another silence fell between them, but this time there was a different look in their eyes. She forgot all her misery, her dread of the future. She lived exultantly in the present.

A moment, or an hour, may have passed; and then Penry leant across the wall, and taking her face between his hands, he kissed her on the lips.

She did not remember when he let her go, nor if any more

was said between them. I do not think that they spoke again. It never seems to have entered their heads to go away together. She had married Rees Lloyd, and was bound.

How he left her, Megan could never recall. When she regained full consciousness, after the delirium of that kiss, he was already a long way off, striding up the valley towards the pass. She was still standing where he had found her, leaning against the inside of her little garden wall. Nothing had changed visibly, except the shadow of the western hill, which now lay across the Cwm. As Penry disappeared from sight, the last glint of sunlight vanished from the tops of the hills.

Not until many hours later did Megan re-enter her house. She remained standing motionless until it became too dark to trace the white line of road in its ascent of the distant pass. Even then she stayed on, staring into the deepening gloom. She was not aware as yet of being acutely miserable. The magnitude of the blow she had received had stunned her, and left her unable to act, or even to think.

Perhaps she would have remained like this all night, had not her parents sent their servant girl to enquire why she had not come to supper. 'I 'on't be comin' to-night,' she managed to say, when she became conscious that someone was addressing her. ''On't you be afraid to sleep here alone?' the girl asked. 'No,' she answered, 'I'm not afraid of anything as can happen to me – now.' It was the sound of a human voice, reminding her of a life which must be resumed, that awoke her from her lethargy.

When she was alone once more, she began to pace up and down in the darkness, sobbing inconsolably like a child. Nothing broke the silence of the hills, that loomed above her, black, on either side, but the pitiful sound of her crying, and the faint sighing of the night wind.

For hours she walked to and fro, and cried, and wrung her

hands. When dawn was turning the sky to a chill grey, she dragged herself into the house, and up the stairs, and fell, exhausted by suffering, on to the bed. She must have fallen asleep immediately, and have stayed in the drugged slumber of worn-out grief, for it was noon when she was awakened by her husband and her mother.

Rees Lloyd had called for his wife at Cwmbach farm that morning; but she was not there. 'There's odd she was last night, too,' the servant girl had told him, 'like as if she's *seen* something.' He had turned to his mother-in-law anxiously and asked her to come over at once to his home with him. They set off together in haste, fearing that Megan might have been taken ill. On their way across the valley they encountered the postman, who passed Cwmbach twice a week on his rounds. He was excited, and shouted to them from a distance. 'Have you seen Penry Price, son of Rhosferig as used to be?' Megan's mother stared, aghast. 'The Lord forbid,' she cried. 'Isn't he dead this long while?' 'Nor, nor,' answered the postman, coming up to them, triumphant that he should be the bearer of sensational tidings. 'Alive he is, and they do tell me as he was in Pontnoyadd yesterday. The folks there was tellin' him as your gal was married to Mr Lloyd here, but he 'ouldn't believe it. "Megan's not one to forget," says he, so he was comin' up by here to see for hisself.' 'Coming here?' Rees Lloyd interrupted. 'Yes, yes,' the postman affirmed. 'Up this road he did come sure. John Jones as was ploughin' close by seed a great tall man passin' by in the afternoon. Findin' out his mistake he was, no doubt,' the postman added, grinning at the old woman. 'Your gal's done a deal better for herself by marryin' a wonderful gifted preacher like Mr Lloyd here. She's not havin' no cause to look back, she's . . .' But Rees Lloyd waited to hear no more. He seized his mother-in-law by the arm, and hurried her on towards his cottage. She stole a glance at his white face and thin tight lips, and was so much alarmed that she began to wail: 'Duw, Duw, why has Penry come back to trouble us all?' Rees Lloyd made no reply, but jealousy and fear tormented him, and he hastened his pace, dragging the breathless whimpering old woman after him. When they reached the house, he flung open the door which he found ajar, and called in a harsh voice: 'Megan, Megan, where are you?' There was no answer and, dreading to find her gone, he rushed upstairs, and burst into the bedroom.

There he found her, fully dressed, but with her hair dishevelled, lying asleep on the bed with shadows under her closed eyes. The lids were swollen with much crying. The fit of murderous jealousy that had possessed him when he heard of her sweetheart's return left him as suddenly as it had come. 'Megan bach, poor Megan bach,' he whispered, and her mother, who had followed him into the room, echoed 'Poor Megan bach, she must have seen him; but indeed,' she added, 'Megan's allus been an honest gal, and she 'on't think no more about him, now that's she's married to you; only do you be gentle with her, Rees bach.' 'I'll be gentle,' he promised, struggling to quell another pang of jealousy at the thought that his wife should have been so deeply affected by the return of Penry.

At that moment Megan opened her eyes. At first she was vaguely conscious of great unhappiness; then, as her mother began to talk, she recalled what had happened the night before, and turning her eyes away from her husband, she hid her face in the pillow. 'I do wish as I might die,' she thought. She lay there too unutterably weary and miserable to move; whilst Rees Lloyd stood watching her, with hatred and pity, love, desire, and jealousy coursing each other through his tortured being. The old woman rambled on, incessantly repeating the phrases about duty and the will of God which she had heard so often in chapel; and outside the little window of the darkened room, the autumn sunshine gilded the hills, and the larks and meadow pipits soared up singing joyfully into a blue sky.

'Let me be,' Megan pleaded at last, 'just for a little while.' At length they left her alone. Later in the day her husband brought her a cupful of something to drink, liquid which might perhaps have been tea, though it had no flavour. He forced it between her lips. She shrank from physical contact with him; but this act of kindness on his part gave her a sort of desperate courage to go on living.

When he left the room, she rose unsteadily, and began to wash her tear-stained face and arrange her disordered hair. It surprised her to find how easily these things could be done, mechanically, whilst the spirit was far away. Having set the bedroom to rights, with the precision of a machine, she went downstairs, and began, as though nothing unusual had occurred, to cook her husband's supper. He asked her no questions, but his sombre eyes followed her wherever she went, with the devotion and suspicion of an illtreated, hungry dog.

In the weeks that followed, she often saw this expression in his gaze, invariably fixed upon her; and she grew increasingly to pity the man of whom formerly she had been afraid. In pitying him she found some solace from her grief. So she picked up the broken thread of her life, and was busy as ever about the house and the chapel, all day long. Only at night-time when her husband had fallen asleep was she able to abandon herself to her sorrow.

There came a day when Rees Lloyd was sitting moodily before the fire with a book of sermons lying unread on his knee. Megan had grown so thin that he had sent her to Pontnoyadd to see the doctor. As he awaited her return, forebodings of disaster assailed him. There had always been something elusive about his wife, he reflected bitterly. Even before the accursed return of Penry Price, she had never seemed wholly to belong to himself. Now perhaps she would cheat him altogether by dying, daring to die for love of another man! It was unjust, he swore, clenching his hands in impotent anger. She had only set her eyes on this interloper once since he left her eight or ten years ago. 'Whilst I,' cried Lloyd to himself, 'I am close to her day and night, watching over her, ready to spend all I have on her, if only she would love me as I love her.' And then he added threateningly: 'And I am her lawful husband. I have a *right* to her affection.' It appeared to him dishonest of her to pine away as she was doing, for this Penry – a vagabond, with no claim on her affection.

Rees Lloyd angrily closed his book. He could not read. When Megan was not there to distract him in person, her sorrowful face haunted his imagination. She, who in the early days of their marriage had quenched his desire when need be, and at other times occupied a safe place in the background of his thoughts, had, through this unforeseen catastrophe, forced herself into his every thought and dream, awake or sleeping. He could no longer concentrate his attention upon his preaching or his prayers. He had chosen her for his helpmate; it was her wifely duty to succour and soothe him, that he might the better serve God. Now that she came between him and his devotion she was beginning to assume the aspect of a temptation sent him by the Devil.

He rose, and was frantically pacing up and down the little kitchen, trying to banish her image, when she herself came softly into the room. He turned on her his black eyes full of lustful hostility. For answer she smiled at him, yet he fancied hardly so much *at* him as *through* him, as though she were smiling at another whom she saw in his place. He scowled, suffering from a sense of unreality, wishing that she might fade away, if only he could be released thus from the nightmare in which he had been living. But she laid her hand on his shoulder. 'I am goin' to have a child,' she announced quietly.

For a moment he was too greatly surprised and overjoyed to speak. Then he took her in his arms and triumphantly kissed her. 'Now you will be mine,' he said, 'wholly mine.' She made no reply. 'When you are the mother of my child, Megan bach, you will learn to care for *me* only,' he assured her.

'You are very kind to me,' she murmured, absently. She was thinking of the child she might have borne, had she been the wife of Penry – blue-eyed and golden haired, splendid to look upon, like himself, and she fancied that she could hear again the infectious happy laugh she remembered so well from her girlhood.

The days passed monotonously, and Megan went about her work as before. But now she wore a mysterious smile, as if she were picturing to herself something which greatly pleased her. She had set herself, scarcely conscious of what she was doing, to form the child of her dreams. Throughout her waking hours she dwelt on her memories of Penry. She rehearsed every word he had spoken to her; she recalled every characteristic gesture, every tone of his voice. They were all stored up in her heart, these precious things. The years had but overlaid them with the dust of lesser matters. When she came to search them out once more, scenes and incidents of her early courtship became distinct again, as on the day when they took place. Her picture gallery of beloved memories grew more vivid as her time drew near.

When her household work was finished, she would put a chair outside the cottage, close to the wall on which she had leant when Penry had returned. She knew the exact spot on which their hands had met; and there, evening by evening in the winter's dusk, she rested her clasped hands, as she sat picturing that last meeting in all its details. Sometimes she fancied even that she felt his parting kiss on her lips. Then, for a long while, she would sit motionless in silent ecstasy, with her eyes closed.

When she had married, she had put away the little coloured daguerreotype of Penry with her other relics of him. She had not thought it right to cherish, yet lacked the heart to destroy them. Now she brought out his portrait, and, carrying it about in her pocket, looked at it secretly a hundred times a day.

Her husband, unsuspecting, watched her covertly, and rejoiced that she should have become, it seemed, not merely content, but cheerful. He was considerate to her in a clumsy fashion. She, in return, was in all things a dutiful, submissive wife. In all things, that is, but her thoughts. These she kept to herself, as the silent hills about Cwmbach have kept the secrets of ten thousand years.

Rees Lloyd and all his kith and kin were swarthy of skin, dark-haired, black-eyed, with the long narrow skulls of a race older even than the Celt. Megan's hair was nut brown, smooth and silky to touch. Her eyes were the colour of the peat streams that ran down her native hillsides, neither altogether brown, nor green, nor amber, but each in turn, according to the light in which you saw them. The child that was born to these two some nine months after the return of Penry was blue-eyed and had a crop of close yellow curls all over his head. When Megan's mother took the crumpled scrap of flesh out of the doctor's hands, she stared at him with grave misgiving; after which she hastened to tell her son-in-law that his firstborn 'favoured' a maternal great-grandfather, the only one of her family whom she could recollect to have had blue eyes. She assured the neighbours that the likeness was remarkable. As the ancestor in question had been dead and buried for half a century, they could not contradict her. Nevertheless, the matrons who went to see Megan's baby whispered about it as they came out of chapel.

Rees Lloyd had a puzzled, incredulous way of staring at the infant; and Megan from the moment when he was put into her arms, as she lay half dead with pain and exhaustion, loved him idolatrously. She would sit for hours in silent adoration of the child in her lap.

Had Rees Lloyd been a Catholic, he might have accepted this miracle, which filled his wife with glad devotion, and have been content to play the rôle of meek Saint Joseph. But being a Calvinistic Methodist, he indulged in no specially tender sentiment about the Holy Family. Moreover, he believed in no miracles excepting those recorded in the Bible. Such things had happened once; this he was constrained to believe on Divine Authority; but that nothing miraculous could possibly occur nowadays, his common sense assured him.

It was not long before rumours of what was being said by his congregation reached his ears, and he began to brood over the shameful suspicion that tarnished his home. He sat watching his wife in her contemplation of the child, and struggled to put all thought of the slander from him as unworthy. He had, however, been trained in the school of thought which holds the human heart to be full of wickedness and guile; and he was afraid of his own more generous instincts. He dared not trust the evidence of his eyes, or believe in the innocence of a possible sinner merely because she had every appearance of innocence. Megan's untroubled manner towards him, and her frank steadfast gaze, became at last, to his fevered imagination, proofs of her deceitfulness. He said not a word to her of this; but he began to preach sermons more threatening than any of his former ones on the need for repentance and of public confession. On the deadly sin of adultery he waxed especially eloquent, and the denunciation of those who transgressed the seventh commandment became his obsession. So great was his fervour and eloquence that women sobbed aloud, and men rose to confess to fornication before an hysterically excited congregation. Strange things came to light in Alpha Chapel. The impressionable young were overwrought; the elders shook their heads. Weak brethen, they declared, committed sins in order to enjoy the notoriety of penitence. Some were even so wicked as to invent sins which they had not committed. But though sober-minded persons disapproved, the chapel collections increased, the groaning and crying of 'Amen' rose louder, and Rees Lloyd thundered ever more savagely his terrible threats of death and judgment and everlasting fire.

Only the woman at whom all this fury was directed, who dominated his every thought, who filled his being with impotent rage, sat beneath his pulpit unmoved and placid, as if in her childlike innocence, above the storm of his anger, she heard the calm music of celestial things.

When the child, whom they had christened Ifor, was two years old, Megan gave birth to another son. He was as swarthy as a gipsy. His mother gave him the same dutiful care which she paid to his father. She spared herself no trouble in the service of these two. Nothing was lacking to them but the warmth of her love. That was all for her firstborn, and Rees Lloyd hated her daily more and more. He found her one day, seated beside the kitchen fire, giving her breast to the black-eyed baby in her arms. He stood staring down at her in a gloomy reverie, when the sound of Ifor's crying reached their ears from the walled-in space before the cottage. In an instant Megan was on her feet, and taking the baby from her breast, rolled it up hastily in a shawl and left it to whimper in its cradle, whilst she hurried out to comfort her loved one.

A gust of fury shook Rees Lloyd. He followed his wife out through the doorway, and the sight of her holding the golden-haired child in her arms drove him to the verge of madness. 'Put down that bastard,' he shouted at her, 'put it down – or I'll kill the both of you.'

She gave him a terror-stricken look, but clung closer to the child. 'Do you hear me?' he cried hoarsely. 'You will drive me to murder, flaunting your shame before me as you do!'

'It isn't true,' she said in a low voice, facing him unflinchingly. For a moment he towered over her, clenching and unclenching his hands as though he would strangle her. Then he turned abruptly away, and strode off bareheaded into the hills. Megan crouched down upon the doorstep with Ifor folded close to her heart; and the wailing of the neglected baby rose unheeded from the house.

When Rees Lloyd returned home that evening after hours of prayer and wrestling with himself in the solitude of the mountains, he came up to Megan and laid his hand on her shoulder. 'I will not blame you,' he said, in a voice from which all the life was gone. 'God knows, we are all miserable sinners, and in danger of hell fire; yet the worst of us may be saved, at the last, by repentance. Confess your sin, and I will forgive you, as I hope myself for pardon.' 'I am not guilty of what you do think,' she answered resolutely.

He turned away from her sharply with a gesture of despair. She followed him across the room, moved to compassion by the sight of his suffering. 'Maybe I have done wrong,' she murmured, 'without knowin' as I did it.' He turned and looked at her with revived hope, waiting for her confession. 'But if I sinned,' she continued softly, ''twas only in thought. I have allus been keeping my marriage vows, and actin' honest by you.' 'Look at the child,' he interrupted her with renewed anger. ''Tis the child of my dreams,' she whispered. He stared at her uncomprehending, and turned away in disgust.

That night he said no more, but throughout the years that followed he returned to the subject which poisoned his mind, with reiterated demands for her confession. 'I am not guilty as you do think,' was all she would vouchsafe him, and he with growing conviction would answer: 'You lie!'

She bore him three more children, all dark as her second, and she listened patiently to his cruel denunciations, his reproaches, his appeals to her to repent. She suffered his moods of passionate desire, and his violent reactions of loathing and self-contempt; and the whole wealth of her love was poured out upon Ifor and the memory of Penry. She was far less unhappy than the man who lived to torment her and himself; for her life was one of resignation, whilst his was a self-created hell of hatred and suspicions.

When the imprisoned winds came howling down the Cwm one night in December, a wizened old man knocked at Rees Lloyd's door. Megan opened it a crack, and a wreath of blue smoke and peat ash went swirling round the kitchen. Rees Lloyd raised his head, as he sat before the fire with a book on his knee. He listened to the whispering of his wife and the man who stood in the darkness outside. Unable to hear what they were saying, he felt an angry suspicion that they were discussing something of which they did not want him to know. He was ready to believe any ill of Megan, since she had so repeatedly lied to him. Presently she closed the door on the storm and the firelit room grew warm and still once more. When she came back into the light he saw that her face was pallid and her lips were quivering. She stared past him with dilated eyes; then caught up a shawl and wrapped it round her shoulders. 'I must be goin' to Graig-fawr,' she announced. 'What!' he cried, 'goin' up to the top of the valley on a night like this?' 'Yes, yes, there is someone dyin' there as do want to see me.'

He asked her no more questions but let her go out alone

into the darkness. Driven by an ill presentiment, he rose and followed her stealthily up the road that was just visible beneath his feet.

The wind came raging down between the hills on either side, and lashed the rain and icy sleet into his face. His hands grew numb with cold; at times he could scarcely draw his breath; still he struggled on, now and then catching a glimpse of the two figures ahead of him. Once the sound of their voices was blown back on the tempest. 'Hurry, hurry,' Megan cried in agonized appeal. 'He may be dead afore we can get there.' The old man shouted at her: 'I am goin' as fast as I can. I can't do no more.' The force of the wind had almost overmastered him and he staggered. She caught him by the arm, and dragged him along. She was endowed with superhuman strength, and would have fought her way through fire and water to the place where Penry lay dying.

Two shepherds had found him lying at the foot of a steep rock, off which he had stepped, blinded by the treacherous mist. They had carried him to a neighbouring farm; and there he lay in an upper room, barely conscious when Megan entered. His eyelids fluttered and lifted slowly at the sound of her voice. His blue eyes seemed to have turned black, for the pupils were dilated to take in the last of light. His face was corpse-pale; but at sight of her, a faint smile hovered over it. She knelt down beside the bed, and motioned away the farmer and his wife who had followed her in to the dimly lit room. They stole out on tiptoe. On the narrow landing at the top of the stairs they encountered the minister, with burning eyes fixed upon the door through which his wife had passed. No one had seen him enter the house, and they exclaimed in surprise and fear at sight of him.

'Go downstairs,' he commanded, 'and leave me be. I will keep watch here.'

They obeyed him in awed silence; and when he was left

alone in the dark, he crept close to the door through which came a faint crack of light. He knelt down beside it, listening, with murder in his heart.

Megan was speaking in low tones. She was telling the dying man the story of the miracle. Her husband could see her, through the crack in the door, kneeling beside the bed, her eyes fixed adoringly on the white face upon the pillow. The haggard man, with bloodstained bandages about his head, did not stir; but he was fully conscious now, and his wide eyes shone with fever's brilliance in the light of the single candle.

'How is it possible you comed to bear a child like me?' he murmured. His lips hardly moved. The words seemed to form themselves in the air. 'We were never doin' no wrong, you and I, Megan.'

'All things are possible to the spirit,' she answered, 'as we are readin' in the Bible. The old folk too, they are tellin' us stories of things they have seen as aren't of this 'orld. I am not laughin' at the old stories, as some are doin'. Folks as have had a bit of education, they aren't willin' to believe in anything as they can't understand. But the wisest are them as are full o' wonder still, like little children.' And she added: 'There is nothin' so strange but what it may come to pass.' This was the summing up of her faith.

Penry nodded his assent, and there seemed to be no further need of speech between them. They remained silent for a time, gazing at each other with comprehension in their eyes. At length he murmured dreamily: 'Your love is wonderful strong, Megan. I do feel as 'twill go with me where I am goin' slippin' – away –' his voice became barely audible, 'away, into – I am not knowing what.'

She bent over him, but could not catch the last words formed by his lips. They had turned the colour of skimmed milk. Silence reigned. He seemed to have fallen asleep, but when she pressed closer to listen to his breathing she found that it had ceased.

She rose quietly and turned away from the bedside. She was not frightened, nor appalled by any tragic sense of loss, for she had suffered all the agonies of parting with him whilst he was yet alive. Rather, she was glad that she had come in time to say to him what she had said. 'He might never have known,' she thought; and then she added: 'but wherever his soul has gone, it must have known *there.*' To her the things of the spirit were stronger and more real than those of the flesh. Had she not proved it to be so?

In the chill of dawn, when she came out of the room where the dead man lay, she saw her husband seated at the head of the stairs with his head buried in his hands. He rose, shivering, as he heard her footsteps behind him, and turning, looked at her with mournful eyes.

'Forgive me,' he said, and suddenly kneeling down at her feet, he put the hem of her coarse skirt to his lips and kissed it reverently. She drew away with an exclamation of surprise and self-depreciation, and taking his hand in hers, raised him and led him downstairs. He wrapped his own coat round her shoulders and her shawl over her head before he took her home; but he did not speak of what had happened that night.

It lay like a mysterious gulf between them, which nothing could bridge. It had been, for him, a revelation of the inexplicable. A chasm had opened under his feet where had been the solid ground of his harsh and concise beliefs. Doubts of all sorts came thronging up from this abyss, doubts as to the finality of his theological creed, the justice of his denunciations, the infallibility of the Bible, or at least of his rendering of it. From that hour until the day of his death he was assailed by questions innumerable and unanswerable. He became daily more morose and absorbed in uncertainty, but gentle in his manner towards Megan, whom, in the light of the miracle, he had ceased to regard as his possession. He was no longer consumed by the flame of jealousy as when he had fancied her unfaithful; but he regarded her as irrevocably lost to him, a saintly being whom he had no right to touch, and for whose love he dared never hope, in this world or the next.

He died of pneumonia before the spring came. As Megan sat at his bedside, he gasped out: 'You are wiser than I am, *diar anwl*. I have been preaching to others about the will of the Lord; but you have kept silent and listened whilst God spoke to you.' 'No,' she said, 'I have only listened to my own heart.' 'Perhaps,' he murmured, 'God speaks to us through our hearts.' He lay still for a time, struggling for breath; his frail hands clenched, and a line between his brows. He was grappling with a difficult, new thought. At last he said: 'I don't know'; and later on he repeated very sadly: 'I don't know . . . after all –'

These were the last words spoken by the preacher who had gained so great a reputation for fiery eloquence and dogmatic fervour. The minister who preached his funeral oration had much to say on the tenacity of Rees Lloyd's faith, in an age of scepticism. 'He stood fast in the true faith,' cried the preacher, 'he was never, for a moment, troubled by doubts on religion, nor on the right conduct of life. He *knew* the right from the wrong. He never admitted that there could be more than one path, the old and narrow road, to Heaven.'

The black-clad crowd that had gathered from far and near to attend the funeral, nodded and murmured 'Amen'. Only one woman amongst them knew the torment of uncertainty through which Rees Lloyd's soul had passed before it left his body; and she was the wife whom for years he had hated for a sin of which she was not guilty. The tears ran down her face as she sat listening to the sermon; but not, as her neighbours fancied, because she had lost the husband whom she had betrayed. 'I was understandin' him, at the last,' she told me. 'And what you do understand you do forgive.'

Before the year was out she had lost Ifor also. 'When he comed to die, I was like a mad 'oman. Sittin' over the fire in my old home here, where I've been ever since, and rockin' myself back and fore, day and night; not able to eat, nor to sleep, nor even to cry for days together; but moanin' to myself and prayin' God in my heart to let me join him. The light was clean gone out o' my life with his honey-sweet hair and that laugh o' his, for all the 'orld like the laugh o' Penry. Father and mother they was takin' it to heart somethin' terrible. 'Ticing me to eat with this and that, and settin' the other children on my lap to try and make me pay heed to them; but nothin' 'ouldn't rouse me. Dyin' I should have been, for I hadn't no wish to go on livin', if they hadn't got me out one day into the sunlight.

'It was springtime, and everything was fresh, and newborn like. The hills was standin' there as calm and grand as ever; and it comed to me, all of a sudden, that we was like their shadows, as do pass to and fro across the Cwm, and are leavin' no trace of theirselves behind.'

I remember that the shadow of the western hill had almost touched our feet as she reached this point in her story. We were still bathed in the afternoon sunlight, Saint Anne and I, but the grass before us lay dark as emerald velvet in the shade.

'Yes,' I said, looking up in wonder at her tranquil old face, 'but did that make you want to go on living?' She shook her head. 'I did not *want* to live,' she said, 'but lookin' up at those ancient old hills, it seemed to me such a small little thing to live out my short span, patient like, to the end o' my days.'

Those words sent a chill through my being. I remember thinking how endlessly long were her seventy years of life. They do not appear to me so now.

'And then,' the sound of her soft Welsh voice broke the stillness, 'little Emrys, as is a grown man and farmin' here now, was fallin' down on the path by my feet, and cryin' something pitiful. I was pickin' him up, and comfortin' him. And after that I was goin' back to my work. There was four little uns to mind, and that kept me from thinkin' overmuch of the one I'd lost. Not that they was ever the same to me, as he'd been; but they had need o' me none the less.' After a pause, she added: 'They are married and with children o' their own now, all dark-eyed, same as poor Rees. Mother died soon after I was comin' back to live here, and I was lookin' after Father, as was gettin' simple. Then I was keepin' house for my eldest boy, after Father was taken too, until the lad was marryin'. Then again there was his children to see to. . . . Yes, yes, I've been busy with one thing and another. And now I'm gone old,' she said placidly, watching the shadow of the hills opposite steal across her feet, and creep inch by inch up her dress. 'I am sittin' here day after day, rememberin' all as is past. There is no trace of Penry, nor of little Ifor, they are gone – like shadows o' the hills.'

When I raised my eyes to hers again, the sunlight had disappeared from Cwmbach.

Saint Anne is gone now also. Last summer I tramped up the road that leads through the imprisoned valley. I found it unchanged. The great green hills stood sentinel on either side. There was the square grey chapel, and the caretaker's cottage, and Cwmbach farm, nestling in its hollow on the opposite side of the angry torrent. Nothing broke the well-known stillness but the sleepy trickling of many streams, that in winter are foaming spates, and the sound of my own footfall along the stony track. I came to the fold gate. There I disturbed a tribe of black-haired urchins, swarthy as Spaniards, who were playing upon the strip of sward on which Saint Anne used to set her chair. The sight of these children brought back my own girlhood, so that I called to them by name – 'Gladys, John Owen, Rees *bach*.' Then I saw that they were watching me with shy curiosity. After a moment they ran away and hid from the stranger.

As I trudged on towards the pass, the shade of the western hill stole across the road behind me, seeming to blot out all trace of my passage; and I remembered the words of the Psalmist that my father had taught me in the Book of Common Prayer: 'Man is like a thing of nought; his time passeth away like a shadow.'

XIV

The Poacher

EILUNED LEWIS

Mr Richard Woodly was a bachelor who flattered himself on never interfering in other people's affairs. Having inherited a pleasant estate in Wiltshire with enough money to carry out the improvements it needed, he was free to indulge his taste for gardening and ecclesiastical archaeology. There was not a church in the county on which he was not an authority, while his glowing herbaceous borders, expensively-run greenhouses and a new water-garden of his own planning, bore witness to a love of flowers.

Every spring or, to put it more precisely, between the time of the bulbs and the flowering shrubs, Mr Woodly would inform his housekeeper and his head gardener that he was going away for a few weeks. As a young man these journeys led him to Italy, Spain or Greece, but with the approach of middle-age, he found himself more and more affected by the beauty of an English landscape and inclined to remain at home.

One April, he had gone to stay in Gloucestershire, and on a certain fine, sunny morning he walked from his inn through the fields where the larks were singing, to visit a neighbouring church.

While he stood in the chancel examining the carved miserere seats of the choir stalls a conversation forced itself on his hearing through the open door of the vestry.

'Well I reckon we needn't trespass on your time any longer.' The man's voice was unmistakably American, and Mr Woodly, who didn't care for Americans, continued to give his attention to the choir stalls.

'It's very good of you to have taken so much trouble,' a woman's voice chimed in and was cut short by, 'Not at all! Not at all!' The words of the last speaker – full-throated, English and parsonic – boomed under the vaulted roof.

'I only wish I could throw some light on the subject. It's a most interesting story. As you see, there were Lovells in the parish as lately as ten years ago, but none, it seems, who fit into your tale. If ever I do discover anything . . .'

The speakers came out through the vestry door – a smartly dressed woman, holding a little girl by the hand, a tall man, wearing tortoiseshell spectacles, and the grey-haired vicar. As they passed down the aisle the child turned and looked at Mr Woodly, who was now studying an almost obliterated wall-painting of the Day of Judgment over the chancel arch. She had, he thought, an elfish face and remarkably large, dark eyes. For a minute or two he stood watching the little creature, with her thin legs and black curls, on her way from the dark church to the sunshine outside.

Perhaps it was the child who made him inclined to be more sociable than usual when the same family appeared at his inn that morning, driving up to the door in a large, closed car, just as Mr Woodly reached it by way of field paths.

In the coffee-room at lunch time they sat at an opposite table, and the child, restless and unwilling to eat, slipped down from her chair before the end of the meal to examine a stuffed fox in a glass case at one end of the room.

She slid past Mr Woodly with a quick grace of movement, and suddenly he wanted to speak to her.

'He looks a wily old fox, don't you think?'

There now! He had startled her. For a fraction of a second

the child hesitated, her dark brown eyes fixed on Mr Woodly; then she fled back to her parents. They were apologizing to him now, with little smiles and gestures. Later, the man strolled over to where Mr Woodly was sitting and introduced himself.

'I'm Ernest P. Wilbur,' he announced. 'Didn't we see you in that li'l old church this morning? I wonder now, could you tell me the exact age of all these churches round here?'

He had come to the right authority in Mr Woodly.

'I guess you know a lot about ancient monuments,' said Ernest P. Wilbur, when Mr Woodly had finished his short history of the Cotswold churches, followed by a few scholarly remarks on the Norman, Transitional and Perpendicular styles of architecture.

'And ancient families, too, I dare say. May I ask you if this is your part of the country? No? Well, then I reckon you won't be able to help me over a problem I've been trying to figure out lately. It's about our li'l girl here.'

Mr Woodly expressed well-bred surprise, adding that he had never seen a more attractive child.

'Yes, sir!' agreed Mr Wilbur proudly. 'In another few years she'll be doing some damage with those eyes of hers, but she didn't get them from either Mrs Wilbur or me.' The big American paused to fill his pipe and with another glance at the quiet face of the Englishman opposite him, leant back in his chair.

'If I may, I'll tell you the story. My wife and I lost our own li'l girl when she was a baby.' He was silent for a moment, trying, it seemed, to get his pipe to draw. Then he went on.

'I thought Mrs Wilbur would never leave off fretting, but after a time we went up into Canada for a change, for she'd been very ill, and in the shack next to where we were staying for the fishing, there was a German family – just poor emigrants, with a whole heap of children. The youngest of the lot was a baby a few months old. The mother was an English-woman who had come there one night and died in giving birth to the child, and the German woman had taken it in and brought it up along with her own children, though she didn't know anything about its history. She told us that the mother was a delicate, soft-spoken lady, and she was so darned sorry for her that she promised to look after the child though there was no money and she had six of her own.'

'And her father?' asked Mr Woodly.

'No, sir. She couldn't find out anything about her father – only that his name was Lovell. I guess he'd gone off with another dame. Well, I expect you've seen the end of my story. I saw it myself after a few days. Mrs Wilbur was only happy when she was looking after that child. It just seemed as though we'd been sent straight to care for her, and she's been like our own daughter ever since, or pretty near. Not just exactly the same perhaps, but there are some things you can't have over again.'

'It's a strange story,' said Mr Woodly. He was more interested than he would have thought possible by the confidence of this complete stranger. So this dark-eyed changeling did not belong to the American couple. She was the child of English parents, of some runaway couple perhaps.

'You said the name was Lovell?'

'Yeah! And I can't discover a darn thing about the family. It sounds a kind of aristocratic name to me, and there's nothing about that child that would make you think it wasn't. She's sensitive – and wild. I guess there was something dare-devil about those Lovells. All this time I've been waiting for a chance to come to England and find things out for myself. I thought it would be easy but it seems it's like searching for . . .'

'What led you to think of this place?' asked Mr Woodly.

'A man on the ship coming over said he'd known of some

Lovells in this part of Gloucestershire, and I found the name in the parish register where you saw us this morning; but that dug-out old parson had never heard of any of 'em going to America.'

'Well, I wish you luck,' said Mr Woodly. 'But I shouldn't be too keen on finding the family. They might want to keep her, you know.'

Next morning the Wilburs left. Over his kidney and bacon Mr Woodly saw the car drive up to the door and Ernest P. Wilbur – very large in his overcoat – distribute tips to the boots, the chambermaid and the red-cheeked waitress. Mr Woodly found himself watching their departure with interest, hoping at the last that the brown-eyed child would turn her head in his direction.

'If they do find her relations,' he remarked to himself, 'I hope for Ernest P. Wilbur's sake they'll be aristocratic.' And, smiling gently, Mr Woodly helped himself to the marmalade.

I have said that Mr Woodly prided himself upon not interfering in other people's affairs. The sentimental quest of Ernest P. Wilbur slipped into a pigeon-hole of his mind; it was of considerably less importance than the stone effigies and fourteenth-century wall paintings in the Gloucestershire churches, and the flowering of his azaleas next month.

The summer that followed was fine and Mr Woodly's herbaceous borders had never looked better. But, by the time the October sunshine was slanting through his beech woods, he had grown restive. This time he chose to visit the Welsh Marches, where an Archaeological Society claimed to have laid bare fresh Roman remains.

Sending his luggage on ahead, Mr Woodly left the train at a border station and walked a dozen miles across the hills. The rich colours of October surrounded him: the scarlet berries of the mountain ash, the tips of the bilberry leaves and the rust-coloured bracken at his feet. There was autumn, too, in the sunset which flamed before him beyond the rugged country cut by innumerable dingles and the dark hills rising one behind the other. The blue smoke of the 'Pencader Arms' rising from the valley was a welcome sight to Mr Woodly as he scrambled down the last hillside and over a stile into a muddy lane.

Mrs Evans, the landlady, received him with the natural courtesy of her race. She was a woman of forty, with dark eyes, a slightly aquiline nose and a soft Welsh voice. The 'Pencader Arms' was a hostelry noted in the district for the comfort of its beds, the superiority of its fishing and the excellence of its bacon and eggs. Mr Woodly found that he was the sole guest, with ample opportunity of relishing Mrs Evans's conversation as well as her cooking.

Next morning the weather broke. Mr Woodly decided that it was too wet to visit the Roman camp with enjoyment, and found his way instead to the village of Aberdulas, where he purchased tobacco at the general store and examined the church with its square wooden tower and sixteenth-century rood screen.

Mrs Evans was distressed at his reappearance.

'Well, well, there's wet you are!' she exclaimed. Then calling to the little maid: 'Quick, Polly, take Mr Woodly's coat. Better take off your boots at once. Sit you down there and ketch into your dinner. I'll make you a nice cup of hot tea.'

The inn parlour where Mr Woodly spent the afternoon was a long, low room where the scent of wood smoke and beeswax mingled with the penetrating flavour of dry rot. Past the distorted glass of the window panes the leaves of the yellowing damson trees whirled by in gusts of rain. Mr Woodly settled himself by the fire with a book on Celtic civilization, but found his attention straying to the rugs which covered the floor round his feet.

They were, it appeared, all that was left of Mrs Evans's late domestic pets. Across the middle of the floor caracoled a white pony skin; near the door lay the fleecy coat of a pet lamb; and something that looked very like a sheepdog crouched at the foot of the tall-boy. From the opposite wall a squirrel in a glass case regarded him with a glassy eye, and a stuffed white ferret bared its teeth in a snarl. At the end of an hour Mr Woodly was in a state of fidgets, and decided to see how the weather looked from the front door.

The bar of the 'Pencader Arms' was far more cheerful than the parlour and Mrs Evans herself, knitting by the fire, was a pleasant sight. She welcomed him to the seat opposite – 'though indeed that old settle isn't very comfortable'.

It was distinctly better than the parlour and the company of the dead, Mr Woodly reflected, crossing his legs before the comfortable blaze, and then the outer door was suddenly and violently opened, and a gust of cold wind and wet whirling leaves blew into the room as a man stepped in.

'If you're coming in, Ned, shut that door behind you,' called out Mrs Evans, with a sharper tone than Mr Woodly had heard her use before. The intruder turned and closed the door, then faced the room, pulling off his hat that was black with rain, and raising a finger to his forehead in salutation. He had the brown eyes, set rather close together, of a gipsy and a quick smile, though his teeth were dark with decay.

'Good day, marm! Good day to you, sir! I've brought you a chub, Mrs Evans fach, caught in the Dulas this morning. Look at the lovely creature.'

He opened his basket and laid a slippery fish on the table where it lay catching the firelight on its steely scales.

'Maybe you'll be coming out one of these days, sir,' the fisherman leaned across the table and smiled at Mr Woodly. 'There's not much in a chub, now, once you've caught it. They're rubbishy fish to be eating – no offence to you, Mrs

Evans – but pretty enough to catch if you've the mind and the wrist that way. Now, if you was to be here when the salmon is up . . .'

'Dear to goodness, Ned,' cried Mrs Evans. 'D'ye think the gentleman has nothing to think of but your old fishing?'

'Not when you're around, marm, I dare say he hasn't,' said Ned with a sly look and a wink at Mr Woodly.

'There's foolish you talk!' remarked Mrs Evans and stepped from the room.

Ned meanwhile had removed his wet boots and padded across the floor in his socks. His lean, wiry frame was clad in the wreck of a tweed jacket and a much-patched pair of corduroy trousers; the red handkerchief at his throat suited his gipsy face. Leaning against the chimney-piece, he pulled out a pipe and set to filling it, one eye cocked in Mr Woodly's direction.

'You've not been to Aberdulas before, have you, sir?'

'No, this is my first visit. It's a pretty country, this of yours.'

'Beautiful, sir. Nothing like these old hills.' The pipe was alight now and giving out a strong smell of rank tobacco.

'I've travelled a bit,' he went on, 'and I've never seen anything to touch them. No, not even the Rocky Mountains, though they're grand enough in their way.'

'Ah, so you've been to America, have you?'

'Canada, it was, sir. Been all over it. I have seen the Falls of Niagara and the Prairies and the Great Lakes – big as the sea. We travelled across them for days – me and my lady wife.'

The outer door opened once more and two farmers stepped in. They were on their way home from market and at sight of Ned their joy was evident.

'How are you, man?' cried one, a red-faced young fellow. 'Get out, dog!' he added, aiming a kick at a nimble little collie that had followed him in; then, nodding to Mr Woodly, he called for drinks in which Ned was invited to join.

The second farmer, an older man with a sallow skin and a cast in one eye, emptied the rain water out of his hat with deliberation, and leaned on the bar. His eye rested on the chub.

'Thee's been up to thy old games again,' he said slyly. 'Where d'ee find that fellow, Ned?'

Ned jerked his thumb behind him and winked.

'Diawl, man,' cried the young fellow, 'tell us about the trout you caught in the brook and old Squire Lloyd watching 'ee through a little small hole in the bank.'

There was a roar of laughter at this sally. Mr Woodly, beginning to think more kindly of his book and the silence of solitude, walked from the room and back to the parlour.

In the gathering dark he read a chapter and rang for a light. Mrs Evans herself brought in the lamp.

'I hope, sir,' she said, placing it on the table, 'that you haven't been disturbed by any noise.' Mr Woodly assured her that he had not.

'Well, I'm glad of that. It's that Ned Lovell again. A glass goes straight to his head and William Jones Pentre is leading him on, as though he wasn't wild enough already.'

'He's an attractive looking rascal,' said Mr Woodly. 'Rather gipsy-looking, perhaps.'

'Half gipsy he is,' replied Mrs Evans, adding: 'Lovell's a gipsy name in these parts.'

At the sound of the name something stirred in Mr Woodly's memory and he asked sharply: 'What was that he said about a visit to Canada and his lady wife?'

'Did he tell you that?' Mrs Evans was startled. 'Why that was poor Miss Frances Lloyd who ran away with him.'

Mr Woodly closed his book firmly. 'I'd be very much obliged to you if you'd tell the story,' he said. 'I have a particular reason for wanting to hear it, as a matter of fact.'

'It's queer you should ask, for I'm the one that can tell you best. I was housekeeper to Jasper Lloyd at Pencader.'

'And these Lloyds,' asked Mr Woodly, 'what were they like?'

Mrs Evans drew a chair up to the table and examined the wick of the lamp.

'They were all of them a bit queer, as you might say, but Jasper Lloyd was the meanest and worst of the lot. Everyone was sorry for his wife, poor lady, but she died when Miss Frances was a little thing. It was a strange house for a child to grow up in. I lived there for three years as housekeeper and I never could abide the place, with the trees crowding close all round and the plaster peeling off the walls. The river runs through the garden, so near that it's no use at all calling to anyone at the farther end; your voice is lost in the rushing of the water over the stones. And at night the noise of it seemed to get into the house. I'd often lie awake listening to it and not able to sleep.

'Old Mrs Lloyd, Jasper's mother, was still living there. She'd been a beauty in her time, but her poor old brain had run all to seed till she forgot the faces of her own family. She'd a liking for raw eggs – "to clear her throat," she used to say. She would steal about the outhouses looking for them and hoard them all about the place in chests and old cupboards.

'Then there was Miss Hetty, Jasper's sister. She's never been right in the head, poor thing, thinking she was still seventeen and always talking of going to her first ball. She'd spend hours of the day at a big old chest up in the attic trying on her grandmother's frocks.

'The Lloyds had been big people in the old days, and there'd been fine goings-on. Old Jasper's father always kept good horses and was fond of driving tandem.

'There were a lot of old dresses up in that cupboard, and Miss Hetty would pull them out and sweep up and down in them – all rustling bombazine and satin, though she was a little bit of a thing. I remember a stiff yellow silk with a sprig on it, and a claret silk shawl with a long fringe, and little old high-heeled satin slippers and a brown parasol with a jointed handle.

'Poor creature, it did her no harm! But Miss Frances, she couldn't abide to see her aunt bedizened in that way. She'd lock the cupboard and hide the key till Miss Hetty would come whimpering to her for it.

'All the rest of the day Miss Hetty would sit curled in front of the fire. She'd a way of covering her face with her hands when she was talking, and then peeping at you between her fingers. She wore a heap of bangles, and if ever it happened that someone came to call – which wasn't often – Miss Hetty would skip upstairs and put on a locket or a bit of lace at her throat, and then she'd trip into the drawing-room, seemingly astonished to find anyone there.

'As for old Jasper, he was the worst landlord in the county, letting his farms fall down before he'd do any repairs, so much as mend a gate or put a slate on a roof. He used to drive about in a high, rickety dog-cart, and all through the winter he hunted once or twice a week on a big old chestnut horse.

'Miss Frances didn't care for hunting – which was just as well, for her father would never have spent the money on her. He didn't part with a penny more than he could help; wore a greasy old green coat and wouldn't buy any new top-boots. His own were so tight that old Sam, the coachman, had a job to pull them off every hunting day; the Squire's language was something shocking.

'Maybe you're wondering what Ned Lovell had to do with all this. Well, every now and then he'd come round to the back door with his fishing tackle and ask if missie (as he called Miss Frances) would like to come out with him. The fish would be rising nicely, he'd say, and he'd seen a big trout as he passed the pool.

'Ned was half gipsy, and he was a young fellow in those days with brown eyes and a way of smiling. He walked loose and springy, like a collie dog.

'He was the best fisherman in these parts and he taught Miss Frances to cast a fly. She'd be out with him for hours and come back wet through, as often as not, and with a spot of colour in her cheeks. "Look what Ned and I have caught for you, Mrs Evans," she'd say, coming in with a basket of fish.

'I blame myself that I didn't suspect anything in those days, but somehow I never did, for Miss Frances had a haughty way with her.

'Yet there was no one else to look after the child, Miss Hetty being so foolish and old Mrs Lloyd getting queerer every day. Why, one evening at dinner she looks down the table at the Squire and says sudden-like: "I seem to know your face. Tell me, who was your father?"

'Old Jasper gives a nasty sort of laugh: "Well, mother," he says, "if you can't tell me, I don't know who can!"

'Miss Frances turned very red, but Miss Hetty goes on counting her cherry stones: "This year, next year, sometime . . ."

'I went away about that time to take over the inn here for my brother and his children, and glad I was to leave that daft house.

'It seems that soon after – one warm evening in May when the fish were rising nicely – Ned Lovell comes to the door. "I've come to catch a trout," says he. "A pretty silver one." (He was always poetical in his way of talking.) "Will you tell Miss Frances I've gone to the river?"

'The servant girl takes the message to Miss Frances.

'"Thank you, Clara," says she, very quiet. And that's the last time she was ever seen or heard of in that house. She and Ned Lovell slipped off together that evening and he must have led her a feckless life, for he was no mate for the likes of her. They went to America, and it seems she died when a child was born, but no one ever knew where or how they lived.

'As for Ned Lovell, he came drifting back in four or five years. He was never any use for anything but fishing and drinking, and it's when he's had a glass too much that he'll tell you of his lady wife.

'And now, sir,' finished Mrs Evans, 'you'll be wanting your supper. It's late, but you've let me run on so.'

Mr Woodly stood for some time, looking into the fire. He was thinking of the dark eyes of a little ten-year-old girl, and of a cheerful American voice that said: 'I haven't discovered a darn thing about the family, but it sounds to me an aristocratic kind of a name.'

XV

Davis

SIÂN EVANS

Fred Davis opened the back door and spat on the manure heap thrown up against the kitchen wall.

'It's no use following me about,' he called into the hollow of the passage. 'Nagging night and day, it ain't my fault, damn you.'

He sighed heavily; his fat, sullen face sagged over a dirty, white rag tied round his throat in lieu of a collar, his hands picked at the edges of his pockets; his hair, yellow and plentiful, hung in tags over a flat red brow.

A shrill voice answered like an echo. 'That's what you always say, you're lazy *and* you know it. Just look at the garden.'

Voice and wife approached through the shadows; a woman thrust her face over the man's shoulder, at the same time pointing with a bony arm so that the fingers only appeared round the lintel of the door.

'Call that a garden, look at that hedge, I'd be ashamed to see my wife doing all the work.'

Davis shook himself and turning round, muttered an oath.

'You clear off, leave me alone, can't you?'

His wife now stood on the weedy path from which vantage point she poured forth a string of invective and abuse.

'What's happening to us? Bills, no money, no beasts, the place rotting over our heads. Oh you lazy pig, I wish to God

I'd never married you. Too idle to mend the hedge or move the horse manure from off the path. God, the place is worse than a slum and *yet* you won't do anything. I can't even find any vegetables to cook but have to buy what I want. Look at all this garden, wasted, while you lean about all day. It makes me sick. I'm through.'

Her voice rose to a shriek, cracked and was silent.

Davis started to shamble off towards the pigsties, standing at the far end of the path.

'You drive me crazy,' he mumbled. 'My life's hell.'

His wife tore at her hair as though with one frantic gesture to release all her bitterness.

'Hell, that's your destination all right, this ain't a patch on what God'll make you suffer in the world to come.'

She turned and disappeared into the house, slamming the, door behind her. Davis leaned on the pigsty wall.

He noticed the cracks in the bricks and how the rotten gate swung from one hinge only.

Moss grew like slime on the walls, the roof leaked, stale pig manure and straw sprouting grass littered the floor.

Again he sighed and the sound seemed ominous as though by his own breath he stood accused.

God, he was tired. Couldn't she see what an added burden it was to think?

Of course she could, the bitch, that's why she kept goading him. Facing him with his demon till his hands were at his own throat.

He groaned; only with an effort could he bring himself to look at the house.

What had happened? The place was going to ruin.

He remembered how it had looked before his father, old Davis, died. White walls, clean paint, plants in the windows, thick doors fitting without the tremor of a draught, flower-beds under the windows, vegetables in neatly dug patches, pigsties with proper roofs.

The yard, too, looked different, in those days a gate divided the cowsheds, stable and ricks from the open patch in front of the house; now yard and garden mingled in a puddly mess of straw, rotten stumps of cabbage and manure.

It had been a prosperous enough place.

Well, something had happened, that was all. A gradual decay.

The garden full of weeds, that large hole in the hedge that made his wife so angry, the patch of horse manure in the middle of the path left when the horse broke in and finished the last of the vegetables, the cracking doors tied together with string.

The yard, unkempt as the garden, standing deserted save for a scraggy horse pulling out tufts of hay from the two remaining ricks, hens scratching in the flower-beds, turning over old tins, cans and putrid scraps.

Yes, something had happened.

Davis made up his mind to remove the horse manure so that his wife shouldn't see it and scream at him every time she came to the door. He pulled out a cigarette and while he stood smoking watched the sun disappear beneath the rim of the fields.

Another day gone, too late to do anything now. To-morrow he'd tidy up the place and mend the hedge.

For a moment his heart seemed to lift in his side, his mind sprang lightly towards the future.

He'd get everything straight, he'd start work seriously.

Again his wife appeared at the door; a lighted candle burned in the passage throwing a beam that revealed her shape and her thin, attenuated arms waving like feelers towards the yard.

'Really!' she screamed, emphasizing each word with a fresh gesture. 'Can't you see that horse eating its head off in the yard? Anyone would think we'd got a dozen ricks to waste. Why don't you put it in the stable or shut it in the field? You've been standing out there for nearly an hour. I warn you, I've had about enough.'

Davis looked at her, at her small body that even when still appeared possessed by a demon of energy, at her hands rapidly unwrapping a scrap of bandage from round her wrist and her face moving round words that poured from her lips in an endless stream.

'Why can't you do your share? Are you ill or what? You don't care about anything, no pride . . . no nothing.'

He bellowed suddenly in a voice choking with anger. 'It's your bloody tongue, you take the relish out of anything, work or pleasure. I'm going out, you've driven me out. You do everything yourself then you can't complain, you always know best, nothing I do's right, you make a man mad.' He turned his back on her, setting off towards the road in a great hurry. His blood beat in his temples like pistons, he clutched at his chest uneasily. All this noise and excitement day in, day out, supposing he had a heart attack?

The thought made him feel sickish. When he had turned a corner in the lane he sat down on the road-side and held his head in his hands. No man could stand it.

A great depression fell on him. He kept asking himself questions although the answers tormented him.

'What shall I do?'

'Work,' came the reply like a stone hurled at his head.

'What's the use?'

'Do you want to die then?'

'No by God!'

'If everything rots over your head how will you live?'

'I don't know, something'll happen.'

'No it won't.'

He began to groan and mumble out loud.

'Things aren't so bad, I'll soon pull them round. I've seen many worse places about.'

Then he heard his wife's voice: 'You're lazy . . . bone lazy.'

He jumped to his feet. 'That's a lie, a damned lie. Nobody but a bitch would say a thing like that.'

He stopped shouting as suddenly as he had commenced.

It was nearly dark, a light mist covered the surrounding fields, standing back the hills were black against a thickening sky. It looked like rain.

Davis turned and stared at the bank where he had been sitting. A distinct patch where the grass lay flattened revealed the spot.

He looked at it with surprise. 'I'm going dotty, anyone would think I'd been drinking . . .'

He walked about for some time unable to make up his mind to go down to 'The Angel' for a pint. At last he made for home.

He remembered angrily that he had forgotten to milk the cows.

Never mind, it wouldn't be the first time, they'd have to wait a bit.

When he reached home his wife was washing the milking pails in the back kitchen.

He poked his head round the door but she kept her head obstinately turned from him. Her tightly compressed lips showed that her silence was the silence of anger and contempt.

He returned to the kitchen and sat warming his feet by the fire. Presently he slept.

His wife woke him. 'Your supper's ready.'

It was late, nearly nine o'clock; he sat up with a start.

'All right, you needn't pretend to be surprised it's so late. You needn't say: "Why didn't you remind me about the cows", because you knew all along I'd do it like I always do.'

The woman set his plate down as she spoke. There were two red spots burning in her cheeks.

She polished the forks on a cloth and then they started to eat. Neither spoke. While she was making the tea Davis watched his wife sulkily, pulling at his hair with his hands and watching her every movement through half-closed eyes.

As soon as the meal was over she hurried out to the sink and started to wash up.

That night Davis couldn't sleep but lay on his back staring at the chink of light showing through the bedroom window.

Outside he could hear the rustle of rain mixed with the lifting and falling of branches blowing in the wind.

If only with one sweep of his hand he could put everything right, if only from nothing wealth rose up like a thing solid to the touch, a thing one could snatch without effort and keep locked behind doors while one slept, ate, idled . . .

His thoughts drifted; he stirred and looked at his wife lying straight and stark beside him; the pallor of her face divided her from the surrounding gloom, her dark hair, braided in two plaits hung outside the bedclothes.

He felt a dim desire, which, as his thoughts lingered grew in urgency; he leaned over and touched her with his hands. 'Mary, let's be friends for God's sake.'

As though through her sleep she had realized his passion, she at once drew away and answered harshly: 'It's useless, quite useless, we can't go on like this.'

He seized her arm and ran his fingers up to her bare shoulders; he could feel the blood beating slowly under his touch. There was a clanging in his veins, all his senses seemed gathering for a final revelation; everything was hastening, hastening . . .

He muttered thickly. 'I'm sorry, Mary, don't be hard; I've thought it all out how I'll start to-morrow; I'll mend the hedge, tidy the garden, in a week I'll get the place straight, honest to God I will.'

His hands enclosed her breast, dimly he heard her cry. 'It's no good . . . no good.'

The lace curtains rustled, swept the fringe of the bed then lay with a shudder, flat against the window.

Davis swore slowly, half asleep. 'I swear it, just you see in the morning.'

His wife answered with a kind of wild intensity. 'I don't mean to be hard. I try to believe in you but you make me so bitter.'

Her voice broke; Davis fell asleep to the sound of her crying.

He awoke and at once he was depressed.

Daylight filtered through the window, it fell on the bed, wide, flat and tousled, on the white counter-pane dipping to the floor, on peeling wallpaper and the washbasin half full of dirty water, standing in the far corner of the room.

He yawned and closed his eyes. Why did the days come on him like a burden?

Downstairs he could hear his wife lighting the fire.

What had he said last night? Something about lighting the fire himself. Well, anyway it was too late now.

With a groan he remembered other promises. He closed his eyes; the warmth in the bed was like the heat from burning logs.

He heard his wife calling out that breakfast was ready. He must have slept again. He turned the clock with its face to the wall and again shut his eyes. His limbs felt like logs.

Drowsily he heard the cows passing under the window on their way to the cowsheds, their feet splashed in the mud, splash, splash, splash.

'Another minute,' he started to count slowly. Nearly sixty. What a fool he was to set a limit on time.

Rain ran down the windows and danced in bubbles on the aerial. One, two, three, no man could work in such weather.

Words ran in fragments to the tune of falling rain, they passed through his head and the pulsing of his blood set a rhythm to utterance. 'Lazy, bone lazy, one, two, three. What were words?'

He buried his face deeper into the pillows. Once more he slept.

XVI

The Pattern

RHIAN ROBERTS

The barefooted boy padded along the warm pavement of the main street. He was carrying his shoes under his arm, pretending he was on the seashore at Barry Island, feeling good inside, his lips stained blue from the blackcurrants he had been eating. He had wanted to walk the length of the street, from the Calvinistic Methodist Chapel at the top to the dance hall at the bottom, just for fun, but he saw the Bracchi shop halfway and halted. His mouth watered. Ice-cream, fruit drinks, fudge, chocolates, buns and meat paste sandwiches. Now he crossed the street, eyes intent on the men licking the creamy ice-cream from the golden brown cones at the edge of the mid-street crossing.

Two cars were tangled up among the cows ambling back from the village farm to their field on Penmynach hill, tails swishing lazily in the warm afternoon. The cars honked horns impatiently but old Bob did not hurry himself nor his cattle. Spat on the ground, shrugged his shoulders, that was all. Some people laughed and the ones who didn't stared at Gwil, their eyes straying to his bare feet. Everyone knew who he was – Gwil Rees son of Ted Rees, the overman, who lived in the New Houses. That's who he was. No-one had seen him walking barefooted down the main street before. Gave them a bit of a surprise, no doubt.

'Oany blackies do that Gwil,' said Mrs Price, eyes big and yellow like a sheep's, 'not nice little boys.'

'Growing up now. Can't do that any more now, you know, bach.'

'What will yore mother say if she sees you, Gwilym Rees?'

'Oany William St. boys do tha Gwil.'

'Better put yore shoes on or get a thorn in them you will.'

'Naughty boy. Get your feet dirty.'

Duw! It made him feel fed up, all this scolding and fussing. It was the same at home. Couldn't take a step outside the house without someone setting about him, couldn't take a step inside the house without Mam lecturing him, correcting his manners.

People in tight shiny shoes looked at him, whispered 'Oany a boy. What can you expect.'

He was puzzled. There was something inside him urging him on, something else holding him back and saying it was wrong, silly, not respectable. Why couldn't he? He'd wanted to do it, to get those hot swollen feet out of the uncomfortable shoes. Willie often did it and no-one scolded him. No-one said 'Don't do it!' Only to Gwil. Getting himself dirty, someone would say 'For shame Gwil' and then laughing at funny people, Mam would say 'Ssh! That isn't polite!' Willie laughed. His mother didn't say 'Ssh!' She laughed too. Mam wanted him to be nice. What was nice? Willie with his grubby face and raggedy clothes was nice. Mr Thomas Schoolmaster, always clean, with his washed face, smart smooth suit and black shoes with the pointed toes wasn't nice. Why?

Now he passed the men outside the shop. Twm Jones of the white muffler trod on his toes purposely with his heavy mining boots and made him jump. The men laughed.

'Look, Joe,' one of them said to Mr Bracchi, 'there's a barefooted beggar boy. Son of Ted Rees too. 'Ave an 'art. Give 'im an 'aypny.' Mr Bracchi bent over the counter, smiled, patted Gwil's head. Then turned, squeezed a big blob of ice-cream into a cone, gave it to the boy.

'Like Angelo,' he said, 'he was barefooted.' No-one asked him who Angelo was. The men began to talk about the pit, and about somebody called Dan Hughes. Gwil had seen him once or twice, this man they mentioned. He was a grand big man. 'Damn Dan Hughes.' 'No guts! – Dirty swine!' Voices became rougher, cursed. All except Mr Bracchi's. He was speaking softly to Gwil, his bald head shining like Mam's copper in the cool shadows of the shop.

Everyone like Mr Bracchi, even the Chapel deacons when it wasn't Sunday. But it seemed to Gwil grown-ups didn't listen much. Always told him their troubles, never bothering about his; always came to him for sympathy and advice, afterwards never gave him a thought. Children listened though. Gwil did, laughed at his quiet teasing, thrilled to the exciting stories he told. Gwil liked him. He didn't say, 'Don't do this! Don't do that!' He was different somehow. Why! Once he'd let Gwil work the pop machine, get the lemonade to swoosh and hiss into the glasses. 'When I grow up,' Gwil said, 'I'll have a shop with a machine like tha'.' How he loved the fizzing and frothing of the pop, the way it bubbled and stung the throat and the cool fresh dairy smell of the shop. Yes indeed, when he grew up he must have a place like this, for somehow here he was away from it all, the worrying nag-nag-nag, the boring daily routine, the practised lines that had now become automatic 'Speak when yore spoaken to! Wash yore hands! Were you a good boy in school today?' Mam, sitting stiffly, speaking stiffly, worrying about all manner of things, large and small and middlesized, a broken saucer, a new dress, his manners. Here he was away from the carefulness, the cautiousness, could be as carefree as a William St. boy.

He remembered Mr Bracchi once telling him about the time he was a boy in that far away land he was always talking about and how he would creep out at night to mountain slopes and play with his friends in the moonlight. And so, remembering this, Gwil had done the same, slipped out of the house at night and played by himself among the small skinny firs in Penmynach wood, wondering at the same time whether he was doing right, knowing when Dad – hardfaced and tightlipped – had found him there, that it was wrong.

The world was all wrongs for some people; nothing ever seemed to be right. Doing the things he wanted to do, he was wrong; doing the things he didn't want to do he was right. It appeared to him that just because he was from the New Houses on Pentwyn hill he couldn't act like any other boy.

Micah Twp, slobbering mouth, shaggy like an old sheep-dog came into the shop, roused Gwil from his thoughts by asking for an ice-cream, stuttering helplessly. The men laughed, cruel laughter that was becoming less puzzling to Gwil's ears as the years passed. Like his laughing at funny people, he supposed, but much nastier. Gwil's cheeks reddened as he heard the old man guzzling the ice-cream, the men laughing louder. He put on his shoes, laced them and left the shop. Running away from things he didn't like, not meeting them, laughing at them, encouraging them like the men in the shop.

'Where have you been?' asked Mam, neat as a pin.

'Bracchi shop!' he replied.

'Spendin' yore money on ice-cream again?'

'Never mind!' said Dad, 'He could be in worse places. Bracchi's a good man, kind to children.'

'All the same,' Mam retorted, 'he keeps his shop open on Sundays; that isn't decent.'

'That's because he's Italian!' Dad said.

'I doan care, I doan hoald with it and I doan think Gwil'd better goa there soa often. Why! The next thing we'll noa, he'll be going on Sundays, buying sweets and ice-cream on the Sabbath like common children. You noa, thoas William St. children who never goa to Chapel at all or Bible class as if they never been christened. I doan want our Gwil to be like tha.'

'Aye,' said Dad looking at his newspaper, 'News looks bad thoa. Wass going to happen I wonder?'

'Yore getting wasteful,' she said to the boy. 'Now what about saving moa money! You've got a money box from Auntie Tillie. You do a bit more saving my lad, or I woan give you yore pocket money to buy sweets with all the time. Save up for a rainy day. Thass what I say. Not that I'm saying Mr Bracchi is a bad man. Far be it from Catrin Rees to run anyone down or say a bad word against even her enemies, but thoa Mr Bracchi is a good man and better than moast in the village, I can tell you, he's a Catholic and thoas Catholics do awful things sometimes.'

Gwil didn't know what a Catholic was but he guessed it wasn't too good the way people talked about it. Yet Mam praised Mr Bracchi. It didn't add up. Seemed as he grew older the world became more bewildering, full of strange worlds like Catholics, Italians, mining agents, good, bad, right, wrong.

'I can't understand,' said Mam, 'really I can't. It seems that the children nowadays are getting too easy a time. It wasn't like this when I was a girl. Oh, noa. If we didn't do just as Taid and Mamgu said, we'd be whipped with the Jenny Fedw and sent to bed. See how good we are to you, althoa you try our patience sometimes with yore daft cammocks. Wasn' like this when we were children was it, Ted?'

'Noa,' said Dad.

'Dearie me, noa! What a silly boy you are indeed! Dad and me here savin' to make somethin' out of you, a doctor, a preacher or somethin' and there you are spending money as fast as we can make it on rubbishy stuff tha' doan do you any good!' Gwil half listening to her words watched Dad's face, the bushy eyebrows drawn low over the eyes, the long jaw hard. 'Oh dear!' Mam paused, then was off again like a steam engine, over and over the same words, weaving the same pattern, padding a little here and there, emphasising her point by slapping her lap occasionally. Fuss, fuss, fuss. Gwil's eyes strayed from his father's face to the window, the hills like fat men sleeping. Now with every word of Mam's a shadow appeared, lengthened at a breath, drew closer.

'Night's comin',' said Dad, 'Nothin' new, there's always night. Look at the darkness of men's thoughts, the depth of their sins. Take these damn dictators now . . .'

Gwil listened without understanding. A whirl of words, all senseless, meaningless. Wish he could be out now with Willie, chasing Mog Parry along the streets. That day they'd pushed him on the slag on the Level, he'd never forget that. Mog poking his tongue out at them, at the next moment sobbing his heart out, his posh suit dirty, his face smudged. That was a sight for sore eyes. Then Joe Bracchi, on his way back home from a walk had come into sight.

'What you done, eh? Two boys setting on one, like two big hounds after a rabbit eh?'

And they had laughed thinking he had intended it as a joke because he was smiling. But then, he was always smiling. He was smiling when he made them give a penny each to Mog Parry but they were not. Mog stopped crying like magic, forgot the mess on his new suit, clutched his pennies tightly, ran to the nearest sweet shop to buy some bulls' eyes . . .

'Dan Hughes an' clique here, they're dictators. Black as night is that two faced potbelly, black as Satan's night. Do him good to get down on his knees and work for a bit instead of orderin' us about like a lot of cattle.'

Dad was talking now, Mam quietly knitting. Like taking

turns at a game. Some people said Dad was wise, some said he was crazy, some said all he could do was beat the air. But all said he was a man of his word, never let you down. Only another man like him in the village, they said, and that was Bracchi. Ted Rees gives you the headache, Joe gives you the aspirin, but both of them are men of their word.

Thinking back, Gwil remembered how the joke about Joe Bracchi had evolved, how he used to dose himself with aspirins, wash them down with pop when he saw blood. He couldn't stand the sight of blood. It made him all sick inside. There had been the day when Sammy the Farm had cut his head against the dance hall railings and was brought into the shop. Purposely, of course, people had said, just to make Joe's stomach turn. The shopkeeper's face had changed colour, his hands had trembled, and they had laughed. Even Sammy the Farm laughed and called him a 'yellowbelly'. Good old Joe! Harmless as a pullet, they scoffed. He'd faint in a fight, scream at a mouse, run away from a sheep. What a man! 'Have you learnt your verse for Sunday school?' asked Mam.

No, he hadn't. He had clean forgotten. He fidgeted and Mam frowned. She took the Bible down from the shelf, wetted her thumb, turned the pages, found a long verse for him to learn for Sunday.

That Sunday everyone was talking about war.

'We must pray now,' Mam said, looking very pious with her hands folded in her lap, 'then the war may be over in a few weeks.'

Praying devotedly in Seiats and Prayer Meetings, eyes closed, hands clenched together, Mam thought the war would end soon. So did Gwil until Dad said it would last for a few years.

'Seen it cropping up,' said Dad, 'Seen it as plain as the fingers on my hand.' Gwil was proud of his father's wisdom, told Willie about it. 'Pah!' Willie exclaimed. 'Data says the same. He did noa weeks agoa oany noabody did listen, cos they wass soft. Less play soldiers!' Gwil began to put his pennies aside from that day. He had seen a toy rifle in Owens', had set his heart on getting it! No sense in playing soldiers if you didn't have a gun. Like a farmer without a farm, a County Schoolboy without his satchel. Mustn't tell Mam though, he thought, or she'll row me. What was it Dad had said once? 'If you doan tell anybody yore plans, noaone can upset them.' He must remember that. If Mam got to know, she'd be in her glory. Never hear the end of it. 'You good for nothin'!' she'd say and take his pennies away from him, put them in Auntie Tillie's money box. So he hid his pennies in the box under his bed upstairs, hid them under a pile of Bible books Mam had given him, the Christmas presents of the years that had passed. Books about Jesus and the Disciples, Moses, Joseph and some of the others. She told him that reading these would make him a good man, a man everyone could look up to and respect, a God-fearing man. Little did she know that under these books he was hiding his pennies, that he counted them every night like a miser to make sure that one was not missing.

That toy rifle . . . it had become an obsession. No more ice-cream, no more sweets, no more twopenny rushes at the pictures on Saturday afternoons. So, little by little, he stopped going to Mr Bracchi's too, resisted the temptations, lost touch with his old pleasures. Mam thought he was coming over onto her side, prided herself on her slow, methodical conquest.

Somehow it seemed years of waiting and saving, of long dreary days. Dad reading his newspaper, commenting on the news, grumbling, frowning, saying what ought to be done, laying down the law, cursing, shouting, table-thumping, repeating the same words, 'Noa man's good. Thass what I say now. Noa man's good when it comes to the test. Killin', fightin', slavin', everythin' rottin' inside, stinkin' with sin . . .'

Mam shaking her head patiently, calmly setting tables, arranging flowers, washing dishes, reading her Bible, worrying about Gwil, tut-tutting when Dad swore.

Gwil thought 'Wait till I get my rifle. I'll shoa it to Mr Bracchi an' the kids on the ashtip with their daft boas and arroas!' Each night counting his pennies, watching his collection grow, counting away the days, the months. The toy rifle had gone from Owens' shop. At first Gwil had been alarmed, and had had a nasty sinking feeling. But fat Mr Owens had smiled at him, comforted him by saying he was expecting some more of them in shortly. Any way, Gwil saw some of them one Saturday in Ponty Woolworths when Mam had taken him shopping with her. There were plenty of guns. He wasn't worried any longer. And just think – no-one knew his secret. 'I doan noa why there's less people in chapel,' Mam said. 'Thank goodness I've got a firm hand on our Gwil. I'll see he woan be like thoas awful screechin' children playin' on the streets on a Sunday.'

'Good man, tha' Dan Hughes,' said Dad. 'Never thought he had it in him. He slapped me on my back yesterday, as chummy as could be, "Hullo Ted," he said, "Come in an' have a talk with me!" Jus' like old pals. Fancy! Me of all people.'

At last, only a penny to go. Gwil was excited, knew it couldn't be long now. Would soon have enough – then, whoopee! Mr Owens said he would keep a rifle for him. They were coming in tomorrow. A special favour for Ted's boy, he said. Regular customers first. Never forget old friends. It was the following afternoon that Gwil discovered that Bracchi's shop was closed, had been for the last week. There were the old dummy chocolate boxes, the empty sweet bottles and tins, and a week's dust on the shelves in the window. He pressed his nose against the glass, wondering if Mr Bracchi was ill. It was funny to see the shop closed, no men standing outside. What could have happened? Yes! He had heard Bracchi's name mentioned quite often during the last few weeks. But surely that was nothing strange. The Italian shopkeeper always cropped up in the conversation somehow. Then, of course, there was the war. We were fighting the Italians, weren't we? They were killing our men weren't they? But he guessed Mr Bracchi must be different. Otherwise he'd be fighting us too. And, anyway, he wouldn't harm a fly. Everyone knew that. Everyone liked him. People said so.

'Hullo Gwil,' somebody said close by. Mr Hughes was standing there, big and posh, dangling a walking stick in his hand, smiling down at him. Mr Hughes! Only important people knew him. Rich as a king they said.

'Shop's closed,' said Mr Hughes, as if Gwil didn't know already. 'We've got to put all the Italians away you know, the ones who haven't been made British. Might be spies for all we know. You go to Simon. You'll get some sweets there.'

Mr Hughes slipped a penny into his hand and winked. Gwil was so surprised he forgot to thank him. One more penny. Just enough. Mr Hughes giving him a penny! That was enough to surprise anybody. 'Tell Daddy I want to see him tonight, will you?' Mr Hughes said.

'Yes sir.'

He patted Gwil on his head, moved on. Gwil walked home in a dream, nursing the penny in his pocket, thinking how mistaken men had been in saying all those wicked things about Mr Hughes when he was so kind, wondering if Mr Bracchi was really a spy. It couldn't be. Firstly he didn't look like a spy. But who could tell? Mr Hughes should know. He was clever.

'Something is up,' Dad was saying in the kitchen. 'It's been stewin' these last few days. I can smell it the way they're actin' today. Anyway, let them have their fling. It'll pass. I suppoas with all this talk about fighting they'd like to have a shoa all on their own, get rid of all the bad feelin'. He's been interned, soa what's the difference. That's all to the good. Noa call to get worried about it.'

Gwil gave Dad the message, touching the penny in his pocket lightly, possessively, secretly. 'I've been saying for a long time,' said Mam, 'that Bracchi's noa good. He's a Catholic. Thass why. Thass what it amounts to, an' you noa how fishy thoas Catholics are?'

'Bracchi was alright,' said Dad, 'but weak as water. A little two-faced, you noa. All Italians are two-faced. I found that out in the last war. Couldn't really trust them, thoas Eyties. No fear.'

Something strange and fearful had happened to Mr Bracchi. Gwil sensed it. It was the way Dad was talking, grimly like a judge, and Mam, nodding sternly. Gwil bent his head, looked into the fire and refused to have his tea. Mam fussed about him now. He might have known. There she was touching his forehead, asking him what was the matter, jumping to conclusions. 'What have you been eating?' she enquired, her voice pitched high, the words clipped and jerky, not natural. Funny how Mam got so easily worked up. Always thought the worst. Had got it into her head now that he was ill.

'That was a long time ago,' Mr Bracchi had said while washing the pop glasses. It was a hot day. Gwil remembered well. The bare hills were baked yellow in the hot season. Throats were dry, sensitive, skins reddened and blistered. The miners coming home from work called in at Mr Bracchi's shop for some cool drinks to quench their thirst and then stopped to talk. 'But then sooner or later everything became a long time ago. More hair on my head then. Younger. When

I come here it was strange, sad and small. People strange too and me sad. People stare and stare at me and wait long time before smiling but one day they come to my shop and buy. All of us friends then. Now everybody come here and talk as if I am one of themselves. Everybody like me now.'

'Thass right,' said Madoc Lewis. 'Yore've settled down now. Yore one of us now.'

'Ah but,' Mr Bracchi said, 'jus' see. This is what I want to say. All the earth is home for wanderers. Make home in Brazil, Bombay. Same, eh? Men are brothers everywhere, good, kind, and friendly. Laugh with you, drink with you. You are as much friend to me as Rabaiotti my cousin in Cardiff, eh?'

Madoc raised his eyebrows, glanced at the other miners in embarassment, turned bewilderedly again to Joe Bracchi. 'Aye! Aye,' he said.

A long time ago . . . Gwil at last relented to his mother's demands, nibbled some bread and butter, slices cut as fine as wafers. Mam watched him solicitously, at last nodded with satisfaction.

After tea he ran upstairs, counted out his pennies, let them slide carefully from his hand into the mouth of an envelope. With his heart thumping he dashed out of the house, down the street to Owens' shop and bought his rifle. As quickly as that! 'Jawch! What will Mam say when she sees it?' he wondered.

And again he began to evolve a plan.

First boy he saw was Jack Meurig, spoilt boy with freckled face and ginger hair from the Bungalows.

'Look at my rifle,' Gwil said proudly.

'Thass nothin',' Jack scoffed. 'I got a tommy gun – that big!'

Somebody could always go one better, Gwil thought. When he had a bar of chocolate another boy had a box of chocolates. When he had won a prize in chapel, someone else had won ten prizes. It wasn't fair. What was the sense in trying, if you couldn't beat someone at something? Strange that he could never get the best, only the second best, or third best.

'Poof!' said Jack Meurig, 'What good would tha' be against a Jerry? Couldn' kill a fly with tha' thing.'

Gwil looked down at the toy rifle in his hand, turned it over, wondered if he had been too rash in throwing his money away. After all, it was only a bit of useless wood. And so small. 'Look!' Jack Meurig suddenly shouted. 'Down there!'

Gwil lifted his head, saw a group of men standing further down the street. They must have come very quickly. They hadn't been there a minute before.

'What they doin'?' Gwil asked, beginning to run after Jack. And yet he knew. Hadn't he heard Dad and Mam talking about it? 'Somethin' stewin',' Dad had said, and here it was, not fierce and mad, but laughing excitedly and grumbling in low voices. 'We didn't ought,' said one.

'Give it a go . . . bloody Eyties . . . see 'em in hell first . . . twister . . . who'll start it off? . . . show 'em . . .'

'Stand back kids,' said one of the men, big burly Watcyn Jones, haulier at the pit. In his hand he held a big stone. At his side was a woman, nursing a baby in a shawl, rocking gently backwards and forwards, humming a little tune. She looked over her shoulder at Gwil, blew back a wayward strand of hair.

'Well, who's agon a do it?' laughed Watcyn, 'Fine thing in it! Us comin' to shoa the Eyties what we're thinkin' of 'em and noa-one with guts. Champion, in it?'

A crowd began to gather.

'Fine ones you men,' scoffed the woman. 'Talk a lot, doan you? Come to the push you carn do a bloomin' thing for yoreselves. If I din' 'ave this baby in my arms I'd do it.'

'Aye an all!' one of the men sneered. People gaping now, open-mouthed, eyes staring. Another woman pushed her way to the front, shook Gwil angrily.

'Come on, you!' she snapped and dragged him hurriedly away.

The colour rose in Gwil's cheeks. All these people turning to look at him.

'Mam, please let me see,' he whispered. 'Huh!' she snorted, shaking him again. She snatched the rifle from his hands. 'You naughty, naughty boy,' she said vehemently. There now. They'd broken the window and he hadn't seen. He could hear the crash, glass splintering, the wild laughs, the throaty cheers. Just now she had to come, of course. He turned and saw people slapping Watcyn Jones on his back, congratulating him, and they weren't running away either. Remember the time he'd thrown a stone at Mog Parry, missed him, got Evans the Grocer's window instead? Jawch! How he'd run! And the rows he'd had, day in and day out afterwards.

'For shame, you!' Mam barked. 'Spendin' yore money on this silly thing. Wait till I tell Dad. He'll have somethin' to say to you about this. Give you a hidin', I shouldn' be surprised. An doan think you doan deserve it.'

She pushed him into the house. 'Look Ted,' she said, brandishing the rifle. 'What do you think of this? An' me thinkin' all the time he was savin' tha' money in his box to please us. I mighta known.'

Dad glared at the toy, glared at Gwil. 'And guess where I found him, Ted. Standing with thoas madmen outside Bracchi's shop.'

'What did they do?' asked Dad, suddenly interested.

'Oh I doan noa,' Mam replied irritably. 'Breakin' the windoa, I suppoas. I didn't stop to see. I'm not like one of thoas common riff-raff. Couldn't be bothered. Fancy our Gwil there, thoa. Shame Gwil. You ought to be ashamed of yourself, indeed you ought. You could have got a bit of glass in your eye.'

Gwil felt miserable, disappointed. She had taken his rifle. Not that he cared any longer. It was no good, a waste of money. Yes indeed, it was. Then she'd spoilt his fun, and now he was going to have a hiding. He was all confused. Didn't know what to make of these grown-ups. One minute they were sweet as sugar, next minute sour as lemons. Always changing with the weather, never the same, always different. Worrying, scolding, fussing. Talking about what was right and what was wrong and how he must fit himself into the pattern. What was right and what was wrong? He'd never know. Grown-ups seemed to know and understand in a queer kind of way, seemed to be able to find their way in this pattern they talked about so much. But he'd never know. He was sure of it.

'Could smell it in the air,' Dad nodded. 'I knew about it all the time. The way the men been actin'. We carn blame them. They got to let off steam someway. Noa I carn say I blame 'em at all. Thass the way of the world for you. Noa sense botherin' about it. It'll pass.'

XVII

The Return

BRENDA CHAMBERLAIN

It isn't as if the Captain took reasonable care of himself, said the postmaster.

No, she answered. She was on guard against anything he might say.

A man needs to be careful with a lung like that, said the postmaster.

Yes, she said. She waited for sentences to be laid like baited traps. They watched one another for the next move. The man lifted a two-ounce weight from the counter and dropped it with fastidious fingers into the brass scale. As the tray fell, the woman sighed. A chink in her armour. He breathed importantly and spread his hands on the counter. From pressure on the palms, dark veins stood up under the skin on the backs of his hands. He leaned his face to the level of her eyes. Watching him, her mouth fell slightly open.

The Captain's lady is very nice indeed; Mrs Morrison is a charming lady. Have you met his wife, Mrs Ritsin?

No, she answered; she has not been to the Island since I came. She could not prevent a smile flashing across her eyes at her own stupidity. Why must she have said just that, a ready-made sentence that could be handed on without distortion. She has not been to the Island since I came. Should she add: no doubt she will be over soon; then I shall have the pleasure of meeting her? The words would not come. The postmaster lodged the sentence carefully in his brain ready to be retailed to the village.

They watched one another. She, packed with secrets behind that innocent face, damn her, why couldn't he worm down the secret passages of her mind? Why had she come here in the first place, this Mrs Ritsin? Like a doll, so small and delicate, she made you want to hit or pet her, according to your nature. She walked with small strides, as if she owned the place, as if she was on equal terms with man and the sea. Her eyes disturbed something in his nature that could not bear the light. They were large, they looked further than any other eyes he had seen. They shone with a happiness that he thought indecent in the circumstances.

Everyone knew, the whole village gloated and hummed over the fact that Ceridwen had refused to live on the Island and that she herself was a close friend of Alec Morrison. But why, she asked herself, why did she let herself fall into their cheap traps? The sentence would be repeated almost without a word being altered but the emphasis, O my God, the stressing of the *I*, to imply a malicious woman's triumph. But all this doesn't really matter, she told herself, at least it won't once I am back there. The Island. She saw it float in front of the postmaster's face. The rocks were clear and the hovering, wind-swung birds; she saw them clearly in front of the wrinkles and clefts on his brow and chin. He coughed discreetly and shrugged with small deprecatory movements of the shoulders. He wished she would not stare at him as if he was a wall or invisible. If she was trying to get at his secrets she could till crack of doom. All the same. As a precautionary measure he slid aside and faced the window.

Seems as though it will be too risky for you to go back this evening, he said; there's a bit of a fog about. You'll be stopping the night in Porthbychan?

– and he wouldn't let her go on holiday in the winter: said, if she did, he'd get a concubine to keep him warm, and he meant –

A woman was talking to her friend outside the door.

You cannot possibly cross the Race alone in this weather, Mrs Ritsin, persisted the postmaster.

I must get back to-night, Mr Davies.

He sketched the bay with a twitching arm, as if to say: I have bound the restless wave. He became confidential, turning to stretch across the counter.

My dear Mrs Ritsin, no woman has ever before navigated these waters. Why, even on a calm day the Porthbychan fishers will not enter the Race. Be warned, dear lady. Imagine my feelings if you were to be washed up on the beach here.

Bridget Ritsin said, I am afraid it is most important that I should get back to-night, Mr Davies.

Ann Pritchard from the corner house slid from the glittering evening into the shadows of the post office. She spoke out of the dusk behind the door. It isn't right for a woman to ape a man, doing a man's work.

Captain Morrison is ill. He couldn't possibly come across to-day. That is why I'm in charge of the boat, Bridget answered.

Two other women had slipped in against the wall of the shop. Now, four pairs of eyes bored into her face. With sly insolence the women threw ambiguous sentences to the postmaster, who smiled as he studied the grain in the wood of his counter. Bridget picked up a bundle of letters and turned to go. The tide will be about right now, she said. Good evening, Mr Davies. Be very, very careful, Mrs Ritsin, and remember me to the Captain.

Laughter followed her into the street. It was like dying in agony, while crowds danced and mocked. O, my darling, my darling over the cold waves. She knew that while she was away he would try to do too much about the house. He would go to the well for water, looking over the fields he lacked strength to drain. He would be in the yard, chopping sticks. He would cough and spit blood. It isn't as if the Captain took reasonable care of himself. When he ran too hard, when he moved anything heavy and lost his breath, he only struck his chest and cursed: blast my lung. Alec dear, you should not run so fast up the mountain. He never heeded her. He had begun to spit blood.

By the bridge over the river, her friend Griff Owen was leaning against the side of a motor-car, talking to a man and woman in the front seats. He said to them, ask her, as she came past.

Excuse me, Miss, could you take us over to see the Island?

I'm sorry, she said, there's a storm coming up. It wouldn't be possible to make the double journey.

They eyed her, curious about her way of life.

Griff Owen, and the grocer's boy carrying two boxes of provisions, came down to the beach with her.

I wouldn't be you; going to be a dirty night, said the man.

The waves were chopped and the headland was vague with hanging cloud. The two small islets in the bay were behind curtains of vapour. The sea was blurred and welcomeless. To the Island, to the Island. Here in the village, you opened a door: laughter and filthy jokes buzzed in your face. They stung and blinded. O my love, be patient, I am coming back to you, quickly, quickly, over the waves.

The grocer's boy put down the provisions on the sand near the tide edge. Immediately a shallow pool formed round the bottoms of the boxes.

Wind seems to be dropping, said Griff.

Yes, but I think there will be fog later on, she answered, sea fog. She turned to him. Oh, Griff, you are always so kind to me. What would we do without you?

He laid a hand on her shoulder. Tell me, how is the Captain

feeling in himself? I don't like the thought of him being so far from the doctor.

The doctor can't do very much for him. Living in the clean air from the sea is good. These days he isn't well, soon he may be better. Don't worry, he is hanging on to life and the Island. They began to push the boat down over rollers towards the water. Last week Alec had said quite abruptly as he was stirring the boiled potatoes for the ducks: at least, you will have this land if I die.

At least, I have the Island.

Well, well, said the man, making an effort to joke; tell the Captain from me that I'll come over to see him if he comes for me himself. Tell him I wouldn't trust my life to a lady, even though the boat has got a good engine and knows her own way home.

He shook her arm: you are a stout girl.

Mr Davies coming down, said the boy, looking over his shoulder as he heaved on the side of the boat. The postmaster came on to the beach through the narrow passage between the hotel and the churchyard. His overcoat flapped round him in the wind. He had something white in his hand. The boat floated; Bridget waded out and stowed away her provisions and parcels. By the time she had made a second journey Mr Davies was at the water's edge.

Another letter for you, Mrs Ritsin, he said. Very sorry, it had got behind the old-age pension books. He peered at her, longing to know what was in the letter, dying to find out what her feelings would be when she saw the handwriting. He had already devoured the envelope with his eyes, back and front, reading the postmark and the two sentences written in pencil at the back. He knew it was a letter from Ceridwen to her husband.

A letter for the Captain, said the postmaster, and watched her closely.

Thank you. She took it, resisting the temptation to read the words that caught her eye on the back of the envelope. She put it away in the large pocket of her oilskin along with the rest.

The postmaster sucked in his cheeks and mumbled something. So Mrs Morrison will be back here soon, he suddenly shot at her. Only the grocer's boy, whistling as he kicked the shingle, did not respond to what he said. Griff looked from her to the postmaster, she studied the postmaster's hypocritical smile. Her head went up, she was able to smile: oh, yes, of course, Mrs Morrison is sure to come over when the weather is better. What did he know, why should he want to know?

It was like a death; every hour that she had to spend on the mainland gave her fresh wounds.

Thank you, Mr Davies. Good-bye Griff, see you next week if the weather isn't too bad. She climbed into the motor-boat and weighed anchor. She bent over the engine and it began to live. The grocer's boy was drifting away, still kicking the beach as if he bore it a grudge. Mr Davies called in a thin voice . . . great care . . . wish you would . . . the Race and . . .

Griff waved, and roared like a horn: tell him I'll take the next calf if it is a good one.

It was his way of wishing her God-speed. Linking the moment's hazard to the safety of future days.

She waved her hand. The men grew small, they and the gravestones of blue and green slate clustered round the medieval church at the top of the sand. The village drew into itself, fell into perspective against the distant mountains.

It was lonely in the bay. She took comfort from the steady throbbing of the engine. She drew Ceridwen's letter from her pocket. She read: if it is *very* fine, Auntie Grace and I will come over next week-end. Arriving Saturday tea-time Porthbychan; Please meet.

Now she understood what Mr Davies had been getting at. Ceridwen and the aunt. She shivered suddenly and felt the flesh creeping on her face and arms. The sea was bleak and washed of colour under the shadow of a long roll of mist that stretched from the level of the water almost to the sun. It was nine o'clock in the evening. She could not reach the anchorage before ten and though it was summertime, darkness would have fallen before she reached home. She hoped Alec's dog would be looking out for her on the headland.

The wind blew fresh, but the wall of mist did not seem to move at all. She wondered if Penmaen du and the mountain would be visible when she rounded the cliffs into the Race. Soon now she should be able to see the Island mountain. She knew every Islandman would sooner face a storm than fog.

So Ceridwen wanted to come over, did she? For the weekend, and with the aunt's support. Perhaps she had heard at last that another woman was looking after her sick husband that she did not want but over whom she was jealous as a tigress. The week-end was going to be merry hell. Bridget realized that she was very tired.

The mainland, the islets, the cliff-top farms of the peninsula fell away. Porpoise rolling offshore towards the Race made her heart lift for their companionship.

She took a compass-bearing before she entered the white silence of the barren wall of fog. Immediately she was both trapped and free. Trapped because it was still daylight and yet she was denied sight, as if blindness had fallen, not blindness where everything is dark, but blindness where eyes are filled with vague light and they strain helplessly. Is it that I cannot see, is this blindness? The horror was comparable to waking on a black winter night and being unable to distinguish anything, until in panic she thought, has my sight gone? And free because the mind could build images on walls of mist, her spirit could lose itself in tunnels of vapour.

The sound of the motor-boat's engine was monstrously exaggerated by the fog. Like a giant heart it pulsed: thump, thump. There was a faint echo, as if another boat, a ghost ship, moved near by. Her mind had too much freedom in these gulfs.

The motor-boat began to pitch like a bucking horse. She felt depth upon depth of water underneath the boards on which her feet were braced. It was the Race. The tide poured across her course. The brightness of cloud reared upward from the water's face. Not that it was anywhere uniform in density; high up there would suddenly be a thinning, a tearing apart of vapour with a wan high blue showing through, and once the jaundiced, weeping sun was partly visible, low in the sky, which told her that she was still on the right bearing. There were grey-blue caverns of shadow that seemed like patches of land, but they were effaced in new swirls of cloud, or came about her in imprisoning walls, tunnels along which the boat moved only to find nothingness at the end. Unconsciously, she had gritted her teeth when she ran into the fog-bank. Her tension remained. Two ghosts were beside her in the boat, Ceridwen, in a white fur coat, was sitting amidships and facing her, huddled together, cold and unhappy in the middle of the boat, her knees pressed against the casing of the engine. Alec's ghost sat in the bows. As a figurehead he leaned away from her, his face half lost in opaque cloud.

I will get back safely, I will get home, she said aloud, looking ahead to make the image of Ceridwen fade. But the phantom persisted; it answered her spoken thought.

No, you'll drown, you won't ever reach the anchorage. The dogfish will have you.

I tell you I can do it. He's waiting for me, he needs me.

Alec turned round, his face serious. When you get across the Race, if you can hear the fog-horn, he said quietly, you are on the wrong tack. If you can't hear it, you're all right; it means you are cruising safely along the foot of the cliffs . . . When you get home, will you come to me, be my little wife?

Oh, my dear, she answered, I could weep or laugh that you ask me now, here. Yes, if I get home.

Soon you'll be on the cold floor of the sea, said Ceridwen.

Spouts of angry water threatened the boat that tossed sideways. Salt sprays flew over her.

Careful, careful, warned Alec. We are nearly on Pen Cader, the rocks are near now, we are almost out of the Race.

A sea-bird flapped close to her face, then with a cry swerved away, its claws pressed backward.

Above the noise of the engine there was now a different sound, that of water striking land. For an instant she saw the foot of a black cliff. Wet fangs snapped at her. Vicious fangs, how near they were. Shaken by the sight, by the rock death that waited, she turned the boat away from the Island. She gasped as she saw white spouting foam against the black and slimy cliff. She was once more alone. Alec and Ceridwen, leaving her to the sea, had been sucked into the awful cloud, this vapour without substance or end. She listened for the fog-horn. No sound from the lighthouse. A break in the cloud above her head drew her eyes. A few yards of the mountaintop of the Island was visible, seeming impossibly high, impossibly green and homely. Before the eddying mists rejoined she saw a thin shape trotting across the steep grass slope, far, far up near the crest of the hill. Leaning forward, she said aloud: O look, the dog. It was Alec's dog keeping watch for her. The hole in the mist closed up, the shroud fell thicker than ever. It was terrible, this loneliness, this groping that seemed as if it might go on for ever.

Then she heard the low-throated horn blaring into the fog. It came from somewhere on her right hand. So in avoiding the rocks she had put out too far to sea and had overshot the anchorage. She must be somewhere off the southern headland near the pirate's rock. She passed a line of lobster floats.

She decided to stop the engine and anchor where she was hoping that the fog would clear at nightfall. Then she would be able to return on to her proper course. There was an unnatural silence after she had cut off the engine. Water knocked against the boat.

Cold seeped into her bones from the planks. With stiff wet hands she opened the bag of provisions, taking off the crust of a loaf and spreading butter on it with her gutting knife. As she ate, she found that for the first time in weeks she had leisure in which to review her life. For when she was on the farm it was eat, work, sleep, eat, work, sleep, in rotation.

I have sinned or happiness is not for me, she thought. It was her heart's great weakness that she could not rid herself of superstitious beliefs.

Head in hands, she asked: But how have I sinned? I didn't steal another woman's husband. They had already fallen apart when I first met Alec. Is too great happiness itself a sin? Surely it's only because I am frightened of the fog that I ask, have I sinned, is this my punishment? When the sun shines I take happiness with both hands. Perhaps it's wrong to be happy when half the people of the world are chain-bound and hungry, cut off from the sun. If you scratch below the surface of most men's minds you find that they are bleeding inwardly. Men want to destroy themselves. It is their only hope. Each one secretly nurses the death-wish, to be god and mortal in one; not to die at nature's order, but to cease on his own chosen day. Man has destroyed so much that only the destruction of all life will satisfy him.

How can it be important whether I am happy or unhappy? And yet it's difficult for me to say, I am only one, what does my fate matter? For I want to be fulfilled like other women. What have I done to be lost in winding sheets of fog?

And he will be standing in the door wondering that I do not come.

For how long had she sat in the gently-rocking boat? It was almost dark and her eyes smarted from constant gazing. Mist weighed against her eyeballs. She closed her eyes for relief.

Something was staring at her. Through drawn lids she felt the steady glance of a sea-creature. She looked at the darkening waves. Over an area of a few yards she could see; beyond, the wave was cloud, the cloud was water. A dark, wet-gleaming thing on the right. It disappeared before she could make out what it was. And then, those brown beseeching eyes of the seal cow. She had risen near by, her mottled head scarcely causing a ripple. Lying on her back in the grey-green gloom of the sea she waved her flippers now outwards to the woman, now inwards to her white breast, saying, come to me, come to me, to the caverns where shark bones lie like tree stumps, bleached, growth-ringed like trees.

Mother seal, seal cow. The woman stretched out her arms. The attraction of those eyes was almost strong enough to draw her to salt death. The head disappeared. The dappled back turned over in the opaque water, and dived. Bridget gripped the side of the boat, praying that this gentle visitant should not desert her.

Hola, hola, hola, seal mother from the eastern cave.

Come to me, come to me, come to me. The stone-grey head reappeared on the other side, on her left. Water ran off the whiskered face, she showed her profile; straight nose, and above, heavy lids drooping over melancholy eyes. When she plunged showing off her prowess, a sheen of pearly colours ran over the sleek body.

They watched one another until the light failed to penetrate the fog. After the uneasy summer twilight had fallen, the woman was still aware of the presence of the seal.

She dozed off into a shivering sleep through which she heard faintly the snorting of the sea creature. A cold, desolate sound. Behind that again was the bull-throated horn bellowing into the night.

She dreamt: Alec was taking her up the mountain at night under a sky dripping with blood. Heaven was on fire. Alec was gasping for breath. The other islanders came behind, their long shadows stretching down the slope. The mountain top remained far off. She never reached it.

Out of dream, she swam to consciousness, painfully leaving the dark figures of fantasy. A sensation of swimming upward through fathoms of water. The sea of her dreams was dark and at certain levels between sleeping and waking a band of light ran across the waves. Exhaustion made her long to fall back to the sea-floor of oblivion, but the pricking brain floated her at last on to the surface of morning.

She awoke with a great wrenching gasp that flung her against the gunwale. Wind walked the sea. The fog had gone, leaving the world raw and disenchanted in the false dawn. Already, gulls were crying for a new day. Wet and numb with cold, the woman looked about her. At first it was impossible to tell off what shore the boat was lying. For a few minutes it was enough to know that she was after all at anchor so close to land.

Passing down the whole eastern coastline, she had rounded the south end and was a little way past Mallt's bay on the west. The farmhouse, home, seemed near across the fore-shortened fields. Faint light showed in the kitchen window, a warm glow in the grey landscape. It was too early for the other places, Goppa, Pen Isaf, to show signs of life. Field, farm, mountain, sea, and sky. What a simple world. And below, the undercurrents.

Mechanically she started up the engine and raced round to the anchorage through mounting sea spray and needles of rain.

She made the boat secure against rising wind, then trudged through seaweed and shingle, carrying the supplies up into the boathouse. She loitered inside after putting down the bags of food. Being at last out of the wind, no longer pitched and tumbled on the sea, made her feel that she was in a vacuum. Wind howled and thumped at the walls. Tears of salt water raced down the body of a horse scratched long ago on the window by Alec. Sails stacked under the roof shivered in the draught forced under the slates. She felt that she was spinning wildly in some mad dance. The floor rose and fell as the waves had done. The earth seemed to slide away and come up again under her feet. She leant on the windowsill, her forehead pressed to the pane. Through a crack in the glass wind poured in a cold stream across her cheek. Nausea rose in her against returning to the shore for the last packages. After that there would be almost the length of the Island to walk. At the thought she straightened herself, rubbing the patch of skin on her forehead where pressure on the window had numbed it. She fought her way down to the anchorage. Spume blew across the rocks, covering her sea boots. A piece of wrack was blown into the wet tangle of her hair. Picking up the bag of provisions, she began the return journey. Presently she stopped, put down the bag, and went again to the waves. She had been so long with them that now the thought of going inland was unnerving. Wading out until water swirled round her knees she stood relaxed, bending like a young tree under the wind's weight. Salt was crusted on her lips and hair. Her feet were sucked by outdrawn shingle. She no longer wished to struggle but to let a wave carry her beyond the world.

I want sleep, she said to the sea. O God, I am so tired, so tired. The sea sobbed sleep, the wind mourned, sleep.

Oyster-catchers flying in formation, a pattern of black and white and scarlet, screamed: we are St Bride's birds, we saved Christ, we rescued the Saviour.

A fox-coloured animal was coming over the weedy rocks of the point. It was the dog, shivering and mist-soaked as if he had been out all night. He must have been lying in a cranny and so missed greeting her when she had landed. He fawned about her feet, barking unhappily.

They went home together, passing Pen Isaf that slept: Goppa too. It was about four o'clock of a summer daybreak. She picked two mushrooms glowing in their own radiance. Memories came of her first morning's walk on the Island. There had been a green and lashing sea and gullies of damp rock, and parsley fern among loose stones. Innocent beginning, uncomplicated, shadowless. As if looking on the dead from the pinnacle of experience, she saw herself as she had been.

She opened the house door: a chair scraped inside. Alec stood in the kitchen white with strain and illness.

So you did come, he said dully.

Yes, she said with equal flatness, putting down the bags.

How sick, how deathly he looked.

Really, you shouldn't have sat up all night for me. He stirred the pale ashes; a fine white dust rose.

Look, there's still fire, and the kettle's hot. He coughed. They drank the tea in silence, standing far apart. Her eyes never left his face. And the sea lurched giddily under her braced feet. Alec went and sat before the hearth. Bridget came up behind his chair and pressed her cheek to his head. She let her arms fall slackly round his neck. Her hands hung over his chest. Tears grew in her eyes, brimming the lower lids so that she could not see. They splashed on to his clenched fists. He shuddered a little. Without turning his head, he said: Your hair's wet. You must be so tired.

Yes, she said, so tired. Almost worn out.

Come, let us go to bed for an hour or two.

You go up, she answered, moving away into the back kitchen; I must take off my wet clothes first.

Don't be long. Promise me you won't be long. He got up out of the wicker chair, feeling stiff and old, to be near her where she leant against the slate table. One of her hands was on the slate, the other was pealing off her oilskin trousers.

He said: don't cry. I can't bear it if you cry.

I'm not, I'm not. Go to bed please.

I thought you would never get back.

She took the bundle of letters out of the inner pocket of her coat and put them on the table. She said: there's one for you from Ceridwen.

Never mind about the letters. Come quickly to me. She stood naked in the light that spread unwillingly from sea and sky. Little channels of moisture ran down her flanks, water dripped from her hair over the points of her breasts. As she reached for a towel he watched the skin stretch over the fragile ribs. He touched her thigh with his fingers, almost a despairing gesture. She looked at him shyly, and swiftly bending, began to dry her feet. Shaking as if from ague, she thought her heart's beating would be audible to him.

He walked abruptly away from her, went upstairs. The boards creaked in his bedroom.

Standing in the middle of the floor surrounded by wet clothes, she saw through the window how colour was slowly draining back into the world. It came from the sea, into the wild irises near the well, into the withy beds in the corner of the field. Turning, she went upstairs in the brightness of her body.

He must have fallen asleep so soon as he lay down. His face was bleached, the bones too clearly visible under the flesh. Dark folds of skin lay loosely under his eyes. Now that the eyes were hidden, his face was like a death-mask. She crept quietly into bed beside him.

Through the open window came the lowing of cattle. The cows belonging to Goppa were being driven up for milking. Turning towards the sleeping man, she put her left hand on his hip. He did not stir.

She cried then as if she would never be able to stop, the tears gushing down from her eyes until the pillow was wet and stained from her weeping.

What will become of us, what will become of us?

XVIII

The Old Woman and the Wind

MARGIAD EVANS

In her grey, blunted garden, with the gutterings of the long slidden turf mounding about her, old Mrs Ashstone was stooping above her broken crocuses.

'Maybe I can rise them up,' she was wailing as she touched their bruised cold petals, 'maybe. But what's the use when that old wind'll only blow 'em all flat agen?'

They were her only flowers – just the one clump of ochre yellow sheaths growing under the cottage wall as close and thick as if they were in a pot.

And even them the wind had smashed as it had smashed everything else. The porch, the fence . . . Mrs Ashstone had nothing pretty or hospitable to look at; nothing but rocks that broke out of the quivering wire grass, and lay about like sheep. Wind! Mrs Ashstone growled, *wind*!

The air was stiff with it – solid and encroaching. Wind more than age was dwindling her sparrow frame. Sometimes it felt as hard and narrow as churchyard mould; others it was like being cuddled by a giant. Wind, always blowing, roaring, pushing at her and her cottage, shoving her out of her place, pouncing on her hair. Cursed wind, too big for the world.

Look how that grass was bending! That melted bank had been a stone wall once. And the stumbling gusts that harshly rocked her tiny body. And the flattened smoke coming down round the chimney's neck in wisps like her own hair. How she hated it, oh how she hated it!

Mrs Ashstone straightened her spine slowly, pushing her knuckles into her knees, her thighs, and then her hips. 'Ah! Ah! Ah!' she groaned, 'if only I could get away from here I shouldn't get old so fast. A nice soft little place in the village now, like what Mrs Maddocks has. Or Mrs Griffiths.'

Mrs Ashstone was seventy-one. She had little to think of after living alone on her hill for twelve years except her own bad luck. She was not stupid, but so ignorant that she imagined 'Mrs' to be a common Christian name and the marriage service a sort of second baptism. She had forgotten that she was called Annie. Mrs Ashstone, Garway Hill, she was, and there she stood with tears in her eyes, stroking her crocuses and wishing for a pathway, box-edged, and a little orchard with a clothes line. It was the hour of evening, which seems made solely for the first slender winter flowers. The shadowless January twilight enclosed and shaped each contour with leaf-like distinctness. The tiny cottage, slapped with limewash, was built under a single flake of rock. Some bloomless gorse bushes and pale bracken patches, that was all. There was no living feeling, but only a heedless and violent solitude.

Under the slurred turf lay half-buried a few heavy stones. Swept and seamed by each gust, the old woman toiled up and down the frail track she had worn from her door to the gap in the mound. Each journey she brought a stone. These she laid round the crocuses lifting their golden pods: 'There, now, if the sun shines, they'll open in the morning,' she said when it was done. Then she raised her face menacingly and flapped her fist. The gesture seemed not hers but the wind's. 'Keep off,' she screamed. 'Keep off 'em now. You go down there and break off some of they great el'um trees.' She went to the step and rested against the door, arranging her dim dress and apron, gripping them down at the knees with fierce self-conscious modesty. She had a little screw of hair on top of her skull, a screw of nose curled upwards like a dead leaf, and small, clutching yellow hands that were always chasing the flying and broken things floating in the wind's wake. Somebody said she looked as if she were forever catching feathers in the air, and it was true that she did.

She turned to face the valley. The soft sound of it was going underground, but up here it was coming a gale. She could feel it in her heart. Every breath seemed too big for her. Her eyes followed the downward path to the village. Ah, it was always still there, always blowing here. Below the oak trees, where the round winds whisked the dead leaves in figure forms, the quietness began. Warmth, sounds, birds' voices. Up here she had to listen through the wind, but after the oak tree was passed things found their own way into her hearing. Voices, footsteps trickling from cottage to cottage through the peaceful lanes . . .

It had been like that this morning. There she had stood and stroked her hair. She'd lifted her face and smelled the sky as if she were smelling at a flower. A flock of birds as fine as dust she'd seen. Then she'd gone on down, cruel rage and cruel envy in her mind, tears in her eyes. Mrs Griffiths's daughter had cancer, they said, but Mrs Griffiths's front path was ruled between primulas and violets. The sunlight touched the dark-green box bush.

'Good morning, good morning,' the ninety-year old woman had nodded cheerfully. Well, Mrs Ashstone wished her no harm, for her son carried the coal up Garway. But, oh, the meadows, the gentle river at her garden side, made tired flesh drag with longing. Old Mrs Ashstone had passed on, not answering the human greeting, but hearing the water's poem, the crow flock's rustling over the elms.

Mrs Maddocks, she was hanging out the washing – sheets,

Fred's shirts. This time it was Mrs Ashstone who stopped. Under the hedge, wide open in the grass of the bank, a constellation of celandines shone at the sun. Five of them, shaped, she noticed, like the Plough. She put out her torn, black foot. She wanted to kill their beauty. But she closed her eyes. The sunlight was red through the flesh. And then she had a vision. A white willow tree in a red world. It was an effort to raise her tired lids. Mrs Maddocks was slapping each garment out in the air. She was standing aslant, empty wash bath on her hip, the breezeless sheets a white screen for her shadow.

'There 'tis!' she cried in triumph. 'But will it dry! Bain't no wind.' Would it dry! Mrs Ashstone sneered to herself as she fingered a twig in the hedge. Would it dry and the sun gloating on the orchard! She pressed her lips together and walked on quickly.

When she came out of the shop some impulse took her up the steps to the churchyard gate. She stood there eased of some of her misery, for it relaxed her just not to hear the grind of the wind. She waited for the hatred to return and help her home. Her feet were on a cracked stone, her hands folded on the dusty gate, when old Captain Ifor and Mr Brewer went by below with their sheepdogs and retrievers, talking.

'Good day, good day,' the Captain called. 'You down from your eyrie?'

She blinked at them mockingly, fumbling with the old spoon latch, clicking it with her thumb, her face expressing only a kind of humiliating wistfulness. What was an ar-ry – and what had it to do with her hill? So she turned her back on them. 'One day I shall lie here, and none to prevent me,' she told herself. Up there, where the greyness roamed the bracken, was her home, looking from where she stood, like a white pebble that a boy had flung out of the river. Later on she trod her way upwards with her groceries and a bucket of shallots Mary Maddocks had run out to give her. They were very heavy, but she stooped to gather a handful of bracken, bending the canes over and over to fit her small grate. The climb made her tremble. The wind took her breath and threw it away as if it were nothing. 'There's no mercy, no mercy,' she began to whimper, feeling her hair blow awry, and her knees clutched invisibly.

That night old Mrs Ashstone had to bolt her door against the boulders of air the wind rolled against it. The latch and bolt jigged with each solid blast: the glass in the window rustled, a beast roared in the chimney, and a wet black mark like a footprint appeared under the door.

She looked at it. 'This is a rare storm that brings me such a visitor,' she said.

The rain tumbled down the chimney on the flames.

'My fire's scalded,' she said.

She sat down on her fender and began to unravel the shallots. Suddenly, letting her hands fall, she called: 'John? John Ashstone?' She thought a voice had spoken to her aloud. She wasn't afraid. She had many voices inside her, but fear had seldom spoken. Her mind turned and talked to her often enough. Yet this had sounded different. It had come in the gale, now all but through the walls, now backing away, moving it seemed with and among the freakish screams, the lumps of wind, and the long dragging sounds that hung back along the earth.

A slate crashed. 'Mrs Ashstone, Mrs Ashstone!'

Mrs Ashstone stood up. 'Be you my conscience?'

'No.'

'Then be you my stomach?'

'No.'

'Then you must be the roof going?'

'No. I'm the wind. And you're a witch.' And the roaring rose all around the room, like heatless flame.

'You may be the wind, but I'm no witch.'

'Yes, you are.'

'I'll pummel ye,' said she. 'Leastways I would if I could see ye. But all I can see is black cobwebs a-shaking in the chimney and soot in the lamp. I never was no witch.'

'You've lived alone, and that makes a woman a witch.'

'Oh, do it? Well, be that your footmark?'

The wind laughed and the sound was like stones leaping in a quarry. Then it seemed to fade, and when it spoke again there was only a tiny, distinct vibration, like embers tinkling and creeping when a fire is left alone.

'Come outside and look at me,' said this sequestered voice. The gale at that moment stopped; it was flat calm.

Mrs Ashstone stood on her doorstep, looking to the south-west, where a low black toadstool of cloud gloated over the hollow. She gazed at this evil web in silence, rubbing her little hands. In the doorstone dent lay a handful of starlit rain.

The old woman shook. She waved her fist and shouted: 'I don't like you. Get away, wind, ugly thing you be!'

The cloud was nearer. Around it the stars shone as in tender piety. 'I cannot abear that thing,' the old woman said, and she went in and closed the door. But the voice bent itself round the chink before she could thud the bolt: 'Where shall I go, where shall I go?' it uttered shrilly and rapidly.

'Go?' screamed Mrs Ashstone. 'Go anywhere. Go down the village and blow down all they great el'ums and rookeries and Captain Ifor's peaches. Haven't them had peace all these years?'

Her words were repeated, but slowly, as a lesson is read, meditatively, engraving the stillness. Then there was silence. She was alone. Her fingers hovered about her ears as if to catch meanings in the lamplight. But she heard nothing except clock, kettle, and mouse. She felt that she lived in these stirrings. Thoughtfully she went to the cupboard, took down the sugar-basin and flipped a mouse-pill out of it with her thumbnail.

When she opened the door again before going to bed she noticed that the darkness had a strange sallow smell. There was a faint wavy noise. She strained to hear. ''Tis like the weir!' she said staring. On the hill it was as still as midsummer, with the sheep cropping the hushed mounds. She saw a star sinking slowly as if someone was lowering a candle to the floor. The old woman put out her hand to catch it . . .

In the morning, looking under the sunrise, she saw the empty floods and the river winding through their vacancy. Red as copper, the dull waters showed seaweed-like patches spread upon them. These were ricks of hay and clover and corn which the wind had lifted and carried away and dropped furlongs from their foundations.

Mrs Ashstone dropped her sticks and ran away down to the village without lighting her fire or even so much as lifting the lid off the bread pan. When she was past the oak tree the breeze fluttered like a flag in her face, but it made no sound at all. She ran into the 'Street', holding her left wrist in her right hand, and then she stopped and listened.

Slates were lying on the paths, trees were down, with their roots that had burst the sod, washed bare of earth, and strange sand bars and pearly pebble beaches rippled across the lane.

Most of the doors stood open on the tightly-furnished rooms, but nobody stood looking out. It was so quiet except for the cadaverous murmur of the flood that she could hear the puddings snuffling in the saucepans.

She ran on round the bend. Then what a sight! The river had cut the village in half. It had felled the bridge, and was rushing over the road fifty yards wide, and rough and red as a ploughed field.

On the side where Mrs Ashstone was running the slope was abrupt and the houses stood clear above the torrent. But on the far side old Mrs Griffiths's cottage was four foot deep, with a broken door and the green velvet furniture floating in the garden. In the greatest danger was Mrs Sate, the baker's wife, at her second-floor window with her baby up against her cheek. For the river divided from the flood at the corner of her chimney wall, and with enormous pressure split into two, islanding the cottage, with the cage of its partly-demolished porch clinging to it like rubble.

Mrs Sate was shouting wildly to the people who stood by the water. They did not seem to listen for they were all telling one another the story of their night. They had remote incredulous expressions on their faces because they could not go to work. The children were crawling out as far as they dared along the broken bridge stones. Captain Ifor was there in a mackintosh cape, prodding the water with his stick. And Mrs Maddocks, shouting at him, her white cotton bosom overlapping her folded arms. And many others.

''Twere more like sunset than sunrise, so wild and lonely 'twere,' Fred was saying.

Then they all turned round, hearing old Mrs Ashstone running. Her footsteps sounded intelligent, as if they brought an explanation. But the old woman was rushing towards the river without any idea, her arms stretched before her as if she wanted to prevent the waters. She ran right up to the end, and then pulled herself up. She put out her foot and gently paddled her shoe in it. Old Captain Ifor cast her a glance, and then once more plunged his stick in it.

'What I do say is it's coming to something when your own roof's blown off you and you're the last to know it,' Mrs Maddocks was screeching at him: 'Sitting there mending Fred's shirt I was, and not a notion in the world what was happening till he comes in. "Mother," he says, "do you know the roof's lifting up and down like a rick-cloth? For God's sake," he says, "come out and see." '

Mrs Ashstone looked at her, and angry as she was Mrs Maddocks politely included her. But a voice that might have spoken out of the group itself, so monotonous and undistinguished was it, began to recite:

'Mrs Sate, she be s'ying as she 'ev nowt with 'er for sustenance but 'alf a pork pie and a crust. And her the baker's wife! Charley, 'e's been at the bake'ouse all night. What 'ool 'appen I can't think, for 'er can't swim to 'e, and what be good o' 'e swimming to 'er? And there bain't no boats in this village.'

'And all the telephone wires are down. I've tried and tried,' said the Captain.

Mrs Maddocks raised her stern voice again: 'Whose fault is this, I said, when I'd seen. Eh? Who won't do the repairs? Eh? Who? Captain, you can take the key this minute if you've a mind, for I'm not a woman that will live under a roof that's tied on me head with wagon ropes as this one be this minute. All me furniture's out.' And she handed the key out from her armpit where she'd been hatching it. The Captain took it gingerly. Mrs Ashstone turned her eyes across the water. She stretched out her arms, and it seemed to her she was stroking the faces in the upper windows. She wanted to say something, but the waters and the gossiping stopped her frail words. Her face was beautiful.

Just then, on the other side, a man came running down the slope in a greatcoat. It was Charley Sate. He threw down the coat by the water's edge. He was in vest and pants. Round his waist he wore a scarf, and tucked into it were two bottles of milk.

'Ah, brave fellow, brave fellow,' clucked the Captain. 'Many waters cannot drown love. Besides they're going down. He'll make it.'

Charley thrust out. His jaw was like a knot under his ear.

He seemed to look into all their faces and to live in the look. The current knitted itself round his neck and his separated hands, walking, as it were, before those dark and frenzied eyes. He plaited his arms in with the water, weaving all three.

In a few minutes he was safe on the shed roof, lifting up a little window under the chimney. Mrs Sate's face vanished. Every one shouted and a little boy dropped a flat stone with a ringing splash.

Captain Ifor nodded: 'Well done, well done!' He propped his stick against his shaking knees so that he could clap. This made him recognize the key. Mrs Maddocks was crowdedly cheering with the rest, and for the first time the old man saw what was in his hand: 'What's this? A key?' His eyes settled on Mrs Ashstone – eyes like smoky glass. 'Want it? She doesn't. Mary always makes up her mind by accident, but when it's done it's done. You're more pliable. You have it. Get you down from that eyrie of yours.'

Mrs Ashstone was no longer beautiful. Her body had dropped that direct expression. She stood twisted in an attitude of crooked secrecy before the Captain, and between their two silent figures flowed a little eddy of air, as it might between two trees.

She shook herself, as you might shake a clock that is stopping, and the slow tired look of secrecy was gradually transferred from one old face to the other, as though by reflection.

And so Captain Ifor and Mrs Ashstone stared silently at each other.

To him it was suddenly revealed that she was not like other old women. At least when you thought of an old woman you did not think of anybody like this one. Old woman in the imagination are all alike. But old Mrs Ashstone was nothing you could imagine. She had a child's distinctness, he thought, yet she looked enfeebled, as though in her old age she saw the world by candlelight.

'Won't you have it?' he said.

She shook her head: 'I have a friend up there. One that do know where I was born. To live with me.'

'A relation?'

'Nearer than that,' she said. And then shyly, and, as it were, *wonderingly*, she took a peppermint like a white button out of her pocket and tossed it in her mouth. She turned away and walked slowly up the road, her feet leaving little quiltings in the thin red mud, where the nails in her soles stuck. Under the oak tree she stumbled over the wind as if it had been a dog asleep. It circled around her, blowing a wren out of a bush.

'Well?' it said out of the grass.

The old woman sat down on a stone.

'If you was a beetle I 'ood stamp on you,' she scolded.

'Oh!'

'Some of them people have been kind to me.'

'Then why didn't you take the key and go and live with them?'

She considered this question as if it lay on her lap with her hands. After a pause she said quickly, '*You* didn't ask me that – I asked myself. I can't hardly sort you out from my thoughts,' she said, 'even when it's quiet like here. I bain't got the *use* of a lot of people and voices. I bin too long on Garway. Down there I couldn't hardly tell whether I was glad or sorry. I couldn't seem to *hear*. And that's the reason as I don't want to change my ways now. I do like to hear even the mice in the cupboard, and the cockroaches, I'm that curious and learned. I 'ave got used to them. I've worked with people, not loved them, and now I be done with work I do want to be shut of 'em.'

'It can't happen again,' said the wind.

'Nor I don't want it should,' said she, rising and beginning to bend over the crackling bracken.

XIX

A Modest Adornment

MARGIAD EVANS

'Bull's eyes are boys' sweets,' said Miss Allensmoore and popped one in her mouth.

She and Miss Plant had lived together for many years in a cottage just outside a small village. It was difficult to guess whether they liked each other; but they didn't seem to quarrel. They didn't seem to be poor and they didn't seem to be rich: they had plenty of food apparently but no clothes, except what they always wore; and they were squalid, eccentric and original. And rather old.

Miss Allensmoore was a fat black cauldron of a woman frequently leaning on an umbrella. She had a pair of little hobbling feet which turned up at the ends and which were usually bare. Miss Plant had great silky green eyes and soft silver hair with yellowish patches in it the colour of tobacco stain. She was very, very pretty with strawberry pink in her thin face, but in her enormous eyes which were truly half blind, there was a curious sort of threat. But she was the meekest of martyrs. She was an odd rambling creature, always dressed in a shawl and a mackintosh, and she used to pass a lot of pleasant time writing letters to the farmer who owned the cottage asking him to send a man to trim the hedge. They were rather peculiar letters. He kept a few to smile at. 'You are such a shy man,' wrote Nora Plant, 'that I don't like to stop you, although I meet you so often in the lane.'

Miss Allensmoore was an atrocious but, alas, perpetual cook. Coming down the garden path to the door which was generally open, their few visitors always heard furious frying or the grumpy sound of some pudding in the pot, bouncing and grunting like a goblin locked in a cupboard. Miss Allensmoore also wrote letters which she sent by the baker and always expected to have answered in the same way. She played the oboe. She played beautifully, and she kept a great many dirty black cats.

Miss Plant only kept silence. A sort of blind silence which was liable to be broken at any moment by her falling over something or knocking something else down. It wasn't a quiet silence; and it hadn't the length or the loyalty needed for music. When Miss Allensmoore played in her presence, Miss Plant would sit looking desultory, like a person who is taking part in a hopeless conversation.

The cottage smelled of soot and stale shawls and burnt kettles.

And now it was January and Miss Plant was dying of cardiac disease. And Miss Allensmoore was standing in the garden on a paste of brown leaves, eating bull's-eyes.

It was very cold. On the bank of the steep fields the broken snow was lying like pieces of china. A wind was going round the currant bushes.

'Cold, cold,' muttered Miss Allensmoore looking down at the snowdrops. It would be nice to pick them and have them indoors, she thought. But on the other hand, if she left them how well they would do for the funeral!

'I won't. It can't be long now,' she said.

She breathed a long silent phrase and moved away her hand.

Miss Plant was, in fact, almost through death. At half past three in the afternoon two days later, the district nurse quietly pulled down her cuff. Miss Plant had parted with her dazed, emaciated body.

Miss Allensmoore was again in the garden, picking some washing off the thorns. Suddenly she heard the nurse calling, so she hastened indoors and met her coming out of the cupboard where they kept the stairs.

'It's over,' said the young nurse uneasily.

Miss Allensmoore looked confident and unchanged.

'Oh, don't be upset,' she said. 'What time did she die?'

'Twenty-nine minutes past three exactly,' said the nurse more powerfully. 'Can you give me a bit of help? That bed's so heavy.'

'Certainly,' said Miss Allensmoore affably, 'it *is* a solid bed. Just let me hang these things up before I put them down somewhere and forget them. There's no reunion so hard to bring about as a pair of stockings which has separated.'

It was dark in the narrow rooms. They lit candles and went upstairs. Castors screeched as the bed was moved out from the wall: a flock of birds flew low over the roof with a dragging sound like a carpet being drawn over a floor. The dust could be felt on the teeth. Presently Miss Allensmoore came out fumbling with her candle and dropping grease on her toes. An unfinished smile tinged her face for a moment before she licked it away with the point of her tongue. It was a fat, proud, eternal face, and the little smile gave it a strange brevity. She was thinking Miss Plant would never send things flying again, reaching for others.

But the nurse having finished, stepped back from the candlelight and gazed at the face above the tallowy folds of the sheet. Beneath were the vivid hands, hands in new green knitted gloves, bunched on the breast almost as if they had been a knot of leaves. A woman from the village who used to come to see Miss Plant had made the gloves for her. And she had asked the nurse if she would do her best, please, to see that she was buried in them.

The nurse again went to the bedside and quietly looked.

There was a kind of daylight on the face which was the colour of the flesh in that pale, plastered light. Poor Miss Plant didn't look wonderfully young, or beautiful as the dead are said to look: she just looked simple and very, very tired. The nurse sighed as she picked up her case.

She went downstairs. Miss Allensmoore squatted on the fender holding a cup and saucer under her chin. She had lit two lamps which were flaring and she was frying chips on an oil-stove. She got up; her naked feet, dark as toads, trod the hundreds of burnt matches which covered the floor.

'All over now. Funeral Friday,' she announced.

'My God, she's a hard old nut!' the nurse thought. She said: 'I'll let the doctor know. And would you like me to call on Billy Prosser as I'm passing?'

'You mean Mr Misery. I simply can't think of him as *Billy Prosser*,' said Miss Allensmoore. 'Oh, yes, please, if you would. I'd sooner not go myself.'

The nurse smiled. The village was a great place for dubbing and nick-naming. People called Miss Allensmoore "Sooner". It stood for Sooner Not Do Anything.

'If you'd be so good,' muttered she, eating chips. They were long and warped and gaunt as talons, Miss Allensmoore's chips were. She threshed them in her gums and spat them at the cats that caused an idiotic darkness by gambolling before the lamps. Wands of flame flew up the glasses and then shrivelled, while the dirty ceiling swayed with clumsy shadows. And the sagging black cobwebs.

The nurse got ready to go. She sidled away saying: 'Not nervous, are you?'

'Nervous? Nervous of what?' demanded Miss Allensmoore, and she added, 'I've known Miss Plant for a great number of years,' as if that were a perfect explanation for everything.

The nurse went, nodding mildly. Somehow she seemed

frightened, Miss Allensmoore thought. In fact she was only relieved, for how dreadful it would be for anybody to have to sit with the old slut in that awful cottage! Every time she walked in the tables seemed more and more crammed with washing up, with crumbs and tea leaves and the hilly horizons of many obstructive meals. And then, the pailsful of refuse, the tusky cabbage stalks, the prowling smell . . . !

So she was gone. And Miss Allensmoore turned the key on her. Ha! She was alone. Now she would gently, gently put out her hand and take up the oboe. Presently she would play. How beautifully she could play! Between the pieces sighs of joy broke from her and loud words that left holes in her breath.

'Ah – ah – my beautiful – when you sing like that . . .' And again she would cry: 'My beloved . . .' Ah, oh – it was the loveliest thing in life, music – the only wise, the only sagacious thing. And afterwards she would play again, until the fire was out and the cats all slept, and something, rain or insects or mice, crinkled in the shapely pauses.

Silence. With her instrument ready, Miss Allensmoore turned to face it. It was to her what the mysterious stone is to its carver who will presently unfurl from it the form which he observes inherent in it. As stone is to the sculptor only a gauze upon the idol of his mind, silence was transparent to Miss Allensmoore. The musicians' dawn she called it. And now she was face to face with the biggest silence she had ever known and all the time the nurse was gathering up this and that she was longing to breathe across it the first dangerous phrase.

With ecstatic anguish she loved the melodious shapes of her breath; she noticed how other people breathed: to her it seemed terrible that most of them used this art only for scrambling about the world and gossiping. Out of breath! She only wished they were! They weren't fit to use the supple air. Or if they were, she reflected sometimes, it was a pity she was obliged to mix such a common medium with her music. For when she played she knew gravity and posture: she felt the formal peace of her heavy body as it centred the encircling grace of Palestrina, Handel, Gluck . . .

Palestrina tonight . . .

'Art is science,' said Miss Allensmoore, 'there is no sloppy art. There are no sloppy stars.'

She talked to Ada Allensmoore every night. It was no use talking to Nora Plant, anyway, even if she happened to be alive, and, she often talked about the stars because for some reason she had decided they were 'scientific and accurate'. In the hours of her playing the universe went round her in satellites of sound, and that irrelevant ingredient, her identity, lapsed into an instinct so rapt and so concise that it amounted to genius. She yielded. She yielded to her breathing, to her transformation. Apart from the Voice, hers, she said, was the most physical form of music. So she gave way, but not lusciously. Always decorously, utterly and unselfconsciously.

Sometime in the night, sitting in her hard chair, her feet crossed, she *noticed* Miss Plant was dead – and then she wondered if one felt dying as one felt music. A giving up, and a giving back, thought Miss Allensmoore. Because she knew the feeling of music was quite different from the listening to it. Of course. Just as different as any two arts could be.

So she laid down the oboe, and she went with a secret intensity to look at Miss Plant who lay hardened to the sudden light in the bed-filled little room.

'Just like a statue of herself,' thought Miss Allensmoore, who had been pondering on stone and sculptors. A statue with hands of vernal green. These, however, she didn't observe. She wanted to ask her a question, and she even prepared a breath for it as for a note, but somehow no question was spoken. Miss Plant's silence had been no more than a continual state of never being spoken to. It was now *her* turn to be superior and uncommunicative.

Miss Allensmoore gazed down upon her friend somewhat severely, as if she were going to lecture her for lying there. Not that she ever had. Miss Plant had been absolutely free. It was just the way Miss Allensmoore looked for a moment. She had, in spite of her chubbiness, strict features, and if momentarily a definite expression replaced her usual abstract glance, it was a disciplinary one.

'But it's nothing after all,' said Miss Allensmoore, her eyes leaving the wistful dead face. And going to the window which the nurse had shut, she opened it, letting in more darkness than her candle could go round. It was nothing.

The nurse had shut the window as she had shut Miss Plant's strange eyes. If they opened now, would darkness come out of them? Ridiculous idea, said Miss Allensmoore leaning out. How a little light does revive one! You feel drowsy and helpless and then someone lights a lamp and then! You're full of energy again.

She saw the lamp from the room underneath shining out on the earth below her. Cabbages had been grown there. There were their gnarled stumps curled like cows' horns. Suddenly she remembered her mother and the way she used to cross the cut stalk with her knife so that in the spring fresh leaves frilled out. Bubbling with green, the garden all round them. And the cuckoo flying over. The sound of summer too in a window which seemed to be its instrument. Rustling rain, and her father's singing . . .

Beyond the yellow light it was as dark as if one's eyes were shut, and as silent as if a bell had just stopped ringing. Every death brought a little more stillness into the world. But what she couldn't command was the feeling that the darkness was Miss Plant's eyes not seeing . . .

The village was only a dozen or so cottages all at corners with one another, each one askew, and each one butting into a neighbour's sheds or gardens. The people, primitive, yet not unworldly, entertained themselves with conversation over the hedges while they hung the washing, set rat-traps, or planted their seeds.

Everything was talked over. Yet there was caution and a native secrecy. A person not of their kind might live among them for at least five years before noticing that the sexton in the churchyard gossiped like a sparrow to people in the lane, and even the ringers nodded news under the bells.

And Miss Allensmoore and Billy Prosser the carpenter and undertaker weren't the only people who had nicknames. There was Squatty Gallipot, the fat little shopkeeper, and there was George Ryder, the postman, a tall crooked-headed man whose height and low opinion of himself made him known beyond even his wide and hilly round as Mr Little-So-Big. The people had, however, a sense of situation and the wryness of circumstances, which at times was apter than the truth. To one man surnamed Beer they had erected a memorial stone inscribed: Tippler of This Parish, which their vicar had caused to be erased, without, however, their permitting it to be forgotten.

The morning after Miss Plant's death a neighbour, calling to borrow something, found Mrs Little-So-Big with a burst washer and a roaring tap. It was getting light. People were cracking morning wood, carrying pigswill and paddling out to feed the poultry. Mr Little-So-Big sat in the least wet patch of the already sodden back kitchen, a candle near his feet on the floor, lacing his boots to go and run for help; while the two women with hands reaching out towards the noise, eyed with disdain the bullets of water bouncing madly from the sink all over everything.

'What're we to do?' screamed Mrs Little-So-Big.

'Tie a scooped out potato over ur,' yelled the neighbour. 'Miss Plant's passed away.' 'Yes, I do know she 'as for I saw nurse go to Misery's. Oh, 'urry you an' get yer boots knotted and go and fetch somebody. No, Nance, I yen't doing anything fancy for meself. Let it run till it do choke itself. Do you s'pose Mrs Webb do know? I bin to see if I could make her out but them weren't up.'

'Oh, her's sure to know.'

The candlelight swaying in the dank draught of the jet made the nimble lips and eyelids of the women twitch. And a cockerel crouching on the copper among a lot of sacks and boxes leapt dustily and rapped upon the whitening window. The daylight which was creeping upon them seemed to cling about their faces and hair, like a fleecy hood. They wrung their hands busily.

At last Mr Little-So-Big, tying an audible knot, jumped up, looked grievously at them, put on his hat, and then took it off again to go through the door.

'Him ought to live in a steeple,' said his wife. 'One thing though, the wind do keep 'is 'air short. Oh, come in, Mrs Webb.'

'Why, what's up yere?'

An elderly thin woman, in a grizzled overcoat was stooping to put a milk tin on the doorstone. 'Why don't you turn it off at the main?' she asked in a shy, rather invalidish voice, which went with her complexion and the sort of pedigree hat she wore.

'Come in – come inside. I've bin three times up the gyarden to see if you was up. So Miss Plant's dead?' gabbled Mrs Little-So-Big.

'No!'

'Why, 'aven't you 'eard? It's as true as Satan's false. Yes. Nurse 'ave bin to Mr Misery's already.'

Mrs Webb had sat down suddenly on a plain old chair,

leaning on the table and arranging her hands finger by finger before her. A nervous colour came into her long cheeks, her eyes filled with tears. Childless, an orphan, a widow, she had been attached to Miss Plant. She had the pallid devoted face of those who naturally develop best in the shade of others. She wore their clothes – clothes which had 'atmosphere' and a vague kind of dignity. Round her neck to-day she had a little fence of starched net, with posts of bone and a cameo brooch; she was as neat and clean in the early mornings, they said, as if she sat up all night watching that no dust fell on her. But for all her differences (and different she was beside their splashed broadly-shadowed bodies) she was as much one of them as were her speech and her brown sensible hands.

'Yes,' said the neighbour. 'Her's as dead as Sooner baint. Ain't it a pity 'twasn't the other one?'

Mrs Webb said nothing. She had a sensitive imagination for which common talk was inadequate, and her timid grief was real.

'Maybe Miss Allensmoore 'ool be sorry now,' suggested Mrs Little-So-Big. 'If you do neglect to do things they do often turn on you at the end. Look at this tap! A was a-dripping all yesterd'y.'

'When did Miss Plant pass away?' Mrs Webb asked.

'Sometime yesterd'y afternoon I'm told. Ah, poor soul! She's gone. I seen Nurse leaving.'

Mrs Webb sat up, saying defiantly: 'Well, I be glad for 'er sake: it were time. Her sufferings was bad.'

'Ay, strangled by her own breath,' declared the neighbour. 'And 'twasn't only that . . .' they cried, 'what a life!'

'Such things. I wouldn't 'ave such things done,' Mrs Little-So-Big said. '*I'm* not afraid to speak. 'Ow do you think that old baggage spent the night – the first night after Miss Plant died, mind you! Why, a-playing on them bagpipes till three in the morning. I do kna-ow because our Arthur 'eard 'er when 'e went up past after an early yowe 'e 'ad twinning. Ah.'

There was a silence. They rested like people close to a weir breathing the cold, wild smell of running water. Mrs Webb thought of trees turning ashen, and the drifting, groping winds of yellow leaves. Like most people, she imagined it harder to die after the turn of the days. Miss Plant would never again hear bees in the orchards, the voices of skylarks, the shy singing of waters in the valleys. However, she had no proof Miss Plant had *ever* heard them . . .

'Them's educated things though, them musical instruments as Miss Allensmoore do play,' the neighbour was saying, 'spite of sounding like our owld cat a'spaggin' the Vicar's. Some folks do say her's a cleverer woman than us working class do realize.'

'What of it! 'Er be an old turnip for all that and can't 'ave no heart for anything 'uman,' retorted Mrs Little-So-Big, 'no education can't make up for that, nor change it. Clever! 'Er's no more clever than a dog as has bin brought up to yet [eat] bread and butter and chocolate and fish paste. It's a dog for all that, any road, yen't it? I say this: you do kna-ow, Mrs Webb, after what you told us. Is it educated to sit on top of a great fire a-frying yerself, and let a body die upstairs without so much as a match? Come on now, Mrs Webb, be it?'

'Pah, education! If that's it I'll wear me eye in a sling,' the neighbour said very angrily.

Mrs Webb didn't answer. Nervously she danced her fingers on the table. Mrs Little-So-Big sneezed and wrung her nose in her apron. The cock again scuffled and gave a dusty crow. He struggled for the light and the bright shadow on the water in the butt outside the window. And there suddenly was nothing in place of the cataract. The jet ceased, the tap coughed.

'George 'as turned it off at the main! Now what am I to fill the copper with? Oh, whatever do us women marry for? If I'd another chance I wouldn't pick George out o' a field o' turnips.'

'I want me breakfast,' said Mr Little-So-Big, walking in.

"Aven't you brought somebody with you? Oh, you 'aven't. Well then, you can go and look for yer breakfast somewhere else. 'Ow am I going to fill the kettle?' his wife demanded.

'There's a bucketful outside,' said Mr Little-So-Big faintly, 'I pumped it.'

'Oh, tha did? George, where was Miss Plant's part? Where did she come from?'

'I dunno. I never yeard anything about 'er except that daft walk to London she done once, years ago. 'Twasn't from yere she done it, mind. Ah. 'Oo do kna-ow if she done it all?'

'Oh yes, she went to London,' said Mrs Webb, 'yes, that's true. She told me herself.'

'She did?' The two women looked at her sharply. She had been several times to sit with Miss Plant while she was ill. It was possible she had the secret. There was, they knew, always a secret when anybody died. Especially a woman like Miss Plant, who had never known people. But Mrs Webb's face was empty. They saw that and went on mutually on a more monotonous level.

'Ah. Yes. Time and agen – yes, time and agen, I 'ave said there weren't anything *to* her. No, as you mid say, there weren't nothing *to* 'er. But that jaunt to London, that's true . . .'

'As I do kna-ow. Our Arthur, 'e asked 'er once. She said, "Ah, but that was long ago!" So 'e said, "What you done it for, Miss Plant?" "Love and scenery," she said. That was what she said, love and scenery.'

'Eh? Did she now? Did 'er s'y that? Poor thing, 'er 'asn't 'ad a lot.'

'Tchah – women!' Mr Little-So-Big puffed, and he wrung

the cockerel's neck in a decided but rather inattentive manner.

'All right, all right, George. It yen't me as you're strangling,' reproved his wife. 'Give yer mind to it, do. 'Tain't as if the bird'll 'elp yer. Ah, if she said that there must a' been a man.'

'I've always thought so,' said Mrs Webb sadly.

'Huh! It must a' bin Adam then, 'twas so long ago,' the brisk neighbour countered, her eyes spell-bound and her deep pink, old-fashioned workbag of a face gathered tightly round her mouth. 'Miss Plant must a' bin forty or fifty a score years ago, I'll be bound. Not,' she calculated, 'not as any a host of women don't go queer in middle life, as we do knaow.'

'Ay.'

'Ah.'

'Oh, they do.'

As they sighed, bracingly, the clock struck. The neighbour stepped startingly out of a pool, and Mrs Little-So-Big seizing a house flannel said she mid as well mop up.

'I must do up me a fire and make me a seven o'clock pudding,' said Mrs Webb, rising. And they separated candidly.

A seven o'clock pudding was a recipe for a mixture of currants, apples, suet and flour. It was called that because it was supposed to take all the time from seven o'clock until noon to cook. But it was long after eight when Mrs Webb sat down in her own kitchen to take off her hat after she had carefully rolled up the blind. Her dog, which had a mouth like red meat, yawned and came and lay down on her feet. Mrs Webb patted him and then she sat with a sedate gravity on her face worrying a little over what she had told people at different times. She *had* been angry – yes there was no doubt. But she had no wish to set anybody against Miss Allensmoore. It wasn't as if Miss Plant had ever *said* anything. Only the eagerness with which she had exclaimed 'Gloves – I should *love* them. My hands get so cold –' Only that. And yes – but it wasn't much – hadn't she said, 'I don't like music, and I don't like cats'? She certainly had, for Mrs Webb perfectly remembered it.

That cold bedroom, Mrs Webb breathed. And Miss Plant with only a faded old-rose velveteen coat round her shoulders! While downstairs Miss Allensmoore had a fantastic great fire, trained up sticks like some gorgeous climbing flower, right up the chimney. Hadn't she seen her sitting there with her bare legs and her sleeves pushed up, with her fat, soft flesh that looked as if it had been mixed with yeast, all naked, and flushing? Selfish and cruel, that's what she was, and didn't she deserve to be disliked? At any rate, it didn't matter surely? Unless – unless it would have grieved Miss Plant?

Mrs Webb was uneasy. Not that Miss Allensmoore seemed the one to care or even to notice. Nance and Ellen had been comic, but it wasn't funny really, what they meant. Hostile feelings in the village could be ugly. And ugliest when it was no more than a look . . . One look, from everybody.

She had unconsciously gathered up a tiny ball of wool – green, the remnant left over from those sad bright gloves, and she tolled it round and round in her palms until it was moist and had a clinging sticky feeling. Tears came into her hazel eyes. Miss Plant had had such lovely eyes! When the lids were quivering, flickering their crescents of lashes against gaunt cheek and brows, they had reminded her of butterflies in summer. It was in summer Miss Plant had walked to London, she'd said. When she told her that Mrs Webb had seen her in a flourish of dust, dragging past the brambles with their thick pink and white blossom, along some highway hedgerow. And then perhaps stooping to wash her face and hands in a roadside stream with a lovely little fish-shape of clear pebbles underneath the water . . .

In this way, and in others, she had often 'seen' Miss Plant. She had always interested her imagination. Sensitive, tender, romantic Mrs Webb, pictured her going those hundred and thirty-seven miles to meet the unheard-of man she adored. Waking because she was afraid to go faster with the fragile words she carried. Looking slowly and quietly about her with her shy, cool light brown hair stirring, at the earth's monopoly of green . . .

'Love and scenery,' said Mrs Webb, feeling for the flour. 'Love and scenery.'

It was strange how certain she had always been of Miss Plant's slow errand long ago, even though she had never before heard her own admittance. It was strange how she guessed at a dominant feeling taken there, a passion which had kept her there, in spirit ever since.

When she had asked Miss Plant why she had gone the answer had been she had forgotten. Mrs Webb wished she hadn't heard that. If she had sounded bitter and suffering it would have been all right, but she hadn't – she looked and spoke as if she *had* forgotten and was indifferent at it. She was, of course, very near death, though.

London! That was a superstitious long way. Once the women of the countryside had collected themselves and taken a trip there in a char-à-banc. They had seen St Paul's and the Zoo, and at the end, the Tower. 'Just a broken-down castle like any other round yere,' had been Mrs Little-So-Big's comment. No one remembered anything very distinctly. The hoardings, the banks of faces, the number of people in a Ladies, a shower, after which one of them had sat down on a seat in the park and dried her shoes with a paper bag – those had been their individual memories, for they weren't old-fashioned enough to be at all aghast, and found London, as a matter of fact, far more like their own cities than they could have guessed.

But Mrs Webb again was different. She remembered looking at some people sitting on the steps of St Paul's and wondering if by any chance Miss Plant had once sat there to rest and listen to the misty whirr of the world. And at the Tower she thought she had never seen, anywhere, brighter April grass. And (this was queerest of all) when they told her some great man had walked across it to have his head cut off, she had seen not a figure out of a story, but poor Miss Plant, in her old brown burberry, the worsted shawl drawn over her stained white hair, wandering over to the tragic corner as she wandered up and down the hedge the farmer wouldn't cut. She *saw* her. She seemed to quaver across the air, across the sunshine, weaving herself, as it were, *behind* the April light.

Coming home, Mrs Webb remembered she had taken off her hat and gone to sleep and dreamed Miss Plant was in the next seat, asleep too and leaning on her. Odd, she thought, to dream that someone else was asleep! Odder still that the time should come when she was telling the dream to Miss Plant. Oh dear, she wished she had gone to see the poor woman long before! But she hadn't liked to: it seemed rather presumptuous, for they weren't 'ordinary' folk, and besides Miss Allensmoore was formidable, and, she had been told, unfriendly. But Mrs Little-So-Big was right: what you neglected turned on you at the end. It made her weep now, to think how solitary Miss Plant must have been. There was something – yes there was – in the way she had jumped at the offer of the gloves, in the tone in which she said she didn't like music – that made Mrs Webb consider whether she wasn't more like one of themselves really? Only she had got marooned with Miss Allensmoore, who didn't encourage people to be neighbourly and who would, now she was left alone, probably end up as one of those queer women who are found dead one day, dressed in newspaper, after they have shut themselves up for years.

'With seven days' milk sour on the doorstep,' Mrs Webb exclaimed. The picture was dreadful and she felt quite sorry for Miss Allensmoore, even while remembering the weeks, when alert with indignation, she had waited only for the chance word to speak her mind. But Miss Allensmoore had utterly defeated her by her silence and her acceptance of things. She sat, or she walked about prodding the garden, and that was all. She had a way of standing in the lane just outside the gate with one hand just lifted as if to seize even a robin's twist of song, and catch it, as one squeezes a gnat. She was listening, anyone could see. She listened to every sound as if it were news. And she leant forward meanwhile in the attitude of one who is prepared to grab anything that comes close enough. At Mrs Webb she even smiled one day when the wind was coming out of the garden, swinging the gate like a white curtain in a window. The smile was even more remote than her speechless indifference to the visitor.

When the pudding was on boiling, peacefully knocking at the saucepan lid in a subdued and proper manner totally opposite to the peremptory frenzies of Miss Allensmoore's fierce creations, Mrs Webb went and peeped through the window into her orchard. The south-west breeze was blowing, the bare boughs all but knotted against the pane were full of the village notes of blackbirds and thrushes, and her troop of hooligan young hogs was galloping crazily over the grass under the trees. The weather was yielding, the snow would be melting off the hills, and there would be water over the road for Miss Plant's funeral without a doubt.

It was in the orchard, walking up and down, she had knitted most of the gloves, while keeping an eye on a hen who had a mind to lay in other folk's hedges. For several afternoons after having a wash and doing up her grate, she had walked and twinkled her needles until it was time to go indoors again to get her nephew's cooked tea ready. She had knotted the last stitch there, close to the old perry pear and then she had brought them indoors to sew on backs, at the table, by lamplight, the sprightly woolly flowers that were to bloom in the grave.

Miss Plant must have been *used* to cold hands, Mrs Webb told herself, in tears again, so that the orchard looked all blurred and warped through the shrunk glass. And the fact that she was apparently determined to be *buried* in Mrs Webb's gift showed that it was not so much for themselves she wanted them as for what they represented. Friendship. Company, Sympathy. Although she had cried joyously when Mrs Webb promised to make them. 'They'll be pretty too . . .'

Mrs Webb thought they were pretty. Not that she had ever seen Miss Plant wearing them, for she grew worse very suddenly as it happened, and after they were finished and taken to the door she had never seen Miss Plant again. She had given them to the nurse and the nurse had brought back the message: 'Thank you. They're a great comfort. She says she'll never take them off. She wants to be buried in them, she says . . .'

'Is she – dying then?'

The nurse nodded: 'She may rally but I don't think it's likely now.'

So Mrs Webb had gone away to wait for the event which was in spite of her foreknowledge such a shock to her. Often and often she thought of Miss Plant lying there under the old dark army blanket which gave her long body the look of a rough image dabbled out of earth. She had known Miss Plant was dying – oh yes. Hadn't she told herself there was a look no one could ever mistake particularly when the face of the sick person was seen in profile? Remembering this and the hair like glass or ice, and the strange fluttering eyes, the shape of which was an intensity in itself, Mrs Webb felt how easy it would be to see Miss Plant's ghost.

Those eyes! They focussed the tiny room, furnished it; and Miss Plant herself became in some strange way only the brink of them. As she grew weaker, their characteristic, passionate stare seemed to withdraw further and further. Rather than being fixed on distant visions, they appeared to be retreating from everything they gazed on. She would lie and look at the small, low window at the foot of the bed where the wind flopped in the shred of coarse white lace. Close to her hand would be a saucerful of peeled orange left by the nurse, her silver spectacles and the book of Common Prayer. Scales off the white-washed rafters fell in among her hair – thin brittle flakes which Mrs Webb would comb out, and pick from the bedclothes. Then one day when she was doing nothing at all and thought Miss Plant was asleep she had suddenly been asked if she would read the Litany. That was the time she remembered best. She had gone very red and hasty as she said, Oh dear, to tell the truth she wasn't a very grand reader.

'Not even with my glasses on. And without them, well, I can't read a bull's head from a duck's foot as I say. I expect I haven't been as well educated as you. We all do say you must be very clever to live with a woman like Miss Allensmoore.'

'Why?' Miss Plant asked, as if she were astonished.

'Well, I mean she – Miss Allensmoore as do play such educated music! Not that I like it if you can understand me. It's above me. A good hymn now – some of us like that. That's about all. Yes, you must be very clever indeed and I'm sorry I can't read to you. But if it's the Litany you want I don't need to. Shall I repeat it to you?'

Miss Plant looked wondering for a moment. Then she closed her eyes and the two women began to mutter the sorrowful rhythmic words. But in the middle Miss Plant suddenly opened her eyes again and in them was a cunning, confidential look – something sleek and furtive and yet rather defiant.

'I don't like music,' she said shortly: 'And I don't like cats,' she added. 'I wonder if anybody *ever* thinks of me?' she speculated faintly.

Mrs Webb looked down, sorting her fingers as if they were skeins and making a row of them on her knee. 'I dreamt about you once,' she said. 'It was the night we were coming home from our tour in London. I dreamt you were asleep next to me in the bus.'

'Music's too good for me,' said Miss Plant bitterly, 'and too queer. Did you know I walked to London once?'

'I have heard you did. Whatever did you do that for, Miss Plant?'

'I've forgotten,' said Miss Plant. 'I've forgotten everything about it except that it was one summer, and I used to walk along in the dusk because it was cooler. I saw owls. They were like moths,' she sighed. 'There were bats too and I was always afraid they'd get in my hair. Tell me, Mrs Webb, do I talk in my sleep?'

Mrs Webb shook her head. 'I don't know, I 'aven't heard you. Why?'

'I feel as if I do. I hear myself. I can't change it though . . .'

'You're free to talk in your sleep if you want to,' Mrs Webb nodded hotly.

'I saw an old woman,' Miss Plant mumbled; 'it was once when I'd lost the road and I went round to the back of a big house to ask the way. I thought I ought to go to the back for that, but I was so frightened always of dogs! I'm very independent, really, you know and I didn't like asking. I saw such a little old woman, pumping. She had on a skull cap. Yes. A big blue apron with pockets and a skull cap. I couldn't make her understand at all. She kept saying, "The mistress is round the gardens, feeding the chickens, if you'll just step that way." No, not step, stroll, was what she said. I've often thought she might have been me. How funny to remember that. I'm sure there were only the two of them living there and they both ate their meals in the kitchen together. And it was such a big house! All the beautiful rooms must have been shut up. Lovely furniture and curtains I'm sure. Eh, don't you think so?'

'Very likely,' said Mrs Webb compassionately. 'Maybe you dreamt it. I know I remember what I dream much better than anything else.'

Mysterious and rambling, Miss Plant shed no intentional secret but lay there talking and letting the irrational light of her sick memory fall here and there on what must have been a coherent life once. And filled with pity, Mrs Webb, tried to arrange her in the bed, to make her eat the eggs she carried to the cottage, warm from the nest, to please and soothe her. Never once did Miss Allensmoore come upstairs. If she had it would have been she who would have been the stranger, Mrs Webb thought. And she calculated how she would get up and where she would stand when Miss Allensmoore came to the bed. Glimpses she had of her, as she went out, sitting on the fender in the kitchen, nursing her foot. Inscrutable glimpses. That was all. Except the smell of burnt toast, and the sound of the sick woman sighing over herself upstairs.

Yes, it was quite warm for January, said Mrs Webb, going to look out of her door, to see if anyone were about. There would be water over the road, surely. She leant far out, right over her doorstone. She heard the slow shuddering calls of the ewes with early lambs, and a wind which was swift sunlight touched the land as with a white flame. And wasn't that Mr Misery coming up the hill on his motor-bicycle? Yes.

He fled past, popping, the silver sidecar flashing a sunspot in her eyes. She listened for the engine to stop, and it did, at Miss Allensmoore's.

Sunlight eddied round the cottage. Through wiry curtain and dusty glass it shone and settled. Under, the thinnest shifting film of shadow, it bubbled and stirred like a spring in the wall at the head of Miss Plant's bed. Presently Mr Misery's stooping head and shoulders obliterated it.

Downstairs, Miss Allensmoore lolled, waiting, turning her head with a turgid movement on its thick neck as she looked for the undertaker to appear. She had planned the arrangements. No relations, no expense. A walking funeral. But the weather worried Mr Misery. Did she know floods were already out in the lower meadows, he inquired? Gumboots, snapped Miss Allensmoore, and if there were any mourners, which besides herself there wouldn't be, they could paddle. Personally – here she looked preoccupied and Mr Misery glanced about him.

'What do you do with yourself all day?' he asked.

'Call the cattle home,' she said lazily. She smiled in her dormant way and added, poking her foot at a cat: 'No doubt you're used to domestic hurly-burlies. Spring cleaning and all that. Now I detest all that sweeping and dusting and polishing. Scrubbing occasionally or washing a floor over I don't mind. In fact it's a sort of pleasure to me.'

'You don't give yourself a treat very often, then,' Mr Misery observed: ''ard on yourself, aren't you?'

'Witty, aren't you?' she retorted: 'it's your calling, I suppose.'

After she had got rid of *him* she went out and picked the snowdrops. She took them upstairs, putting them in a cup on a small table that looked as if it were made of wet hay. She sat down with a drowsy sigh, blinking as she watched a sunbeam dazzling itself in the mean little mirror. Soon all would be quietly over . . .

She gave Miss Plant's feet quite an affectionate pat.

A few days later, in her shaggy black, with her healthy wide open gaze which seemed to refuse to mourn, Miss Allensmoore followed the coffin of her friend alone as far as the village. The bearers *were* in gumboots, and, listening to them going champ, champ, champ, along the lane, she smiled to herself.

'A lot of melancholy indiarubber elephants,' she thought, delighted.

But when they came to the village where glass, stone, and slates were giving back a greyish reflection of the flat afternoon light, there was quite a crowd waiting. Quietly, and rather drolly, as if someone else had made up her mind for her, Mrs Webb came forward carrying a wreath of moss and aconites which she had made the night before. Mr and Mrs Little-So-Big and one or two more who were standing by, also wandered up and began vacantly to follow until gradually a funeral shaped itself under the serious and wand-like gestures of Mr Misery, over whose tall black hat and deft flexions, Miss Allensmoore's ironic eye perpetually tripped in spite of her straightest efforts.

'What can they all be looking so peculiar about? Surely it's what called a "happy release",' she reflected, twirling the identical snowdrops, laughing a little in her bottom chin as she saw aside, other figures trying to catch up. There was a child, alone, who seemed happy, who seemed to think that such a procession must mean a celebration, and who began most respectfully to dance, while all the rest walked silently, with a touch of fame, with transparent gaze and opened lips, as in a story, down to the edge of the thin water where its blue and brownness flowed over the lane.

There they paused a moment as long as a leaf might take to sidle to earth from the top of a tall tree, before the bearers' loaded feet stepped into the flood.

'Oh, will they be drowned?' the child quavered, in her high drawling voice.

As clearly as if the coffin had been glass, Mrs Webb saw the green hands curled in Miss Plant's breast . . . she scrounged up her skirts. The water was in truth hardly deeper than the heel of her shoe, but psychologically she seemed to require emphasis.

Miss Allensmoore stopped. What revelation possessed her she didn't, for a moment, fathom; it was something *warranted,* something far too assured in Mrs Webb's action which convulsed her into perceiving, for the first time, the people who surrounded her.

She stopped. She would *not* share this absurd funeral with that woman or anybody else.

'Can't go any further,' said Miss Allensmoore. 'Here, will you take these?' she addressed Mrs Webb directly, with a most uncharacteristic courtesy. And she looked past her at the coffin now being slowly borne up the hill, with a terrible expression on her face, like the obstinacy of death. In that second her sight became myriad. She saw Miss Plant, who had somehow at the last moment contrived to amass an undreamed hostility against her. She saw the stupid, avid stares, the dancing child moving only her hands and her eyelids, in her mimicry of joy, the church steeple poking through a hill like a giant darning needle, and five white and golden hens pricking proudly over a swell of winter wheat . . . She saw the onyx clouds, the beautiful wind that came so suddenly that it was carved like lightening in the silver water fields . . .

Mrs Webb didn't turn, so the snowdrops fell on the water and gaily nudging one another, rippled into the ditch.

'Well!' cried Miss Allensmoore furiously. Trumpets of rage and grief sounded for her. She went so pale that many of the small crowd thought she would faint. But not she, not Miss

Allensmoore. There, in the middle of them she stayed, staring with paralysed eyes until the coffin and its few followers were round the bend. Then she moved, and prodding and pushing the road behind her with her umbrella, she climbed to a point from which she could see them creeping to the churchyard across the ribbed fields.

The church gate was open making a gap in the wide stone wall that was flung like a noose round the top of a hill. And the coffin was being borne forwards like the huge fated black stone that was to fill up the space. On and on they crept . . .

'That woman –' Miss Allensmoore said to Miss Plant. 'That woman! You *talked* to her. Coming up day after day, lying and spying. Both of you up there *talking.* And who *knows*?' cried she passionately, 'who's to judge? What *could* I do? What use is a wise friend to a fool? People. I hate them! I'd sooner shut meself in and tar my windows than ever endure the sight of one of 'em again.'

As she stood on the hill, watching Nora Plant's body being taken to the earth, it was useless telling herself she was going back to silence, useless to say the uproar was over and there would be no more crashes, no more fidgetings, no more nurses and neighbours coming. For the foundation on which she had suffered these things to be, was gone, and nothing was significant any more, and perhaps never would be again. Miss Plant had, she believed, destroyed that profound, if secretely weary, fidelity which had bound them, and in so doing had revealed the astonishing reality of her own quaint affection. She could not speak: her outcry was mental only. There, leaning on her umbrella, she stood, speechless, as when, with her oboe, she turned towards silence with the first low summons to the hordes of sound, as when, all those years ago, Miss Plant had come to London just to say to her, 'I can no longer bear to live away from you.'

XX

A View Across the Valley

DILYS ROWE

What was left was a presence in a room where all the wood was scrubbed white. The presence, already disembodied, had assumed a power it never had before. It was hard for those present to know what they felt in the presence of an event so difficult to understand, so impossible to reconstruct. Feelings ran like mercury between compassion and awe. Fortunately routine provides a set of phrases and even a tone of voice which concealed this confusion. Time that morning was short. The man considering the case said he must ask himself what else it could be but misadventure; he found no answer, he said. No one unfortunately would have been likely to pass by that place, not at that time of day and on a Sunday. He paused again and found the next part of the formula. All too often, he went on, in that place the deaths of children came before him, but it would have been unfair in this case to expect the parents to start a search immediately because a girl whose habits must have been a little out of the ordinary did not return in time for her lunch. He sighed and made a gesture with his open hand. He was disgruntled like a good workman who had not been given the right tools for the job. He was returning this verdict, he said, because they did not know what went on up there.

The child had been alone on the slope of the hill. She drew all her hair down before her face, pressed her chin to her neck, and knelt there for something to do in the brazen afternoon. Through the back of her neck the sun drove a boomerang of light grown solid, a creature consumed by light, as light had consumed the pieces of white hot metal pulled out of the furnace to amuse her as she stood at the foundry door. They would pick them out for her on the long tongs, shapes like toys distorted and fantastic, shapes pure with light and possessed by it; they held them out to her so that the heat flew at her face like an angry swan restrained. She felt the white-hot boomerang now probing through her neck to meet her chin at the other side. She pressed her chin still closer. She created dusk with the heavy curtain of hair, and at the day's height she put out the sun. It was a new state of being, and labouring with her breath she enjoyed to the full its exquisite pain. She opened her eyes to the thick falling hair, blew on it and felt the moisture returning from it to her face. She shook it three times. It swung in its own weight like a pendulum, and then hung still. Sweat started on her forehead and spread. When it became unbearable she raised her head and through the hair falling back around her face she saw the scar cut by the valley white after her own dusk, until in a moment the sun drenched it again.

She hitched up at her waist the green pleated skirt which the last wind before the heat of the day blew against her legs. Haze was beginning to rise on the summer Sunday. Occasionally gorse cracked in the heat. It must have been between one and two o'clock because below nobody was moving in the toy streets. She saw the tower of feathers where a train crawled on its stomach amongst the black hulks of the steel works and the bright red boxes of the new factories. A car visible only in the sun's searchlight moved where a road must be. From the cemetery something too small to see, a glass shade it may be with two dirty joined hands inside it, flashed her the living sun from amongst its deaths. No one moved in the streets. They were all in their houses stifling in the fumes from roast beef, lamb and mint, hot jam and rhubarb. The valley had life as a wound has microbes, but not on a Sunday between one and two o'clock. Stripped of its power, it lay harmless and neutral in the sun.

She was high above it where woods had been, where there was nothing to wreck. Somewhere behind her foxes and badgers played, and beyond that further than she could walk there was a lake. But only men with their heads in the clouds and gentle happy madmen would use this right of way with wind strumming in their ears when there were other ways in and out of the valley. And so it was no part of the landscape where the girl was now. Where she was four white clovers might spring up in all her footsteps, or she might be a girl conjured for convenience out of flowers. But she was not. She was a girl who was out at a forbidden time on the muted Welsh Sunday.

From her pockets she took the six bracelets. She put three on each arm and shook them towards the sun. She held her thin arms out and admired them hanging at her wrists, then pushed them hard up her arm as far as each would go. The sharp edges cut into the white freckled flesh. She had chosen them carefully for their graded sizes, two from jam jars, two from jars of chutney and two from jars of fish paste. She pulled them down again to the wrists and ran her fingers through the grooves of the red weals, three on identical places on each arm. She sat on, above the valley, shackled in the six bracelets.

From here the river was only a river, winding its way on a map through the lie of the land. Its banks were not doomed by memories of old deaths; it was not a place where pitiful drowned dogs covered with the grey plush that is left of them show the holes of their eyes. Down the valley the viaduct leapt in three great bounds across it, and she could see now that when trains stopped on it, sprawled in their monstrous immobility, people would be up there with their heads well out of the smoke, parcelled eight at a time in little boxes. In a musty book which might have been the only one an illiterate old man long dead had in his house for sentimental reasons, she had once seen a drawing on a page hanging off the thin cords of the binding. 'A landscape in Tuscany,' it said, showing a long arched bridge in the fields with hills behind it. This might have been a landscape in Tuscany under the sun.

Time in this new dimension of sun and space was long and vacant, solid so that she felt she could have cut it into little blocks. She was appalled by the length the afternoon would be. She cupped her hand and called, not seriously thinking that at this time it would bring the others up to her from the valley. Calling still she beat her hand against the sound. She was the child the children follow in the streets; when they form their little groups conferring against walls, it is she who bends the lowest in the centre and walks first away, upright carrying the threat and the secret of the destruction they have planned. If she says there are to be no spitting games today nobody spits for the furthest, the longest, the slowest, although the game has been devised by her. To this call they did not come.

But it was then for the first time that the hare showed itself, its haste less like fear than the movement of a dance. Seeing her he ran back to the slope below all in the flick of his tail. She went to the place where she had left her shoes and made on them the two crosses for seeing a hare. She took them off again, and threw herself down with her face into the sun. Turning she watched the leather of her shoe lapping up the crosses for as long as, in a more familiar dimension, a kitten would take to drink its saucer of milk. Then time came over her again, and pressing her fingers to her eye-balls she walked about in the yellow halls behind her eyes in the greatest nothing she had never seen.

Into the depths of this endless time she threw at random one thought after another and watched them ripple slowly outwards and outwards in the lazy afternoon. It was between one and two o'clock on a Sunday in the whole long history of the world, and the moment that had just passed and this minute had gone for ever into the whole world's past. There would never be another time when one girl and one only, 13 years and 6½ days old, would be lying alone on the hill hungry and damp from the sun between one and two o'clock. She thought of valleys which are green and fruitful and yellow with corn; a slow river would be winding through green banks. Cowslips would be lying like newly-washed children around it and poplars and larches would be beyond the water meadows. This valley was not green, but sometimes a piece of slag would have the print of a fern stamped deep into it. Sometimes a stream would turn red with copper like the biblical sea or yellow like the Tiber with filth. When the snow came the birds left their confident footprints on the slag heaps mistaking them for hills. When it was two o'clock the hooter sounding between hills sent packs of soiled and sweating men moving through the valley. And when it was dark the furnace opened its inflamed mouth and caught stars for flies.

The vaporous halls behind her eyes turned solid, and through the skin of her lids she saw the cloud that was passing for a moment over the sun trailing with it a wind that was no more than a message. She sat up. Purple lights blocked her newly opened eyes. When they cleared the hare came again running in the arc of a circle from below. She called to him, and crossed her shoes and ran to where it had disappeared. Licks of flame were playing in the bracken and in the grass at its edge. Over its blazing purity the river was full of the thick and various filth it collected, there were leprous deaths on the grave stones and the black hulks of the steel works were crusted with barnacles of soot and grime. On the canal she could pick out the galleon, the treasure boat, with the gold breast plates and the rings with stones like blood on the sandals and the bracelets. It was rotting and sodden, the coal barge that had not been used for thirty years. Every year of her life its swollen timbers had become a little more decayed until now their ends were fraying. Sitting in the sun with the fire beginning she remembered one of many deaths. Men stood with ropes and poles for the whole of a day; children looking for sensations as hens peck for anything that comes out of the ground were shooed away only to gather again and again. The boy lay only where he had fallen in the discoloured yellow water. He did not get himself destroyed in a lonely place. He fell quietly, almost under their eyes, with a low wall between him and the road, and the path was there for anybody to be walking on at a lucky time.

But where he fell the barge imprisoned him, weeds parcelled his nine year old body with the awful precision of accident, and the men dragged in shallow water through a whole day, and when they were meant to find him they did find him tangled in weeds. The canal is not like the sea, the powerful destroyer, returning its dead when the deed has been accomplished. The canal only gives them reluctantly after a struggle covered with the long green slime with which it brands the bodies of dead dogs. The girl was dappled in sunshine and hatred for his wilful destruction. And the hare came again.

He was running now in no hurry, as children run to music when they expect it suddenly to stop. The afternoon had reached its turning. The sun was a blatant disc of light, from which the wind had snatched the warmth to give it to the fire. The fire burnt now on three sides of the hare. The child thought she would look at the sun through a flame. She ran into the middle of the hare's circle to catch a sight of this miracle of miracles. She lay outstretched in the middle of light and the soft unburdened flame leaping and the tireless hare running in his sacrificial pleasure as far away from her as he could go. They all lay about her like gifts she did not deserve. She felt the angry swan straining again for her flesh. She saw the hare moving in now closer to her than he had dared. He was beyond caring now for her presence or she for his. Pleasure moved inside her mounting from the pit of her stomach to her throat in waves of exquisite agony. The wind changed on the turning of the afternoon tide. The fire was already a great bracelet all around her just open for the arm. She lay enchanted, and the circle closed.

Notes on the authors and their texts

I. **Anne Beale** (1815-1900)

Anne Beale, born to an English farming family in Somerset, came to Wales in 1841, initially to work as a governess in a Welsh clerical household. She settled in Llandeilo, Carmarthenshire, and embarked upon a long and successful career as a novelist. *Gladys, the Reaper* (1860), *Country Courtships* (1869), *The Pennant Family* (1876), *Rose Mervyn, of Whitelake* (1879) and other of her fictions set in Welsh locations were generally appreciated by her contemporaries as sympathetic and well-informed portrayals of rural Welsh life. Her first published prose, *The Vale of the Towey; or, Sketches in South Wales* (1844), is presented to its readers in her preface as virtually a piece of oral history, the 'simple annals of simple folk' that she observed about her in Llandeilo. She later re-worked this material and twice republished it under different titles, as *Traits and Stories of the Welsh Peasantry* (1849) and *Seven Years for Rachel, or Welsh Pictures sketched from life* (1886). The version of 'Mad Moll's Story' included in this anthology comes from *Traits and Stories of the Welsh Peasantry*, and preserves many of the characteristics of oral record in its reportage of an incidence of child abuse and its consequences.

None of Anne Beale's novels are currently in print, but for further information on their author, see Moira Dearnley, '"I came hither, a stranger": A view of Wales in the novels of Anne Beale', *New Welsh Review*, 1, no. 4 (1989), 27-32.

II. **Mallt Williams** (1867-1950)

Born Alice Matilda Langland Williams, to an English-speaking family of Welsh – and reputedly noble – descent, Mallt Williams was reared in Aberclydach House, near Talybont-on-Usk, Brecknockshire. There she and her sister Cate became acquainted with their neighbours, Lady Llanover and her daughter, fervent supporters of Welsh and Celtic revivalism. Under the Llanover influence the two sisters espoused nationalistic and pro Welsh language causes, adopted Welsh versions of their own names, becoming Alis Mallt and Gwenffrida respectively, and began together to write patriotic novels, which they published under the pseudonym 'The Dau Wynne'. Alis Mallt also published a few articles and short stories independently, signing herself 'One of the Two Wynnes'; 'David' appeared under that pseudonym in Owen M. Edwards' English-language journal *Wales* in 1896. The story's focus on a heroic and martyred central figure is characteristic of the Dau Wynne's Romantic bent. But the persecution which David endures for the sake of his Methodist beliefs is more likely historically to have occurred a hundred years before the story's publication, rather than 'fifty years ago', as the text itself suggests. According to the religious census of 1851, 75% of the Welsh population were Nonconformists by the middle of the nineteenth century, with Calvinistic Methodism as one of the largest single denominations. It is unlikely, therefore, that in 1846 a Methodist convert could have suffered the degree of persecution which afflicts David in this tale.

Neither of The Dau Wynne's two novels, *One of the Royal Celts* (1889) and *A Maid of Cymru* (1901) are currently in print, but for further information on Mallt Williams, see Marion Löffler, 'A Romantic Nationalist', *Planet*, 121 (1997), 58-66.

III. **Sara Maria Saunders** (1864-1939)

Sara Maria Davies was born and reared in Cwrt Mawr, Llangeitho, Cardiganshire, the daughter of a local magistrate Robert Joseph Davies and his wife Eliza. In 1887 she married a Calvinistic Methodist minister, John M. Saunders, and started to publish short stories in the Welsh-language journals of the day. Characteristically, she produced series of stories, linked by locality, narrator, and recurring characters, and signed 'S.M.S.'; these stories were collected and published as three separate volumes in 1897, 1907 and 1908. Her favourite localities were rural villages, like the one in which she herself was brought up, with most of the community's activity centred on the Methodist chapel and its meetings. From 1896-9, she also published an English-language series of tales, 'Welsh Rural Sketches', which appeared sporadically in the journal *Young Wales*, the English-language mouthpiece of the Welsh 'Home Rule' movement of the day. Set in the village of Pentre-Rhedyn, with the local school-master as their narrator, 'Welsh Rural Sketches' focuses primarily on a long-standing feud between the chapel's severe 'big deacon', Mr Morris, and a kind-natured lay preacher, Mr Rogers. So bitter has their opposition become that when Edward, the Morrises' only child, woos and wins Nancy, the preacher's daughter, Mr Morris vows that neither he nor his unfortunate bullied wife will have anything to do with their disobedient son again. 'Nancy on the warpath' begins at this point in the series, and was published in *Young Wales* in 1897.

None of Sara Maria Saunders' writings are currently in print. For further biographical reading, see *The New Companion to Welsh Literature*, edited by Meic Stephens (University of Wales Press, 1998).

IV. Gwyneth Vaughan (1852-1910)

'Gwyneth Vaughan' was the pseudonym of Annie Harriet Hughes (née Jones), a miller's daughter from Talsarnau, Meirionethshire, who, after a paltry education and an apprenticeship as a milliner, married the son of a local tradesman, and left with him for London, where he trained as a doctor. But her husband fell prey to alcoholism, and, after the family's return to Wales in the early 1890s, Gwyneth Vaughan struggled to support their four children by working as the editor of the *Welsh Weekly* and the *Dowlais Gazette*, and as a free-lance journalist, public lecturer and novelist. She published two Welsh-language novels and a number of serialized journal and newspaper fictions, while at the same time contributing energetically as an organizer and publicist to the Welsh Home Rule campaign of her day, and to the women's suffrage and temperance movements. She also contributed English-language articles to *Young Wales* and the *Celtic Review*, but 'The old song and the new' appears to be the only piece of English-language fiction she penned. It seems not to have been published during her lifetime, but was found as a pencilled manuscript amongst her papers deposited in the Gwynedd County Archive Library. The manuscript is undated, but, given its pan-Celtic theme, it is likely that it was written at the turn of the century in support of the Celtic Congress movement, which held its first gathering of Scottish, Irish, Welsh, Breton and Manx representatives in Dublin in 1901. The story's similarity, in terms of theme, tone and technique, to the Welsh-language allegories published by Gwyneth Vaughan in the journal *Cymru* in 1902 and 1905 also suggests an early 1900s date.

None of Gwyneth Vaughan's writings are currently in print. For further biographical information, see *The New Companion to Welsh Literature*, edited by Meic Stephens (University of Wales Press, 1998).

V. **Allen Raine** (1836-1908)

Anne Adaliza Evans, who was later to take the pseudonym Allen Raine, was the daughter of a Newcastle Emlyn solicitor. Well-educated, in Cheltenham and London, in 1872 she married Beynon Puddicombe, a London banker with Welsh connections. In 1894, in her late fifties, she commenced on what was to prove a highly successful authorial career through winning a serial story competition in that year's National Eisteddfod. From then until her death, Allen Raine published regularly: eleven novels and a number of short stories followed one another in quick succession, and won her fame. By 1908 just under two million copies of her novels had been sold in the United Kingdom alone, and her work was also popular in the States. The majority of her tales appear to be located in or around the rural seaside village of Tresaith in Cardiganshire, the holiday home of her childhood which became in 1900 her permanent home, after her husband's early retirement for reasons of mental ill health. 'Home, sweet home' was published in 1908 in *All in a Month, and other stories*, a collection of shorter fictions which her publishers put together after her death.

Honno Press has just republished Raine's 1906 novel *Queen of the Rushes* in its 'Classics' series. For further information on the author, see Sally Jones, *Allen Raine* (University of Wales Press, 1979), and Katie Gramich's introduction to the new Honno edition (1998).

VI. **Jeannette Marks** (1875-1964)

Jeannette Marks was an American, born in Chattanooga, Tennessee; but soon after her birth her family moved to Philadelphia, where her engineer father was appointed to a professorship at the University of Pennsylvania. Marks followed her father into academic life, and took up a post as instructor in English literature at a Massachusetts women's college, Mount Holyoke, in 1901. There she was to remain for the rest of her working life, settled in life-long partnership with the president of the college, Mary Woolley. According to her biographer, Jeannette Marks 'fell instantly in love with Wales' when she first visited the country in 1904. She returned in 1906, 1907, and 1910, and set many of her short stories and plays in Wales. 'An All-Hallows' honeymoon', which first appeared in her collection *Through Welsh Doorways*, published in Boston in 1909, was subsequently re-worked by its author as the one-act play 'Welsh Honeymoon', and published in *Three Welsh Plays* (1917). Marks dedicated this last volume in the warmest possible terms (*'Calon wrth Galon'* – Heart to Heart) to the Welsh National Theatre, which in 1911 had awarded her one of its first prizes for playwriting.

None of Jeannette Marks' work are currently in print, but see, for further information on her life, Anna Maria Wells, *Miss Marks and Miss Woolley* (Boston: Houghton Mifflin & Co., 1978).

VII. Bertha Thomas (1845-1918)

The daughter of a Glamorganshire clergyman, Bertha Thomas moved from her childhood home in Wales to England in 1862, when her father was made Canon of Canterbury Cathedral. In the early 1870s she started to contribute articles and stories to English literary magazines, such as *Fraser's*, *The National Review* and *Cornhill*; *Proud Maisie*, the first of her eleven novels, appeared in 1876. She never married, but was clearly considered a literary woman of some note during her day: she was asked, for example, to contribute a biography of the French woman novelist

George Sand to the Eminent Women series, a volume which duly appeared in 1883. Many of her fictions include reference to the political topics of her day, and demonstrate her interest in the suffragette movement and early socialism. In her last published book, *Picture tales from the Welsh hills* (1912), she returned to the scenes of her childhood. 'The madness of Winifred Owen', one of the tales included in that volume, explores with sensitivity a topic which was of personal interest to Bertha Thomas: she was herself the offspring of a mixed Welsh/English love match, as her mother was an English woman.

None of Bertha Thomas's writings are currently in print, but see for further biographical information, *The Feminist Companion to Literature in English,* edited Virginia Blain et al (Batsford Books, 1990).

VIII. Ellen Lloyd-Williams

Between 1923 and 1925 a handful of short stories and a few poems by Ellen Lloyd-Williams appeared in *The Welsh Outlook,* a patriotic periodical which had announced itself on its first appearance in 1914 as 'A Monthly Journal of National Social Progress'. Earlier, a few of her poems had also been anthologized in A. G. Prys-Jones's collection *Welsh Poets: A Representative English Selection from Contemporary Writers* (1917). Although Lloyd-Williams's literary output was slender, 'The call of the river', published in *The Welsh Outlook* in 1924, bears comparison with many of the better-known stories collected in this anthology, in its haunting evocation of the triumph of nature worship over the utilitarian purposes of men and women.

IX. **Kathleen Freeman** (1897-1959)

Born and educated in Cardiff, from 1919 to 1946 Kathleen Freeman taught Greek at the University of Wales, Cardiff, where she had earlier gained undergraduate and research degrees. Under her own name she published a number of critical and historical monographs on classical Greek culture, and of translations into English of Ancient Greek texts, as well as a few works of fiction. Under the pseudonym Mary Fitt she also published over twenty detective novels between 1941 and 1958. Both aspects of her career won recognition in 1951 when, in one and the same year, she was both appointed to the chair of the Philosophical Society of Great Britain and made a member of the Detection Club. 'The coward', which was first published in her collection *The Intruder and other stories* (1926), would appear to indicate that she was also an early student of Freud; the foreman road-mender who recounts his history in this tale seems to have been held captive throughout life by a pronounced Oedipus complex.

None of Kathleen Freeman's novels and short stories are currently in print, but see for further biographical information, *The Dictionary of Welsh National Biography 1951-1970*, edited by E. D. Jones and Brynley F. Roberts (Cymdeithas y Cymmrodorion, 1997).

X. **Dorothy Edwards** (1903-34)

The daughter of an Ogmore Vale schoolteacher with strongly socialist leanings, Dorothy Edwards was educated in Howell's High School Cardiff, and took a degree in Greek and philosophy at Cardiff University. Her home base for the rest of her short life was in the Cardiff suburb of Rhiwbina, with her widowed mother, but she also travelled in Italy, and lived for a period with David Garnett and his wife Ray, members of the Bloomsbury group in London. The publication of her collection of short stories *Rhapsody* (1927) and her novel *Winter Sonata* (1928) brought her early recognition as a writer, but she seems to have found it difficult to establish an authorial voice which could at once express her strong Welsh nationalist and socialist leanings, and yet still engage the interest of the London literati, whose views were of significance to her. Her writings are curiously stifled in tone, and seem intent on concealing both the gender and nationality of their author, let alone her political affiliations. In January 1934 she burned her unpublished papers before committing suicide by throwing herself under a train, leaving a farewell note which apparently read 'I have received kindness from many people, but I have not really loved any human being'.

'The conquered', which was published in *Rhapsody,* will be familiar to readers of Welsh short story collections, as it has been much anthologized. But it is by far the most interesting of Dorothy Edwards' stories from a Welsh point of view, and one which could not be omitted from a collection like this one, which aims to integrate previously established and little-known writers.

Both *Rhapsody* and *Winter Sonata* were republished by Virago Press in 1986, with a foreword by Elaine Morgan, but are by now once again out of print. For further reading on her life and work, see Luned Meredith, 'Dorothy Edwards', *Planet,* 55 (1986) and Christopher Meredith, 'The window facing the sea: the short stories of Dorothy Edwards', *Planet,* 107 (1994).

XI. Nansi Powell Price

'The heads of Coed Uchaf', which was published in *The Welsh Outlook* in 1925, is of interest as an apparent precursor of Margiad Evans's 1932 novel *Country Dance.* Like the novel, this Border counties' tale pits a Welsh man against an English one, in their love rivalry over a young woman of mixed Welsh and English parentage. Though the mood of this story is much more lightly humourous than that of Margiad Evans' novel, yet it still manages to convey both the ease of cross-border alliances and the intensity of racial tension which could co-exist within relatively isolated rural Border communities. The 'Commortha', which provides the setting for the tale, would appear to refer to the wide-spread Welsh rural '*cymorth*' (help) tradition, in which neighbouring communities met to assist one another with such tasks as the ploughing or reaping of the fields. Nansi Powell Price, whose name would suggest that she herself hailed from the Welsh side of the border, seems to have published little else except this tale.

XII. Mary Webb (1881-1927)

Mary Gladys Meredith was born in the village of Leighton in Shropshire, her father of Welsh descent and her mother a Scot. Her father ran a boys' preparatory school, and Mary was well educated, first at home and then in a finishing school in Southampton; later she attended Cambridge University Extension classes in Shrewsbury. Encouraged by her father, to whom she was strongly attached, she started to write poems in her teens, but little of her work was published before her first novel *The Golden Arrow* appeared in 1916. By this time George Meredith, her father, was dead, and Mary married – unhappily, as it turned out – to Henry Webb, another Shropshire schoolteacher. She went on to publish four more novels and a collection of essays before her relatively early death from Graves' disease, a disfiguring ailment with which she was first afflicted in 1901. Best known for her evocative depictions of the Shropshire landscape, the author of *Gone to Earth* (1917) and *Precious Bane* (1924) is, of course, a Border writer rather than a Welsh one. Nevertheless her sense of identification with Wales and the Welsh through her father seems to have been strong. Two of her novels, *Seven for a secret* (1922) and the unfinished *Armour wherein he trusted*, were set in Wales, and, from the evidence of its characters' surnames at least, the short story 'Over the hills and far away', included in this volume, also appears to have its location on the Welsh side of the border. The story was published in *Poems and the Spring of Joy* (1928), a selection of her poems, prose and shorter fictions put together by her publishers in response to her sudden posthumous fame. For, after a lifetime of much unhappiness and of critical neglect, Mary Webb became a best seller once she was dead, and her writings have remained fairly readily available ever since.

For further biographical reading, see Gladys Mary Coles, *Mary Webb* (Seren Press, 1990). The 'Peri', to which the central character of 'Over the hills and far away' is compared, was originally a genie from Persian mythology; in Mary Webb's story it appears to denote a super-natural being which haunts, yet is not part of, human society.

XIII. **Hilda Vaughan** (1892-1985)

Born in Llanfair-ym-Muallt, Brecknockshire, to a land-owning family that traced its descent back to the seventeenth-century poet Henry Vaughan, Hilda Vaughan left her home during the First World War to serve as a nurse with the Red Cross and later as an organizer for the Women's Land Army. Subsequently, in 1923, she married the London-based novelist Charles Morgan, and started publishing her own fictions. Many of her novels, for example *The Battle to the Weak* (1925), *The Invader* (1928), *Her Father's House* (1930) and *The Soldier and the Gentlewoman* (1932), are set in rural Welsh locations. 'A thing of nought', which is generally recognized to be one of her finest pieces, was originally published on its own, as a novella, in 1934. A note by its author on the dust-jacket of the first edition describes the origins of the story as follows:

> A friend of mine, to whom I told the plot, asked me where I had come by it. I said, and as far as I was aware I spoke the truth, that I had made it up. She then told me that she was sure the principal characters, at least, must have had their counterpart in real life. I assured her that not only the characters, but the setting of this story, like that of most of my novels, were entirely invented. When I came to reconsider the question, however, I suddenly remembered what I had long forgotten, and was not even conscious of when I wrote this story. One day, perhaps fifteen years ago, I was riding up a lonely little road between two high walls of hills in a remote Welsh valley. A stream ran beside the road, the noise of its peat stained waters, and the mewing of a solitary buzzard overhead were the only sounds that broke the stillness, except the occasional bleating of a mountain sheep, and the sighing of the west wind. Suddenly, round a bend in the road, I came across one isolated farmhouse. It was whitewashed, the only white object in a vast green landscape. Facing it, upon the other side of the stream, was a gaunt square chapel, built of grey stone, with the caretaker's cottage clinging to its side – as a little shell might do to a strong rock. Something about those two lonely dwelling places and that chapel, to which I imagined black-clad men and women coming from far away

> along the solitary road on a Sabbath, stirred my imagination. Many years afterwards, the seed dropped into my mind at that time bore fruit in the tale entitled 'A thing of nought'.

None of Hilda Vaughan's novels are currently in print, but for further biographical reading see Christopher W. Newman, *Hilda Vaughan* (University of Wales Press, 1981).

XIV. **Eiluned Lewis** (1900-1979)

Born to a landowning Welsh family based near Newtown, Montgomeryshire, Eiluned Lewis worked as a London journalist with the *Daily News* and *Sunday Times* until her marriage to Graeme Hendrey in 1937. Earlier, she had started publishing short stories and poems in the *Welsh Outlook* in 1929-31, and her first novel, *Dew on the Grass*, appeared in 1934. Like her second novel *The Captain's Wife* (1943), it is set in Wales and draws heavily upon her childhood memories, and those of her mother and grandmother. She turned to more contemporary events for the plot of her third and last novel *The Leaves of the Tree* (1953), which is set in France during the Second World War. The collection *Morning Songs* (1944) includes the majority of her poems. 'The poacher', which was first anthologized in the Faber collection *Welsh Short Stories* in 1937, relies for its plot, and its subtle commentary upon social snobbery, on the fact that one of the longest established gypsy families of Wales goes by the surname 'Lovell'.

For further biographical reading, see the introduction by Glen Cavaliero to Boydell Press's 1984 edition of *Dew on the Grass*. See also, for autobiographical material, Eiluned Lewis, *A Companionable Talent: Stories, Essays and Recollections* (Goudhurst: The Finchcocks Press, 1996).

XV. Siân Evans (1912-)

Nancy Esther Whistler, who later, under the incitement of her sister Peggy, took the name Siân Evans, was born in Uxbridge, London, to a mother of English and Irish extraction, and an English father, whose grandmother, Ann Evans, was believed to be Welsh. Owing to her father's ill health, which necessitated his early retirement from his post as an insurance company clerk and left the family in some financial difficulty, at the age of seven Siân Evans spent a year living with her sister Peggy near Ross-on-Wye, on the Welsh border, in the care of an aunt. This experience of immersion in the Border countryside was formative for both sisters. The next year their parents moved to the village of Bridstow, just west of Ross-on-Wye, and the family home there remained Siân Evans's base for the next sixteen years. Towards the close of this period, inspired perhaps by the publishing success of her sister, she started to write short stories. She was still writing during the time in which, after her father's death in 1935 and the family's enforced departure from Bridstow, she and her sister Peggy kept a guest house in Walford, a little further south down the Wye valley. 'Davis' was published in the Faber anthology *Welsh Short Stories* in 1937, and three years later was chosen once more by Gwyn Jones for inclusion in his 1940s Penguin collection *Welsh Short Stories*. It is the only story which appears in both the 1937 and 1940 anthologies, apart from one tale by Gwyn Jones himself which he chose to repeat. Siân Evans's story writing, then, met with some success – understandably so, as 'Davis' is a very vivid and convincingly detailed study of Welsh Oblomovism. What is surprising, given its quality, is that it constitutes one of the very few pieces published by this author.

XVI. Rhian Roberts

It would be good to know more about Rhian Roberts, who published short stories in the journals *Life and Letters Today* and *Wales* in the 1940s. 'The pattern' first appeared in *Wales* 7 (1947). Given that the central character in this story refers to 'Ponty', or Pontypridd, as his local market town, its setting would appear to be one of the industrial villages of the Rhondda, Dare or Cynon valleys during the Second World War. The accumulation of convincing local detail in the tale, along with its valiant attempt to convey the Valleys' dialect on paper, suggest that Rhian Roberts must herself have come from this locality or have lived in it. But so far attempts to find out more about her have been unavailing.

XVII. Brenda Chamberlain (1912-1971)

Brenda Chamberlain was born in Bangor, to an English father – a railway bridges' inspector – and a mother of Irish and Manx origin; her mother, a socialist and a supporter of the women's equal rights movement, became the town's first woman mayor. At school Chamberlain excelled at art, and won a place to study at the Royal Academy in London; there she met John Petts, whom she married in 1935. With Petts she returned to Wales, to live in an isolated hillside cottage near Llanllechid in Caernarfonshire, and to attempt to make a living through painting and print-making. Together they set up the Caseg Press, and with the poet Alun Lewis produced a series of Caseg Broadsheets in 1941-2, a combination of Lewis's poetry and Petts' and Chamberlain's art work. By this time Brenda Chamberlain had herself started to write; and during the 1940s she published poems and prose pieces in the Welsh and English literary journals of the day. In 1947, after the break-up of her marriage, she moved with a Frenchman, Jean van der Bijl, to settle on Ynys Enlli, the island of Bardsey, off the tip of the Llŷn peninsula, and lived amongst the dozen or so inhabitants of that isolated community for the next fifteen years. *Tide-Race*, her illustrated prose account of life on the island, was published to some critical acclaim in 1962. Her other publications include *The Green Heart* (1958), a collection of poems; a semi-autobiographical novel, *The Water-Castle* (1964); and *A Rope of Vines* (1965), an account of the year she spent living on the island of Ydra in Greece from 1964-5. In 1971, back in Bangor, Brenda Chamberlain ended her own life, with sleeping tablets.

'The return', was first published in *Life and Letters To-day*, 54 (1947); the 'Island' of the story is Ynys Enlli. *Tide-Race* has recently been republished by Seren Books (1987), but none of Brenda Chamberlain's other works have reappeared in print. For further biographical reading, see Kate Holman, *Brenda Chamberlain* (University of Wales Press, 1997).

XVIII and XIX. Margiad Evans (1909-1958)

Peggy Eileen Whistler, who later adopted the name Margiad Evans, was born in Uxbridge, London (see above, in the note on her younger sister Siân, for details of her parentage and early years). After leaving school at the age of sixteen, she spent some months teaching English in France before returning to attend art classes in Hereford School of Art. Her first involvement with publishing was artistic rather than literary: she illustrated an anthology of Indian stories, *Tales from the Panchatantra*, in 1930. But soon it was to be her own fictions that she would illustrate. With her first novel *Country Dance* (1932), a tale about Welsh and English love rivalry set in the Border country, she early established for herself a reputation as an Anglo-Welsh writer. *The Wooden Doctor* which followed in 1933 is partly set in Wales, and describes an adolescent girl's unrequited obsession with her local doctor. *Turf or Stone* (1934) and *Creed* (1936), both set in the Border Country, are similarly concerned with doomed and destructive passions. By 1936 Margiad Evans had published four relatively well-received novels and was still only twenty-five, but soon both her literary output and her life history were to change direction. In 1939 she married a Welshman, Michael Williams, and settled down with him in Llangarron, two miles east of the Welsh border near Ross-on-Wye. She wrote no more novels, but did publish two volumes of autobiographical reflection, *Autobiography* (1943) and *A Ray of Darkness* (1952); the latter was primarily the record of her responses to the fact that in 1950 she developed epilepsy, and in 1951 gave birth to her first and only child. Her poems were collected during these years in two volumes, *Poems from Obscurity* (1947) and *A Candle Ahead* (1956), and her short stories in the volume *The Old and the Young* (1948), from which come both the stories by Margiad Evans included in this collection. In 1958 Margiad Evans died of a brain tumour.

None of Margiad Evans's writings are currently in print, but Seren Books is planning to bring out an edition of *The Old and the Young* shortly. For further reading on her life and work, see Moira Dearnley, *Margiad Evans* (University of Wales Press, 1982), and Ceridwen Lloyd-Morgan, *Margiad Evans* (Seren Books, 1998).

XX. **Dilys Rowe** (1927-)

Dilys Rowe was born in Landore, an industrial village in the Swansea valley. Her father, a clerical worker in Baldwin's local steel works; came from Carmarthenshire where his originally West of England family had settled some generations back; her mother's family was Welsh, and Welsh-speaking on the grandfather's side. She started writing early and had one story published before she embarked on an English Literature degree at the University of Wales, Swansea. After graduating she sought work as a free-lance journalist in order to fund her writing, and moved to London. She worked for the *Guardian* and the *Times,* and during the late 1950s and early 1960s was editor of the *Observer*'s women's page. Her story 'A view across the valley' first appeared in *Pick of today's short stories*, 6 (1955), edited by John Putney. Married to American writer David Dorrance, Dilys Rowe now lives in the south of France.

The figure of the hare, which proves mortally enchanting to the central protagonist in 'A view across the valley', draws upon medieval and folkloric representations of the hare as a supernatural creature associated with witchcraft.

ABOUT HONNO

Honno Welsh Women's Press was set up in 1986 by a group of women who felt strongly that women in Wales needed wider opportunities to see their writing in print and to become involved in the publishing process. Our aim is to publish books by, and for, the women of Wales, and our brief encompasses fiction, poetry, children's books, autobiographical writing and reprints of classic titles in English and Welsh.

Honno is registered as a community co-operative and so far we have raised capital by selling shares at £5 a time to over 350 interested women all over the world. Any profit we make goes towards the cost of future publications. We hope that many more women will be able to help us in this way. Shareholders' liability is limited to the amount invested, and each shareholder, regardless of the number of shares held, will have her say in the company and a vote at the AGM. To buy shares or to receive further information about forthcoming publications, please write to Honno, 'Ailsa Craig', Heol y Cawl, Dinas Powys, Bro Morgannwg CF64 4AH.

ALSO AVAILABLE
IN THE HONNO CLASSICS SERIES:

Queen of the Rushes
by Allen Raine

With an Introduction by Katie Gramich

Allen Raine (Anne Adaliza Puddicombe) was one of the most popular authors of the turn of the century, with her books selling over a million copies in Britain alone. *Queen of the Rushes*, first published in 1906, has been out of print for over fifty years, but now Allen Raine's powerful and accomplished novel can be enjoyed again. Set in a seaside village in West Wales at the time of the 1904 Revival, the novel relates the enthralling tale of the lives and complex loves of Gildas, Nancy, Gwenifer and Captain Jack. Eminently readable, and with touches of humour, this is nevertheless a serious attempt – one of the first in English – to map out a distinctively Welsh literary landscape.

Katie Gramich's fascinating introduction situates Allen Raine's last novel against its literary background and points to its significance in the Anglo-Welsh tradition and in Welsh women's writing.

£7.95 ISBN 1 870206 29 0